THE WAY TO BRIGHT STAR

Dee Brown

A TOM DOHERTY ASSOCIATES BOOK
NEW YORK

THE WAY TO BRIGHT STAR

Book design by Orit Mardkha-Tenzer

A Forge Book
Published by Tom Doherty Associates, LLC
175 Fifth Avenue
New York, NY 10010

www.tor-forge.com

Forge® is a registered trademark of Tom Doherty Associates, LLC.

Library of Congress Cataloging-in-Publication Data

Brown, Dee Alexander.
    The way to bright star / Dee Brown.
        p. cm.
    "A Tom Doherty Associates book."
    ISBN-13: 978-0-7653-2255-5
    ISBN-10: 0-7653-2255-2
    1. Circus—Fiction. 2. Circus performers—Fiction. I. Title.

PS3503.R79533 W39 1998
813'.54—dc21
                                                                98014621
                                                                    CIP

First Hardcover Edition: June 1998
First Trade Paperback Edition: October 2008

Printed in the United States of America

0 9 8 7 6 5 4 3 2 1

Praise for Dee Brown

"With an unerring eye and unflinching irony, Mr. Brown shows how history, myth, and business work hand in hand. . . . As loaded with nuggets as the streambed at Sutter's Mill."
—*The New York Times* on *The American West*

"This tale of America's Gilded Age is told with a vigor and irony that do full justice to its excesses, energies, venalities, and dreams." —*Newsweek* on *Hear That Lonesome Whistle Blow*

"It is obvious from the outset that Brown knows the Civil War period as well as he knows the Indian War and the taming of the West. . . . A consummate storyteller. The rivers flow, the winds blow, the nights are full of secrets, and the days pulse with real life."
—*The Washington Post* on *Conspiracy of Knaves*

"*The Way to Bright Star* is an old-fashioned yarn, an adventure story and a love story, an epic and a picaresque, a quietly exciting romantic tale spun out unhurriedly and beautifully, with sweetness and dignity and marvelous humor, about life as it was lived in middle America a long time ago." —*Arkansas Times*

"A spectacular tour of middle America during and after the Civil War." —*The Oklahoman* on *The Way to Bright Star*

"Take two camels, two Texans, an Egyptian, a traveling peddler, a vengeful bank robber, and a runaway, plunk them down in southern Missouri during the Civil War, and toss in an aging man's memories of battle, journeys, and the circus. In the hands of historian Dee Brown, the mix bakes up into the delightful treat that is *The Way to Bright Star*." —*The Anniston Star*

"Sweet-natured, vigorous, colorful entertainment, and a compelling portrait of the frontier."
—*Kirkus Reviews* on *The Way to Bright Star*

ALSO BY DEE BROWN

NONFICTION

Fighting Indians of the West (with Martin F. Schmitt)
Trail Driving Days (with Martin F. Schmitt)
Grierson's Raid
The Settlers' West (with Martin F. Schmitt)
The Gentle Tamers: Women of the Old Wild West
The Bold Cavaliers: Morgan's Second Kentucky Cavalry Raiders
Fort Phil Kearny: An American Saga
(republished as *The Fetterman Massacre*)
The Galvanized Yankees
Showdown at Little Big Horn
The Year of the Century: 1876
Bury My Heart at Wounded Knee:
An Indian History of the American West
Andrew Jackson and the Battle of New Orleans
Tales of the Warrior Ants
The Westerners
Hear That Lonesome Whistle Blow
Wondrous Times on the Frontier
When the Country Was Young

FICTION

Wave High the Banner
Yellowhorse
Cavalry Scout
They Went Thataway (republished as *Pardon My Pandemonium*)
The Girl from Fort Wicked
Action at Beecher Island
Teepee Tales of the American Indians
Creek Mary's Blood
Killdeer Mountain
A Conspiracy of Knaves

To
the surviving manual typewriters
and those who still
use them.

A NOTE TO THE READER

~

In the matter that follows, the chapters titled "Ben Butterfield" were set down by him in the early months of the twentieth century. All other chapters consist of a narrative of events occurring forty years earlier, in the year 1862.

The Way to Bright Star

I

BEN BUTTERFIELD

~

Thinking about the circus coming to town led me to pull out this shoe box full of faded photographs that I keep in the bottom drawer of Old Man Fagerhalt's desk. I have not looked at them for a long time, maybe a year or more. I just now found my favorite, the one of Queen Elizabeth Jones, of course, and there she is—in her white riding tights, her golden hair done up halo style, her lips parted in that joyful smile that is like none I've ever seen on any other human being's face.

In the picture she is standing in front of those two damned camels. Those poor cursed evil-smelling beasts! Detest them I did, but it was they that brought me to Queen Elizabeth Jones, placing me in debt to them forever.

I would like to brood over the picture and dream again of the time and place where it was made and the life I led then. But I hear Hilda Fagerhalt out in the hardware store chattering with a customer, and I know that any minute now she will be traipsing down the hall, her slippers slapping on the hard boards, thrusting her Swedish head through the open door to remind me sharply to prepare an order for that keg of ten-penny nails I forgot about. "Remember the post office closes at six o'clock, Ben, and don't forget the horse collars for Jack Bilbrew's dray teams, either."

I call her Fagerhalt, but she's used my name, Butterfield, since Old Man Fagerhalt caught her in bed with me. And me at the time with a leg so badly shattered I knew I'd never ride in the circus again with Queen Elizabeth Jones. When Hilda crawled into my bed, she was only trying to comfort me and ease the cruel pain of mending bones. She is a great comforter, I'll allow that. But Old Man Fagerhalt saw me as the spoiler of his daughter's virtue, although she was the one who came into the bed. Maybe he just wanted to get her married and off his hands.

The desk before which I sit—this handmade oaken desk with its innumerable cubbyholes filled with useless papers and trinkets—Hilda now refers to as mine, although I will always think of it as Old Man Fagerhalt's desk even though he has long been interred in Mount Holly cemetery out on Broadway.

Those camels! Omar and Tooley. I peer again at the old picture of them and recall the day after the battle, the one the Yankees named Pea Ridge and the Rebels call Elkhorn Tavern. No photographs were made there, but I'll forever remember the face and arrogant stance of Captain Solomon Lightfoot as he took the measurements of Johnny Hawkes and me and talked about the camels being contraband of war.

Well, I'd better put this shoe box of photographs back in the bottom of Old Man Fagerhalt's desk before Hilda comes in here and finds me musing over them. She hates all reminders of my youthful past, especially the gaudy circus posters I keep on the walls around me. Above the desk is a tall poster of a woman in white tights jumping a horse through a large hoop. Around the hoop is a circle of big scarlet letters: QUEEN ELIZABETH JONES. THE WORLD'S GREATEST EQUESTRIENNE! Every new season Johnny Hawkes used to send me posters carefully rolled into pasteboard tubes. A few years back, when Hilda still liked to tease me, she would draw mustaches in ink on the poster faces of Queen Elizabeth Jones.

I think I hear her coming now, prancing, her loose slippers slapping the floor, and I remember Captain Solomon Lightfoot, Quartermaster Department, U.S. Army. Popinjay, carpet knight, and flimflam artist.

II

PEA RIDGE, OR ELKHORN TAVERN

~

They were gathered in a little clearing on the edge of a corn-field where withered brown stalks from the last autumn's crop lay across the rows. It was midmorning of an early March day. Clots of wet snow were still melting in shaded places. With challenges of shrill songs, birds that had been frightened away by two days of blasting cannon and an almost continuous rattle of firearms were returning to resume the claiming of springtime territorial boundaries.

The boy sat on a recently felled log, facing a dying woodfire. Above the coals an iron pot hung from an improvised frame. Beyond the fire Johnny Hawkes lay outstretched in his fringed buckskin jacket and tan jeans, his head propped on his boots. Off to one side a dozen Cherokees, in gray linsey-woolsey jackets and trousers that served as Confederate uniforms, were sitting huddled under a leafless oak tree. Not far from them were five white Confederate soldiers playing with a jackknife that they took turns flipping in the air above a grassless spot of ground. Back in the trees several horses were held in a rope corral. Near the horses two dromedary camels rested on the ground, calmly chewing their cuds. A dark-skinned man wearing a dusty yellow turban and a travel-worn wide-striped wool blouse that was long enough to cover his knees was propped against a nearby stump, his eyes closed.

They were all prisoners. Their guards in dark blue uniforms, with forage caps on their heads, rifles held carelessly, watched their charges in attitudes varying from uneasiness to uncertainty. Suddenly the guards all came alert, looking off to the edge of the cornfield where a Union cavalry platoon led by an officer was winding slowly toward the clearing.

The boy pulled his floppy, wide-brimmed dragoon hat more securely to his head and stepped upon the log to have a clearer view of the approaching riders. Not since leaving Fort Davis in Texas more than a year ago had he seen an army officer in blue. This one was a captain, and when he dismounted, his movements were so awkward that in the eyes of the boy his importance was diminished. The captain's uniform was brand-new, no dust or sweat, no mud stains, no battle smudges. Except for a narrow line of dark mustache, he was clean shaven, and the boy guessed he might have slept last night on a bed in one of the surrounding farmhouses. Not until he was on the ground did the captain remember to order his platoon to halt and dismount. His gaze fixed upon Johnny Hawkes, who in one easy motion had slipped his boots on and stood upright. Hawkes was a foot taller than the captain, but he had worked around army posts long enough to assume an attitude of respect when in the presence of officers, regardless of his private opinion of them.

"You must be the man with the camels," the captain said.

"Yes, sir. John Hawkes at your service, sir." His reply was crisp, his body held almost, but not quite, in the posture of military attention.

"You are not wearing a uniform," the captain said accusingly.

"I'm not in their army, sir. I hired out as wagon master to move baggage and supplies. The camels was in the train."

"Nonetheless, you aided the enemy." The captain turned to look around the clearing, asking, "Where are these camels?"

Hawkes motioned toward the trees and then led the way to the camels. The boy followed at a respectful distance.

The camels, continuing their placid chewing, ignored the visitation. With obvious keen relish, the captain kneeled to examine the two animals. He paid no attention to the turbaned dark-skinned man in the wide-striped blouse who gradually drew nearer the camels as if to protect them. "Male and a female," the captain said. "Perfect pair. And they appear to be in good health."

"Yes, sir. When you release us, I reckon they're ready to head back to Texas."

"I think not," the captain replied. "Your camels are contraband

of war, Mr. Hawkes. Property of the United States government."
He glanced at the dark-skinned man. "Who is this furriner?"

"Name's Hadjee. Our cameleer. Come over from Egypt with
the second lot."

"Oh, yes, I know all about old Jeff Davis and the Camel Brigade. How many of the animals are left now?"

Hawkes shrugged. "I couldn't say, sir. Several of the females
bore young. Before we left Texas, a few was wandering out in the
brush country around Camp Verde. They say some are still way
out west in California where they went on the first crossing."

The captain rubbed his hands briskly together. He kept looking
back at the camels with a covetous expression. "Who ordered the
camels added to your baggage train?"

"General McCulloch. He rounded up every beast of burden and
serviceable wagon around San Antonio for the march up here. My
train started weeks later than the troops. Three camels was in it,
but one got split when her hind legs straddled. Had to be shot.
The quartermaster boys at Camp Verde overloaded her."

"You don't say!" The captain seemed disappointed. "And now
your General McCulloch is dead. He walked right up to one of
our rail fence breastworks. Wearing a big white hat, I hear. A
perfect target. Must have been a damn fool."

"That's what we heard, sir." Hawkes ran his fingers across his
unshaven chin. "I always figured General McCulloch to be a fearless sort of man." He looked straight at the captain. "Ben and
Hadjee and me, sir, are not a part of this war. Hadjee has no horse,
but he's light enough to ride behind Ben, and we'd like to start
home to Texas today. With your permission, sir."

"Who the hell is Ben?" The captain's voice had turned edgy.

"Oh." Hawkes turned to the boy who was standing close
enough to hear everything yet still was at what he considered to
be a respectful distance. "Ben Butterfield, sir," Hawkes said. Ben
came to attention, yet there was something comical about his attempt at dignity. The boy's face was half hidden beneath the flop-
brimmed hat, with his reddish hair pushing out like wild grass
around the edges. His posture did not suit the dark blue tunic,
obviously cut down from an officer's blouse to fit his smaller figure.
His faded sky-blue dragoon trousers had also been remade and
patched at knees and seat.

"What's the little ragamuffin to you?"

"I'm responsible for him," Hawkes replied. "I was given that bounded duty by Miz Sergeant Peddicord while she was dying."

The captain shook his head in puzzlement and then appeared to lose any further interest in the boy. "I must be about my own obligations," he said, as though talking to himself. "Must get these prisoners over to the temporary stockade and the captured horses to the corral."

A few moments later, when Johnny Hawkes realized that the captain was going to take away his and Ben Butterfield's horses along with others that had been captured, he protested strongly. "That pair are not army horses, sir, they're mine and Ben's. Best of mustang stock. Bought at San Antonio with our money."

"They're contraband of war," the captain retorted harshly. "We need good riding mounts to replace ours killed in the battle." He turned to a sergeant, lowering his voice as he spoke.

Well aware of the power of army officers, especially over underlings or civilians viewed as enemies, Hawkes tried to check his anger. "We ain't contraband of war, too, are we, sir? I mean me and Ben and Hadjee?"

Taking his bridle from one of the guard soldiers, the captain mounted in silence. A corporal already had the prisoners formed into a column of twos and was marching them out along the edge of the cornfield, with the captured horse herd behind them. "Look here," the captain called back to Hawkes. "I'm leaving you with the camels. I've given the sergeant of the guard orders to shoot you or your two minions if you try to escape." He slapped his horse into motion. "I'll be back before dark."

For the boy, the afternoon passed with abysmal slowness. He remembered the stockade at Fort Davis where prisoners were kept, the appalling misery of the place, and the open loathing the soldiers held for it. He feared being locked away in some dreadful dungeon like those Miz Sergeant Peddicord had told him about in the stories when he was younger. As the hours dragged, he kept waiting for Johnny Hawkes to present some whispered plan of escape before the captain returned. But Johnny did not want to talk. Whenever Ben sidled up to him, Johnny would draw away, to spend most of his time catnapping or teasing the guards.

On the previous day, one of the guards from Missouri who

knew the country well had gone deep into the woods and killed a deer. The soldiers had cooked some of the meat over the fire and shared it with the captive Confederates, most of whom were Missourians too. Soon after the captain went away that morning, the guards asked Johnny to roast a leftover haunch, and during the late afternoon they all stuffed themselves with venison.

From what he had heard the soldiers say, Ben knew that during the night most of the Rebels had marched away on the road toward a place called Huntsville, leaving their debris of battle in woods and fields. Along a sandy trail barely visible through the trees he saw occasional Confederates hurrying along, usually in pairs. Johnny said they must have become separated from their regiments, lost their bearings, and were searching for familiar comrades. The Union soldiers made no effort to pursue them. The sergeant of the guard had remarked that the battle was over. The Rebels were beaten and unlikely to return. As it was, the sergeant added, the prisoners they already had in hand would be a burden on the Union Army. Any more taken would also have to be fed and guarded; better to let them go.

Observing and listening to all this, Ben knew that he and Johnny and Hadjee could expect no rescue from the Texans with whom they had marched north or from any other Rebels. The only hope was Johnny's cleverness. After all, it was Johnny who had been foxy enough to find both of them a home at Camp Verde after the army closed out Fort Davis. But as the day drifted away, and Johnny kept avoiding him, he wondered if the mess they were in might not be too much even for a smart fellow like Johnny Hawkes.

In a chilling March dusk, the captain returned alone. Ben caught the smell of whiskey when the officer passed between him and the fire. He greeted Hawkes quite amiably, grasped him by one arm, and led the way into the trees toward the camels. When he spoke he slurred his words, and as they moved away from the fire, Ben could not hear clearly what he was saying. The boy got up and followed them tentatively into the darkening wood. He stopped and leaned against a tree, letting his backside slide to the ground.

"My name is Lightfoot," the captain said. "Solomon Lightfoot." He hesitated a moment and then continued. "I have a farm in Indiana, outside the town of Bright Star." He bent toward one of the camels, caressing the side of its hump. "A year or so ago I was visiting a cousin down in southern Alabama. Have you ever been to Alabama, Mr. Hawkes?"

"No, sir."

"Soil is rich there. Corn and cotton grow like weeds." He looked fondly at the camels but seemed disappointed, perhaps offended, by their continued indifference toward his presence. "Well, sir, a plantation owner, a neighbor to my cousin, imported some camels. Two-humped, Bactrians. Now this one-hump pair you have here must be dromedaries."

Hawkes glanced at the Egyptian who was silently nodding his head. "Yes, sir, they're dromedaries, Arabian camels," Hawkes replied, and added, "I'm told they're better for riding than the two-humped Bactrians, faster, but can't carry as much weight."

"That's exactly what the plantation owner told me," Lightfoot said. "He was planning to import two or three dromedaries. I don't know if outbreak of war changed his plan. But he was sure sold on camels over mules or draft horses. They don't eat much of anything, do they?"

"No, sir. A little graze, or a handful of plain old coarse hay, with a bite of grain paste now and then, dough balls. Hadjee knows how to fix them from barley."

Lightfoot stood erect and faced Hawkes. "I'll get to the point. This war is about done up. Rebels on the run everywhere. Before this year of 1862 ends I expect to be out of uniform and back in broadcloth and home in Bright Star, Indiana, maybe harvesting the autumn crops. I aim to start with this pair of camels on my farm, and if they prove out I'll get some two-humped ones for hauling corn from my fields to the railroad."

"You said these camels is contraband of war. Does that mean they're your property, Captain?"

Lightfoot shook his head and winked. "Not yet. They'll be auctioned off at Springfield, along with other captured trappings. I'll get them for a trifle. It pays to be in the quartermaster corps."

Hawkes laughed. "Well, sir, you're sure welcome to the camels. I'll be damned happy to be shed of the beasts. But what use to you are Ben and Hadjee and me? You took our horses, but we'll walk it back to Texas if we have to."

"I need you, Mr. Hawkes. The other two can go. I need you to drive the camels to Springfield."

Hawkes laughed again. "I couldn't get them critters a mile up the road without Hadjee, sir. Camels won't obey nobody but Hadjee. And Ben, he goes wherever I go."

"I should have had the lot of you herded over to the prisoner stockade." Lightfoot's voice had turned petulant. "But I reckon I won't. It's seventy-five miles to Springfield. Can you get the camels there in three days?

"Easy," Hawkes replied.

"All right, the three of you will have to live partly off the land, pick up some cornmeal and bacon along the way. I can give you a few legal tender notes, army vouchers, to pay for what you need, but I should warn you that not many of these hill natives will accept notes as real money."

"Can we have our horses back? Hadjee can ride one of the camels, but me and Ben don't take to the pitchin' and rollin' of a camel's amble."

The captain shook his head impatiently but added, "I might put you with one of our commissary wagons heading north."

Sensing that he had some sort of advantage over Lightfoot (the captain had said he *needed* him), Hawkes took a step or two closer to him and stretched his lean height so that the captain had to look upward at a sharp angle to meet his deliberate gaze. "Suppose I say we won't take the camels to Springfield—unless you give us back our horses?"

"Then you'll go as shackled prisoners. And on to long confinement in a St. Louis stockade."

Hawkes grinned, his face still close above Lightfoot's. "Suppose I say we'll go, and then up the road a piece we just bob out and head into these hills and you never see us again?"

Reaching inside his blouse, Lightfoot withdrew a small leather pouch. "I trust you, Mr. Hawkes," he said, loosening the rawhide ties on the pouch and withdrawing three gold coins, which he held up in the dimming twilight so that Hawkes could see their worth. "These will be yours when you bring the camels into the stockyards at Springfield. There I will write you out a parole so you and your minions can return unmolested to Texas."

"Done!" Hawkes cried and offered his hand. "When do we start?"

Lightfoot turned and shouted an order to the sergeant of the guard. "You start in the morning," he said.

Within minutes the camp in the little clearing was abandoned. Hadjee put the camels in motion, and the soldiers who had been guarding the three prisoners marched out behind them. Hawkes and the boy carried their blanket rolls on their backs, with saddle-bags slung over their shoulders. Off in the distance where the Union Army was encamped around Elkhorn Tavern, fires glimmered against the deepening dusk.

As though he did not wish to be observed, Lightfoot followed backcountry trails that took them farther and farther from outposts of the main encampment. Once they came upon a road almost completely blocked by trees that had been felled by one of the opposing forces to slow the progress of the other. They turned off, skirting a dilapidated fence depleted of almost half its split rails that must have been used for cooking fires.

The boy was beginning to shiver in the chilly dampness of nightfall when they reached a farmhouse and barn. Lightfoot called to the sergeant to open the door of the barn. "We'll fasten the camels in here," he said, dismounting and handing the reins to one of the soldiers.

That night, for the first time in his life, Ben Butterfield slept in a barn, and although the hay piled on the upper flooring had been cut and dried months before, its fragrance still permeated the old log building. Not until he awoke at daylight did he smell the repellant and all too familiar ammonia scent rising from the camels in the stalls below.

Johnny Hawkes had spent the night in the farmhouse with Captain Lightfoot, but both men were out before sunrise making everything ready for the long march to Springfield. The captain showed Hadjee the grain bins in the rear of the barn, and although the containers were almost empty, the Arab managed to scrape a small supply of barley and oats into the camels' saddlebags. "Spoils of war," Lightfoot said and then watched with intense interest while the cameleer adjusted his wooden saddle upon pads on the male Omar's back.

Ordering Omar to kneel, Hadjee mounted and followed Lightfoot out the barn, with the female Tooley close behind. On horseback, and without his platoon, the captain led them to a junction with the main road to Springfield, and there they found a staging depot for wagons preparing to transport wounded northward.

Arrival of the camels created considerable excitement among the bored soldiers and wagon drivers, as well as some perturbation among the more skittish horses. After the camels were halted and Hadjee had dismounted from his exotic saddle, a noisy crowd gathered around, much to Captain Lightfoot's annoyance. The captain hurriedly forced his horse through the mob until he found an officer in charge of loading and dispatching wagons.

After engaging the officer in a hasty and heated exchange of words, Lightfoot wheeled his horse, shouted to Hawkes, and motioned excitedly for him to bring the camels forward. "Mr. Hawkes, do you see that wagon up there by the tent?" the captain cried hoarsely. "It's being loaded with wounded. You will be the driver to Springfield. Your camels can follow behind."

When they reached the tent, Lightfoot explained with grim humor that Hawkes's wagon would be hauling "sitting up" wounded. Wagons carrying "lying down" wounded usually had an attendant assigned to them, he added, and this attendant had the power to order the driver to a slow pace and to make frequent stops. Progress would be much faster with the "sitting up" wounded.

There were eight men in the wagon, most of them wearing bandages made from torn shirts and blankets. Floating around and above them were heavy fumes of whiskey that drifted over the wagon seat where Johnny Hawkes and Ben Butterfield awaited orders from Captain Lightfoot to move out for Springfield.

III

BEN BUTTERFIELD

~

Hilda Fagerhalt Butterfield, my good wife, wanted me to go to church with her this morning, but I mumbled my usual excuse, "My leg hurts so, my dear, that I could not sit still in the pew," and she was kind enough not to press the matter, although she knows I can sit still for hours here in front of Old Man Fagerhalt's desk trying to set down the story of my wasted life.

We are all a bundle of memories, each memory related to others, like vines running across the ground in all directions, fruiting vines mingled with prickly vines. Good and bad memories. When a human being grows older, like me, about all that's left are memories and shriveled dreams. It was this faded photograph that I came across of Socrates Drumm boring a hole in the belly of a Percheron that led me to remember the wounded Union soldiers in the wagon.

Socrates called himself Doctor Drumm, and maybe he was one at some time, during the Civil War likely. A surgeon, he said. When Bell Brothers Wild West Show combined with French's Bavarian Circus and Menagerie, the doctor was hired to look after the many animals that Mr. French had assembled. The first poster for this new, enlarged circus boasted of the largest collection of wild animals on earth, and they did keep Socrates Drumm busy tending their ailments and injuries.

This all happened during my last months under the big tents, but like warnings of the great smash-up that was coming to me, I began having a series of little mishaps—a sprained elbow, a torn knee, a hip bruised against a post, frazzles that would not have mattered much had it not been for the exactness of control that each horseman had to maintain during the rip-roaring dashes and gallops and jumps we had perfected for the finals of the stagecoach holdup that had made us famous even among our fellow showmen. Any rider missing a cue endangered the lot of us. Sound legs and arms were absolute necessities.

When I told Queen Elizabeth Jones, who was the leader of this daring stunt, that I had a bad elbow, she made me go to see Socrates Drumm. He had his own wagon, with a sleeping place up front and a storehouse of liniments, ointments, painkillers, enormous pills for purges, and other nostrums for men and beasts. He had two small facing seats of wicker, padded but backless, in front of his boxed store of cures and surgical instruments.

Dr. Drumm was a heavyset man with a face as wide as it was long. Many wrinkles creased the lower part of his face just above and below the jawline. When convenient he shaved daily, but he seldom bothered to cut the beard hairs within the wrinkles, and as his hair was still dark this gave him an oddly striped sort of facial appearance.

When Dr. Drumm was attending any of his animals, he had no time for visitors or small talk, but when everything was quiet, he enjoyed having the circus people come with their scrapes and cuts and coughs and wheezes, and while he was treating us he liked to talk about his experiences. For my pains he usually sold me a bottle of his Kickapoo Secret Formula Herbal Liniment. This stuff applied to aching flesh and bone burned like fire for a few minutes, and then when the flames died, it was such a relief that the original pain did not seem so bad.

Sometimes he would keep me for hours, reminiscing and occasionally confessing how little the surgeons in the Civil War knew about treating wounds or diseases. He had the figures in his head: 140,000 died in battle, twice that number from the care of military surgeons. A soldier was better off most of the time, he said, if he kept away from doctors. They could set broken bones just fine, but if it was a gunshot wound in an arm or leg, they would give the patient a painkiller, if one was handy, and then amputate. Although they knew little about antiseptics or infections, the doctors somehow discovered that dousing a wound with whiskey would keep it from going into gangrene. Pouring a gill of the stuff down a wounded man's throat also helped deaden the pain and shock, temporarily.

When I told him about my Civil War experience with the wounded soldiers in the wagon starting out for Springfield, he was not surprised to hear they were suffused in whiskey.

I also told him about the runaway wagon. When Hadjee brought the camels up, for some reason—probably all the bustle at the crossroads—they turned suddenly frisky and swung themselves right up beside and then in front of the horses. Now, some horses don't mind a camel much, but that pair of bony nags must have thought they were seeing four-footed demons from hell. In simultaneous panic motions, the horses sprang forward, jerking the reins out of Johnny Hawkes's hands and snapping one of the traces. Johnny and I were both flung forward and then backward out of the low-backed seat, tumbling about amongst the alcohol-soaked wounded men in the wagon bed.

I never heard such swearing before or since as came pouring out of the mouths of those injured men. Some of them being Germans from St. Louis, they used oaths I'd never heard before, but they sounded bloodcurdling, certainly to me. Every bump and bounce discommoded at least one or two of the floundering soldiers. They tried to keep their splinted and bandaged limbs out of the action, but I guess it was impossible.

Meanwhile Johnny had got himself back over the seat and down on the wagon tongue to recover the reins. At that time we were going up a pretty steep hill, and that slowed the runaways considerably, but because of the slant in the wagon the wounded men slid down to the wagon gate, and there they had to hold on for dear life to keep from falling out entirely.

Just as we were rattling to a stop, Captain Lightfoot galloped alongside, mad as hell, adding his profanities to the soldiers' chorus in the wagon. Way back down the slope of road, maybe a mile away, I could see the camels, with Hadjee rocking along on Omar, and Tooley tailing behind.

Strange how this old yellowing photograph of Socrates Drumm, relieving a Percheron of a bad bellyache, made me remember all that. I don't know who took the picture or why. You can't see what kind of instrument Socrates was using to bore a hole into the horse's distended abdomen to remove the gas, but that is what he was doing. My fading memory tells me the Percheron recovered, but I would not bet on it.

There goes the bell on the front door. A peek out the window tells me that Hilda Fagerhalt is back from church, bringing that perky little widow lady, Mrs. Valentine, who likely will warn me of the fires of hell for not going to church and then talk my ears off. Ah well, as Socrates Drumm used to say, C'est la vie.

IV

TO JOLLIFICATION IN MISSOURI

~

After the frightened and exhausted runaway horses were brought to a standstill, and Hadjee and the camels caught up with the wagon, Captain Lightfoot gave Hawkes a stern lecture about keeping the camels to the rear and out of sight of any working horses. Lightfoot then assured Hawkes that he would meet him at the Springfield stockyards in less than a week. With a jaunty wave of his hand, he turned about and started at a gallop for the crossroads they had left behind so precipitately. Whereupon Hawkes shouted the fidgety team into motion, and they moved off toward the north.

By this time the wounded men were adding groans to their profanity. At Johnny's suggestion, Ben climbed back over the seat and offered to help them. Some of the soldiers had lost their slings; others were bleeding through their bandages and needed assistance in tightening them. Ben had seen wounded men before, but this was his first occasion to minister to them, and it gave him a feeling of important participation, if not absolute equality with the victims. He could barely understand the three Germans from St. Louis. When one of them complained that his leg was carrying a jagged piece of shrapnel fired from his own artillery battery, the others joined in and said they had all been under fire from a Union battery on a hill. "Ve tink it vas Osterhaus," said one, but another disputed that assertion and declared it was a green bunch of cannoneers from Peoria, Illinois. "Anyway," the first man said, "ve could not vithdraw because of Rebels pressing from our rear, and to move forward vould have brought only vorse shelling from our own cannons."

As the day passed, some of the men grew morose and silent. Others recovered their spirits in spite of the constant jolting of the wagon; they joked and laughed about the camels following close in the rear. Near sundown, as they were passing a church, Hawkes noted a pile of firewood, and he quickly turned the wagon into the churchyard, announcing that they would camp there for the night.

Before dusk fell, two other wagons joined them. A surgeon accompanied one of the vehicles. He ordered a large fire built to give him sufficient light to amputate a leg that was beginning to suppurate.

In order to get an early start on the other wagons, Hawkes had coffee boiling before daylight. He had found a bag of coffee beans and several boxes of hardtack under the wagon seat. Some of the wounded slept in the wagon, and with Ben's help he roused the others who were in the church. All complained about being awakened in the dark chill, but after washing down their hardtack with coffee, they brightened up and took their places in the wagon. At sunrise they were on the road again.

About midmorning they came upon a cart that had been converted into an ambulance; it was spraddled square in the middle of the road. Standing placidly in front of it was a pair of small spotted ponies. A cavalry captain was leaning against the vehicle, watching a corporal work at one of the front wheels that was turned at an unnatural angle. Hawkes gave the reins to Ben and shouted back to Hadjee to keep the camels in the rear. He then dropped down and approached the crippled ambulance.

"Breakdown, sir?" he asked politely.

The cavalry captain grunted an affirmative. His face was sullen. The shoulders of his shell jacket were adorned with new epaulettes, his sleeves with intricate galloons. A pistol rested in a holster attached to his wide belt. His boots appeared to be freshly polished. "My corporal says the axle is broken," he said in a grudging and complaining tone as though blaming all present for his misfortune.

Hawkes needed only a glance at the axle to tell him that it was indeed broken, too badly to be even temporarily mended.

The captain spoke again. "The men in your wagon—" When he saw the camels for the first time, he stopped the rising inflection of his voice. "What in thunderation are those camels doing here?"

"They're contraband of war, sir," Hawkes replied. "Come from Texas. I've been ordered to deliver them to Springfield."

"On whose order?"

"Captain Solomon Lightfoot's."

"Never heard of him." The captain frowned. "Look here, are you in charge of the wounded men in that wagon? As well as the menagerie?" Without waiting for a reply he hurried on, "I must get Major Withers to the railhead east of Springfield as quickly as possible. He's wounded and must reach St. Louis to be in the care of his physician. How badly wounded are your men? They appear to be alert."

"Mostly broken bones and flesh wounds," Hawkes said. "But they've had a rough time."

The captain turned and raised the canvas curtain on the ambulance. A pale-faced, hollow-eyed major stared out at them. He was lying on a feather bed beneath an Ozark quilt, both evidently contraband of war seized from some luckless farm wife. One of the major's ears was clotted with dried blood that had turned black.

"I think we'd better move you to the wagon behind us, Major," the captain said. "This ancient hack is played out."

Grumbling over the intrusion, Major Withers sat up and rolled himself out of the bedding. He still wore his boots, and the spur on one of them had cut into the feather bed. Goose down floated after him as he followed the captain to the rear of the wagon. "Good God, Jack," he cried huskily. "Camels! Have we run into an overland circus here?"

"They're contraband," the captain explained impatiently. "En route to Springfield." He unlatched the wagon gate and let it down. "See here, you men," he said to the wounded, "we need room for the major. Two of you get out. You can use the ambulance wagon."

None of the soldiers volunteered to transfer. They knew they might be there indefinitely waiting for repairs. They cast their gazes in various directions.

"All right," the captain cried. "All of you, out!" He placed his right hand on the butt of his holstered pistol.

The wounded men shifted unwillingly toward the opened wagon gate. A man with a bandage around his forehead and another with his arm in a sling dropped down first.

"That'll do," the captain said. "The rest of you stay where you are." He called to the corporal who was still standing beside the ambulance, "Bring the major's bedding."

In a remarkably short time, the efficient cavalry captain had the major and the two officers' belongings aboard the wagon. He ordered his corporal to take over the reins, rousted Ben Butterfield from the seat, and took the place himself. Although Johnny Hawkes protested mildly over being left with the broken-down ambulance, the captain paid him not the slightest attention. As the wagon rolled away and turned out to pass the abandoned vehicle, the captain shouted back a peremptory general order: "Get that ambulance repaired. And guard it well. It's military property!"

And so there they were, Johnny, Ben, Hadjee with the camels, and a pair of ambulatory wounded soldiers, Germans from St. Louis who communicated only in very broken English.

After the soldiers crawled into the ambulance and lay down on the two parallel straw-stuffed canvas pallets, Johnny and Ben took another look at the axle and quickly agreed that only a blacksmith could repair it. Meanwhile Hadjee had brought the camels into a grove of cedars bordering the road, taking care of them out of sight of the patient ponies.

About this time, a farmer who had observed the camels passing his cabin a mile or so in the rear came striding along the road. He had never seen a camel before, he said, but had heard them spoken of by the circuit-riding preacher who had described the animal for him. Sure enough, they did have humps. Did they give milk? Jacob the Prophet had thirty milk camels, the Bible said. And the Apostle Matthew said it was easier for a camel to go through the eye of a needle than for a rich man to enter into the kingdom of God. That was true, sure enough, he guessed, but for the fact he did not know any rich men. Can you make raiments out of these camels' hair? Raiments, that's clothing, don't you know. John the Apostle had raiments of camel hair. The Bible said so. And the three wise men, they must've had camels to carry all that gold and stuff for baby

Jesus. With a gesture of elation, the farmer declared that it was sure a blessing for him to be in the presence of these holy animals.

A skinny little man in worn jeans, he would have babbled on for hours, his Adam's apple bobbing up and down, had not Johnny Hawkes stopped him in a loud voice, inquiring if he had a blacksmith's forge on his place. No, he had no blacksmith forge, but there was a blacksmith up at Jollification. His name was Pybolt, Temporary Pybolt.

"Jollification, you said?" asked Johnny. "That's a place?"

"Yup. Little village."

"How long would it take you to get there?"

"Don't know. Don't have a timepiece."

"Well, how far is it?"

"They say about five miles from my cabin."

Johnny glanced at Ben. "You're fast on foot, Ben. Or you could ride Omar over there."

"I'll walk," Ben said. He'd been nauseated too many times on Omar's back. Seasickness, Johnny called it.

Johnny thought it might be a good idea for Hadjee to take the camels on to Jollification. They'd be that much farther along toward Springfield, and in the meantime maybe another military vehicle would come by with an officer present to take charge of the ambulance. He'd like to be shed of those two Dutch-talking soldiers and that broken-down vehicle, but he'd stay with them, as he'd been ordered to do by the cavalry captain.

When the Ozark farmer learned that the camels were leaving, he offered to go with the mission to Jollification. Climbing back into his saddle, Hadjee took the animals off at a fast rate, leaving Ben and the skinny little man walking determinedly behind them. At first, Ben was annoyed by the persistent flow of words from his companion. "What was the fighting like, over there in Arkansas?" the man asked. He'd heard cannons thundering far away and felt some trembling from the ground, and the last day or two he'd seen a few wagons going north with wounded men in them. Couldn't make out what it was all about, the shooting. Must be a mighty big feud.

The ceaseless monologue did make the time pass more swiftly, and after an hour or so Ben sighted a village nestling in a hollow between forested ridges. "Yes, sir," the little man continued, "last night I saw the brightest of stars sparkling big up in the heavens. I knew it was a sign. It was a sign them holy animals was coming. The Lord sent them to stop all that shooting, and it did stop, didn't it?"

"Yes," Ben said, "the shooting stopped after the Lord told the Rebels to skedaddle."

The blacksmith shop was on the edge of Jollification, a whitewashed building with an odd collection of plows and wheel rims and rusted farm tools strewn along one side. Above a pair of sagging double doors that appeared to stand permanently open was a crude sign: T. PYBOLT SMITHY. A steady clanging from inside ceased abruptly as Hadjee halted the camels outside. Two boys who had been fishing from a nearby stream flung down their poles and came up to stare at the apparition.

A blacksmith wearing a leather apron stepped cautiously out of the wide doorway. He recognized the approaching farmer. "Where'd you get these camels, Henry?" he asked.

"They come from Bethlehem," Henry replied. "They followed a star. They come to stop the war."

"Maybe so," the blacksmith said, his eyes on Ben, studying the floppy hat and the faded refashioned tunic and dragoon trousers. "Is that boy one of the soldiers?"

"He's with the broke-down little wagon," Henry explained.

Ben stepped forward. "Sir, I was sent to ask you to come fix the axle. It's broke too bad for us to fix. We got two wounded men. A captain and a major took off with our wagon and left the broke-down one for us to fix."

"Yeah, they stopped here for water a while ago. Prideful bastards." The blacksmith looked undecided. "Who you with, boy? And who owns these camels?"

"Johnny Hawkes is in charge. We're taking the camels to Springfield for Captain Solomon Lightfoot."

"Who is this Hawkes? Is he Union or Rebel?"

"Neither. He's a Texan. A wagon master. I work for him."

Temporary Pybolt, the blacksmith, scratched his black-bearded chin in puzzlement. "If he's a Texan, why ain't he Rebel, boy?"

"I never asked him," Ben answered.

"Well, since Wilson's Creek, I been for the Rebels," Pybolt declared. "Henry, have you picked a side yet?"

"I'm for Missouri," Henry said.

"Well, hell, Henry, half of the Missourians are Union, half Rebel. You better pick a side or you'll get caught in the middle."

"I'll think on it, Temporary," Henry said.

The blacksmith still looked undecided. "This Hawkes fellow, has he got any hard money, boy? Can he pay in coin of the realm? Silver or gold?"

"He won't get the gold coins till we take the camels to Springfield. But he's got some silver."

"Which axle is it that's broke?"

"Front," Ben said.

"All right." Pybolt looked with amusement at the gathering crowd of townspeople, come to see the camels. "Boy, you charge everybody a penny to look at your circus," he said, "and you can pay me handsomely." He turned to the farmer. "Henry, give me a hand with my hitch team. If what that boy says is true, we'll need to pull the broke-down wagon back here to repair it."

By the time Temporary Pybolt and the farmer were ready to go, most of the inhabitants of Jollification were gathered around the smithy to watch the camels. Ben warned them several times not to come too close, but a boy with a dog darted in to touch Tooley. She immediately threw herself at the dog, which barely escaped being crushed, and at the same time she spat a stream of cud upon the boy's head. The dog ran off yelping, the boy following with an indignant howl.

At this, Hadjee took Tooley's halter and backed her against the wall of the smithy, muttering "khrr, khrr" until she kneeled. Ben then made Omar kneel beside Tooley, and he and Hadjee sat in front of the animals. After that, whenever one of the spectators came too close, Hadjee would shout "Bite, bite!" Ben would echo the cry and then speak firmly about the ferocity of dromedaries.

V

BEN BUTTERFIELD

~

I sat here this morning for an hour trying to remember the sin-
gular name of the blacksmith at that little Missouri village of
Jollification. After all these years the name finally came to me. Temporary Pybolt. He was a brawny man, with a low forehead over
thick black brows, but he was not the dolt he may have appeared
to be.

Johnny and Hadjee and I, and the two wounded soldiers from
St. Louis, spent the night in his blacksmith shop, and he kept us
up late telling of his wandering life. In his youth he apprenticed to
a blacksmith in Philadelphia, and it was there he saw his first
camel. Some well-to-do Philadelphians imported a few wild animals for a menagerie, and he was hired to build cages and pens.
Of all the animals, he said, he liked the camels best, but when
Johnny and I pressed him for a reason he could give none. I spent
enough of my young life with camels to last forever. I do not care
for them. A camel is always grumbling or crying real tears about
something. I can't put up with that in people, so why tolerate com-
plaints from a camel? Truly I would not take the time to look out
my window to see one.

A quarter of a century after hearing Pybolt tell of building those
first cages for the menagerie in Philadelphia, I found myself in that
city with the Great John Robinson Circus, which exhibited for a
week there during the Centennial. One morning Johnny Hawkes
and Queen Elizabeth Jones and I went to see the Philadelphia Zo-
ological Garden. While looking at some of the confined animals
we noticed the beautifully fashioned ironwork on some of the older

cages. I suddenly remembered Temporary Pybolt and wondered if some of the cages were not his creations.

Pybolt had told us that before he reached full manhood he began following the trails and rivers to the West, stopping briefly to blacksmith at Pittsburgh, Cincinnati, Louisville, St. Louis, and dozens of towns that were cities by the time I first saw them years later while traveling with circuses. It is odd how some human beings, encountered casually, will stick in the mind, especially if one meets and is impressed by them in early youth. Although I was around Pybolt for only a day or two, I sensed he was a man who took pride in his work and had a great curiosity about everything in the world. In knocking about this country since that time, I've observed that people who are interested in everything in the world are seldom mean-spirited. It's those who are wrapped up all the time in themselves who are mean.

Pybolt wanted to know everything we could tell him about the camels used in the Camel Brigade and how it came into being. Which reminds me that perhaps this is as good as any time to set down something of that long-forgotten military venture and how Johnny and I played a little part in its ending.

Rain has been pouring all morning, so nobody is coming to the hardware store. Hilda Fagerhalt is out front knitting bootees for Lucy Markham's baby daughter and is not likely to bother me. She has been talking to me about subscribing for one of those newfangled telephone machines with their ringing bells and voices that sound like they are coming out of a tin can. Hilda says customers could order things from the hardware store that they need in a hurry, but my God, everybody is in too much of a hurry as it is. She said something about putting the telephone machine on Old Man Fagerhalt's desk so I can answer the goddamned shrilling bells. I'll fight that to the death. She thinks I have nothing to do but sit here and woolgather. It does no good to tell her this is the way Thomas Edison thought up his wonderful inventions, any one of which is a great deal more useful than Alexander Graham Bell's silly telephone machine.

Well now, the Camel Brigade. I remember pretty much the way Johnny Hawkes told it to Temporary Pybolt, because that's the first time I'd ever heard the beginning and middle and end. Around the time of the California gold rush, the U.S. Army was responsible for guarding the trails and transporting supplies to forts in the far West—posts like Fort Davis in Texas where I spent most of my early years. Some of the generals thought camels might be just the ticket for crossing the desert country of the Southwest. When President Pierce appointed Jefferson Davis to be his secretary of war, Davis wheedled some money out of Congress and sent an expedition commanded by Major Henry Wayne to Egypt and other camel countries. Wayne brought back a shipload of the beasts, with a few Egyptian cameleers, and established them at Camp Verde near San Antonio. Later on, a second shipment was brought over, and soldiers were assigned there to get accustomed to working with the animals.

I remember well the arrival at Fort Davis of the first western camel expedition under command of a Lieutenant Beale. They were en route to California and had to stop at the fort for two days to get wagons repaired, so we saw quite a lot of the camels. When Johnny Hawkes was telling all this to Temporary Pybolt, he said his eyes about popped out when he saw camels eating screwbeans, a desert plant that's covered with thorns longer and more prickly than any rosebush. To get at the beans the camels pulled the thorny limbs through their teeth, stripping off the ugly briars. Johnny said that when he saw them doing that he knew camels were something special and would never starve to death even in the desert country.

The last night the expedition was at Fort Davis, some off-duty soldiers from the Camel Brigade visited the sutler's and spent the night drinking snake-head whiskey. Just before reveille they awakened me with their singing and hollering as they passed the enlisted men's quarters, and about the same time I looked out the window slit, a bugle sounded from their camp half a mile away. It was an amazing sight to see the soldiers trying to run to the assembly place. They floundered and stumbled and tried to hold on to each other to keep from falling down, which most of them did anyhow.

The Camel Brigade, sad to say, did not get much support from the U.S. Army after old Jeff Davis left the War Department. Yes, he is the same unlucky man who later became president of the Rebel Confederacy. I think the army could use camels in some of the wilder places of the West to this day, but the brigade folded its tents for good at Camp Verde. Except for the three camels that Johnny Hawkes and I started out with the supply train across Indian Territory, the Confederates made no use of them. The animals just wandered off into the Texas hill country and must have been shot by frightened settlers, or maybe perished from old age. They sure would not have starved to death.

A word about why riding a camel makes me heave up my cud. A horse, now, can give me a sore tail or chafed legs if I've been too long out of a saddle, but I never was stomach sick from riding a horse all day. Fifteen minutes on a camel, though, oh, my! You see, a camel don't move its legs the way a horse does. It goes sideways and forward and backward at the same time—as Johnny said, it was like riding a ship on a rough sea.

Another thought: Maybe I have made too much mention of the crowds gathering around the camels whenever we brought them into a new place. There was hardly any of that coming from Texas across Indian Territory because most of that country was so thinly populated. We seldom saw an Indian village, and if there was one we usually went around it. In Missouri the camels must have been a big surprise, appearing unexpectedly, especially to people who had never seen one. I will skip mentioning the presence of crowds unless there is some special reason for it.

Well, the rain has stopped, and here comes old Hughie Snow carrying a basket of turnips and greens. He'll be wanting to trade that garden truck for one of Hilda's pullets, so I better flip the lid shut on my inkwell, unhitch from this desk, and hobble down the hall to the store to mind the cash box while Hilda's transaction takes place out in the backyard henhouse. Selah.

VI

TO SPRINGFIELD IN MISSOURI

~

Temporary Pybolt was a friendly man, but he was also a wiser man than Johnny Hawkes believed him to be. The next morning after the blacksmith finished replacing the axle on the light wagon, he named his price, and Johnny took from his shirt pocket one of the army paymaster's vouchers given him by Captain Lightfoot and cheerfully presented it.

"Ah, no," said Pybolt, "that's not coin of the realm. The boy here said you had some silver pieces."

"My own stash," Johnny replied. "This wagon is army business, Mr. Pybolt. It don't belong to me. This here note is good as silver, or gold."

"Not to me, it ain't," Pybolt said firmly. "Since the armies've been marching around here, the woods are full of this paper. Merchants at Springfield won't take any more of it, and I don't aim to go all the way to St. Louis to cash in. I'm regretful, Hawkes, but it's hard money for me, or else I keep the wagon till somebody redeems it with hard money. I don't know about that pair of spotted ponies, either. They must belong with the light wagon."

Johnny shrugged. "I reckon me and my party will be camel-backing to Springfield. Look after the two Dutch boys, will you, Mr. Pybolt. Maybe we'll be seeing you on our way back to Texas."

"You'd be welcome. No hard feelings?"

"Nah. Not after you fed us so well. A man's got to make a living." He offered his hand, and they exchanged good-byes. "Wait a minute," Pybolt said and went hurriedly into the living quarters of the blacksmith shop. He returned with a slab of bacon and refused Johnny's offer to pay for it with silver.

After Hadjee was mounted on Tooley, they started north through the town, Johnny and Ben walking on opposite sides of Omar. A long line of small boys trailed after them until they crossed a ford and started up a steep hill.

They had lost a full day on the journey to Springfield, but time did not seem to be pressing. Captain Lightfoot had said he would be in Springfield in less than a week, and that could be as much as three or four more days.

The morning turned warm, the sun's power lifting springlike fragrances from the earth, and a stirring of air brought a spicy scent from cedars bordering the road. Stopping to relieve himself, Ben fell behind the others. As he came round a bend in the road, he noticed a quick movement beside a cone-shaped cedar. He was sure that only a large bird or some animal could have made such a shaking motion in the bush, and when it was repeated he strode across the brown sedge grass, hoping he might surprise a deer. Instead a young man appeared, holding one arm upward. His other arm was wrapped in a dirty strip of linen, the bare hand inflamed to a fiery red. He was wearing a makeshift gray uniform. "I'm surrendering to you, boy," he said. "Are you with that circus just passed?"

"It's not a circus," Ben said.

"Well, I'm surrendering to you, anyhow. I'm hungry, my arm hurts bad, and I suffer chills and fever."

Ben did not know how to reply. No one had ever offered to surrender to him before. After a pause, he asked. "Who are you?"

"Rafe Linkous. I'm in the Third Missouri Confederate Infantry. We got shelled."

"What are you doing way off here?"

"Going home. Live near Springfield. Are you willing to take my surrender? You're Union, ain't you?"

"Nah, I'm Texan."

"How about one of them up there with the circus animals?"

Ben shook his head. "Johnny's Texan, too. And Hadjee is Egyptian."

"Aw hell. I need to surrender before somebody shoots me."

Up ahead in the meantime, Johnny had glanced back and noted the stranger. He stopped the camels, waiting for Ben and the Rebel soldier to overtake them.

After Rafe Linkous explained his situation, Johnny suggested that the Missourian accompany the camel party for protection until possibly they might overtake or be overtaken by a Union Army officer who might take his surrender and write out a parole. Linkous expressed his gratitude and walked along between Johnny and Omar, asking the usual questions about camels.

Around noontime they stopped for half an hour to refill their canteens from a rock-bedded stream of clear cold water and to nibble on pieces of hardtack and dried sausage that Johnny had appropriated from the ambulance wagon and stowed in his saddle pack. He had just distributed the rations when a man riding a gray mule appeared in the road ahead. The rider stopped the mule, took a telescope from his bag, and obviously was examining the camels and the human members of the party. After a moment, the mule resumed its unhurried and apparently reluctant gait until it brought the rider close enough to converse. The man wore a black broadcloth suit, a tall-crowned black hat, and a knitted lemon-colored scarf, all a bit dusty.

"I say," the man cried, "are you circus people?"

Before replying, Hawkes finished chewing his piece of cold sausage. "No, we're not circus people."

The man dismounted, tied the mule to a sapling, and walked closer. "It is surprising, don't you know, to come upon a brace of camels in this wilderness. My name is Frank Fogerty. Special correspondent for the *New York Graphic*."

Hawkes stood up, took the newspaperman's offered hand, and gave his name. He patiently explained the reason for the presence of the camels in the Missouri "wilderness" and then added, "Would you care to partake of a bite of cold meat and hard crackers, Mr. Fogerty?"

The correspondent declined the offer, saying that he had dined on boiled eggs provided at a farmhouse back up the road, a place where he had spent the night and unfortunately overslept. "My newspaper telegraphed me several days ago at Jefferson City—the capital of this benighted state, don't you know—and advised me of a rumored impending battle somewhere below Springfield.

Travel is most difficult in this weary wasteland, don't you find it so, Mr. Hawkes?"

"No worse than Indian Territory, I reckon," Johnny replied.

"Ah, so you have been out in the Indian country? Any adventures I might dispatch to my newspaper?"

"Well, we all come near drowning while fording Red River."

"You don't say! Any fights with the redskins?"

"Didn't see any Indians till we got to Arkansas. Cherokees. They fought in the battle. Crossing the territory, the backcountry trails took us away from Indian villages."

Fogerty pulled a notebook and a pencil stub from an inside pocket of his natty jacket. "From what you told me about these camels being contraband, and your Captain Lighthead—"

"Lightfoot," Hawkes corrected.

Fogerty wrote the name in his notebook and continued, "I judge there was some kind of a fight."

"Oh, hell yes," Hawkes said. "They banged away at each other for two days."

"Any people killed?"

"Hundreds, I reckon," Hawkes replied. "Maybe thousands."

"You don't say! Then it must've been a real battle. What regiment did you fight with?"

"Didn't fight," Hawkes said with a grin. "I'm a wagon boss."

Fogerty removed his hat and placed it on a hummock of brome-grass and then glanced in his notebook. "I need names of regiments that fought heroically—for my dispatch. You must've been attached to some regiment, a General Sam Curtis, General Sigel, Colonels Davis and Dodge and Carr. Were you a wagon boss for one of their outfits?"

"No. You might say I drove for General McCulloch. He got killed."

"If a general was killed, it must have been a very big battle. How do you spell that name? I never heard of him."

"Don't know exactly how McCulloch spelled his name. He was from Texas."

Fogerty looked up in surprise. "Good God! You're Secesh!"

Hawkes shook his head. "No, sir, I'm Texan. Ben Butterfield, there, and Hadjee, we're not in this war. That lad lying over there with the swollen hand is a Missourian Rebel, trying to get home. He was in the fighting. Bad, as he tells it."

The Missourian, Rafe Linkous, rose up, his face filled with anger, his eyes frightened. "You shouldn't've told that, Mr. Hawkes," he said accusingly and then looked imploringly at the newspaperman. "Can you take my surrender, sir? I been trying to surrender, but nobody will listen. I'll be shot if I don't surrender."

"No, no," Fogerty said soothingly. "Nobody will shoot you, lad. So you were in the fighting? Did you see your fellow Rebels die bravely?"

Rafe Linkous sniffled and rubbed his nose against a gray sleeve. "They didn't have no chance to die bravely, mister. A shell exploded right in the middle of the company. If I hadn't been back of the tree line, behind a big oak, I'd be pieces of meat like them." Linkous stopped and wiped his running nose again.

"Well, go ahead," Fogerty insisted. "What you say, lad, is of good substance." He scribbled in his notebook. "I take it that some of your comrades were killed."

"Blown to bits," Linkous said.

"I like that phrase," Fogerty cried. "Blown to bits. How many men were lost, would you say?"

"All of them except us still in the woods."

"You have no casualty number, I suppose. Tell me what the explosion of the artillery shell was like."

Linkous blinked his eyes, trying to keep tears from showing. "Nothing but a big flash and a big bang and lots of smoke. We wasn't expecting it, you see. The captain was marching us down the slope toward the field. Next thing I saw was bloody arms and legs and Will Dean's head where they'd been flung up along the tree line."

The newspaperman smiled a smile of false sympathy. "You could say they died bravely, could you not, lad? Could you tell me why you are now so far from the scene of the fray? Why a Rebel is so deep behind enemy lines?"

"Truly, sir, I have left the Rebel army and am trying desperately to surrender. Soldiering ain't what it's cracked up to be. It is just hell, and I am going home to help my pa with spring plowing."

Nodding with approval, Fogerty continued his scribbling.

"Good, good." He smiled again at Linkous. "Now, pray tell me, what is your name?"

Linkous's face turned angry again. "I ain't telling my name till somebody takes my surrender. In writing," he cried.

"I have not that authority," the correspondent said, winking at Johnny. "You, Mr. Hawkes, may I quote you as 'Traveler from Texas' witnessing this great battle? You saw heroes die for the cause. You saw Union commanders lead their men to victory. Magnanimous men, stainless, undefiled, devoted patriots, the Union's brightest stars and purest jewels. Loved, honored, and admired by every true-hearted son who marched under their commands." As he spoke, Fogerty was busily writing down his own words.

Johnny's face was a study in perplexity. "No, sir, as I said, I saw none of the fighting."

"No matter," Fogerty replied. "Some other 'Traveler from Texas' must have seen it that way."

Johnny stood up, stretching his arms. "I ain't looked at a newspaper since we left San Antonio last January," he said, "but I sure hope I can see the one you make words for. Well, Mr. Fogerty, we got to be moving on toward Springfield."

The correspondent spoke hurriedly. "I say, could you do me a good turn? Post a dispatch for me at the Springfield telegraph office? I'll dash it off this moment." Without waiting for Hawkes to reply, he turned to a fresh page in his notebook, reciting the words as he wrote: "Bloody battle south of Springfield. Thousands slain. Glorious victory for the Union. Rebels blown to bits by Union cannon. Rebel General McCulloch killed. Secesh fleeing in all directions. So desperate they used camels in assault. Full account to follow. Signed, Fogerty." He ripped the page out, folded it carefully, and handed it to Johnny. "Just tell the telegrapher to send it collect to the *New York Graphic*. And be sure he gets my name in."

VII

BEN BUTTERFIELD

That professional veteran of the Civil War, Colonel Preston Boggs, just left this office, after giving me the official losses of the Battle of Pea Ridge, or as he calls it, the Battle of Elkhorn Tavern. Colonel Boggs would like to change everything about the Civil War, including its name to the War Between the States, and even its outcome, I suspect. Through the years he has also changed his rank. I am told on good authority that he ended the war as Lieutenant Preston Boggs, but during his career as a professional veteran he has promoted himself to colonelcy. My reliable informant tells me that at last summer's Confederate Reunion at the McNeil campgrounds, he was introduced more than once at speechmakings as "Brigadier" and made no effort to disown the rank.

But no matter. Preston Boggs is a useful member of local society. He maintains a library filled with statistical records of what I call the War of the Rebellion, and scarcely a day goes by that he is not asked by somebody to settle an argument about a certain campaign or a commander or a field of battle. He is accepted as the final arbiter on numbers of killed, wounded, or blown to bits in any and all engagements.

In addition to this essential function, Colonel Boggs is recognized as having no equal far and wide in the art of penmanship. So beautiful are the letters formed by his hand, every certificate and diploma issued to students in the public schools, as well as to graduates of the medical college, are inscribed by Preston Boggs—names, dates, and honors. My dear wife, Hilda Fagerhalt, has one of these masterpieces with her name in bold cursive strokes framed behind glass on a wall in our bedroom, and she boasts that it was one of Colonel Boggs's earliest efforts, done two or three years after he returned from the battles of Virginia.

What else Colonel Boggs does with his time is not in my ken; perhaps his duties as professional veteran and inscriber of documents leave him with no hours to spare. He is a widower, the owner of a small hotel on lower Louisiana Street, but his unmarried daughter, Blossom, is mistress of that establishment. He lives there and dines there and can be seen on the veranda on almost any clement day holding forth from a massive rocking chair in his capacity as professional veteran, listening to or talking with other survivors of the great conflict.

In this small city there are veterans of both armies, although most by far were soldiers of the Confederacy. The few Union veterans call themselves the Grand Army of the Republic, and whenever a parade is held, those that have had blue uniforms tailored to fit their aging girths march right behind the men in gray. For their annual reunions, however, the GAR must entrain to St. Louis. Four years ago in '98 they attracted considerable attention with their sprightly marching in a local parade to mark the inauguration of President William McKinley. Afterward there was some talk in both veterans organizations about holding joint reunions at McNeil. Colonel Boggs, however, was firmly opposed. His objection was said to be based on the fact that the McNeil campground was the site of a skirmish between a regiment known as the Texas Rangers and an Iowa cavalry squadron. After exchanging a few shots, both outfits fled the field, but the blood of several Texans was shed there. In Preston Boggs's view that incident so hallowed the ground that any official presence of the GAR or any other Yankee patriotic society should not be encouraged. Individuals, of course, are always welcome, provided they do not wear blue uniforms.

During the summer, twenty-six years ago, I visited Philadelphia with the Great John Robinson Circus. The veterans of both armies were holding a reunion together beside the Centennial Exhibition grounds. But then maybe Philadelphia is not hallowed ground. Anyway, the local GAR still goes all the way to St. Louis for their reunion instead of to the nearby McNeil campgrounds.

But all this is beside the point. The purpose of this interruption is to insert the proper number of losses of soldiers at Pea Ridge, or Elkhorn Tavern. I never had a chance to read the report of the battle written by Frank Fogerty of the New York Graphic, but I would bet real money it was filled with gross exaggerations. When I get to the part in this narrative about Omar and Tooley being auctioned in New York City, Frank Fogerty will reappear. He was a master at stretching the truth, a fault of far too many writers for newspapers, but it's a great godsend for publicizers of circuses and other fanciful creations of mankind.

Now to get around to the casualties at Pea Ridge, which Fogerty surely stretched into the thousands: The Rebel Army lost about eight hundred dead and wounded and two or three hundred more who were either captured, deserted, or blown to bits. The Union Army, which kept more exact records, reported 203 killed, 980 wounded, and 201 captured, deserted, or blown to bits. Colonel Preston Boggs came here in person to present me with these figures, written in his exquisite hand upon a sheet of ruled yellow paper.

While the colonel was discussing the battle's importance and its failed opportunities, I noticed he kept sniffing the air in a gentlemanly manner, and I finally realized that he was inhaling the fragrance of turnip greens cooking on Hilda Fagerhalt's stove and drifting from our living quarters into the hardware store and down the hall to this office. When I gave Colonel Boggs the opportunity, he launched into a tribute to expertly cooked greens and then delineated the differences among turnip greens, collards, and mustard greens.

He was disappointed when I told him that I could not abide collards or mustard greens, but that Hilda's skill as a cook had made me a devotee of turnip greens. Never in my youthful years in Texas forts or during my career with the circus had I been served any kind of greens.

Colonel Boggs declared there was no greater delicacy then cornbread dipped in the pot liquor of greens properly seasoned with fatback pork. He was fairly salivating when he left me and marched down the hall to bid farewell to Hilda in the store. A minute ago I heard the entrance screen door slam shut as he departed with what sounded like a gleeful chortle.

So I am not surprised to hear Hilda Fagerhalt's voice coming down the hallway, which acts like a giant megaphone. "Brigadier General Boggs is coming to dinner with us, Ben. Get over to Lora Valentine's house, and tell her to join us. Tell her the brigadier will be here." She pauses and adds, "If we had a telephone now, I could ring her. A telephone would save wear and tear on your leg, Ben."

Like so many women, Hilda Fagerhalt is a born matchmaker. Using turnip greens and cornbread and pot liquor to bring together the town's most prominent widower and widow, Hilda will become a creature of soaring spirits. She will fancy that what she is doing is a work of the purest art.

VIII

WAITING FOR CAPTAIN LIGHTFOOT

~

As they came nearer to Springfield, Ben noticed that the cabins and small fields carved out of the forest were closer together. Although Rafe Linkous, the homeward-bound Confederate Missourian, was feverish from his swollen hand, he began walking with a brisker step. Each fresh recognition of a familiar farmhouse brought a low cry of relief from him.

"How far to your place, Rafe?" Ben asked him.

Linkous allowed it was about five more miles to the Springfield square and about another mile on the other side of town to his pa's farm. He hoped that he could find a Union soldier in Springfield who would be willing to take his surrender.

Holes had been worn in Ben's stockings, and one of his heels was so badly chafed he almost decided that if there were many more miles to go he would have to ride one of the camels. From time to time, Hadjee dismounted to walk for a few minutes beside Tooley, but Ben knew that riding in that saddle could be as nauseating as a bareback ride on Omar.

"What side of Springfield is the stockyard on?" Johnny Hawkes asked Linkous.

"Oh, you just turn at the courthouse and go down the hill a ways," he replied. "It's where all the roads come into Springfield, and Pa says all the roads in Missouri come to Springfield."

Although they were close to their goal, the sun and their hunger told them that the time was well past noon. At the end of a log bridge up ahead, a man and a woman seated on the ground beside two saddled horses appeared to be eating something. Nearby them a thin plume of smoke spiraled upward from a little fire. Johnny sniffed the air and decided that they should halt and join the strangers.

Before Johnny could gain consent to use the cooking fire, the man and woman were on their feet, staring at the camels. The man was dressed in a greasy deerskin coat belted at the waist with a huge brass buckle. The hem of the long coat reached the knees of his trousers that were stuffed into a pair of heavy boots that bore traces of bear's grease in the leather cracks. His wide-brimmed, low-crowned hat was weathered gray, but in the band a bunch of birds' feathers dyed a brilliant red added a flash of gaiety. His hair and short beard were the color of straw; he did not appear to be yet forty.

The woman stood shyly behind his burly frame, but Ben, curious as always, shifted to one side so that he could see her face, which was round as a full moon. She was Indian but was different from the Kiowa and Comanche women he had seen in Texas. She was quite young, a bit plump, her dark eyes continuing to peer at him from a winged calico bonnet. She wore a simple beaded buckskin dress.

After the usual exchange about the camels, the man welcomed them to use his fire and bent to toss a few more dry branches upon it. "I'm Will Cornwall," he said. "Trapper by trade. This is my woman, Lucy." His voice was deep, echoing as if it might be coming from a cavern.

"You trap in these hills, then?" Johnny asked.

"Most years I trap out in the Rocky Mountains. Blackfeet country. But beaver's gettin' thin out there, and what skins I take have to be brought all the way down to St. Louis for decent prices. This winter my woman and me we come out here for closer pickins, but hellfire, this country's so filled up with people, the best fur animals done run off." He shrugged his heavy shoulders. "But I did get me a young b'ar yestiddy, juicy with winter fat." He stopped abruptly. "I see you got some salt bacon thar. Want a trade?"

They swapped meats, and when Hadjee got a pot for coffee out of the camel pack they all settled down for a long nooning. Will Cornwall's woman, Lucy, made herself busy at the fire, but she never spoke. Cornwall, on the other hand, was extremely loquacious, words tumbling out as though they had been dammed up within him for weeks, which was probably the case. Lucy was Arapaho, he said. She'd been captured by a band of Blackfeet, and he'd bought her from them.

"Little mirrors," he said, "no bigger than a silver dollar. Blackfeet's crazy about mirrors. Young men especially. They'll sit and look at their faces for hours. Mirrors are better than money." He wanted to know where Johnny had found the coffee. "I took my pelts into Springfield t'other day, hopin' to trade some for coffee, but they ain't a bean in the town. We been drinkin' tea from sassafras root till we must be turnin' pink inside."

When Johnny told him the coffee had been obtained from the Union Army, the trapper showed intense interest. "Maybe you can tell me about that army. Fellow in Springfield says to me they pay you to carry a gun. And more pay if you shoot people. Is this right, friend? What is this ruckus about?"

Johnny laughed. "It ain't a simple thing, Mr. Cornwall. People on both sides get mighty stirred up about it. Some say it has to do with the Negro slaves, but since the shootin' started I've traveled two ways across Texas and then across the Indian Nation and into Arkansas and the Missouri hills, but I'm damned if I've yet seen a free or slave Negro. Some say the shootin' started when some Rebels fired a big gun into a fort somewhere on the Atlantic Ocean. I'd wager you silver money that not one of the boys tryin' to kill each other over there at Pea Ridge ever laid eyes on the Atlantic Ocean, no, sir. Some of the Texans I come north with spoke a lot about their stained honor and their duty to God and country, but none of that troubles me."

With his calloused fingers, Will Cornwall lifted a strip of greasy bacon from the sizzling pan and nibbled it slowly through his beard into his wide mouth. "You ain't a regular soldier then, Mr. Hawkes? A feller in Springfield told me they pay ten dollars in gold for every man you kill. Why, that's considerable more than I can gain trappin' beaver or anything else. I'm a good shot, too."

"It ain't that way," Johnny said. "They make you wear a blue outfit if you're Union, or a gray outfit if you're Rebel. And you got to do what they tell you and go where they tell you. Till the fighting stops, if it ever does. If you decide to bob out and go home or some'eres else, they'll hunt you down, say words over you, and then likely shoot you."

"I wouldn't tie to that," Cornwall said with a grimace. He fingered another strip of smoking bacon from the pan and then took the tin cup of coffee offered by Hadjee. "But I reckon me and Lucy will head on down to where the shootin' is." He reached out with one of his enormous hands to pat the Arapaho woman's rump. "Maybe there's more skins to be found farther on. Bear and deer ain't too precious in St. Louis. The animals easiest to find in these forests and the hardest to kill are the wild boars. Razorbacks the hill folks call 'em. Dangerous as grizzlies if you're not ready for 'em. Mean little red eyes over a nasty long narrow snout, they'll run right at you as fast as a bird can fly. Some days back I managed to kill one of 'em. Surprised him, I did, but had to put three shots in his ugly head with my Sharps afore he quit tryin'. Meat tough as rawhide and the skin ain't worth two bits."

Johnny laughed. "Yeah, we saw a bunch of wild hogs running for life when the armies begun shooting cannon there at Pea Ridge."

Cornwall took a ragged fold of linen from a coat pocket and wiped his greasy fingers and lips, burlesquing the elaborate motions of a jack-a-dandy and winking at Johnny as he did so. "You know, Mr. Hawkes, you can tell a lot about folks by the animals they admire. Indians, now, they like eagles and bears and buffalo and even coyotes. Most such animals are good medicine to an Indian. They'll draw pictures of 'em on their tepees and elsewhere. But a boar hog, razorback, Christ-a-mighty, they'd never admire such a vile, bloody-eyed, snouty beast. Maybe the trashy white folks in these hills might put razorback signs on their amulets and good-luck charms, but the lowest-down Indian out in the Plains and the Rockies would see' em as nothing but bad medicine, you can bet your boots."

While Will Cornwall continued his monologue—interrupted only occasionally by an interjection from Johnny—Ben finished eating his slice of gamy bear meat and transferred his attention to the horses tied at the end of the bridge. They had been unbitted so they could browse on early shoots of native grass along the edge of the road. One was a handsome chestnut stallion. The other was a small gray pony bearing an odd-shaped saddle covered with buffalo rawhide. Decorative buckskin fringes hung from pommel and cantle. Ben walked closer to examine the saddle.

"That's a Blackfoot saddle, boy," Cornwall said. "Made to fit a woman's arse."

"I saw saddles like that when I was at Fort Laramie some time ago," Johnny said. "A bunch of Crows come there to trade. But I been admiring that chestnut of yours. Never saw a horse built quite that way."

"Kentucky breed, Mr. Hawkes. You wouldn't think, looking at his flanks, he'd be much of a jumper, would you now? Well, that chestnut can out jump any horse I ever rode. Want to see him?"

"Wouldn't miss a good horse jump," Johnny said.

After adjusting saddle and bridle, Cornwall mounted. With thumb and forefinger separate about an inch and raised almost to his eyes, he studied the grassy approach to the right of the bridge and appeared to be measuring the width of the stream. Then he trotted the horse back down the road, a hundred yards or more, and turned and started back in a quickening gallop. Both Johnny and Ben had seen faster horses in Texas than the chestnut, but they perceived the raw power in every motion of the animal as it drove faster and faster toward them. With the Arapaho woman they crossed over to the left side of the bridge. Hadjee waited with the camels in a low spot on the right side, well out of the way of the grassy approach to the stream. Both camels were down, resting. Perhaps it was the beating of hooves on the hard clay road that aroused Omar's curiosity. Just before the horse swept past, he raised up, crooking his long neck around. The horse shied, trying to slow its forward plunge. Before Cornwall could regain control, it reared, lifting its forelegs in the air, almost falling backward, then steadied and raced straight across the bridge and down the road toward Springfield.

"Goddamn them camels!" Johnny shouted. He glowered at Hadjee and the dromedaries, both of which were now on their feet. He walked out on the bridge and waited there until horse and rider returned.

"Them furrin beasts spooked him," Cornwall said as he dismounted beside the dying fire.

"Yeah," Johnny said. "Our apologies, Mr. Cornwall."

Cornwall grunted and began a careful examination of each hoof and leg of the chestnut. "No harm done," he said after a few minutes. "We'll give it another try, I reckon, if you'll hide them misbegotten beasties."

After Johnny sent Hadjee and the camels across the bridge and some distance along the road, Cornwall repeated the galloping approach, and this time the chestnut soared like a mythical flying horse, floating above grass and stream and landing gracefully on the greensward beyond.

Shortly afterward, the members of the two parties bade each other warm farewells, the trapper and the woman heading south on horseback, while Johnny and Ben and Rafe Linkous hurried on foot to overtake Hadjee and the camels. All the way to Springfield they talked of nothing but the aerial jump, offering various estimates of the distance covered, the length of time the chestnut was in the air, the monetary value of such a horse, the near disaster at the bridge, and the animal's miraculously calm recovery.

Late in the afternoon they entered the Springfield square. On one corner was a tavern, with half a dozen uniformed officers loitering beneath a sign: TURNPIKE INN. Dominating one side was the county courthouse. Facing it was a row of shops along a raised plank sidewalk, parts of which were shaded by weather-stained canvas awnings. Lines of stumps along both sides of the street marked the recent deaths of shade trees cut for fuel by occupying soldiers of alternate armies. The broad open area teemed with unhurried motion—men mounted on horses and mules, men on foot sauntering or reposing against posts along the sidewalk, a pair of hogs wallowing and grunting in mud beneath a leaky watering trough. Dogs were everywhere, some sleeping on the wooden walk, others ambling from post to post, smelling and urinating leisurely, as though time might have stopped forever.

"It's most big as San Antonio," Ben said.

Johnny laughed. "And just as lazy looking."

Very few women were on the street, most of them wearing sunbonnets and calico dresses so long that the hems dragged with each step. Except for an occasional convalescing young soldier in blue, most of the men were bearded and long haired. They carried pistols of various sizes holstered to their belts. Some were riding horses and mules, all moved with a slow-footed pace.

The sudden appearance of the camels, of course, brought everything to a standstill. A man astraddle a low-backed donkey came closer. His legs were so long that his toes kicked against the ground. He dismounted by stepping over the donkey's bowed head. He was armed with a pair of silvery revolvers.

"Where you all come from?" he demanded, and Johnny had to go through his explanations for the presence of the camels and to deny that they were the vanguard for a circus coming to Springfield. "We're heading for the stockyard," he added, "and I got to send a telegraph. Where is the telegraph office?"

"Why, right across thar on the corner. You see that Yankee soldier setting on the bench? Right thar."

They had to make their way through a gathering crowd of curious spectators, frightening a dog and a horse or two that were pressed too close to the camels. During the commotion, Rafe Linkous whispered to Ben, "Maybe that Yankee soldier will take my surrender."

The soldier was a sergeant. He had been dozing, and the arrival of the small mob startled him so that he dropped his crutch on the board sidewalk with a loud clatter that alarmed the camels. Hadjee quickly brought the animals to a standstill. The confused soldier stood with one leg propped against the bench while he pummeled the air with this fists as though defending himself from attack.

Rafe Linkous stepped closer to the sergeant yet kept out of reach should he resume the fisticuffs. "Sir," he said earnestly, "I am Rafe Linkous, Third Missouri Infantry. Would you kindly take my surrender?"

The big sergeant blinked, his face showing puzzlement. "What you doing here, boy? You're not in uniform."

It was true that somewhere along his journey, Linkous had lost his military forage cap to which had been attached a brass insignia with regimental markings. His plain gray blouse was streaked with dirt; his trousers, also soiled, were ordinary jeans. He stammered something unintelligible.

"Look," the sergeant said, "I'm Eighth Regiment Indiana. What do you mean you want to surrender to me?"

"Well, I'm Confederate Missouri."

The sergeant's mouth opened in astonishment. "You mean you want to be my prisoner? Hell, boy, I'm a convalescent, and from the looks of that swole-up hand you ought to be in the hospital, too."

Johnny Hawkes moved in closer. "The boy lives nearby," he explained. "He needs a parole so he won't be shot for deserting."

"Aw, I see." The sergeant touched Rafe's infected hand very gently. "Hot as fire." Then he leaned down and retrieved his crutch. "You follow me, boy, and I'll take you to Doc Fields, the surgeon. Likely he'll lance that paw of yours and then write you out a parole."

The crowd made way for the sergeant and Linkous, and as soon as they had moved away across the square, Johnny went into the telegraph office, leaving Ben to help Hadjee protect the camels from the increasing throng. When Johnny came out, he good-naturedly asked the crowd to give them room to drive the camels to the stockyards. "They're government property," he explained. "Got to turn them over. Who's in charge down there?"

"Just ask for Pat Halfacre," somebody replied. "You'll be taken care of all right." For some reason this remark brought a snicker and what sounded like a derisive cry from the crowd, but Johnny ignored the response. He helped Ben and Hadjee force the camels past a hitching rack and turned them down a sloping street. The few spectators who continued to follow gradually thinned out as they approached a stockaded log fence. Clouds were thickening in the west, and distant flashes of lightning played across the darker sky. A strong breeze arose suddenly, bringing a heavy leathery odor of horses, urine, and manure.

"Smells like a cavalry post," Johnny said. "Don't it make you homesick for old Fort Davis, Ben?"

"Could be," Ben replied. "Did you send the telegraph for that fancy-talking man from New York?"

"All I could do was leave Mr. Fogerty's message with the operator. He said guerrillas had cut the wire somewhere between here and a place named Rolla. He promised to send it as soon as the wires are fixed."

"What's a telegraph look like?" Ben asked.

"It's a kind of key that they tap up and down with their fingers. They signal with a code that spells out letters and words. Beats me what makes the clicks go over the wires, but they sure do."

They had reached the entrance to the stockyards. A squared sign, crudely lettered and crudely spelled, was nailed to the closed gate:

LivRY baRn & stOkyARd
p. hALFAcre, ProP.

———

ARMy RemOUnt

A bored soldier, armed with only a holstered pistol, came abruptly to life when he saw the camels.

"We're looking for Pat Halfacre," Johnny said.

"State your business," the soldier demanded rudely.

"My business," Johnny replied testily, "is to deliver these animals to proper authorities by order of Captain Solomon Lightfoot."

With a sullen look, the soldier turned, slid back the iron bolt on the heavy gate, and kicked it open. "Inside," he said. "You'll find Pat Halfacre t'other side the barn. Where the shootin' is."

The repetitious crack-crack of a small arm resounded from the direction of the barn. A closer roll of thunder overrode the firing. Johnny led the way past rail-fenced pens of riding and draft horses, some of which had recently been branded "U.S." As they turned the last corner of the barn, they came upon the shooter, holding a long-barreled Colt revolver. The target was a sheet of newspaper tacked to the top log of a feeding rack; the paper's center was pocked with a concentration of bullet holes.

Dressed in a red-checked shirt and brown jeans, she appeared at first glance to be a male, but the full breasts and wide hips and the sandy curls on her shoulders blurred that image, and when she spoke in a soft contralto, they knew she was female. "What in hell are you boys bringing in here?" She looked hard at the camels, and one corner of her full lips lifted in half a grin. Her eyes were black as the eyes of a pair of dried field peas, and her face was sprinkled with tiny freckles.

"We're looking for Pat Halfacre," Johnny said politely.

"That's me, mister. Sometimes called Patsy Halfacre." She gave him a complete grin this time.

Johnny explained who they were and why they were there. "Maybe you know Captain Solomon Lightfoot of the Army Quartermaster."

"Indeed I do," she said quickly. "A pure son of a bitch, if you'll excuse my unladylike expression."

Johnny chuckled. "That description has crossed my mind more than once." He decided he liked Miss Patsy Halfacre and wondered if she claimed a man somewhere around. "You're shooting with a Texas gun," he said. "That's a Walker Colt."

She looked at him in surprise. "Yeah, my pa brought it back from Texas, a present for me. Say, you wouldn't be interested in a shooting match, would you? Money wagers."

Johnny glanced at the riddled newspaper target on the rack, then walked across the feed lot to examine it more closely. Ben, curious as always, followed him. "Johnny," he whispered, "look, she didn't never miss the center. If she fired every shot on this target, she'll be hard to beat."

When Johnny brought the sheet of newspaper back to the side of the barn, Patsy Halfacre was trying to talk with Hadjee, making signs with her hands and slowly pronouncing words by separate syllables.

"I think he understands you, ma'am," Johnny said, "but he don't know how to speak many of our words." At this Hadjee gave her one of his rarely dispensed smiles and bowed slightly.

"He's a strange pumpkin," Patsy said. She snatched the newspaper target from Johnny's hands. "Not my best shooting," she cried airily and grinned at him.

"I'd be pleased to match you, Miss Halfacre," he said, "but the Yankee soldiers took my Dragoon Colt and must've named it contraband of war the way they did our horses and the camels."

"What a pack of nonsense," she countered. "We've got dozens of shooting irons. I'll just call your bluff, Johnny Hawkes."

Thunder boomed overhead, and a few drops of wind-driven rain pattered upon them. "I need a place to put these camels," Johnny said hurriedly, "until Captain Lightfoot comes." She motioned for them to follow her around to the open entrance of the barn. They took shelter just in time before a downpour descended like a gray curtain.

While they waited in the barn, Johnny and Ben learned that the "P. Halfacre" on the stockyard's sign was Patrick Halfacre, Patsy's father, who had gone off to southeastern Missouri to buy mules. The market for horses and mules was so good at Springfield, she explained, that they could not keep enough on hand. As fast as her father could buy and drive them in, she sold them—to jayhawkers

from Kansas, to the Missouri militia, to an occasional wary agent
for the Confederate Army, and to the U.S. Army, which had also
promised to pay for yard pens in which they kept replacement
animals. That is how she had met Captain Lightfoot, she said, a
man who drove flinty bargains, exploited the power of the military,
and did not treat her like a lady, not even when she changed from
her working britches into dresses. Johnny wondered for what reason the jack-a-dandies of Springfield back in the square had made
derisive noises when her name was mentioned. Was she too independent for a female? Had she made herself unavailable to them?
So far she had been friendly enough to him.

By the time the rain slackened, darkness had fallen, and Johnny
asked her to recommend an inn where he and Ben might spend the
night. "Hadjee will stay with the camels," he said. "To him they
are like little children, but me and Ben need forage and a dry place
to sleep."

"If you don't mind sleeping on straw, there's room next to Pa's
and my quarters. He puts his drovers in there when they bring in
stock. Straw's clean, no bedbugs. You and the boy can take potluck
with me."

"We'll pay you when Captain Lightfoot comes," Johnny said.
"He's promised us enough in gold to take us back to Texas."

She gave him a pitying look. "That Lightfoot's promises ain't
worth a penny, unless you got it in hand."

The Halfacres' quarters was a shedlike structure adjoining one
side of the barn. Patsy lighted a lantern and showed them to the
drovers' room. While they were stowing their saddlebags, someone
knocked loudly on the front door, summoning her in a loud, peremptory voice.

Johnny, acting in his best chivalrous manner, and Ben followed
the girl into the front room, where she cautiously opened the door.
Rain was falling again, steadily. A soldier's wet face showed in the
lantern light. "A man in a queer sort of wagon, Miss Halfacre, says
you know him. Name sounded like Vinegar. Shall I let him in the
gate?"

"What's he look like?" she asked.

"Little bit of a duck. Thick black eyebrows, short black chin
beard."

"Oh! Dr. Pingree! Let him in."

"Shall I search his wagon?"

"No, no. He's just a harmless peddler."

She got a coat from a closet and went out into the rain, saying there was no need for anyone to come with her, but they both went, Johnny carrying the lantern.

Out of the darkness the wagon creaked and groaned, then loomed in the form of a towering box with a little man seated upon the shelflike driver's seat, holding the lines that guided a matched pair of giant sorrel-coated Belgians. As they moved into the lantern light and through the barn's entrance, raindrops sparkled on their flaxen manes. Artistically designed and colored lettering on the wagon's side proclaimed to the world: DR. PINGREE'S CHARIOT OF WONDERS.

The movement of the disturbed camels, and probably their unfamiliar odor, set the Belgians to stomping their huge hooves until Dr. Pingree, with Patsy Halfacre's efficient help, unhitched and led them off to stalls on the opposite side of the barn. The introductions were brief and disorderly. Johnny was cordial enough, but he was slightly provoked that Patsy had transferred all her attentions from him to the tiny, aging peddler.

Ben was astonished at the dimensions of the wagon, quite the largest he had ever seen, and when he faced Dr. Pingree to shake his hand hastily, he was surprised to find himself slightly taller than this grown man with the thick black eyebrows, black goatee, thin aquiline nose, and bright penetrating eyes.

"What wonders did you find for me in Jefferson City, Dr. Pingree?" Patsy asked him while they were stabling the Belgians.

"Ah," he replied in a voice so deep and strong that it was inconsistent with his slight physique. "For you, some beautiful rings and brooches brought to Independence from Santa Fe, some reading books I obtained at a bargain from a dying merchant, much Indian goods, Kickapoo medicines that will cure all ailments, but of course you need none of those."

"Saddles," she said. "Pa told me to buy any good saddles."

"A few old ones, but mostly good. Pingree does not buy or sell things that are of no value."

She asked him if he needed food, but he said he did not, that sleep was what he most required after the long day's journey from the north.

Johnny and Ben were surprised that he did not accompany them back to the house. "He could share the drovers' room with us," Johnny said to Patsy.

"Oh, no," she replied quickly. "Dr. Pingree sleeps in his wagon." She laughed. "It's like a fine palace in there. I'll ask him to show it to you tomorrow."

Next morning the rain had turned to a cold dismal drizzle. No stock buyers came, nor any military officers, and after Patsy saw that her stableboys had properly fed and watered the livestock, she began teasing Johnny about a shooting match. Dr. Pingree, dressed in a fancy india rubber coat, walked up to the Springfield square and soon returned to report that the town was deserted. "Until the sun comes out," he said, "useless for me to take the wagon up there to peddle."

By this time Johnny and Patsy had decided to set up targets—a pair of old rusted tin plates—opposite the rear window of the barn. In this way they could stand inside out of the nasty weather and fire away as they pleased. From the Halfacres' collection of pistols, Johnny chose a Starr six-shot .44. The weapon did not feel as well-balanced in his hand as had his confiscated Dragoon Colt, but after a few trial shots he announced that he was ready to take on Patsy. For a while Ben and Dr. Pingree watched them and then acted as judges when the targets were brought inside. They declared Patsy the winner by a small margin, and she took one of the silver coins that Johnny had wagered. She must have guessed the low state of his purse, however, because instead of proposing another contest, she introduced some trick shots that she claimed to have invented and said she wanted to teach him. They included the use of mirrors, quick-draw shots at potatoes swinging on strings, and extinguishing the flames of candles.

After a time Ben wearied of watching, and Dr. Pingree invited the boy to visit his Chariot of Wonders. Ben was amazed that so many objects could be assembled in one wagon. Weather vanes in the shape of roosters, mirrors of all sizes, candles and brass candlesticks, flower-decorated chamber pots, bandboxes, baskets, brooms, coffee grinders, cooking pots, inkwells, tankards, lanterns, blankets, carpetbags, clocks, axes, bells, combs, spices, saddles, cigars, shirts, hats, caps, moccasins, Indian leggings, buffalo robes, pistols, jewelry, dolls, Jew's harps, tiny painted wooden animals, liniment and other medicines, jars of honey, and a tin box filled with balls of spiced hard candy, one of which Dr. Pingree presented to Ben.

Every article appeared to have its place, in kegs or on hooks or fastened upon shelves. A narrow walkway the length of the wagon divided the treasures. At its end was a pull-down step up which Pingree led Ben to a cell-like room furnished with a chair, a cot, and a washstand.

"I live like a tortoise," the peddler said. "My house on my back." The little man obviously was pleased with his own handiwork. As they came back down the steps he asked, "Can you read, boy?"

"Yes, sir. Miz Sergeant Peddicord taught me."

Pingree's thick black eyebrows raised slightly. "Now, who would Miz Sergeant Peddicord be?"

Ben told him that she was a soldier's wife at Fort Davis who had helped take care of him after his father left him there.

"And what did she have you read from?"

"We started with the Bible. That's all she had, till the commander sent her a few with some newspapers and magazines.

"Well, King James's Bible and Shakespeare, they're the best for reading. Too bad Miz Sergeant had no Shakespeare." He stopped in the middle of the walkway, bent down, grabbed a semicircular handhold, and lifted the planking to expose a short ladder. Ben peered into a shadowy recess that was like the hold of a small boat. Pingree led the way down.

Ben found that the ceiling was so low he had to stand half bent over. A small board window, propped open, was at one side. "My dog used to sleep down here," Pingree said, "but she died." A few crates and a box or two filled half the space. In one box was a stock of cheaply printed paper-covered books with crude drawings on the covers. The peddler took one off the top and handed it to Ben. "They come from England," he said. "Penny dreadfuls. You're welcome to borrow this, but don't believe a word of it." Ben read the title, *Jack Sheppard on the Spanish Main*. The illustration showed a pirate skewering another with a sword. "Thank you, sir, I'll take good care of it," Ben said.

When they left the wagon, the occasional crack of a pistol shot came from the other end of the barn. Ben looked at Dr. Pingree.

"Sir," he said, "do you think my pard Johnny is getting sweet on Miss Patsy?"

The peddler tugged at his short black goatee. "Well now, I don't know about him, boy, but I'd say Miss Patsy is getting sweet on your Mr. Johnny Hawkes. She don't take a fancy to many young fellers the way she does him."

That night Johnny didn't come to bed in the drovers' shed until long after Ben fell asleep while waiting for him to leave the company of Miss Patsy Halfacre in the front part of the house.

On the second day after their arrival in Springfield, the sun was out with unusual brilliance and warmth. At breakfast in the Halfacres' kitchen, Patsy told Ben that if he would help the stableboys fill the corn racks in the feed lot she would pay him two bits. Patsy's generosity and kindness pleased him as much as possession of the coin. She was much more agreeable, he thought, than the yellow-haired woman in San Antonio whom Johnny had been sweet on before they left with the supply train.

That afternoon, after filling the racks with corn ears, Ben walked up into the town. Dr. Pingree had brought his Chariot of Wonders to the center of the square and appeared to be quite busy peddling his wares to a constantly moving crowd, more than half of them women in sunbonnets. While walking along the wooden sidewalk, Ben came suddenly upon the pair of ambulatory wounded soldiers from St. Louis who had been left behind at Temporary Pybolt's blacksmith shop. They recognized Ben immediately and began chattering in their broken English about the whereabouts of the camels. As best he could make out they had obtained a ride on an ox-drawn wagon and had found their way to the army's hospital in Springfield where their wounds had been properly attended. They exhibited their spotless linen bandages with obvious pride.

Ben asked if they had seen a very young Confederate soldier named Linkous who was suffering from a badly swollen hand. Neither could recall such a patient, but they suggested that Ben return to the hospital with them and make a search for the boy.

The hospital was only a short distance from the square. Originally a church, it had been expanded with hastily constructed warrens of pine planking. The St. Louis Germans proved to be of little help in finding Rafe Linkous. Only one surgeon had been assigned to the hospital by the Missouri military authorities, and he depended on the assistance of recuperating soldiers and a few women of the town who were acting as nurses. No one had taken the time to prepare a complete list of patients, and if Ben had not chanced to see the big sergeant from Indiana sitting on a bench, he probably would not have learned why Linkous was no longer there.

"He ran off. To home I reckon," the sergeant told Ben.

"Was his hand better?" Ben asked.

"Nah, he must've feared they'd cut if off. The surgeon told him that amputation likely would be for the best."

As the day was growing late, Ben decided to return to the stockyards and ask Johnny if he thought they should do something to help Linkous, perhaps try to find his pa's farm. Johnny, under Patsy's direction, was busy cleaning out the big fireplace where she did most of the cooking, but he promised to help Ben find Linkous the next morning.

Soon after sunrise, however, Captain Solomon Lightfoot came knocking at Patsy Halfacre's door, interrupting a pleasant breakfast they were having in front of the fireplace.

IX

BEN BUTTERFIELD

~

From my window I see an advancing Letitia Higgins, who must be as buxom a bed partner as any male could desire but who as far as I know bestows her favors only upon Yancey Higgins, who is probably the least deserving male of all in this community, a worthless ne'er-do-well scamp.

Because Yancy cannot, or will not, entirely support Letitia, she does laundry for certain families, including my own, approaching the task in as genteel a manner as if she were a member of the royal-born on a mission of mercy. She is at this minute entering the hardware store, with her empty wicker basket, and for the next several minutes will be exchanging gossip with Hilda, who will quietly and unobtrusively fill the basket with our soiled clothing and linens. What I must do before Letitia Higgins leaves with the filled basket is to confront her with humble and indirect pleas to reduce the amount of starch she puts in my shirt collars. I did this once before, weeks ago, and it was a searing experience for both of us because Letitia cannot bear to admit that she launders anyone else's clothes besides hers and Yancey's. To ask her bluntly to reduce the amount of starch will never do. I must go in and compliment her in some manner, and then I will say, "Miss Letty, I'm having this trouble with my collar buttons. In your opinion, could it be the fault of the buttons or the collars? Do you think the collar holes might be filled with too much starch?"

Truthfully it is not the fault of the buttons or the holes. The collars that Letitia Higgins launders are simply so damned stiff and sharp-edged with starch they cut into my neck, painfully. But at least in this manner of approach perhaps I will avoid embarrassing Letitia, and myself as well.

In the meantime I will enjoy studying an old photograph. Regretfully I have only this one likeness of Will Cornwall and Patsy Halfacre, and it has faded to a pale yellow, but I can make out their smiling faces as they pose standing in front of their horses with a big tent of the Great John Robinson Circus in the background.

You see, Johnny Hawkes never forgot people he loved and admired, and after we joined the circus Johnny arranged for Patsy to come to St. Louis while the show was there. She demonstrated to the manger what she could do with pistols and rifles and was hired on the spot.

Finding Will Cornwall took a while longer. Johnny figured that some of the fur trappers would know where he might be found, and he hired a detective in St. Louis to work through the fur companies there. The detective found people who knew Will Cornwall, but nobody had seen him recently. Finally, just by chance, the detective ran into an old trapper who had come down on a boat from Omaha. Will Cornwall, the trapper said, was helping build the Union Pacific Railroad. As it turned out, that wasn't quite right. Cornwall was capturing wild mustangs, breaking them, and supplying them to the railroad builders. Johnny's detective found Cornwall in Cheyenne, and many months later while the circus was showing in Omaha, the world's greatest horse jumper came strolling into our mess tent one noon. Like Patsy, he also was hired on the spot.

For a while Patsy and Will performed separately, and then the circus manager decided to team them, combining the riding and shooting. They were never as dramatic as Queen Elizabeth Jones and her bunch of wild riders of which I was one, but they certainly pleased the crowds. In time, Queen Elizabeth Jones became a bit jealous of Patsy, and there was some bad feeling occasionally between Will and Johnny. I'm sure both were sweet on Patsy, just as Johnny and I were both sweet on Queen Elizabeth Jones. At the end of a season, Will and Patsy announced that they were getting married and joining Buffalo Bill's Wild West Show. Anybody who's seen that show knows pretty well who Wildjumper Will and Sure-shot Patsy are.

We never did find out for certain what happened to Cornwall's Arapaho woman. Johnny told me that while Will and he were drinking heavy one night, Will said he thought the Indian woman just couldn't stand the railroad and ran off to Colorado Territory to try to find her people.

Looking at this old picture of Will and Patsy reminds me of that time I spent in Springfield, and I still wonder whatever happened to Rafe Linkous. Did he ever get his parole? Did he get well? Or did he lose his hand? His life? Looking back now, Rafe reminds me in some ways of how I was at that time—just a know-nothing blunderheaded whelp caught up in a world full of grown-ups gone mad.

Oh, hell, there goes Letitia Higgins across the street with her basket full of our soiled clothes, including my collars that she'll bring back with the edges so sharp with starch they'll cut my throat from ear to ear.

X

BANK ROBBERY AT MARSHFIELD

❧

Patsy Halfacre admitted Captain Lightfoot into the house, but she did not welcome him, and for the next few minutes seemed to be pretending that he did not exist. He greeted Johnny with a false heartiness and said that he was eager to see his camels.

"The camels are in good health," Johnny replied and swallowed the last of the coffee in his mug. The brew was made from the beans that he had confiscated from the army's wagon of wounded soldiers. He had made a present of the coffee bag to Patsy.

"Let's go and have a look," Lightfoot said impatiently.

"Fair enough, if while we are looking we complete the business between us."

The captain made no reply to that but edged toward the door. He was carrying a short polished stick that he kept slapping against one leg.

When Johnny reached for his coat, Ben grabbed a biscuit from a plate and prepared to follow him. Keeping a discreet distance, the boy walked behind the two men until they entered the barn door.

Dr. Pingree and Hadjee were seated on the raised tongue of the big wagon, quietly smoking cheroots. The camels were at rest and rose with obvious reluctance when Captain Lightfoot approached them, rapping his stick along the side of a feed trough.

"As you say, Hawkes, they appear to have survived the march here," he observed somewhat begrudgingly. "A bit lean-fleshed, though."

"And now, sir," Johnny said cheerfully, "I'll take my payment for the task."

"You'll get your gold pieces, Hawkes. Bridle your impatience." He reached out and patted Tooley's shoulder. "Now I must get this fine pair to my farm in Indiana."

"What about the auction?" Johnny asked.

"Oh, that was done last night. In the quartermaster's rooms at the Turnpike Inn." He winked at Johnny. "I was the only bidder. A reasonable enough sum for contraband goods."

Ben wondered what Lightfoot had paid for the camels, but he did not dare ask and was disappointed when Johnny did not. Instead Johnny said, "Well now, Captain, this means that Hadjee and Ben and me no longer have any duties with these animals. You pay us off with the gold pieces you showed me at the battlefield, and we'll be on our way home to Texas."

Lightfoot frowned and tapped one of his knees with his stick. "I'm awaiting funds from St. Louis headquarters. The telegraph company refuses to transfer money to Springfield. Can't blame them, I suppose. This is not a civilized place. War has demoralized the people. Secesh brigands roving everywhere. Our paymaster's wagon is coming from Rolla with a cavalry escort. Should be in Springfield before noon, I hear."

"But you *had* the gold pieces."

"I won't be put upon, Hawkes," the captain retorted sternly. But seeing the anger on Johnny's face, his voice turned to a whisper that Ben could barely hear. "Damn it, man, I lost two of 'em in a seven-up game. The other one went for the camels."

"Oh." Johnny tried to conceal his dismay.

Lightfoot slapped him on the back. "Tell you what, Hawkes. You come over to the Turnpike Inn around noontime. If the paymaster arrives you'll have your money, with a bounty added. And I'll buy you a drink at the bar."

After another look at the camels, Lightfoot again slapped Johnny on the back, and with an imperious nod to Dr. Pingree and Hadjee, he left the barn.

Later that morning, when Ben saw Johnny damping his hair with water and slicking it down with a brush, he quickly donned his blue tunic and prepared to follow him to the Turnpike Inn.

"Hold on, Ben," Johnny said. "No reason for you to go."

"You may need me," Ben replied.

"What for? You can stay here and read on that book Dr. Pingree loaned you. When I come back, we'll go make inquiries about young Linkous and try to find him."

Ben shook his head slowly. "Miss Patsy don't trust that Captain Lightfoot. I aim to go so's I can remind you of that. I won't bother you none, just be some'ers nearby."

Johnny shrugged. "All right, but don't go butting in when we're talking and drinking." He sighed and went out the door and started toward the stockade gate without waiting for Ben to catch up to him.

The Turnpike Inn's double-door entrance led straight into a large parlor and bar. A high desk and a wide stairway were at the center of the room. On one side was a billiard table, but its felt covering was so badly damaged from the cue thrusts of inexperienced or drunken players that it obviously was no longer in use. A number of chairs in various states of disrepair were scattered across the uneven plank flooring between the billiard table and a fancy bar. On the shelves behind the bar were long rows of bottles, cut-glass decanters, and goblets of all shapes and sizes.

Captain Lightfoot was seated beside a small table upon which a long-necked bottle of whiskey stood guard over half a dozen shot glasses. Opposite him was another officer, with large searching eyes, a black drooping mustache, and arms so long that one of his hands was pressed against the floor. Lightfoot glanced disapprovingly at Ben, who immediately turned behind the chairs and faced the wall along which framed drawings had been mounted in double and triple rows.

"Take some whiskey, Hawkes?" Lightfoot asked without bothering to stand.

"Don't mind if I do," Johnny replied.

"Drag up a chair," Lightfoot ordered and filled one of the glasses. "John Hawkes, I want you to meet a special friend, Captain Phil Sheridan."

Sheridan, also without rising, extended one of his long arms and shook Johnny's hand. He turned to look back at Ben, smiling slightly, evidently amused by the pieces of cut-down uniforms the boy was wearing.

"Captain Sheridan has been buying horses for the army from Pat Halfacre," Lightfoot declared. "He's awaiting travel orders to Michigan to organize a new cavalry regiment back there."

"Yes," Sheridan said. "Telegraphic communications out here are very uncertain. Brigands everywhere. Taking advantage of the turmoil of war."

"Captain Sheridan also is late receiving *his* pay," Lightfoot said with a slight laugh.

"And the pay wagon bound for Springfield," Sheridan added, "we just learned has been diverted to proceed directly to General Curtis's field headquarters in Arkansas. In the military, Mr. Hawkes, rank is power."

"So I have previously observed, sir," Hawkes replied. "I worked for the cavalry at Fort Davis in Texas."

"Fort Davis, eh? I was posted through there en route to California from my first assignment at Fort Duncan. In '54 I think it was."

"Eagle Pass," Hawkes said. "I know the country around Fort Duncan well."

"Were you a civilian scout, Mr. Hawkes?"

"They hired me because I could speak a little Comanche. Learned it from my uncle's Indian traders. On the Santa Fe Trail."

Sheridan offered Johnny a cigar, which he accepted. "Most of my time out there," the captain continued, "was spent in California and Oregon territories."

Ben meanwhile had been listening to the talk, his back turned to their chairs while he sidled along the display of framed pictures of the presidents of the United States from George Washington through James Buchanan. The absence of Abraham Lincoln made him wonder if the inn's proprietor might not be a Rebel sympathizer. Below the presidents were drawings from *Harper's Weekly,* most of them being theatrical personalities and scenes from plays. He was especially intrigued by a tinted drawing of a half-clad woman bound to the back of a woolly maned horse charging up a mountain. Mazeppa, or the Wild Horse of Tartary, the caption read.

He heard Captain Sheridan excusing himself in order to attend some pressing business, and then the long-armed officer was suddenly beside him, smiling. "I see, young man," he said gruffly, "that you've served with the Dragoons."

Ben felt his face flush, and he looked down in embarrassment at his unkempt tunic and baggy faded-blue pants, patched at the knees. Sheridan patted him on the shoulder. "An admirable arm of the service, the Dragoons. Mr. Hawkes tells me that you helped bring Captain Lightfoot's camels up from Pea Ridge."

Ben swallowed hard. "Yes, sir."

"I must get out to the stock pens and see those camels," Sheridan said, and then he turned and strode away to the stairs.

Johnny and Captain Lightfoot were also talking about the camels. "Five or six days," Johnny was saying, "if Rolla is that far."

"And remember this, Hawkes. I'll guarantee double pay for both drives, the one here to Springfield and the one to Rolla. Captain Sheridan has granted me some of the new Quartermaster greenbacks for expenses. They are real money instead of the signed vouchers we've been using. They'll buy you whatever you need."

"When do I get these greenbacks?"

"Probably this evening. Phil Sheridan and I will be going down to the yards. I'll see you there." Lightfoot reached for the whiskey bottle, upended and drained it. "Once we've loaded the camels into a stock car at the Rolla railhead, you'll be paid in gold. Four times as much as you expected to get for bringing them here."

"Splendid!" Johnny cried but without much enthusiasm in his voice. From his manner, Ben guessed that Johnny was beginning to feel mellow as a result of his constantly refilled shot glass. The boy decided he'd better move into Johnny's line of sight, just to remind him that Captain Lightfoot was not to be trusted. As soundless as a cat, he crept around the chairs and sat on the floor with arms and legs crossed, facing the two men. Captain Lightfoot scowled at him, but Johnny apparently was so accustomed to seeing him around he showed no sign of awareness that Ben was there.

"You know, Captain," Johnny was saying, "when I come back this way from Rolla, I may stop here and seek work with Patsy Halfacre's pa. She says he may return to Springfield in a week or two."

Captain Lightfoot laughed scoffingly. "Don't bet your buttons the old man will hire you on, Hawkes. I know he damn well wouldn't let you work around the yards. He's too grudging of that scrumptious daughter. Old Pat don't want any handsome young fellow like you—or me—hanging about the apple of his eye." Lightfoot stopped to take a final long swallow from his glass. "Patsy told her pa I was too bold with her. The Halfacres tried to bar me from the yard until I threatened to cut off the army gravy they get for our remount use."

Johnny tried to conceal a flare of anger at the captain's remark. "Well, Captain," he said flatly, "I must be going. Some last matters to attend."

Lightfoot arose, staggering slightly. He did not bother to offer his hand. "I can count on you driving the camels to Rolla? You'll leave in the morning?"

"You bring me the greenbacks and we'll go in the morning." For the first time Johnny appeared to notice Ben's presence. He reached down and caught the boy by the sleeve, tugging briskly. "Let's go, Ben."

Once they were out on the street, in the bright afternoon sunlight, Johnny said, "You and Patsy are right, Ben. That Lightfoot can't be trusted."

"You going to Rolla anyway?"

"We got no choice. We need the money. But we'll be back."

When they returned to the Halfacre house and found Patsy warming homemade cheese soup over the hearth fire, Johnny told her about his new plans. She shook her head disapprovingly. "That man could lead you to the moon, Johnny, if you let him. Tell him to hire somebody else to drive his damned camels to Rolla. You stay here and work for my pa."

Ben could tell that Patsy was truly sweet on Johnny and did not want him to leave. During the time Ben was eating his soup and bread, only halfway listening to the talk, he wondered what it would be like working around a stockyard and livery stable. No worse than a cavalry post, he told himself, and maybe better in some ways.

After the late meal, and a short spell of bantering with Patsy, Johnny declared that if Captain Lightfoot brought him the promised greenbacks he would be leaving at first daylight for Rolla. "We'd better go tell Hadjee," he added. "And then we'll see about tracking our wounded friend, Linkous."

When they left the house and turned toward the barn, both

noticed that a previously empty holding pen was now filled with horses. Most of them had fresh "U.S." brands on their shoulders. Johnny clucked his tongue. "Captured Rebel mounts," he said. "Hey, looky there, Ben! Ain't that my Little Jo?"

"Sure looks like him," Ben replied.

Johnny went to the edge of the fence, whistled a sharp high note, and called, "Little Jo!" A bay mustang with white spots on its flanks pushed its way through the other horses and trotted straight to the fence. "Little Jo," Johnny repeated and gently caressed the animal's forehead. "He's mine," Johnny cried triumphantly. "Ain't no U.S. brand going to take away the best pacer I ever rode."

Ben meanwhile was circling the pen, looking over the fence in hopes of finding his pony, but it was not there.

They went on into the barn. Dr. Pingree's Chariot of Wonders was no longer in its customary place, but neither of them could recall seeing the vehicle in the Springfield square. Nor was there any sign of Hadjee and the camels.

"Vamoosed," Johnny said. "Everybody's vamoosed."

From the lot behind the barn, however, they soon heard the soft voice of Hadjee talking to Omar and Tooley. He was brushing and exercising his charges.

In his disjointed bits of English, mixed with Arabic that was unintelligible to his two listeners, Hadjee made them understand that their new friend, Dr. Pingree, had driven away in his wagon to a mysterious place called Rolla. Upon learning this, Johnny and Ben managed to inform Hadjee that the three of them also would soon be traveling to Rolla. This news seemed to please Hadjee, who began repeating the word "east." To Hadjee "east" had come to mean Egypt, and the cameleer evidently had learned from Dr. Pingree that each step he took toward the rising sun brought him that much closer to his native land. Johnny wondered aloud if the poor homesick Arab had forgotten that a great ocean also lay between him and his goal.

They were interrupted in their necessarily prolonged dialogue by Patsy and a young lieutenant who was carrying a large sealed packet encircled with a narrow strip of red ribbon. "You are Mr. John Hawkes?" the lieutenant asked with deliberate pomposity.

"I am," Johnny replied.

"You must count the contents of this packet and sign the tally sheet," the lieutenant said in a high-pitched voice that he tried but failed to make imperative.

Inside the packet Johnny found a leather sheath containing a few greenbacks with an army quartermaster stamp on their faces. After counting them, he wrote the total on the tally sheet with the lieutenant's pencil and signed his name. Performing a mock salute, the lieutenant turned and marched away with an air of great importance.

Johnny unfolded the think sheet of official army paper that had been wrapped around the quartermaster's greenbacks and read it aloud, for the benefit of Ben and Patsy:

John Hawkes, Esq.,

These legal tender notes will pay expenses for you and your drovers for the overland drive of official quartermaster livestock from Springfield to the railhead at Rolla, Missouri. This action is of the utmost urgency and should be commenced as soon after receipt of this order as is practicable. At Rolla, after loading animals into railroad stock cars, you will be paid in full for services rendered.

> Signed: Solomon Lightfoot,
> Captain U.S.Q.
> acting for
> Major Zebulon
> Bridges 22nd Indiana
> Volunteers

Scrawled across the bottom of the form was a brief note: "Leaving at this hour with Captain Sheridan in a confiscated stagecoach for Rolla. Will await your arrival there. S. Lightfoot."

Patsy moved close enough to Johnny to snatch the leather sheath from his hands. She quickly counted the few greenbacks. "This won't pay more'n half your needs for grub and feed all the way to Rolla," she cried. "Everybody between here and Rolla will discount this paper, and Rebel sympathizers likely won't accept it at all." She handed the sheath back to Johnny. "If it was me, I would not go."

"I've got no choice, Patsy," he replied. "We need Captain Lightfoot's money to get back to Texas."

"You could stay here and work for my pa."

He grinned at her. "Oh, we'll come back. Maybe your pa will be here by then."

Johnny decided not to wait until morning to start on the road to Rolla. The reason for this was Little Jo, his spotted mustang. He first told Ben that they would have to wait until they returned to Springfield to search for Rafe Linkous. Then in a conspiratorial whisper he revealed that soon after sundown he was going to cut Little Jo out of the corral and take him along with the camels. "I'll hang my blanket over the U.S. brand," he added, "and lead him right by the gate guard."

Not until after supper did he tell Patsy that they were leaving that evening. She protested, demanding to know why he could not wait until morning. He did not tell her the real reason, of course, but gave her an extemporaneous lecture on the habits of camels, which included several invented examples of their preference for nocturnal travel. He summed it all up in a one-sentence prevarication. "They see better at night," he declared. Yet he could tell from the dubious expression on her face that she did not believe a word of what he had been saying.

With Ben acting as guard, Johnny quickly slipped Little Jo out of the corral, put a rope bridle on him, and led him into the barn. En route from Texas the mustang had spent considerable time in proximity to the camels, but Johnny wanted to avoid any skittish actions that might attract attention. To put Little Jo at ease with the camels, he brought him right up to their stall. After rubbing his hands along the backs of Tooley and Omar, he caressed the horse's muzzle with them.

As soon as darkness fell, they started for the gate, Hadjee leading Tooley, Ben leading Omar, with Johnny between them riding the mustang. Johnny would have liked to stop and say good-bye to Patsy, but he thought it best that she did not know that he was taking Little Jo.

As they turned toward the gate, however, he saw a flare of candlelight from the Halfacres' front door as it was flung open. "You ungrateful wretches," Patsy cried. "You would flee in the night like land pirates without so much as an if you please." Her silhouette moved out from the open door and melded into the darkness.

Johnny quickly slid off the mustang and slapped its rump. "Go on!" he groaned softly. The horse continued moving forward between the camels.

He turned and caught Patsy by the shoulders. "I didn't want you to know," he said.

"Know what?" She saw the shapes of the three animals then, black against the rays of the guard's lantern at the gate.

"That's my horse," he said. "It's not a Rebel horse. The Union Army had no right to take it."

Her face was very close to his. "I see no horse," she said. "I see a wild Texan babbling." She kissed him hard on the lips but kept free of him. Reaching in her coat pocket, she drew out a pistol. "The Walker Colt," she said.

"I can't take your best gun."

"I'm only lending it to you, dunce. You'll need it through the rough country between here and Rolla." When he took the pistol, she brought out a handful of cartridges and thrust them in his jeans.

The guard was waving his lantern and shouting a loud, "Halt!"

"You'd better get up there and pacify that soldier," she said.

He grabbed her, quickly returned the kiss, and hurried toward the gate.

"If that trooper gives you trouble, Johnny," she called after him, "I'll make jerked meat out of the saphead."

"You stay out of this," he muttered over his shoulder.

Johnny was relieved to see that the soldier holding the lantern was not the same man who had been on duty the day they brought in the camels with no horse accompanying them. All the guards at one time or another had visited the barn to see the exotic animals, and the only query raised by the one on duty made no reference to the mustang. He wanted to know why Captain Lightfoot's camels were being taken out at night.

"They see better in the dark," Johnny said with a note of condescension in his voice, as though the soldier was too dull-witted to know such a patent fact.

The guard began writing on an army form, asking for names, destination, ownership, everything that some seasoned bureaucrat in the nation's capital had conceived of to burden soldiers as well as defenseless citizens. When Omar nudged Ben up closer to the gate, the guard handed his lantern to Ben, asking him to hold it while he wrote down various particulars.

"What kind of horse is that?" the guard asked.

"Mustang," Johnny replied in a patronizing tone.

"Color?"

"Bay."

"Any marks?"

"You don't see none, do you?"

The guard finished writing, placed the form in a box under the tiny shelter, and opened the gate. "On your way, gentlemen," he said.

Johnny mounted the mustang, and turned and waved good-bye to Patsy. They moved out under a star-filled sky.

After they left Springfield, Johnny and Ben took turns riding bareback on the mustang. Johnny complained constantly about the lack of a saddle, but Ben had learned to ride bareback, and he had no trouble controlling Little Jo with the rope bridle. They were several miles out into the country before they halted. Starlight revealed the remains of several old haystacks inside a rail fence, and in a matter of minutes they took down enough rails to pass inside. They tethered the animals and unrolled their blankets on the musty hay.

At first daylight they were out on the road again. By midmorning they were remembering with regrets Patsy Halfacre's savory breakfasts. They met a small caravan of military wagons, and when the drivers stopped to stare at the camels, Johnny was tempted to ask for food handouts, but his pride got the better of him and he did not.

About noontime they reached a small crossroads settlement—a church, three or four log dwellings, and a harness shop. A preacher and his wife, who lived in one of the houses, provided a full farm dinner for the three of them, and corn for the animals, in exchange for one of Johnny's greenbacks.

At the harness shop, the owner—a suspicious hulk of a man—was less willing to accept a greenback in exchange for a dusty old saddle that Johnny found in a pile of secondhand gear.

"Ain't you got no metal money?" the man asked.

"This old saddle is not worth a good United States greenback dollar," Johnny replied indignantly. "The leather's cracked, the fastenings are rotten. If you don't want my greenback, you can keep this worthless piece of saddle."

The man quickly relented. After the transaction, he followed his customers out to watch the saddling. "That's a U.S. Army horse you've got there," he said.

"It is," Johnny answered curtly. "I'm on U.S. Army business."

"Why ain't you got a saddle, then?"

"Saddle got lost in the battle at Pea Ridge." Johnny looked at Ben, but Ben knew the answer was only half a lie, half the truth, and he did not change his expression.

"Heard about that battle," the man remarked with disinterest, and after one more searching look at the camels, he went back inside his harness shop.

Late that afternoon, sudden but brief sprinkles of rain were frequent annoyances to their progress. When a farmer on horseback stopped to look at the camels, Johnny asked him how far it was to a town where they might stop for the night. "About five mile to Marshfield," the man said. "Good livery stable there, prices reasonable."

Near sundown they reached the Marshfield livery stable. With a steady springtime drizzle falling, the building's dry interior looked inviting. Ben was especially pleased to see Dr. Pingree's Chariot of Wonders standing inside. They had a pleasant reunion, and as soon as greetings were exchanged all around Ben said shyly, "If I'd known you was leaving Springfield, Dr. Pingree, I would have returned your book about Jack Sheppard on the Spanish Main. I finished reading it. It's in my saddlebag."

Pingree's black eyebrows danced up and down appreciatively. "You could've passed it to a friend, boy."

"Johnny read it and Miss Patsy read it, but Hadjee don't read our words."

The peddler smiled. "I'll dig out another book from the bottom of my wagon."

They were all seated on a hewn log bench facing the wide and doorless entrance of the livery stable that looked out upon the main street of Marshfield, the opening's rectangular shape framing the scene like the proscenium of a stage. As they talked, the drizzle thinned to a mist, the late light of day creating an air of unreality.

A hundred yards down the street was a brick building with FLANIGAN'S MERCHANDISE painted in large white letters on its wall. Beyond that was a sign over the sidewalk: BANK OF MARSHFIELD. Beside a watering trough, two saddled horses, one gray, one almost black, stood facing the building. A boy loitered with the horses. The animals kept moving away from the trough so that the boy had to nudge them back into their previous positions. Ben wondered why the boy did not hitch the horses to the trough and save himself the trouble of watching them so closely.

Out of this tranquil scene came abruptly the sound of gunfire— one, two, three shots. A big man wearing a black duster stumbled from the bank, stepping high in an erratic course toward the un-hitched horses. The boy who had been standing beside them was already in the saddle of the gray horse. In one great leap the running man got his boots into the stirrups of the black one. The two riders swung around in unison and galloped out of sight down a cross street. As they vanished, a long-haired young man who must have been on the sidewalk opposite the bank mounted quickly and dashed away as though in pursuit. Two men came out of the bank, one holding a rifle, the other a pistol. They moved about in a foolish manner as though they were dazed.

This had all happened so quickly that none of the four who had been sitting on the rough-hewn bench in the livery stable spoke at all until the street was clear of action. Ben was first on his feet, followed by Johnny, who finally shouted, "God almighty, they robbed that bank!"

"And so far, clean got away," Dr. Pingree said. "Likely we won't see them again."

But the peddler was wrong, at least about two of the riders. A minute or so later the boy on the gray horse galloped back into the main street and sped directly toward the livery stable. The crack of a pistol sounded from behind him. Spurring the gray horse, the boy came on faster than before, zigzagging skillfully to avoid the shots. Far behind him came the long-haired rider, mercilessly lashing his slower mount.

Just as the gray horse appeared to be ready to lunge through the wide door of the livery stable, its rider pulled up, dismounted in a run, and sent the horse away down an alley. As though propelled by some marvelous force, the boy almost flew into the stable. His smooth cheeks were ruddy from excitement, and he was breathing hard. He wore brown linsey-woolsey trousers, a brown shirt, a checked waistcoat, and an old militia cap that was barely hanging to his straw-colored bush of hair that looked as if it had been cut with sheep shears. He stopped only inches from Ben. "Hide me!" he shouted. "For God's sake, hide me!" While Ben stared in astonishment into the imploring blue eyes, the boy continued pleading. "I done nothing wrong. It was Uncle Sims's doing. Hide me, or Billy Goodheart will kill me dead for sure!"

After a quick glance at Dr. Pingree, Ben motioned to the near door of the Chariot of Wonders. "In there," he said hoarsely. The boy barely entered the wagon when his long-haired pursuer rode up, scowling fiercely. His young-old face had a feral quality about it—thick lower lip drooping so that he appeared to be sulking, pale blue eyes empty of all feeling, a nose that obviously had been broken at some time in the past. He dismounted quickly, dropping the reins on the ground.

"Where'd that rascal go?" he demanded, swinging his pistol in an arc.

"Run through here like a skittered deer," Johnny said. "Must've gone out the back door."

The long-haired Billy Goodheart also tried to run through the stable, but his warped, run-down-at-heels boots made him sway as he moved. As soon as he was beyond hearing, Dr. Pingree whispered, "That one has a mean and angry look. Maybe I better stow that young boy in the lower deck." Like a wizened grasshopper, the peddler jumped toward his wagon.

Meanwhile, the street below had filled with horsemen, their shouts echoing loudly in the damp air. At the sound of sharp commands, they began assembling in a rough formation of a dozen or more. Brandishing rifles, they rode off down the cross street.

Dr. Pingree was out of the wagon and back with the others only moments before Billy Goodheart reappeared. "Found that damned gray horse moseying off toward the hills," Billy said to no one in particular. "No canvas bag on him. No sign of that rapscallion. Must be hiding in here somewhere." He jerked open the rear door of the Chariot of Wonders, held his pistol level, and stepped through. They could hear him poking about inside and then shouting curses as he stumbled on the steps to Dr. Pingree's sleeping quarters on the upper level of the wagon.

When he came back out, his face was darker with rage than before. Without a word he went off through the livery stable, searching stall by stall, laughing crazily when he found the camels. He returned, then, wanting to know where the other circus animals were.

Johnny patiently began his standard explanation for the camels' presence, but Billy Goodheart soon lost interest. He apparently had no further concern for the camels, his mind quickly returning to the bank robbery and the two missing bandits. "You fellers help me find the robbers and you'll share in the Mexican silver dollars. Hundred and hundreds of 'em." He scratched at his crotch, his pale blue eyes searching each of their faces. "Say, did you notice anything like a canvas bag when that gray horse come by here?"

"No, sirree," Johnny replied. He turned to the others. "Ben, Hadjee, Dr. Pingree, any of you see a canvas bag?" They all shook their heads. "A canvas bag full of Mexican silver dollars," Johnny continued, "would be mighty heavy. That rider who came by here could not have run so fast—like a streak of lightning off his mount—if burdened with a bag of minted silver."

"It's been stashed. Somewheres." Billy Goodheart turned toward his horse and rocked across the hard earth flooring of the stable in his unsteady boots. He mounted and then gave each of them a separate searching stare. "I'll be watching out," he said, a threatening edge in his mountaineer's twang.

Darkness came down like a falling curtain over the proscenium through which they had been viewing the town. "My stomach's complaining," Johnny said. "Let's go find that inn the livery stable man told us about."

The Marshfield Inn offered venison and ham with biscuits and gravy served at a long table with benches along each side. To their surprise they found Billy Goodheart already there, with half a dozen other local males and a pair of Union soldiers who had stopped for the night. Goodheart was seated across from Johnny and his companions, his pale blue eyes regarding them with suspicion and dislike. His presence made it impossible for them to discuss the plight of the boy they had hidden in Dr. Pingree's big wagon. Most of the time they listened to the chatter of the other diners, who seemed to agree that a man named Sims Jones was the perpetrator of the robbery and had surely cleaned out the coffers of the Bank of Marshfield.

While he was eating, Ben thought about the boy in the wagon, wondering how hungry he might be. Twice he slipped hunks of bread into the side pocket of his tunic, believing himself to be unobserved. But when they stood up to leave, Billy Goodheart challenged him. "What you aim to do with that bread in your pocket, boy?"

Ben flinched as if he had been struck a physical blow. "I-I get hungry on the road," he stammered.

Johnny joined in, "We have a far piece of travel tomorrow," he said. "Ben's belly growls if he can't eat between breakfast and supper." He led the way to the registry desk and surrendered to the innkeeper another one of his evaporating greenbacks.

On the way back to the livery stable, they talked about the frightened boy and the missing Mexican silver dollars. "Young Ben thinks the boy is still hiding in my wagon," Dr. Pingree said. "More likely he's decamped."

"Yeah," Johnny agreed. "By this time he's lit out for the hills."

"We could make bets," Ben said.

"Hey, listen to the gambling man." Johnny laughed and pulled a folded greenback out of his pocket. "Anybody want to wager a whole dollar?"

"Not I," Pingree said.

"How about you, Hadjee? What's your desire?"

Hadjee grimaced and spread his hands. "Mebbe so, mebbe no."

"I'll bet he's still there," Ben said.

"Where's your bankroll?" Johnny demanded teasingly. "Tell you what, Ben, if he's in the wagon, you get this greenback. If he's not there, you'll owe me a dollar of your share of Captain Lightfoot's pay when we get to Rolla."

"It's a bet," Ben said.

They were entering the dark livery stable. The wagon stood silent in the building's black immensity. Dr. Pingree found his lantern beside a rear wheel and lighted it, handing it to Ben. "Go ahead, boy."

Ben stepped inside and walked down the narrow aisle to the

indented handhold. He grasped it and lifted the planking. Lowering the lantern, he peered into the recess.

"You owe me that greenback, Johnny!" he called triumphantly and looked back at the three silhouettes outside the wagon's entrance. "He's here. Either dead or sound asleep. I'm leaving this bread for him."

XI

BEN BUTTERFIELD

~

O n the street near the post office this morning I met Hereward
Padgett, a young man of perhaps twenty-five, thirty-five, or
maybe forty. He greeted me with his usual gladsome enthusiasm.
Pounding me on the back with unnecessary force, he dredged from
his eccentric remembrance a dozen happenings over the past decade
in which we had both shared. Most of these incidents I would have
forgotten long ago were it not for an occasional, and unplanned,
meeting with Hereward Padgett, who has a phenomenal memory
for the trivia of human interactions.

Otherwise, Hereward is completely bughouse, unable to sustain
himself at any occupation, and on some days requiring assistance
to dress himself properly. In his youth, after half a dozen years of
futile efforts by public school teachers, he was declared a permanent illiterate and freed from classroom attendance. In brief,
Hereward Padgett is the village idiot, or in the case of this small
city, he is one of three local idiots who are permitted to roam the
streets and in certain ways entertain the public.

The second idiot is the son of one of the dozen or so First
Families who rule this community socially and financially. He pos-
sesses rare mathematical abilities; in fact, I have been told that his
excessive preoccupation with the science is what drove him to madness. His vocabulary consists almost entirely of profane nouns and
verbs of the barnyard class, which he mixes with mathematical
terms while conversing. His acquaintances, upon confronting this
odd human being, humor him with challenges of multiplication,
algebraic and geometric puzzles, and riddles, which he can solve

with remarkable accuracy and celerity. Yet, like Hereward Padgett, this offspring of highly placed parents has no other positive qualities in his makeup above the symbol of zero and is totally dependent upon others for his sustenance.

The third idiot is a female about which the least said the better. An ethereal blonde in appearance, she is so compliant that from time to time she disappears into a local asylum to give birth to a child, but because of her sunny nature she is always released from confinement and again appears upon the streets, offering her loveliness and love to the world.

I mention these idiots to illustrate my belief that almost all human beings of that class possess one strong element among their peculiarities, and only one. That was the case with Billy Goodheart, the first idiot to my knowledge that I encountered in life. Billy's strong point was a tenacious avarice, a fixation upon a single entity that drove him night and day so that he disregarded everything else—food and drink, physical discomfort, weariness, loss of sleep—until nature rebelled and forced him to satisfy demands on his physical being.

In my collection of fading photographs in this old desk I have none of Billy Goodheart. Memory of him leaves me with shadows because he became a shadow, an illusion. He lives in the darkness, an unsubstantial pursuer. More than once in that time I saw Billy Goodheart in nightmares, visualizing him as I first saw him on the day he appeared in the livery stable at Marshfield—long greasy hair to his shoulders, crooked nose, thick protruding lower lip, scowl, large pale blue eyes that bulged with frustration and anger, an untamed ageless face. And, as I came to know, an idiot's face.

In some ways on that seemingly endless journey in the spring and summer of 1862, I became like Billy Goodheart, foolishly and stubbornly persevering, without reason.

XII

THE MYSTERIOUS JACK BONNYCASTLE

~

Ben meant to be up at first daylight to satisfy his curiosity about the yellow-haired boy. When he had bedded down in one of the livery stable's hayracks, the boy was still sleeping soundly in the lower part of the Chariot of Wonders. Ben overslept, however, and while he was buttoning his clothes he heard Dr. Pingree humming to himself in the stable recess that was used as a smithy. The peddler had fired up the forge and was frying eggs and sausages on a griddle.

"Is he still in there?" Ben asked.

"He was before I went down the back road to forage this provender," Dr. Pingree replied.

"I'll go have a look."

When Ben walked around to the rear of the wagon he found the boy sitting on the back step, rubbing his eyes.

"Hello," Ben said.

The boy looked up quickly, a flash of fear appearing and disappearing on his face. "You seen anything of Billy Goodheart?" he asked.

"Not this morning," Ben replied.

"Thank you for the bread you left me last night. Your name's Ben, ain't it?"

Ben nodded. "So I woke you up when I shined the lantern on you and put down the bread?"

"Yeah, but I'm still hungry as a treed bear."

Ben smiled. "Come on. Dr. Pingree's cooking up a mess for us."

"I ought to be setting out," the boy said.

"Come on," Ben insisted.

Turning toward the smithy, they met Johnny walking into the main entrance from the street. He was carrying two loaves of hard bread.

Johnny grinned at the boy. "How's our young bank robber this morning?" he asked.

"I ain't no bank robber, mister," the boy protested. "That was Uncle Sims's doing."

"Yeah, and they caught Sims Jones last night," Johnny informed him. "They're looking for you, boy. They think you have the Mexican silver dollars."

"I never saw any silver dollars."

Johnny laughed. "Well, you sure didn't have any when you galloped up here yesterday evening. Let's go eat."

"Are you going to take me to the sheriff?"

"That depends on what you have to tell us. Come on, let's eat."

"Is Billy Goodheart down there in the town?"

Johnny frowned as he led the way into the smithy. "You ask too many questions, boy. It's our turn to be asking you some."

Hadjee had come from attending the camels, and he stopped to wash his hands in the smithy tank. The yellow-haired boy stared at the Egyptian's turban and long-tailed striped shirt. "Who is *he*?" he asked Ben.

Ben explained who Hadjee was, adding that after breakfast he would show him the camels.

"Hold on, Ben," Johnny interrupted. "I want to know more about this young fellow before you start parading him around."

After Dr. Pingree served eggs and sausages in tin plates brought from his Chariot of Wonders, they all found wooden boxes to sit on. Johnny placed his seat so that he faced the boy directly.

"What's your name, boy?" he asked.

Hesitating only a moment, he answered, "Jack Bonnycastle."

Ben, who was facing Dr. Pingree, wondered why the peddler looked so surprised at the sound of the name.

"Jack Bonnycastle," Johnny repeated. "And Sims Jones, the bank robber, is your uncle?"

"Yes, but I didn't know he was going to rob that bank, I swear."

Johnny bit into a hunk of bread, chewed slowly, and swallowed. "We saw you holding the horses for him. You kept them untied and ready to make a dash for it."

"He told me to keep the horses untied."

"And when he come running out of the bank and mounted, you rode off with him."

"Only a short piece. He shouted at me to turn and come back this way. Said he'd find me later in this livery stable."

Dr. Pingree glanced up from his plate. "Maybe he needed you to draw off some of the pursuit. Did he have a canvas bag full of silver?"

The boy gave the peddler an uneasy look. "I-I don't know, sir. Everything went so fast. I didn't get a good look at Uncle Sims."

Johnny walked over to an oaken keg, dipped a tin cup of water from it, and drank deeply. When he finished he turned to the boy and asked, "Is Sims Jones a man to be afeared of, Jack Bonnycastle?"

"No sir, Uncle Sims is a kind man. Been good to me. My ma died a long time ago, and after my pa was killed in that battle at Wilson's Creek last summer, Uncle Sims took me in. Provided food and shelter. I helped him with his horses."

"Is he a stockman?" Johnny asked.

"Raises horses and trades some. He gave me Champ, that gray horse. I want him back soon as it's safe to track him down."

"You're afraid of Billy Goodheart, ain't you?" Johnny stood spraddle-legged, looking down at Jack Bonnycastle.

The boy shivered slightly. "Billy would as soon kill you as shake your hand. He threatened me more'n once out at Uncle Sims's house when I was alone there. The reason Billy wants to kill me now is he thinks me, instead of Uncle Sims, got the Mexican silver dollars. It wouldn't do any good to tell him I don't know where the dollars are. He wouldn't believe me. You see, Billy was in with Uncle Sims when they was planning the bank robbery layout. Billy would come to the house three or four times a week, and they'd sit out on the porch and talk in low voices so I could not hear. I thought they was planning some kind of slick horse trade. Billy did sell a few ponies for Uncle Sims, but he was rotten, so mean to every horse I saw him ride. If it had been up to me I wouldn't have allowed him in the pens."

Jack Bonnycastle stopped long enough to take a bite of food off his plate. He sighed, and an expression of disconsolation filled his face. "You don't want to hear all this stuff," he said almost in a whisper.

"No," Dr. Pingree said, "we want to know why Billy Goodheart was across the street from the bank when the robbery occurred."

"Well, a few days ago Uncle Sims fell out with Billy. I think it started on the front porch when Billy rode up one night drunk as a wood tick full of blood. Before that, Uncle Sims several times told Billy he had nary sense when drunk, and he didn't want him coming around roostered like that. Billy got mad when Uncle Sims told him to leave. He got down off his horse, full of fight, but Uncle Sims knocked him to the ground with one blow. Uncle Sims hoisted him back in his saddle, roped his legs together, and gave his horse a good starting kick. When Uncle Sims saw me standing in the door watching, he just said in his calm way that Billy Goodheart was a scalawag and he wanted nothing more to do with him. Then yesterday Uncle Sims told me to saddle Champ, my gray horse. He said he wanted me to ride into Marshfield with him. I didn't ask him why, I just did what he said, and when we come into town, he rode straight to the bank. He told me to hold the horses, not tie them, said he was in a hurry and would be right back."

Jack Bonnycastle's head was down as he finished talking. He looked up, his bright blue eyes wide open as though daring any of them to challenge him. Dr. Pingree was gathering up the tin plates. He handed the griddle and the plates to Ben. "Wash them in the smithy tank, Ben, and stow them in the wagon. I've got to harness my team and get the wagon moving. Lebanon is a long day's journey." He turned and walked out of the smithy recess, with Ben close behind. Hadjee muttered a few unintelligible words and went into the stall to ready the camels for the road.

Jack Bonnycastle looked up at Johnny. "None of you believe a word I said, do you? Or care?" His voice was thin, and he looked as if he might burst into tears.

"Oh, we believe some of it," Johnny replied. "If the sheriff wants you, he can find you. We won't take you to him." He leaned down to tighten the fastenings on his boots. "What are you going to do now, Jack Bonnycastle?"

Dr. Pingree and Ben suddenly reappeared in the smithy entrance. "That Billy Goodheart fellow is coming up the street," the peddler cried hurriedly.

"He's riding your gray horse," Ben added.

The color in Jack Bonnycastle's ruddy cheeks drained away. He looked first at a window, then at the door, as if trying to decide in which direction to run.

"Get back in my wagon, son," Dr. Pingree ordered quickly. "Ben, you fasten him in the hold."

The pair scurried for the rear of the wagon.

"I've got to harness my team," the peddler said to Johnny. "You take care of that young Cassius with the lean and hungry look."

Johnny laughed. "You must be talking Shakespeare again, old man." He looked out the wide opening of the livery stable. Reflections from the rising sun turned the pale light in the street to primrose. The rider on the gray horse was approaching in a slow canter.

Leaning against one end of the log bench, Johnny waited patiently for Billy Goodheart to halt and then dismount.

Goodheart rocked across the hard clay flooring in his old boots, giving Johnny a sour look. "I reckon you seen nothing of that rascal thief."

"Nope. If you'd stolen a thousand Mexican silver dollars, would you linger around this town?"

"Maybe. If I knowed where the silver dollars was stashed. And *somebody* knows."

A clinking of harness metal announced the return of Dr. Pingree and his Belgian draft horses. With only a brief glance at Goodheart, the peddler swung the big sorrel horses around to the wagon tongue.

"You'uns leaving this morning?" Goodheart asked Johnny.

"Yup. And I got to be saddling my horse." Johnny gave him a mock salute and started toward the stable.

"Where you journeying to?" Goodheart called after him.

"East."

"I'll be watching out."

"You do that," Johnny retorted without even a glance back at him.

By the time Johnny returned with his saddled horse, Billy Goodheart was gone. Dr. Pingree had his team hitched, and Hadjee was bringing out the camels. The light over Marshfield and the empty street was now a pale yellow.

"Which direction did he go?" Johnny asked the peddler.

"Around the other side of the livery stable."

"Are Ben and the boy still in the wagon?"

Pingree nodded. "Still there."

"I wish I knew more about that boy," Johnny said.

"Well, I know one thing," the peddler declared. "His name is not Jack Bonnycastle, for sure."

"How do you know?"

"That's for you to find out. Anyway, I suppose we'd better take the lad with us."

"Yeah. Can't leave him here with no place to go or hide. If it's all right with you, Doc, we'll travel with you as far as Lebanon."

XIII

BEN BUTTERFIELD

~

When you read about circuses in a newspaper, or anywhere else, you have to discount half of the tittle-tattle because it is written by masters of the big yarn. Some of these ink slingers become so good at stretching the truth and bring gullible folk flocking to swap their money for admission tickets that the circus owners pay them bigger amounts than they give the performers. So this morning when I opened the paper and saw a piece about the circus coming, I discounted most of it, excepting the paragraph about the world's greatest equestrienne, Queen Elizabeth Jones. Nobody has ever been able to exaggerate her accomplishments.

The arrival date of the circus is still several weeks away, but the masters of the big yarn start tickling the desires of the populace months ahead, if they can persuade a local newspaper to cooperate, and they usually accomplish this by offering plentiful free passes and the promise of paid quarter-page advertisements later on. Although I did not believe half of what I read, I was pleased to learn that our town had not been canceled. That happens occasionally even with railroad circuses. A storm or a wreck can cause delays of a day or two, and that means a town somewhere down the list has to be dropped out of the schedule.

So far we have not been cut out, but if that happens I have already made up my mind that I will travel to the nearest city of performance, Fort Smith or Memphis if need be. I must see Queen Elizabeth Jones ride one more time. I cannot help wondering if she has not slowed down. After all, she is about my age, and even if I did not have a shattered leg, I would not dare to try those fast-paced stunts we once performed when we were young and fearless and fancy-free. Perhaps she keeps riding because she never stopped and does not know how to stop now.

Yes, this morning I was so drawn into memories of Queen Elizabeth Jones that I doubly resented the intrusion of a rather pleasant young man named Theo Drumgoole. I resented not only the intrusion but also the enterprise he represents, the telephone company. Over my strongest protests Hilda Fagerhalt invited the telephone people to send a representative to estimate the costs of installing one of these beastly machines in the hardware store.

Theo has been knocking and tapping on the walls in this room and then making measurements around Old Man Fagerhalt's desk to determine the most strategic point for the wires to culminate and feed electricity into the devilish black receiver and voice box. Theo Drumgoole, a prototype man of the forthcoming mechanical twentieth century, views the telephone as a beneficent creation, but he expressed puzzlement over Hilda's decision to install the gimcrack (my word, not his) on this desk instead of on a wall or counter in the hardware store. I told him that my dear Swedish wife has my interests at heart; she wants to bring me out of my splendid insulation into the world of commerce. By placement of the telephone on this desk, I will be kept awake by the jingling of the bell and the tinny voices of men, women, and children who are too lazy to walk or take the electric streetcar to Louisiana Street and see what Hilda has for sale in her hardware store. At breakfast this morning she was speculating on the possibilities of delivering telephoned orders to customers' homes. The telephone is indeed an afreet, not only destroying peace, quiet, and privacy but dissecting days and nights into shreds of time, spreading madness across the earth. I see myself someday in the future driving a horsecart about the town, delivering nails and door hinges and pots and pans or whatever objects the slothful folk may command over the telephone's wire.

One score and five years ago, when Johnny Hawkes and Queen Elizabeth Jones and I were in Philadelphia with the Great John Robinson Circus, the three of us spent some time during the mornings viewing the wonders of the Centennial Exposition. In one of the enormous buildings, Memorial Hall, I think, we stopped to rest our legs at a magician's stand. He performed a few simple tricks, then offered the paraphernalia of legerdemain for sale in little packages. When he stopped for a few minutes, two well-dressed gentlemen at an adjoining exhibit began touting their telephone machine. Most of the people who had been watching the magician moved on down the hall, but we three stopped to see how the newfangled contraption worked. One of the men handed a receiving device to Queen Elizabeth Jones while the other went behind a screen and said a few words over the wire to her. Johnny, and then I, took the receiver and listened to what sounded like a man talking through his nose far, far away. "What a funny toy," Queen Elizabeth Jones said as we walked away. And that is what it should have remained—a toy for children to play with. One of the men at the exhibit may have been Alexander Graham Bell, and it is the bell on the damned thing that riles me. I was in Dr. Barrell's office the other day, and the bell rang so shrilly on his wall telephone that I almost jumped out of my chair. I'd sooner listen to a certain shrieking virago complaining to Hilda about some piece of hardware that failed to measure up to her standards.

Well, well, I see tripping on the sidewalk outside one of the town's genuine beauties—Miss Betty Hesterly, wearing her wide-brimmed white hat with multicolored artificial flowers on the band. She is the nighttime central for the telephone company; that is, she connects the phones when someone calls a number at night. She has a bed up there on the second floor of the telephone exchange. Theo Drumgoole told me this morning that she has to keep a listening device clamped to her head when she goes to bed, and Theo should know. He and Betty Hesterly are engaged, and I'd bet they're already doing some sleeping together.

There goes Theo out to meet Miss Hesterly. Her voice sounds very much like Queen Elizabeth Jones's when she was at that age and I was Theo's age. Maybe a telephone won't be so bad with a central voice like hers. But as Theo tells Hilda, we can't have a machine in this building until some more poles and wires are installed down Louisiana Street. Perhaps a month or two of respite.

XIV

"THE RIGHTEOUS SHALL GROW LIKE A CEDAR IN LEBANON"

~

King Solomon made himself a chariot of the cedar wood of Lebanon," Dr. Pingree said. He looped the driving lines around a peg on the headboard in front of him and let the Belgians choose their own pace. The road was straight and fairly level through the high plateau country. Most of the land was forested, with undergrowth barely recovered from past fires so that long stretches were parklike under great spreading oaks and tall hickories. From time to time they passed thick groves of cedars, varying from conical to ovoid in shape. These evergreens and a road marker indicating that Lebanon was fifteen miles ahead led the peddler to meditate on biblical passages.

After a stop for nooning, Pingree had invited Jack Bonnycastle and Ben to ride on the wide driver's seat beside him. The young pair traded headpieces, Ben wearing Jack's Missouri militia cap. Because Jack's head was smaller than Ben's, the floppy dragoon hat almost concealed his eyes and ears.

"Ben," Pingree said, "you told me the lady out in Texas taught you to read from the Bible. Every time I come peddling this way, to Lebanon, I'm reminded of a verse—from the Book of Kings I believe. I'm going to recite it for you, and if either one of you boys can tell me what it means, I'll give you a hard candy ball from my jar at the very next stop. Listen close: 'The thistle that was in Lebanon sent to the cedar that was in Lebanon, saying, Give thy daughter to my son to wife: and there passed by a wild beast that was in Lebanon, and trode down the thistle.'"

After a long silence, Jack Bonnycastle said, "I can read some, but I never read much of the Bible."

The peddler recited the verse again. "Tell me what it means, Ben."

"Well, sir," Ben replied, "I don't reckon I know the meaning."

Dr. Pingree laughed, very loud, in his basso voice. "Neither do I, son, neither do I. We'll have candies all around anyway." The Belgians were slowing, and he unlooped the lines and slapped the team to a faster pace. "One of you boys stand up and look back to see how far away Johnny Hawkes is."

Both boys stood upright on the wide seat, looking back over the long top of the wagon. "A furlong maybe," Jack Bonnycastle said. "The Egyptian seems to be having trouble with one of the camels. He's kicking it on the shoulder."

"Tooley," Ben declared. "Hadjee says she's off her feed. May be going to bear a calf. That's why he put the saddle on Omar today."

"Hadjee's merely guessing about that," the peddler interrupted. "Yesterday he said he thought she'd eaten too much dewy grass. All right, you two, sit down. I'll let the team dawdle again till they catch us up."

Jack Bonnycastle began humming a tune. All day his spirits had been rising with each mile added to the distance between him and Marshfield. Not since noon had he asked Dr. Pingree if he thought Billy Goodheart would come in pursuit.

"I recognize that tune you're humming," the peddler said. "Heard it at a minstrel show in St. Louis. Do you know the words, boy?"

Jack Bonnycastle looked up at Pingree from beneath the wide, uneven brim of Ben's hat, and he smiled for the first time since the evening of the bank robbery when he had galloped up to the livery stable. He began singing in a clear and flawless treble:

> "Your lips are red as poppies,
> Your hair so slick and neat;
> All braided up with daisies,
> And hollyhocks so sweet.

It's every Sunday morning,
When I am by your side,
We'll jump into the wagon,
And all take a ride."

Dr. Pingree added his deep voice enthusiastically to the repetitive chorus:

"Wait for the wagon,
Wait for the wagon,
Wait for the wagon
And we'll all take a ride."

"Sing it again," Ben urged them. They went through the chorus twice more.

"I suppose that song's got no war flag connection," Pingree said. "A man, especially a man hawking goods like me, has to be careful what songs he hums or whistles in this mixed-up border country. Or females either. In Springfield the other day a Union soldier called down some girls singing about the bonnie blue flag and southern rights hurrah. How about you, Jack Bonnycastle, are you north or south?"

"You tell me what you are," the boy replied, "and I'll tell you what I am."

"Well-spoken," the peddler replied. "So far I'm neutral. Have to be in this peddling business. But one of these days, we'll all have to take a stand. Now Ben here and Johnny Hawkes, they claim to be Texicans. Furriners like."

The afternoon sunlight was beginning to slant through the woods, illuminating the tree trunks. At the top of a dead pine, a woodpecker hammered away with determination. Bluebirds and cardinals made streaks of color as they darted from tree to tree. Then, as if in a dream, a gray horse seemed to float through the woods on the left side of the road, twisting and turning so that only the head and neck, or hindquarters, or the saddled rider, could be glimpsed at any single second of time, appearing and reappearing like flickering pictures.

"Champ!" Jack Bonnycastle cried. "My horse! And Billy Goodheart's on him!" As he cried out, the boy slid quickly down into the tight floor space between seat and headboard. "What's he do-ing? Is he coming to get me?"

"He's just sashaying through the trees," the peddler replied. "Looking us over."

"You think he's seen me?"

"Couldn't have recognized you under that big hat of Ben's."

"God almighty!" Ben cried. "I bet he thinks I'm Jack." He quickly removed the militia cap from his head and held it in his lap.

"Let him think it for a minute," Pingree said calmly. "Put the cap back on."

The gray horse dashed suddenly into the road fifty paces ahead of the Chariot of Wonders. Holding his pistol pointing skyward, Billy Goodheart shouted at the peddler to halt the wagon.

Dr. Pingree reached for his seldom used driving whip and began twirling it, then quickly brought it down with a loud crack just above the backs of the Belgians. Startled, they lunged forward and quickly increased the speed of the wagon. Billy Goodheart shook his long hair angrily.

"Stand up, Ben," Pingree said, "stand up and wave that cap at him. We're coming close enough so he can see you plainly and know you're not Jack."

Ben did as the peddler ordered, and he not only managed to keep a frozen smile in place but dared to bow mockingly to Billy. To avoid a collision, Billy swung his horse aside, cursing, and then fired his pistol. The bullet zipped somewhere between the driver's seat and the rumps of the Belgians.

"Damn him!" Dr. Pingree shouted, angry and surprised.

"I told you," Jack Bonnycastle said from his crouching position. "He'll kill us if you don't stop the wagon."

At that moment the beat of hoofs on the hard-packed road signaled the hurried arrival of Johnny Hawkes. As soon as Johnny swept past the wagon, he fired Patsy Halfacre's Walker Colt, aim-ing well above Goodheart's head. The gray horse and rider dashed immediately for the woods, disappearing beyond a screen of wild grapevines and a copse of cedars. After a cautious pursuit, Johnny returned to the road. Dr. Pingree stopped his wagon until Hadjee brought the camels up, and for the remainder of the journey into Lebanon, Johnny rode as an alert flanker.

As they neared Lebanon, the road deteriorated. Barked slabs of lumber had been laid across mud flats, showing the progress of the wagon and the camels. Still keeping a wary watch for Billy Goodheart, Johnny rode a few yards in front.

When they reached a livery stable on the edge of the town, the sun was setting behind them, casting bright streamers of light against the houses on an uplift of land.

At the entrance to the livery barn, Johnny dismounted, and at the same time Dr. Pingree stepped down from the high wagon seat. As if by prearrangement, they strode across the graveled yard to face each other.

"We must shed ourselves of that slyboots rascal Goodheart," the peddler said. "He might hit somebody with that big shooting piece of his."

"Yeah," Johnny agreed. "I've been figuring a way to saw off his horns. You've been to this town before, Dr. Pingree. D'you know anything about the head law dog in Lebanon?"

"Matter of fact I do. He gives me my permit to peddle. Name's Marshal Tuttle."

"Sharp man, friendly man, or hard man?"

Pingree laughed. "I reckon if necessary he can be any of them. You ain't bringing charges against Goodheart for shooting at us?"

"Not exactly. I aim to cast suspicion of bank robbery on him. Soon as we get the animals settled, we'll go see your Marshal Tuttle."

Lebanon's town marshal had gone home to eat dinner, but his house was only a long block from his office and the jail. He welcomed his visitors into his parlor, remembering Dr. Pingree from previous visits to Lebanon, and he was evidently eager for any news of the bank robbery at Marshfield. "I received a telegraph today from Marshfield," the marshal said. "They've caught one of the robbers but are looking for a young boy. I've passed the word around Lebanon to notify me of any suspicious young fellows passing through."

"That's why we come right over to see you," Johnny said. "We have reason to believe that boy is traveling this way, or is already somewhere in town."

"You have a name, a description?" the marshal asked.

"His name's Billy Goodheart. Chunky kind of fellow, maybe five and a half feet. Long hair to his shoulders. Got a mean eye on him. He could be about twenty." Johnny kept his voice serious as he embellished his story, adding very solemnly, "He may have a gang with him, Marshal Tuttle. They may be up to more than just bank robbery." From inside his shirt he drew out the folded sheet of official army letter paper that Captain Lightfoot had given him. He handed it to Marshal Tuttle. "As you can see, sir, I'm on official business for the United States War Department."

The marshal squinted at the handwriting; his eyesight was evidently poor, and he read very slowly. He finally handed the sheet back to Johnny. "What animals are these you are herding to Rolla?" he asked.

"Camels, sir."

"Camels!" the marshal cried in a tone of disbelief.

"Yes, sir. The United States Army is testing camels for long marches."

Marshal Tuttle gave him a quizzical look. "I reckon you don't know that half the folks in Lebanon don't favor the United States Army. But I'm a loyal man." A faint smile showed on his face. "How many camels in the herd?"

Johnny grinned. "Only a pair. But more will be coming later." He hesitated briefly. "What I was driving at, sir—that there may be more than the bank robbery in this—it is our suspicion that this young robber and his gang may be planning to steal the camels in my care. They could get good money for them from the Secesh. We saw signs of these marauders today along the road. Shots were fired at us, but my attendants and I drove them off."

"I see." The marshal looked at the peddler. "Are you in this, Dr. Pingree? One of Mr. Hawkes's attendants?"

"Oh, no, no. Mr. Hawkes was traveling behind my wagon, and I gave him what assistance I could."

Marshal Tuttle rubbed a hand across his deeply furrowed brow. "I'd like to see them camels," he said. Then he added, "Do you need any help tonight, Mr. Hawkes?"

"I can't say, Marshal. I don't know how many men Billy Goodheart may have in his gang. If only two or three show—over at the livery stable where we're bunked down for the night—my attendants and I can handle them. But if there are a dozen, or even a half dozen in this band of robbers, they might overrun us."

The marshal remained silent for a few moments as if studying the matter, then spoke firmly. "I expect I'd better deputize two men I know well and trust. They're the best shots in Lebanon. It's our duty to keep the peace, and besides, I'd like to catch this Billy Goodheart."

"We'd be mighty grateful, Marshal. Let me warn you, though. Billy Goodheart is a foxy one. When we first encountered him—back at the stables in Marshfield right after the bank robbery—he was running for cover and tried to throw suspicion off himself by actually accusing us of being accomplices in the robbery. Said we must be hiding the stolen Mexican silver dollars!"

Clearing his throat loudly, the marshal interrupted. "The law over at Marshfield still ain't found the silver."

"Billy Goodheart knows where it is," Johnny declared. "But likely he won't say, even if you catch him. He'll point his finger at somebody else." Johnny arose, offering his hand to Tuttle. "Well, we better be getting back to the livery stable. Night's coming on and we need to prepare for the Goodheart gang."

"Soon as I eat my supper," the marshal said hurriedly, "I'll bring my deputies. I sure do want to see them camels."

When Johnny and Dr. Pingree left the marshal's house, neither spoke until they were some distance away. Pingree broke the silence first. "You laid it on thick as axle grease Johnny Hawkes. From now on, I'll be unable to believe a word you tell me." He laughed, softly at first, and then remembering some of Johnny's fabrications, his laughter became so loud and resonant that he attracted the attention of a man and woman seated on the porch of a house they were passing.

"And camels to be tested by the army," the peddler added in a teasing tone.

"Well, the United States Army used camels before. Maybe they ought to try camels again. Anyway, we want that Goodheart rattlepate off our backsides, don't we, Doc? You said so while ago."

"For sure. But all that talk about a robber band! Goodheart's got no gang. If he had one he couldn't direct it."

"How else was I going to be sure the marshal would bring his men over to the stables tonight? Billy Goodheart still believes we have the Mexican silver dollars, or he thinks Jack Bonnycastle knows where the money is. He's not going to leave us alone until he's sure one way or the other. I figure he'll make some kind of move tonight."

Dr. Pingree sighed as he started up the slope to the livery stable. "Most likely you're right, Johnny. But I wish to hell I was not mixed up in this bank robbery mess. I need to do some peddling in Lebanon tomorrow, but if there's going to be a shootout between the lawmen and Billy Goodheart's band of robbers, I dare say I might as well haul my Chariot of Wonders on to the next town."

Before the marshal and his deputies arrived, Johnny again stowed Jack Bonnycastle into the wagon hold, warning him to be as silent as the grave. Dr. Pingree then took three old unloaded muskets from his stock in the wagon, issuing one each to Ben and Hadjee and keeping one at hand for himself. "We must appear to be prepared," he explained, "for the robber band."

Marshal Tuttle and his two deputies—lean and alert young men with the predatory eyes of hunters—at first were more interested in the camels as objects of curiosity than in defending them from Billy Goodheart and his desperados. They were also intrigued by Hadjee, the very presence of an exotic foreigner from the land of the Holy Bible, in the town of Lebanon, Missouri. Johnny Hawkes gave them an inspired spiel about the virtues of camels as transporters of goods and men and as engines of agriculture, and he soon had the three lawmen believing that within a short time— whether the war continued or not—they would see files of dromedaries marching through Lebanon as frequently as horses and mules.

When Johnny finally steered them around to the serious business of a night defense, he suggested that he and his partners would guard the livery stable and its valued government livestock while Marshal Tuttle and his deputies concealed themselves on an outer perimeter. "During my service with the cavalry in Texas," Johnny said, "we always had pickets concealed outside our night camps. We trapped us many a prowling Comanche that way."

"We'll be glad to oblige you as pickets, Mr. Hawkes," the marshal replied. "And we'd be appreciative of your experience to advise us of the best placements for this—ah—ambuscade I suppose you'd call it."

"My pleasure, sir." Johnny looked through the open barn door at the night that was thickening to blackness. "Shall we move out?"

Dr. Pingree, Ben, and Hadjee, with lanterns lit, had been seated at the rear steps of the big wagon, listening to the talk. After the lawmen and Johnny vanished in the darkness, Pingree sighed. "Lord, Lord," he said, "I hope Johnny Hawkes knows what he's doing."

"Usually he does," Ben said. He held his unloaded musket between his knees. "But Johnny was yarning the lawmen pretty good. I never heard of any Comanches being caught trying to sneak into the cavalry camps out of Fort Davis."

"No, I thought not," the peddler said.

After about an hour's absence, Johnny returned. He was whistling a tune that sounded vaguely like *Dixie's Land*. "Pickets posted," he said with a grin. "Now let's see what happens."

"What do we do now?" Ben asked.

"You all can go to bed," he replied. "I'll stand the watch."

"I wouldn't miss this show," Dr. Pingree said.

Ben got up from the wagon step. "I'll go keep Jack Bonnycastle company," he said.

Hadjee pressed his folded hands against one cheek, imitated the sound of snoring, and trotted off toward the stables to join his camels.

For a while Johnny and the peddler played mumblety-peg with Johnny's jackknife on the soft earth behind the wagon. Then they stretched out with a lantern between them, swapping stories about their widely dissimilar experiences.

The first gunshot from outside was followed by a loud cry, and then four or five more shots sounded from different directions, echoing against the barn. Johnny extinguished the lantern and strode hurriedly into the night, with Pingree close behind him. Along the rim of a slight rise, silhouettes began to form, accompanied by excited voices and an occasional burst of swearing.

One of the deputies was the first to arrive. He was half dragging a fat man with grizzled hair and beard, obviously quite drunk. Dr. Pingree relit the lantern.

"I reckon this is not the critter we was looking for," the deputy said. "I recognize him, now. Old Pard. Gets drunk every night and wanders around."

The second deputy brought in a ferret-faced little man, caught in the act of sneaking chickens out of a poultry shed.

Profanity in torrents announced the approach of Billy Goodheart and Marshal Tuttle. The marshal had stripped off Billy's shirt and used it to tie the captive's hands behind him. Tuttle was holding a pistol in one hand and was leading a gray horse with the other.

"That's him," Johnny said. "Billy Goodheart."

"You thieving peddlers!" Billy shouted. "You're the ones oughta be hog-tied! Not a hardworking, honest horse trader such as me."

The marshal ignored the remarks. "We saw no signs of others, Mr. Hawkes. Just the drunk and the chicken thief. Lebanon folks. We'll lock this blaspheming young whelp in jail, and I'll telegraph Marshfield we've caught him."

Next morning Dr. Pingree was up early, debating with himself whether he should take his wagon into the town to peddle or start on the road to Waynesville, his next stop. When Johnny joined him, the peddler said, "If I stay in Lebanon to sell my goods, that blathering Billy Goodheart may gab his way out of jail. He might even convince the marshal that we're the bank robbers. On the other hand, if I don't stay in Lebanon to do some peddling, the marshal might get suspicious on his own over our sudden departure. Maybe you and the boys ought to head out for Rolla."

Johnny shrugged. "You worry too much, Doc. Take your wagon on into town. I'll mosey down to the marshal's office and see what's happening. I'd like to be there if he gets a telegraph reply from Marshfield."

"That's another thing," Pingree said. "A description of Billy Goodheart sure won't match a description of Jack Bonnycastle—which ain't that boy's real name anyway."

"How do you know that's not his name?"

Pingree waggled his short chin beard and laughed. "If you kept a sharp eye out and read more, you'd know."

Shortly after eight o'clock, the Belgians pulled the Chariot of Wonders beneath a spreading oak at the crossing of Lebanon's two business streets. Morning sunshine on the young leaves of the tree spread a thin dappling of shadows over the wagon.

Ben wanted to go with Johnny to the marshal's office, and Jack Bonnycastle wanted out of the wagon hold, but Johnny convinced the boys that none of them was completely out of danger yet. Jack would stay where he was, and Ben would help set up the peddler's wares.

When Johnny entered the marshal's office beside the jail, he found Marshal Tuttle seated in a hickory rocking chair contentedly smoking a large pipe made of corncob and cane. "How's the prisoner this morning?" Johnny asked cheerfully.

"Sleeping off a night that by all accounts was clamorous." The marshal idly tapped a deck of cards against the rough surface of the table he used as a desk. "That boy knows more blasphemous words than any man twice his age." With a flourish he spun the playing cards out on the table into a tight semicircle. "I tried twice to telegraph Marshfield, but the wires are down again. Rebel marauders likely. They know the Union Army depends on the telegraph."

Johnny tried to conceal his relief and elation by clicking his tongue disapprovingly. "Shameful," he said. "Could be Billy Goodheart's bunch."

"May be. They didn't offer him any help last night, though."

"Pack of cowards."

The marshal pushed the playing cards together. "You aim to travel on toward Rolla today, Mr. Hawkes?"

"Later. After Dr. Pingree finishes his peddling. Safety in numbers, you know. He says Waynesville is too far to reach in one day anyhow. So we'll have to make a night camp about halfway."

"I should warn you about Waynesville. The town is still controlled by Secesh sympathizers."

"I didn't know that."

"The road takes you right through the town, and your camels will attract a lot of attention. If I was you, I wouldn't let on they're United States Army property. The Waynesville Secesh might confiscate them—and you too." The marshal showed his teeth in a roguish smile.

"I appreciate your advice, sir." Johnny started to rise from his chair, but the marshal motioned for him to stay seated.

"You have some time on your hands, I guess, waiting for Dr. Pingree. Do you play poker, Mr. Hawkes?"

"Stud poker is my game sir. But I have only greenbacks in my possession. Are they acceptable for the jackpot?"

Marshal Tuttle showed his teeth again. "Greenbacks are money in Lebanon. But if you're as good at stud playing as I think you are, you'll win your greenbacks out of the pot before us country boys get our hands on them." He chuckled as though there was something humorous in what he had just said. "Two or three of my friends come over every morning for a quiet low-stakes game before taking our noon dinners. You're welcome to join us, Mr. Hawkes."

Johnny's poker luck ran out before twelve o'clock, but Marshal Tuttle invited him to have noon dinner at his house. The food was excellent, but, as Johnny said later, he could have enjoyed it more if he had been a winner instead of a loser.

When he and the marshal returned to the office, Ben was waiting there for him. And in the jail adjoining, Billy Goodheart was now wide awake, shouting curses and banging a chair against the bars of his cell.

"Dr. Pingree sent me to tell you he's ready to go," Ben said.

After an exchange of friendly farewells, Johnny took his leave of the marshal. Dr. Pingree was waiting in the shade of the oak. "You and that marshal must be getting mighty friendly," the peddler said.

"Aw, hell no. Marshal Tuttle and his deputies just plain hornswoggled me. Invited me to a poker game but didn't bother to lay out their rules. Didn't tell me they cut off the game at twelve o'clock high noon, no matter what. There I was, way down, after trying to figure out their style of play and ready to start winning big when all of a sudden the marshal picks up a dinner bell and rings it to signal high noon. The jackpot was divvied up, and my share was one greenback out of the bunch I'd put in. Goddamn it, that sure won't buy us grub and grain to Rolla."

Dr. Pingree began untying the Belgians. "Beware the pig in a poke," he said, "or gamesters in their natural habitat."

"The worst thing is," Johnny continued, "I was aiming to use my winnings to buy Champ—that gray horse of Jack Bonnycastle's—so the boy can ride back home to Marshfield."

"Did you tell the marshal that Billy Goodheart stole the gray horse from Jack Bonnycastle?"

"Nope. I just said the horse was surely used in the Marshfield bank robbery. And I put the notion in Tuttle's head that anything a captured robber owns can be sold to pay for his keep in jail. He agreed to sell me the gray horse for three of my five greenbacks. But after that poker game I don't have but one."

With Ben's help the peddler removed the chocks from the wagon wheels. "Come on, Johnny Hawkes," Pingree called. "We'll never get to Waynesville standing around here talking."

Johnny joined Pingree and Ben on the wide driver's seat. The peddler wheeled the wagon into the middle of the street and started up the slope to the livery stable where they added Hadjee and the camels to the caravan.

With Johnny's permission, Ben freed Jack Bonnycastle from the lower part of the wagon. "Down there in the town," Jack said, his eyes blinking in the sunlight outside the livery stable, "I could hear people outside nearby the wagon talking about the capture of Billy Goodheart and how the marshal had him locked in jail waiting for a lawman to come from Marshfield. Nobody said nothing about Champ, my horse." He looked strangely forlorn, with bits of straw clinging to his checked waistcoat and to the bill of his militia cap that was pulled down to block the sunlight from his eyes.

"Your horse is in a pen with the marshal's, right behind the jail," Johnny said. "If I had the money I'd bail him for you."

"You mean we've got to go off and leave Champ here?" The boy's face looked tortured, his eyes moist with incipient tears.

Dr. Pingree stepped down from his driver's seat and motioned to Johnny to follow him into the rear door of the wagon. As soon as they were inside, the peddler closed the door. From an inside pocket he withdrew a small doeskin pouch. "I'll go half for the gray horse," he said.

"I ain't got half," Johnny said.

"I know." Pingree handed him three gold pieces. "This is full amount. Coins, not greenbacks. Now you go and make the marshal reduce the price because he's getting gold instead of paper. When we come to Rolla, you give me your share from what that Captain Lightfoot pays you."

Johnny grinned. "You're hunky-dory, Doc." He buttoned the gold pieces carefully into a shirt pocket. "I'll go right now and bail that horse."

While Johnny was saddling his mustang, the Chariot of Wonders moved out on the road toward Waynesville, the two boys again on the front seat with Dr. Pingree, while Hadjee and the camels brought up the rear.

Returning to the marshal's office, Johnny acquired the gray horse, its accoutrements, a lead rope, and a few small coins in exchange for the peddler's gold pieces. Within an hour he overtook the wagon and set the two horses into a steady lope to pass the vehicle and the Belgians. When Dr. Pingree brought the wagon to a stop, Jack Bonnycastle bounded from the seat, laughing and crying as he ran toward the gray horse. "Champ! Champ!" he shouted and stood on tiptoes to put his arms around the animal's neck. After nuzzling its jaw he turned toward Johnny who had dismounted. He tried to hug Johnny around the waist, but Johnny cried "God almighty!" and drew away. Tears that had been repressed all morning ran down the boy's ruddy cheeks. "God almighty," Johnny repeated, "you got no cause to act like a mama's darling, Jack Bonnycastle. If you want to thank somebody, go thank Dr. Pingree. He furnished the wampum."

Pingree, who sat impatiently on the driver's seat, shook his head. "Don't truckle to me, boy. Johnny got your horse for you so you have a means to travel home. We'll provision you with enough for a couple days."

Jack Bonnycastle stood beside his horse, his head cocked up to face the peddler. "I got no home to travel to, Dr. Pingree. You all said Uncle Sims was in jail for robbing the bank. Nobody out there on his place 'cept old Deaf Camp, who looks after the horses. I can't live there with that mean old bastard."

"We didn't take you to raise, boy," the peddler said firmly.

Johnny looked first at Ben, whose face showed how sorry he felt for Jack Bonnycastle, and then he looked hard at Dr. Pingree. "Look, Doc, he can go on to Rolla with us. Soon as Captain Lightfoot pays us, Ben and Hadjee and me will be heading back this way anyhow. We'll need that gray horse to swap out rides."

Pingree jerked his head up and down, his voice revealing his exasperation. "All right, John Hawkes, he's your responsibility. Now move out of the way so I can get my wheels rolling to Waynesville."

XV

BEN BUTTERFIELD

~

Across Louisiana Street, in the yellow sunlight of morning, walks Colonel Preston Boggs (or is his rank now brigadier?), and I fear he is heading this way, not for so stodgy a task as buying an article of hardware in the store but to call upon me, after paying his gentlemanly respects to Hilda Fagerhalt, my dear wife.

When I read the piece in the daily Gazette this morning about the future Edward VII's coronation date being delayed, I realized instantly that Preston Boggs would want to talk about this event with someone who has an interest in the matter. His concern for Edward VII is purely ancestral, his father having been an emigrant from Britain not long after Victoria was crowned queen. Although Preston Boggs was born in America, throughout his youth his father infused his brain with Briticisms. All his life he viewed Queen Victoria as a distant grandmother.

Last January when the queen died, Preston Boggs went into mourning for a month and for a while put aside his duties as a professional veteran of the American Civil War to speak endlessly with me and a few others about the future of the Empire of Great Britain, Ireland, and India. Now the inheritor, Edward, is ill and must be repaired by surgeons (always hazardous) before the crown can be placed upon his head with appropriate ceremony. Preston Boggs will be apprehensive this morning, gloomy perhaps, and filled with endless rumors gleaned from the St. Louis newspaper he always follows during days of crisis.

He is seeking me out now because we have previously talked at length about my visit to Great Britain some years past, a journey *he has never made. This trip was after my first bad accident, during winter rehearsals, when a falling horse crushed my rib and separated my shoulder. Dr. Socrates Drumm attended me and declared that for the following season I would be unable to continue with the Queen Elizabeth Jones performances in Bell Brothers & French's Circus and Menagerie. Somehow or other Patsy Halfacre and Will Cornwall—who had joined Buffalo Bill's Wild West Show—heard about my misfortune. They telegraphed me that if I wanted to go to Great Britain with the Wild West Show, they would arrange for me to be listed as wrangler for their personal horses, with light duties. Well, I wasted no time in hastening to a telegraph office to wire an acceptance message because Bell & French had already dropped me for a season without pay. I not only wanted to eat regularly, but the thought of shipping to Britain with Buffalo Bill was enough to make me jump up and down and shout heigh-ho rickety jo in spite of my broken body.*

Of course on the voyage across the Atlantic I did become violently seasick, but I restrained myself from leaping overboard. I was mighty happy to sight land at a place called Gravesend, appropriately named, I thought. Buffalo Bill set up a big camp outside London, and many important Britons came to see it and meet the performers. After a few rehearsals, Buffalo Bill invited the prince of Wales—the same Edward VII previously mentioned—for a special showing. The prince brought along a bevy of princesses and royal children. Rains had muddied the grounds, but Edward trooped through the muck, asking to meet the Indians and such stars as Patsy Halfacre and Will Cornwall.

And then, as soon as the show was solidly put together, with horses and stagecoaches and spanking-clean costumes, Queen Victoria came for a special performance. We were told that for more than twenty-five years the queen had been mourning her dead husband, Albert, and during all that time she had eschewed going to public exhibitions. Because of her great curiosity about the Wild West Show, however, she announced that she would come—but for one hour only.

Well, now, an hour was barely half the show, but Buffalo Bill speeded the acts along for her, using only the more exciting stunts. At the start an amazing thing happened when the massed riders aligned themselves and presented a giant American flag, as was

always done at the opening of the show. Queen Victoria surprised
everybody by rising from her seat and bowing to the Stars and
Stripes. That gesture, of course, brought her entire retinue to their
feet to join in the salute. I don't know whether it was true that
this was the first time since the United States declared its independence that a British monarch honored our flag, but Buffalo Bill
said it was, and that made it true for sure.

Another surprise came when at the end of the hour the queen
decided to stay to the finish of the show. This meant, of course,
that we had to make a lot of quick changes, devise some im-
promptu acts, and engage in a few bits of repetition.

When the performance finally ended, Victoria commanded the
lead members of the Wild West Show to be presented to her. Not
being a leading member, I did not approach Her Majesty but joined
many other commoners to gather discreetly in the background. In
a drawing that was printed in a London magazine I can be seen
as a shadowy figure in the background far behind Bill Cody, two
or three Indian chiefs, Patsy Halfacre, Will Cornwall, and others.

Some years ago when I showed this pictorial treasure to Preston
Boggs, he lusted for it to such a degree that I traded it to him for
two of his hotel's twelve-course venison dinners. Now that I've
reached the sere-and-yellow-leaf period of my life, I believe he got
the better of the bargain. That drawing belongs with my collection
of old photographs. For Preston Boggs, however, the mere fact that
my eyes once gazed upon the living face and form of Queen Victoria transformed me into an amulet of priceless value, and the
drawing gives him some proof of that. Actually there are times
when Boggs will briefly defer to me. Yet when I compare his British
queen with my Queen Elizabeth Jones—poor Boggs, he has very
little to idolize.

Right now in the hardware store I hear his voice, beginning to
waver a bit from age as he makes courtly gestures and knightly
remarks to Hilda Fagerhalt—always in his Southern manner so
that one never knows whether it is genuine or affected. I'm sure
he has long lusted for Hilda as he lusted for my drawing of Queen
Victoria at the Wild West Show, and Hilda may lust for him, for
all I know.

Only a fortnight ago Preston Boggs visited us, spending more
time with her than with me, but when he came into this room he

expressed what seemed to be a keen interest in my life with the
circus in the years when we traveled overland in our wagons instead of on a railroad train. That was Boggs's earliest recollection
of circuses, he said, the wagons rolling into town either mud-coated
or dust-covered, the camels tripping sedately, elephants moving
forward with determination, heads and trunks slowly rocking.

I told him that circus travel by roads was pure hell, never a
moment's rest, wagon wheels collapsing, thunder and lightening
frightening the animals, floods on unbridged streams threatening
our lives and delaying our passage. Because we traveled so slowly
we had to stop occasionally at towns so small they barely paid
expenses. I recalled one summer month when the Great John Robinson Circus was split in two, one section traveling on a riverboat
across the northern part of the state of Missouri, the other section
crossing the southern part overland. We were to rejoin in Kansas
City.

I was in the southern section, but Queen Elizabeth Jones and
Johnny Hawkes were on the northern route, and I missed them
terribly. I especially missed them when we came to Rolla and
passed Big Piney and Waynesville and stopped at Lebanon. To my
surprise, the town of Lebanon had moved itself a mile or more
from its beautiful little hill to straddle the new railroad track on
flat terrain. The world changes. Having a few minutes to spare I
went in search of Marshal Tuttle, arousing some suspicions among
the lawmen because the marshal had gone off to war ten years
earlier and never returned.

I told all this to Brigadier Preston Boggs, but he did not seem
very interested. Here he comes now, the hard heels of his boots
tapping a shaky military beat on the hall flooring, ready to regale
me with comments about the prince of Wales, the future King Edward VII if he survives the royal surgeons.

XVI

NARROW SQUEAK IN WAYNESVILLE

~

On the long journey to Waynesville, clouds brought an early dusk, and with rain threatening, Dr. Pingree advised that they make camp before descending into a darkening valley ahead. After the evening meal was finished, Jack Bonnycastle announced that he would prefer sleeping outside the wagon for a change. Pingree sniffed, muttered something about folks who did not appreciate a good bed when it was offered, cast a glance at the blackening western sky, and entered the wagon to ascend to his snug aerie.

Around midnight, a bright flash of lightening and a crack of nearby thunder brought the outdoor sleepers upright in their blankets. Moments later, a rush of wind and rain sent all but Hadjee scurrying inside the wagon. The Egyptian tied the camels to the wagon tongue and crawled beneath the vehicle.

Inside, Johnny stretched out on the floor of the narrow passageway while Ben and Jack Bonnycastle curled up in the lower deck. Because of the storm, the single narrow window had to be kept closed, and Ben, who had grown accustomed to sleeping out-of-doors, found the air stifling. He tried to talk with Jack, but the latter quickly fell asleep, breathing with soft fluttering sounds that kept Ben awake for what seemed like hours.

At dawn the sky was still cloudy, but the rain had ceased. Saddles and harness and everything else were thoroughly soaked. After a breakfast of hard bread and lukewarm coffee, they resumed the journey to Waynesville. About midmorning they met a short train of military wagons hauling supplies to the Union Army below Springfield. When the drivers saw the camels, they halted, of course, to gape and ask the usual questions about the exotic animals.

Near noontime they came upon a migration of box turtles, hundreds of them, little turtles and big turtles, all crossing the muddy road from right to left. Dr. Pingree slowed the wagon, but there was no way to keep the Belgians' enormous hoofs or the heavy wheels from crushing several of the crawling reptiles that seemed driven by some irresistible natural force.

When Ben asked the peddler where the turtles were going, he replied that they might be seeking tender spring vegetation or perhaps a place to mate. "Look off down the road, a furlong or so, where the rainwater's collected on both sides. Snapping turtles may live in there; they like mud. Good eating, snappers. Taste like rare beef. If they're migrating with the others, we'll capture two or three."

Sure enough, the snappers were also crossing the road. When Pingree halted the team, Jack Bonnycastle and Johnny came up alongside on their mounts. "Get my water bucket out the back, Ben," the peddler said, "and drop a pair of big ones inside. But watch your fingers. The rapscallions will try to snap them off."

Jack Bonnycastle dismounted and helped Ben capture two of the snappers. After the little caravan moved on a mile or so to drier ground, Pingree turned the wagon off the road.

"We could drive on to Waynesville and cook the turtle meat there," he said, "but I've got an all-fired hunger for some right now. If we get a hot fire going, we can boil a good mess in an hour or so and still reach Waynesville before dark."

Ben and Johnny pronounced the turtle meat to be more tender than Texas Longhorn beef. Jack Bonnycastle said he had eaten it all his life, but Hadjee was wary of the unfamiliar viand and gingerly sampled only a few bites. "Not same as meat of camel," he muttered, with a few Egyptian words thrown in.

As they neared Waynesville the road became muddier and muddier. Numerous oxcarts coming and going had cut the surface into deep ruts. A few dwellings on the edge of the town had just appeared in view when a stagecoach overtook them, the driver shouting angrily at Dr. Pingree to make way for the hurrying vehicle.

Soon afterward they came to an unbridged stream broiling with runoff from the night's downpour in the Ozark uplift. Pingree stopped the wagon. "Roubidoux Crick," he growled. "Running full and with force." He waited until Johnny came alongside and shouted to him, "I think we'd best turn up that trail to the left. High ground up there and a good spring for a night camp. By morning the crick should be down."

With an affirmative upward jerk of his thumb, Johnny waited for the wagon to turn. The Belgians strained to pull the heavy vehicle up the slope. Then the ground leveled, and below through greening trees, Ben was surprised to see a town spread along the base of a line of cliffs. "Waynesville," Pingree said. "You ever hear of Mad Anthony Wayne, Ben?"

"No, sir."

"A great hero of the American Revolution, although I don't know if Mad Anthony was crazy or just angry. The town was named for him."

As the sun was setting it broke through the clouds to brighten patterns of varicolored rocks in the opposite bluff, and then moments later it shone upon a square of business structures. From the front gable of a courthouse a large Confederate flag hung in the heavy air.

"By gad, they're defiant, flying that flag," the peddler said. "Perhaps it's just as well we did not cross the Roubidoux this evening."

The wagon swung around a clump of trees, and there beside a spring bubbling from a wall of rock stood a stagecoach, the one that had passed them so arrogantly on the road. The vehicle's horses had been unhitched and hobbled a few yards distant. In an instant the four men on the ground came alert, one taking a rifle from the stagecoach seat, another drawing a pistol from his belt. When they saw the camels, they relaxed, all four smiling. They were dressed plainly, like ordinary townsmen.

"You must be circus people," a man with a black spade-shaped beard said. Ben recognized him as the driver who had shouted at Dr. Pingree to make room for the passing coach.

"Not exactly," Johnny replied. "We're heading for Rolla."

"You don't live in these parts, do you?" asked a man with dark reddish-brown hair. He was still holding a rifle.

"Nope. So we'd like to share this spring and a piece of the ground for the night."

The man with the spade beard looked as if he'd been offended. "We meant to stop at the town's inn," he said, "but the creek is running too high for our stagecoach. D'you know anybody in Waynesville?"

Johnny deferred to Dr. Pingree, who said curtly, "I peddle goods there sometimes. I've met the sheriff but don't recall his name."

The auburn-haired man, still swinging his rifle, walked closer to the camels. "Do you use these animals in your peddling work? A show perhaps?"

"If the occasion suits," Pingree replied flatly.

Meanwhile Johnny sidled closer to the stagecoach, which had been unhitched so that it stood at an angle near the spring. He read aloud the markings on its side. "I see this is a regular Amburgh Line coach," he added casually, then grinned at the four men who appeared to freeze in whatever positions they were in when Johnny named the stagecoach company. "Most likely you gentlemen confiscated this coach—by authority of the United States Army."

"That's our business," the man with the spade beard said sternly.

Johnny laughed. "I happen to be on special duty for a Union captain from Indiana. He and his comrades pulled the same trick to get to Rolla in a hurry."

"Name this captain," the auburn-haired man ordered. "I happen to be an Indianan."

"Captain Solomon Lightfoot."

"That popinjay," said the bearded man. "I know him, but he's not in my twenty-second Regiment. A politico officer."

Twilight was turning swiftly to nightfall, and Dr. Pingree with the help of Ben and Jack Bonnycastle began gathering twigs and sticks for a supper fire.

As the evening progressed, the four men grew more friendly, offering to share their rations. One of them brought a small folding table from the stagecoach boot. Dr. Pingree provided stools from his wagon and lanterns to light the surroundings. The addition of a few bottles of porter's ale supplied from the well-stocked stagecoach added merriment to the pastoral scene.

Distant lightning began playing above the western ridges, and the two boys, wary of another rainstorm and sleepy from the long day's journey, decided to bed down in the hold inside the wagon. And as on the previous night, Hadjee fastened the camels to the wagon tongue, rolled himself into a blanket, and slid beneath the vehicle.

After Johnny showed the four men his official order from Captain Lightfoot, they informed him that they were all officers from Indiana volunteer regiments and had been ordered to make a reconnaissance, in mufti, of the county of Pulaski and its seat, Waynesville. "A nest of Rebels," the spade-bearded man said. "You saw that Secesh flag flying over the courthouse. We had hoped to size up their strength by spending an evening right in their lair. But the flooding creek—"

"Risky, anyhow, taking that stagecoach into town," Johnny said. "If I figured you for Yankee soldiers, the Waynesville Secesh would do the same."

The auburn-haired man laughed. "From what I've seen of these hill folk, Mr. Hawkes, they're way out of it. Feather-headed yokels. Now in your case, you say you scouted for the cavalry. You learned to observe things these hill people wouldn't see at all."

"Like a confiscated stagecoach?"

"Yeah, Mr. Hawkes," the spade-bearded man said. "How'd you come to be scouting Indians for the United States Cavalry anyhow?"

"Fell into it. Learned a little Comanche and less Kiowa while I was working for my uncle in the Santa Fe trade. We traded some with the army. Word got around the Texas posts that I was a bright young fellow, a real pippin. Colonel at Fort Davis hired me. Damn good pay and tolerable food, and I earned it."

"Dangerous, I reckon," the man said.

"Not so dangerous as playing poker with lawmen in these civilized parts." He went on to tell them of his experience with the Lebanon marshal and his deputies.

A slender young man who had said very little during the evening smiled appreciatively. "I've been trying to learn the game of poker since I was twelve years old. Nine out of ten times I come out the loser."

Johnny cocked his head. "In that case, my friend, maybe you need some practice."

"In that case," Dr. Pingree echoed somewhat caustically, "I

think I'll be off to bed." He got up and started toward the wagon. The lightning in the west had ceased, and strong upper winds were brushing the clouds away so that an almost full moon shown brightly down upon the camp aground.

Within minutes, cards were on the table, and a game of stud was under way. The four officers apparently carried plenty of greenbacks, and Johnny managed to stay ahead of the play so that he never had to reveal that he possessed only one greenback at the beginning. Five hands around brought him three fairly rich pots. After his winnings, however, play slowed considerably, the officers turning cautious and distrustful of him. They studied their cards carefully in silence, and the springtime night was disturbed only by the musical sounds of frogs and insects until a loud snap of deadwood, like a footstep upon a fallen branch, brought Johnny alert. The sound had come from the flat-topped rock that rose for some yards like a wall behind the purling spring.

None of the other players paid any attention to the sound, but when it was followed by two successive thumping noises, the spade-bearded man's eyes met Johnny's. Possibly it was a stone inadvertently kicked by a boot toe, Johnny thought, and rolling down slope until it bumped against another stone. "We'd better douse the lanterns," he said quietly.

"Why?" the bearded man asked. "Must be a raccoon or a fox up there."

Johnny blew out the lantern on his side of the table and motioned to the man to extinguish the opposite one.

"Is this a poker trick?" the auburn-haired man demanded. "To put us in the dark?"

"No fox or coon up there," Johnny said almost in a whisper. "That was a two-legged varmint."

The spade-bearded man reached reluctantly for the other lantern.

A throaty voice boomed down from above them. "Go ahead and blow it out, Yankee. In this moonshine we can see you all clear as day. A dozen guns are pointed at your heads. Sit still or we'll blow holes in them."

From all sides, men walked slowly out of the woods. They were armed with rifles, old muskets, and pistols. The poker players sat motionless. Johnny dropped his cards facedown on the table and noticed lying on one corner the folded sheet of U.S. Army paper—Captain Lightfoot's orders—that he had taken from his shirt pocket to show the officers. With one hand he pushed the paper off into the shadows so that it fell beside one of his boots. By the time the armed men ringed the table, he had concealed the paper by pushing sand over it with slow motions of his foot.

None of the armed men spoke until the one who had shouted from the heights above the spring came into view. He shambled slowly down a steep pathway, bringing a shower of loose gravel with him. In the moonlight, a silvery mist of white hair and beard were visible below a wide-brimmed hat that might have been gray by daylight. He was wearing a long-tailed military blouse that also may have been gray. He was carrying a long-barreled rifle.

"So," he said in his raspy voice, "we trapped you doltish Yankee spies like roosters in a chicken house." He laughed. "You didn't even have a picket guard out." He walked close to the table. "That's a might sparse poker pot. I reckon you boys better put some more Yankee greenbacks out there."

He picked up the lantern and handed it to one of the men. "Isaac," he said, "you and Ned go through that stolen stagecoach and see what you can find." Glancing at the Chariot of Wonders and the camels, he said as though to himself, "By God, old Doc Pingree must be collecting a circus together. Camels, by God, camels. Anyway, let's roust the peddler."

Awakened by the clamor, Dr. Pingree had already hurriedly dressed. He opened the rear door of the wagon and stepped outside before the band of Waynesville Confederates could force an entry. At about the same time one of them launched a hard kick upon Hadjee's blanketed legs beneath the wagon and reached down to pull the Egyptian upright.

"What's this?" the white-bearded man in the military blouse cried as he stared hard at Hadjee, and then glanced at Pingree for an explanation.

"He's my cameleer," the peddler said.

"Cameleer!" the man echoed mockingly. "Are you adding a menagerie to yur peddling wagon, Doc?"

"A bit of entertainment to please my customers," Pingree replied easily. "And you've got my partner mixed in with the four you've captured." As he spoke, the peddler walked slowly toward the five poker players who had been disarmed and were seated in a row beside the coach under an alert guard of twice their number.

With his rifle slung over his shoulder, the white-bearded man followed the peddler. "All five of them scoggins was playing poker," he said. "Merry as grigs."

Johnny, who had heard the exchange, adeptly took his cue. "I'm a Texan far from home," he said. "I was just trying to win me some Yankee greenbacks."

At that moment the two men who had been rummaging inside the stagecoach stepped outside. Their arms were filled with rifles and miscellaneous loot. "Found their Yankee uniforms," announced the one named Isaac.

"How many?" the white-bearded man asked.

"Four sets. And four canteens with Indiana regiment markings."

"That makes four spies for sure," he declared, then looked down at Johnny. "What you doing so far from Texas, traveling with a peddler, two boys, and them camels and that furrin cameleer?"

"I escaped from Yankee captivity," Johnny explained in his usual facile manner. "Dr. Pingree needed a man, so I offered to go with him as far as he wanted."

"If Doc Pingree says you ain't Yankee, I reckon you ain't Yankee," the white-bearded man said. "Git yourself off'n the ground and git over to the big wagon where you belong." He looked at the peddler as though he felt obligated to offer some explanation for what he was doing. "We'll take these four spies across the footbridge upstream. Into Waynesville. My men'll come back and git the stagecoach tomorrow. Roubidoux Crick oughta be down by morning." At his signal, his followers began marching the four prisoners up the steep pathway beside the spring. He stood aside until all had gone ahead, and then in his rasping voice he called back to Pingree and Johnny, "If'n a judge don't come to pass sentence on these spies, I'll be at the square tomorrow to watch y'r camel show."

Because of the sudden realization of what they must now do on the morrow, Pingree and Johnny stood in a bewildered silence staring at each other and almost failed to return the Rebel leader's salute of farewell.

～

Ben and Jack Bonnycastle slept soundly through the entire night incident. Very early in a damp and chilly dawn, Dr. Pingree roused everybody, warning that they must offer some kind of entertainment to please the Rebels of Waynesville. "I stuck my neck in a loose noose last night," he said to Johnny. "I did it to save you from being executed as a spy. Now it's your turn to do me a favor."

"D'you think they'll shoot them four fellows from Indiana?"

"The citizenry hereabouts prefer hangings over firing squads. Although it will depend on the judge. Likely they'll diddle and dawdle for a few days, maybe exchange for some prisoners on the other side. But now, we have to think up a camel show. And quick. Roubidoux Creek is back in its bed, and after last night you can bet everybody in Waynesville knows we're coming to put on a show."

Pingree's prediction proved to be correct. When he drove the Chariot of Wonders into the small square adjoining the courthouse, a considerable crowd was already gathered beneath the big Confederate flag fluttering in the morning breeze.

Naturally the camels attracted the most attention, and as a part of the entertainment, rides were offered aboard the saddle strapped to Tooley's hump. Hadjee had wanted to keep the saddle on Omar. He indicated with hand signs and by pushing out his belly that he believed Tooley might be pregnant. But Johnny vetoed that proposal; he himself had been ejected from the obstreperous Omar's back more than once, and he wanted no arguments with any hot-blooded folk of Waynesville who might suffer bruises from a fall off a camel. The gentler Tooley would have to be the burden bearer.

The price for rides was five cents for adults, two cents for children, and a line formed almost as soon as the camels appeared. Johnny collected the money, and Ben and Hadjee walked along on each side of Tooley to make certain that no one fell from the saddle. To Dr. Pingree's surprise, he was kept busy handing out more than the usual number of articles from his wagon and collecting payment for them. As for Jack Bonnycastle, he was a part of the show.

Before they had left the campground that morning, Pingree told

Jack that his part in the hastily planned performance would be to sing "Wait for the Wagon."

"No, sir, oh please, no sir," Jack Bonnycastle protested.

"And why not, young man? We feed you and protect you, and now you must do something for us."

"But I might be recognized, sir. Standing in front of the townspeople while I sing! Marshfield is miles away, but somebody—"

"I thought of that," the peddler replied. From his pocket he took a bottle cork, walked over to the dying campfire, and knelt down to hold it against a live coal for a minute or so. "Come here, lad," he said gently.

Rubbing the burnt cork over Jack Bonnycastle's face, he soon covered the boy's ruddy complexion with a dusky hue. "Johnny, Ben, would you recognize this lad now?" he asked.

"His hair don't cover his pink ears," Ben said. "They look funny."

"We'll fix that." He burned the cork again and soon had Jack Bonnycastle's ears as dark as his face. "Go on in the wagon, boy, and look at yourself in one of my mirrors."

While Jack was in the wagon, Johnny said that the boy's golden hair did not match his facial coloration.

"True enough," the peddler agreed, "and that cap of his does not cover enough of it. Ben, you'll have to lend him that droop-brimmed headpiece of yours."

And so that is how Jack Bonnycastle, looking as though he had been plucked from a minstrel show, made his first public appearance as an entertainer. Dr. Pingree introduced him to the crowd while juggling a few items chosen at random from his peddling stock—a doorknob, a darning egg, and a small bottle. He said afterward that his dexterity had grown rusty, but the crowd did not seem to mind his occasional bobbles. At the end of Jack Bonnycastle's song, the listeners cheered mightily.

The silvery-bearded Rebel of the previous night's confrontation pushed his way up to the wagon, and after purchasing a brass spittoon from Dr. Pingree, he congratulated the peddler on the performances. "Stay another day, Doc. We don't git such delights in our town more than seldom. I would linger now, but I'm busy hunting down a judge to try them Yankee spies."

He started to leave, but after a hard look at Johnny's mustang,

Little Jo, that was hobbled in front of the wagon, he stopped and commented in his grating voice, "Looks like you nabbed yourself a Yankee horse, Doc. That critter carries a fairly fresh U.S. brand."

"That's Mr. Hawkes's mount," Pingree said.

Johnny spoke up quickly. "I captured the beast when I escaped," he explained.

"Admirable, admirable," the Rebel declared and went on his way.

About midafternoon the crowd began moving to the other side of the courthouse where the captured Indianans were jailed. Intermittent shouts and jeers echoed eerily from adjacent buildings. Business around the wagon slowed perceptibly. Almost everyone who wanted to ride the camel had done so, and no more people came to buy the peddler's goods.

Pingree spoke in a lowered voice to Johnny, "Let's hitch and ride. I don't like the feel of things."

In a similar undertone Johnny replied, "No use of us getting mixed up in a lynching bee."

They all went quietly to work, repacking the wagon, hitching the Belgians, and saddling the two riding horses. As the sun lowered in the western sky, they moved out of the little square, heading eastward. Only half a dozen young children followed, for a hundred yards or so. Soon the sunlit colors of the bluff above Roubidoux Creek were behind them, and when they turned down a hill through a forest of freshly greening oaks, the Confederate flag above the Waynesville courthouse disappeared from their view.

XVII

BEN BUTTERFIELD

~

Sometimes I sit here thinking about all the fragments of life I have encountered—the beginnings and middles of actions, whose endings I never knew. To this day I do not know the fate of the four Indiana soldiers who were captured by the Rebel bushwhackers at Waynesville, Missouri. In circus life or any other sort of migratory or nomadic existence, the world unwinds like a great turning panorama such as one that I saw in St. Louis—paintings of the Mississippi, scenes along the whole course of the river, unfurling past me as though I were at the center of the universe.

Even if one remains fixed in place, as have I much of the time since the accident, I have not yet seen, nor perhaps ever will see, the endings of numerous tableaux vivants of which I have been a witness and sometimes participant.

Only last evening I enjoyed either a beginning or an isolated encounter with the buxom Letitia Higgins, a gentlewoman if ever there was one, yet who persists in putting too much starch in my shirt collars. It came about through the endeavors of a pair of remarkable sisters, Maude and Annie Grimsley—the Sisters Grimsley, as they are known in the town. Their father was a carpetbagger who was sent down here after the Civil War from some distant corner of New England to set things right in the conquered Confederacy, and here Mr. Grimsley put together a fortune by the time he expired. The Grimsley House, over in the best residential section of Scott Street, is considered an architectural jewel. Even so, because of their carpetbagger taint, the Sisters Grimsley did not have an easy time of it growing up. Perhaps that is why neither of them

married—or have not yet married (they are in their early thirties).
Or perhaps they are simply wary of fortune hunters. Both are
hearty types, not pretty but healthy and energetic and friendly, and
democratic enough to invite such people as Hilda Fagerhalt and
me, and Letitia Higgins and her worthless scamp of a husband,
Yancey, to entertainments in their splendid mansion.

The Sisters Grimsley wear bloomers to ride bicycles through
the park and around town, and certain members of the local bon
ton frown upon this. Another group of suspicious watchers of the
sisters' behavior are even more disapproving of their latest fancy,
which is dancing the waltz. Some months ago the sisters imported
a dancing master from St. Louis, and after they learned to waltz
they kept him in town to give lessons to their friends.

Now, I learned to waltz some years ago while we were in circus
winter quarters outside New Orleans, Louisiana. We wanted to
have a big celebration for Christmas, and someone suggested that
we erect the big tent and have a ball. Even that late in the century
many Americans considered the waltz to be sinful, highly injurious
to morals, because of close physical contacts by members of the
opposite sex. Circus people had no such prejudices. The waltz was
taught to me that Christmas by a high-wire aerialist named Geor-
giana, and when she was done with me she complimented me on
my artistry.

After the accident, I did not think I would ever dance again,
but two or three weeks ago when the Sisters Grimsley came by the
hardware store on their bicycles to invite Hilda and me to their
home for lessons, I decided to have a try at waltzing again. Hilda
wanted no part of dancing of any kind and warned me of the
danger to my crippled leg, but when she realized that I was determined to go, she went along with me. Like most wives in this town,
she is fearful of the Sisters Grimsley. Their rich dowries are believed to be overly tempting to all greedy males, wed or unwed.

If I was going to graze in greener pastures I would choose Letitia Higgins—who is penniless most of the time—over either of
the wealthy Grimsleys, but fortunately Hilda does not know that—
so far.

Anyway, when I first went out upon the polished floor of the
Grimsley House's ballroom, I was very nervous. Naturally I tended
to favor my crooked leg, but the dancing master was a good sort,

and the Sisters Grimsley chimed in with blandishing assurances, calling me their "dancing lame prince." Actually, I believe Hilda had a great deal more trouble than I did in perfecting the steps and movements. She has well-shaped Swedish legs, but there is a residue of the puritanical in her soul, and she has this reluctance that I think is reinforced by her dear friend, Lora Valentine, who believes most of the joys of mankind are sinful.

I am not certain how much pleasure Hilda derived from last evening's reception at the Grimsley House. I believe she enjoyed the music provided by an ensemble of violins, violas, and clarinets. I waltzed with her three or four times, and Colonel Preston Boggs waltzed with her at least double that number. Because of my bad leg I could not risk the whirling Viennese even with Hilda, and she was too modest to try the dipping Boston, which suited my disablement quite well. The Sisters Grimsley loved the dip and did not seem to mind my weight upon them—which I could not avoid because of my leg—but every time I danced with either of them, Hilda's watchful, disapproving face inevitably appeared from the sidelines of chairs or over the shoulder of whatever partner she might be dancing with.

I must confess that I waltzed more times with Letitia Higgins last evening than with any other lady present. As long as the dancing continued, I could not stay away from her. I changed partners occasionally, of course, going sometimes to Maude or Annie Grimsley, both of whom glided with such vigor I feared my poor leg would fail me, and then always there would be Hilda's disapproving frown appearing and disappearing like the Cheshire cat's. Oddly enough she did not object to how often I held Letty Higgins in my arms; in fact, Hilda twice praised me for "rescuing the poor creature from her rogue of a husband."

As for Yancey Higgins, he evidently had a flask concealed somewhere because he gradually became more and more inebriated as the evening progressed. He spent the first hour pursuing Betty Hesterly, the telephone central, but Theo Drumgoole, the telephone engineer, was always at hand to rescue her. Miss Hesterly is indeed a tasty morsel, more articifial than real, however, while Letitia Higgins is luscious in a quite different way and far more real than artificial.

By the time Letty Higgins and I were waltzing every other set, *or sitting and talking with various guests between, Yancey had turned to pursuing the Sisters Grimsley and probably had forgotten that his wife was present. At least he never gave any indication that he was jealous or resentful of my constant attention. After Yancey became fairly well muddled, the sisters lured him into a side room where they stretched him out upon a sofa where he fell asleep. They posted Hereward Padgett, our local idiot and genius, to watch over him.*

Letty was aware of these goings-on, I'm certain, but she paid no attention, and I suspect that throughout her marriage she has endured such behavior until she has reached the point where she can pretend none of it is actually happening. Perhaps last evening she looked upon me as a means of escape. Anyway, whenever a new waltz was called, she was always at hand, ready for me to sweep her around the ballroom as best I could on my impediment. Buxom though she is, Letty is quite light on her feet. Her style is the whirl, and progressively through the evening she allowed her body to touch and retouch mine more and more intimately, as we whirled and dipped and whirled.

From time to time she would face me directly, her lips full and smiling. Her black eyes at times were like pinpoints, studying me as though she wanted to question me but dared not. Before last evening we'd had no more than two or three conversations in our lives. One day when she came for the laundry, Hilda was not here, having gone to visit Lucy Markham who was ill, and I was in charge of the hardware store. After I had given Letitia the basket of soiled laundry, she suddenly began asking questions about my life with the circus. I was surprised that she knew of that, or cared. She said that her secret girlhood wish was to run away with a circus, wear pink tights and spangles, and swing from trapezes. I told her that life in the circus was not the glitter that it appeared to be. "It's a hard life," I said, "especially for women."

"Oh, I would not mind that," she said. "Life has never been easy for me. Running off with a circus would have been an escape to freedom."

Dr. Socrates Drumm, who attended my bruises and ailments while I was with Bell Brothers & French's Circus, once told me that the way he appraised women was by the feel of their flesh. "If a woman has pneumatic legs and arms," he said, "she goes in my book."

Well, Letitia Higgins has pneumatic legs and arms, and she goes in my book. Sitting here today, that is all I can think about. But by God, my aching leg from ankle to hip, all night and all day, is the penalty I must pay for discovering Letitia's natural seductiveness.

Was last evening a beginning with an ending in the future, or was it only a fragment of my life, like the encounter with the four Indiana soldiers we left besieged by Rebel bushwhackers in the Waynesville jail some forty years ago?

XVIII

THE END OF JACK BONNYCASTLE

~

The morning after they left Waynesville, rain began falling, not hard but steady. Muddy roads slowed the wagon and the animals, and by late afternoon everyone was wet and chilled. Ben was riding on the front seat with Dr. Pingree, but the overhang was of little benefit against frequent gusts of spray. From what he could see of the countryside through mists and fogs, Ben decided it was the greenest and hilliest land he had ever passed through.

About sundown a narrow streak of blue sky appeared along the eastern horizon, and the rain slackened. Ahead of the wagon, the road coiled sharply down toward a stream. Dr. Pingree halted the Belgians and waited until Johnny Hawkes and Jack Bonnycastle came alongside on their horses.

"Big Piney down there," the peddler said with a jerky forward motion of his arm. "May be running high at the wagon ford, and it'll be near dark before we can get set for the crossing."

"You want to camp here?" Johnny asked, looking around skeptically at the rocky uneven ground.

"No. Somewhere down this slope I remember a warm spring. Good for bathing. I feel the need for a bath. Suppose you and Jack Bonnycastle canter on ahead and find that spring."

"Will do," Johnny replied and motioned for Jack to fall in beside him.

Several minutes later, Ben and the peddler sighted their two companions waiting on their horses beside the descending road. Johnny signaled for them to come on.

"The warm spring is right in here," Johnny shouted. "Maybe

a hundred paces in. It's steaming in the cool air. Plenty of room for the wagon."

The passage from the road to the spring was not muddy but was so rough with stones that the Chariot of Wonders rocked from side to side like a boat in a rough sea. Johnny guided the Belgians in close beside the spring. The pool that had been formed was set in a crescent of mossy green rocks and was almost as large as the wagon. Vapor rose several feet above the water's surface.

By the time the horses were unhitched, unsaddled, and fed, a brownish dusk had settled over the surrounding forest of oaks and pines. Dr. Pingree brought out a box filled with small cakes of soap and passed them around. In a few minutes, the peddler, Ben, Johnny, and Hadjee were stripped naked and splashing merrily in the warm water. Not until they came out and were drying themselves on strips of muslin—again supplied by the free-hearted Dr. Pingree—did they notice that Jack Bonnycastle was stretched out on the ground behind the wagon, still fully clothed.

"Hey, Jack, you better go bathe yourself," Ben said. "The water's fine and warm."

"Yeah," Johnny added. "All of us are clean and sweet-smelling. We can't have you stinking up the party."

"I'm wore out," Jack Bonnycastle replied. He sat up, blinking his eyes at the others.

"Maybe we ought to toss you in the spring, smelly clothes and all," Johnny threatened. He finished buttoning his jeans and took a step toward Jack.

"No, no, I'll go wash off in the spring," Jack promised. "Word of honor. Just let me rest another minute."

"Leave him be," the peddler said and began gathering sticks for a cooking fire.

Jack Bonnycastle rested for more than a minute He lay on his stomach in the grass until the darkness—relieved only by the small fire—enveloped everything. Then he stood up and, with no word of explanation, walked over to the spring. The others, busy at the cooking, paid little attention to the languid splashing, and then he was back, carrying a wet shirt, wringing it out tightly and then holding it close to the fire for drying.

Ben had hoped to bed down that night in the open, but they had scarely finished supper when the rains returned in freshets. And so back to the wagon hold he went. As usual, Jack Bonnycastle fell quickly to sleep, his mouth opening slightly to make faint little bubbling sounds before he began a slow rhythmic breathing. The night turned quite chill, and in a half sleep the bedmates struggled continuously for possession of the blankets.

Some time late in the night, Ben awoke to find Jack Bonnycastle clinging to his back, arms around him, whimpering and then sobbing. Aromas assailed him—the sweet perfume of Dr. Pingree's soap, the unfamiliar spiciness of clean human skin and hair, the muskiness of his own body. He jabbed an elbow into Jack Bonnycastle's side. The boy cried out, fearfully, in his sleep.

Next morning the sky was cloudy, but no rain fell, and they moved on to the Big Piney. They crossed the stream and then began climbing until they reached a flat-topped ridge that gave them an overlook view of deep blue-green valleys, swift, foaming stream, and occasional clearings. Some fields below had been planted with corn, and rows of green seedlings gave a verdant tinge to the dark, rain-soaked earth.

The road dropped easily into the valley of the Gasconade River, but before they reached the roiled ford, they sighted an oncoming column of soldiers in blue, some marching on foot, others riding in wagons, a few on horseback. A small horse-drawn cannon brought up the rear.

At the first wide shoulder of the road, Dr. Pingree pulled the wagon to one side. In a minute or so the camels and the two riding horses came up and halted behind it.

A major, red-faced and perspiring from exertion, swung his mount to a stop beside the wagon, and after a quick rearward survey of his men who were still splashing across the ford, he lifted his hat and inquired if this was a circus that he had encountered. Johnny, who had dismounted, assured him that they were not a circus, but that he was on special duty for the United States Army, engaged in transporting the two camels to the city of Rolla.

"Why—?" The major stopped with the one word and then asked hurriedly, "Did you travel by way of Waynesville?"

"Yes, sir, we did, and come near being taken prisoners by a bunch of Rebels. They made captives of four Indiana soldiers."

The major nodded. "My orders are to drive the Rebels from the town. Are they still flying the Confederate states flag?"

"The flag was on the courthouse when we left," Johnny replied with a grin. "They all behave like Rebels. You'd have to drive the whole town out."

"The brazen rascals," the major declared and turned to shout a command to a mounted sergeant. The column was a Missouri volunteer company, obviously green recruits in the main. Those who had crossed the Gasconade on foot were wet almost to their waists, and none of them appeared to be enjoying the unfamiliar military life. Although the sergeant trotted his horse up and down the slope, shouting curses, the column remained in very ragged formation.

The major shook his head and smiled sourly at Johnny. "You say the Rebels made prisoners of Indiana soldiers?"

"Yes, sir. They were talking about trying them for spies before a judge. You may be too late for them."

The major sighed. "We're doing our damnedest." He frowned at the straggly column behind him. "Pray for us." He raised his arm and gave the command to move forward. The soldiers, with their wagons and cannon, trudged slowly past the Chariot of Wonders, each man giving a quick glance of surprise at the cud-chewing camels resting patiently beside the road.

As soon as the column passed, Dr. Pingree put his wagon in motion. After fording the Gasconade, they followed the river valley road north until it turned straight eastward. During their nooning stop, the skies cleared and the sun began burning down as though rehearsing for summer. About midafternoon they came upon a grove of widely separated cottonwoods and river birches. Beyond these trees, a fringe of yellow-green willows screened the river. The setting was parklike, and when Dr. Pingree assured Johnny that they could easily reach Rolla the next day, they agreed to make an early camp there.

"Besides," the peddler added, "we need to restock provisions. A couple of miles ahead is a stage stop with grocery."

The idyllic camping area was deserted except for a two-wheeled cart with the points of its shafts resting on the ground. Its wide-rimmed wheels were made of wood, and its contents were covered with sun-faded sailcloth roped down tightly.

Johnny dismounted and intently examined the vehicle. "First time I've seen a carreta since leaving San Antonio," he said. "I'm bewitched how one got way up here in Missouri."

"The owner should not be too far away," the peddler said. "Ask him." He unharnessed the Belgians and ordered Jack Bonnycastle to lead them down to the river for water. "Now, anybody hanker to go with me to the stage stop for supplies?"

Ben and Johnny volunteered immediately. Jack said that after watering the horses he intended to lie down for a rest, and Hadjee made signs that he wanted to brush the camels. Tooley, the Egyptian declared in a mixture of languages, most certainly was enceinte and needed his attention.

Dr. Pingree borrowed Jack's gray horse, Champ, and attached a saddlebag. With Ben riding pillion behind Johnny, they set off down the road.

Little Jo, the mustang, strongly objected to two riders, tossing his head and kicking up his heels, but Johnny settled him down by the time they turned a bend in the sandy road and sighted the trading post.

Three or four wagons and several saddled horses were drawn up around a weathered gray building. The long sloping roof was covered with hand-hewn shingles; the walls were barked logs chinked with mud that had aged stone-hard. A corral containing a dozen stage line horses was at one side. An old Overland Stage Company sign was nailed above the grocery's entrance.

With their saddlebags in hand, they pushed through a battered door into the fragrant interior. Several men were clustered around a crude bar on the left; a few women sat on a long bench to the right. The grocery store and stage stop was obviously a social gathering place for the neighborhood. Every face turned to observe the three strangers who had entered.

Recognizing a primly dressed gray-haired woman behind the counter on the right, Dr. Pingree nodded politely to her. "Mrs. Mack, is Mr. Mack occupied at present?"

"Oh, Lord, Dr. Pingree," she replied. "Mr. Mack went south to join Pap Price's army."

The peddler looked surprised. "Did he indeed? Running off to join the Confederates and leaving you with the trading here? I'm pure flabbergasted."

A gangly man with a black chin beard and a long, thin, bony nose moved in closer to Pingree. "What's it to you what old Mack done?" he demanded.

An expression of displeasure clouded the gray-haired woman's face. "Oh, this is Mr. Tom Thistle, Dr. Pingree," she said. "Mr. Thistle bought Mr. Mack's share and kindly let me stay on to help."

Tom Thistle did not respond to the peddler's extended hand, but he growled in a threatening tone, "You're that Yankee peddler comes through here to take trade away from us, ain't you?"

"I had an understanding with Mr. Mack. I bought produce from him, and he bought from me things he didn't have. We traded discount. I peddled nothing to his customers." Pingree motioned to a row of jugs on a shelf behind the gray-haired woman. "I'll trade for two dozen of the jugs of sorghum there."

"You pay the earnest price, or no trade," Tom Thistle replied. "I ain't looking for business with *Yankee* peddlers."

"I'm a *Missouri* peddler," Pingree said calmly.

"Righteous Southerners don't peddle," Tom Thistle declared. He ran thumb and forefinger along his thin nose as if sharpening the bladelike bone.

Dr. Pingree reached down and picked up the saddlebag he had dropped on the floor. He tipped his hat to the gray-haired woman. "A good day to you, Mrs. Mack," he said and motioned for Ben and Johnny to follow him out of the store.

Outside, as they were mounting the horses, he swore softly. "I was craving after some buttermilk," he said. "My stomach's been cutting up a shine. Mr. Mack always kept a churn of fresh buttermilk. Good for settling the bowels. But I would not trust anything to my belly traded from that Tom Thistle fellow."

On the way back to the campground, whenever they passed the marks of wagon wheels or hoofprints turning off the road into the woods, the peddler would stop the gray horse and peer through the trees. At one of these turnoffs, he gave a grunt of satisfaction. "Take a look, Johnny, Ben. Either of you see a heifer and calf yonder by that cabin?"

"Sure enough," Johnny replied.

The peddler dismounted, opened a saddlebag, and took out a lidded tin pail. "Wait here, boys. I'll be back in a minute."

When he returned, he was carrying the pail with an air of triumph. He tested the lid and fitted the pail carefully into his saddlebag. He then looked up at Johnny and Ben, his thick black eyebrows dancing, and said in a voice that was even deeper than usual, "The simple pleasures of the poor. The kind lady over there gifted me with a mugful of delicious thick buttermilk and then she filled my pail. We'll have flapjacks tonight!"

As they rode into the grove, they were surprised to see a donkey tied beside the Mexican cart. Beyond the donkey a stranger was standing before an easel that had been set up facing the Chariot of Wonders. In his left hand the man held a palette, in his right a brush, and he was daubing paint quite rapidly upon a canvas. Not much taller than five feet, he wore a scarlet fore-and-aft cap with long bills both front and back, a pair of tightly fitting elkskin trousers, and a long-tailed coat. When he heard the horsemen approaching, he gave one impatient glance at them and continued his painting. Hadjee as usual was near his camels, seated cross-legged on the ground, head bent forward. Jack Bonnycastle sat motionless upon a log some distance away, apparently absorbed in what the stranger was doing. When Johnny dismounted and started striding toward the painter, Jack jumped up and trotted toward him, shaking his head. "He don't want to be disturbed," Jack said in a loud whisper. "Allows he's got to get the picture done before sunset."

"Well, he'd better hurry some," Johnny declared. The sun, enlarged and dark orange, was dropping perceptibly into the hills on the western horizon.

"Who is he?" Ben asked.

"Mr. Bonaparte. Says he's an artist," Jack replied.

"He has the looks for it," Dr. Pingree said. "But why does he want to portray my Chariot of Wonders on his canvas?"

"Oh, it's the camels he's hopping about," said Jack. "He and Hadjee can talk together in some kind of gibble-gabble."

"He don't look Egyptian," Johnny said.

"No, he said he's Froncy."

"Froncy?" Dr. Pingree looked puzzled for a moment. "Oh, Français, French maybe. Could be from St. Louie." He carefully lifted his pail of buttermilk. "Come on, you boys get a good cooking fire going while I mix the flapjack dough."

The painter joined them at the fire just before Dr. Pingree was ready to start dropping dough on the griddle. Apologizing for his apparent impoliteness and earlier reluctance to leave his easel, the man explained that he was fascinated by the presence of exotic camels in a pastoral setting in the heart of America. "I knew I must depict them for the world to see, and I feared there would be no later occasion. *Par bonheur,* I was able to work during the best light of day—that is, in the declining rays of the sun that turn *le monde* into a place of magic."

His name, he said, was Bonaparte, not Louis or Napoleon, but simply Jean. A distant relative of the famous kings and emperors and soldiers, but he hoped to earn equal renown with his art. In Paris some years earlier he had met the American artist, Monsieur George Catlin, who was there with an exhibition of paintings and *peaux-rouges,* red Indians. Monsieur Catlin had suggested that if he, Jean Bonaparte, traveled to America, he could find many fresh scenes and subjects to paint in the Indian Territory. Monsieur Catlin himself had painted Comanches and Pawnees there, but since his visit, the United States government had forcibly confined many more tribes in the territory. Various artists had traveled up the Missouri River and into *les Montagnes* Rocky, Monsieur Catlin told him, but few had painted in the territory. Truly he had found such a variety of human faces and costumes there, but alas, because of the perturbation of removal from their homelands, there was much *tristesse,* sadness, much sickness, much destitution.

Jean Bonaparte spoke in sharp nasal accents, pronouncing *th* as *zs.* No, he informed Dr. Pingree, his home was not in St. Louis, although he had stopped there to visit family connections while on his way to the West. He was a Frenchman, and his home was in France.

Johnny wanted to know where he had obtained the carreta and donkey. "Ah," he replied, "in the valley of the River Rouge. I came upon this *garçon de Metigue* with carreta and donkey. *Le bon garçon* was going to Santa Fe with a train of wagons. He no longer needed cart and donkey. *Un bon marché,* a bargain for me."

By this time, Dr. Pingree was tossing flapjacks off his griddle onto tin plates, and he asked the Frenchman if he would join them for supper.

"Ah, I am so *distrait,* absent of mind." With his knuckles he struck both his temples a hard blow. "I have *poisson.* Fish? Took several from river this afternoon. I meant to invite your party to share them."

"No matter," the peddler said. "We can share your fish at breakfast. Just keep them in cold river water." He handed a filled plate to Bonaparte. "These cakes have morsels of ham cooked in them. Delicious with honey. Ben, pass the honey pot to Mr. Bonaparte."

Darkness settled slowly over the woods and the river, which during the rare lapses in the talk could be heard rippling faintly beyond the willows. Most of the conversation was between the Frenchman and Pingree. For once, Johnny Hawkes seemed to be daunted by the presence of so beguiling a stranger. As for Ben and Jack Bonnycastle, they were both out of their depth, but they sat politely listening as they finished eating the last of Dr. Pingree's flapjacks.

"I have a request to make of you, Mr. Bonaparte," the peddler said. "I would like to see your painting of the two camels that you found on the banks of a river in the heart of America."

"Yes, most *certainement*." Bonaparte explained that the painting was not yet dry, but he would bring the easel to the light of the fire so that it could be seen.

In his painting Jean Bonaparte had used the rear of the Chariot of Wonders, with its identifying lettering, to balance the camels and Hadjee on the right of the scene. The Egyptian had been captured in his long-tailed striped shirt with his turbaned head bent forward in a natural pose of weariness as he guarded the pair of contented dromedaries.

"Come morning," the Frenchman said, "I shall show you some of my portraits and landscapes packed in the carreta."

"I would like to purchase this one," Pingree said. "I believe it is the only existing depiction of my wagon."

Hadjee, who had come closer to view the painting, showed his teeth in one of his rare smiles. He began gesturing and chattering in broken French to Bonaparte, evidently expressing pleasure at what he saw on the canvas. In reply, the Frenchman spoke slowly in his language and then in an aside to Pingree said, "His French is no better than my English. It seems he was in a French camel corps *militaire* somewhere in *Afrique du Nord*. Algiers, *je crois*."

Pingree and Bonaparte had just begun bargaining over the price of the painting when they were interrupted by the thudding of hooves. Several horsemen were approaching from the road. The riders formed a line and halted, facing the fire and the campers. To Ben, they seemed even more menacing, being mounted, than the band of Confederates on foot who had surrounded them in the moonlight outside Waynesville. These intruders' faces were brightly illuminated by the light from the fire that had been enlivened with dry wood in order that the Frenchman's painting could be clearly seen.

One of the horsemen was Tom Thistle, the trader from the stagecoach station. "Yankee peddler," he said in a tone that was more like an animal's growl than a human voice. "Yankee peddler, you annoyed Mistress Byford in her home this evening and took cow's milk from her."

Dr. Pingree stood up straight, facing Thistle, and his voice was edged with anger. "I offered to pay the good woman," he said. "She would take no money from me."

"She feared you," declared a huge-bellied man seated on a black mare. "She feared for her virtue and her life."

The peddler rubbed his eyes in disbelief. "She showed no fear of me," he said, "I—"

Tom Thistle cut him off. "Don't deny Gabe Byford. He's a churchgoing man and a truth-speaking man."

Like a falling sack of grain, the rotund Byford slid off the mare. He was wearing rawhide boots that flared at the knees. He came and stood with his great protruding abdomen directly in front of the painting on the easel. "What's this picture, now?"

Nobody spoke. Jean Bonaparte was staring with astonishment at the big man, who reached out and rubbed a thumb across the undried paint. Byford spat a mouthful of chewing tobacco and saliva upon the canvas. He turned to face the Frenchman and then broke into raucous laughter. Some of the other horsemen joined in with snorts and jeers. Pointing a finger at Pingree, Byford then roared, "You come near my woman again, peddler, and I'll kill you dead." He strode back to the mare and mounted with considerable difficulty.

"More than that," Tom Thistle declared. "Listen, you lot of Yankee spies. If you ain't clear of this county by high noon tomorrow, there'll be hangings. That's you, peddler, and you Texan with the U.S. brand on yore pony, the two whelps with you-all, that black furriner with the furrin camel beasts, and you clod-pated, fool-talking French-Mexican and yore purty pictures." Tom Thistle cocked his head to one side and grinned at Gabe Byford. "If we wasn't fair-minded citizens we'd hang you all to-night. But now we've given you warning." He raised one arm and looked along the line of horsemen. "Let's ride out of this stench and away from these trash." He turned his horse, and the others followed.

As soon as they were out on the road, with the sound of their hoofbeats steadily diminishing, Johnny hurried across to the rear of the wagon, opened his saddlebag, and took out the Walker Colt that Patsy Halfacre had loaned him when they left Springfield. "From now on," he said, "I'm carrying this gun on me night and day. If I'd had it in my belt just now, I could've cleaned their plows."

"And likely got us all shot full of holes," Pingree replied. "Every man of them was armed and had us twice outnumbered."

Jean Bonaparte, his face still expressing astonishment, spoke for the first time. "Theatrical!" he cried. "My God, what a country this is. Every man does as he pleases."

"It's the damned war," Pingree said. "Brings out all the old hates of families and clans in these hills."

"Which side would they be on?" the Frenchman asked.

"Their own side. Maybe Secesh, Confederate, although they could not tell you why, except maybe they like being in rebellion. Those jackasses who rode in here, they'd be on whatever side had the largest numbers in their bailiwick."

The Frenchman sat down on one of the stools from the Chariot of Wonders, facing the fire. "Their bombast," he said, "reminds me of the comic villains of Shakespeare."

"That big ox, Byford, destroyed your picture. The one I treas-ured. What's comical about that?"

"Oh, no, no. I can restore the painting tomorrow." He shrugged. "*Le tabac* and saliva may bring a patina to the scene." He laughed. "They *were* Shakespearean in their vulgarity. More English than French. The big man, Byford, is Falstaff *régénéré*."

"That Byford's got a paunch on him like a cow," Johnny said. "Has to throw his shoulders back so he can pack it around." With a scrap of muslin Johnny began a deliberate cleaning of the Walker Colt and added, "Byford needs a hard poke in his belly and balls."

"I did not know," Pingree said, "that Frenchmen cared enough about Shakespeare to understand him well. I keep a tattered volume of his plays by my bed in the wagon."

Bonaparte straightened himself on the stool and began quoting, using such care in his pronunciation there was almost no trace of his usual accent. "Here we will sit, and let the sounds of music creep in our ears—soft stillness and the night become the touches of sweet harmony."

"*The Merchant of Venice,* last act," Pingree declared. "Do you know this one? 'All the world's a stage, and all the men and women merely players. They have their exits and their entrances, and one man in time plays many parts.' "

Bonaparte chuckled. "Of course. It is *As You Like It*. The melancholy Jaques. And then there is Rosalind, 'the fair, the chaste, the inexpressive she.' I have often puzzled over why Shakespeare liked to dress his female characters as boys."

"Easy wantonness? For that Globe Theatre audience? But Shakespeare knew women, or at least as well as any man does. When Rosalind wonders if her lover knows that she is wearing man's apparel in the forest, she observes that her true sex cannot be concealed. 'When I think,' she says, 'I must speak.' "

The fire died rapidly as its dried wood fell to white ashes while a rising moon restored the light to silver. Johnny finished polishing the Walker Colt, reloaded it, patted the barrel as though it were a living thing, and thrust it into his belt. "I'd like to read that Shakespeare of yours sometime, Doc," he said.

"Anytime," the peddler responded.

Jack Bonnycastle arose from the grass, yawned audibly, and started for the wagon. "I'm sleepy," he said. "You coming in, Ben?"

"Nope. Sleeping out," Ben replied.

"I reckon we'd all better start our night dozing," Pingree said. "Your Shakespearean villains, Mr. Bonaparte, will likely be on our heels after sunrise, chasing us to the county line. And I don't know where that line may be, or how far we have to travel to prevent Falstaff and his cronies from hanging us to a tree."

"*Bon soir,* Dr. Pingree," the Frenchman said. "My most enjoyable evening since I left St. Louis."

"Ah, sir, excepting for the visit of the mountaineer blackguards, I can say the same."

In the crimson-gray light of dawn, Dr. Pingree yelled everyone out of blankets. Across the parklike grove the Frenchman was also up and dressed and had started a breakfast fire between his cart and the wagon. He shouted that he was panning his fish and would have them ready for serving within the hour. The group around the wagon set about their usual morning preparations for travel—feeding and watering the animals, checking harness and saddles, packing utensils and gear. A summerlike warmth was already in the air, portending a hot day.

"Where's that Jack Bonnycastle?" Dr. Pingree demanded somewhat testily. "He took my Belgians and the two riding horses down to the river at sunup. I need to start hitching. That boy's too lackadaisical for my taste."

Ben, who was busy roping utensils into a canvas cover, looked up. "You want me to get him?"

"Finish what you're doing," Johnny said. "I'll get young Bonnycastle and the horses."

In less than ten minutes, Johnny came jogging back through the willows, driving the Belgians and his mustang before him. Upon his face was a strange look of surprise, of shocked wonderment.

"Where's Jack Bonnycastle?" Ben asked. "And his horse?"

Johnny exhaled a long breath of air. "There ain't no Jack Bonnycastle," he said. "Not no more."

"What do you mean?" Ben asked in alarm.

Johnny motioned to Dr. Pingree to come closer. "He's a female," Johnny said in a tone as though he were divulging some dark and horrible confidence, his voice almost a whisper.

"I suspected so," Pingree said, with less solemnity. "She's one of Will Shakespeare's Rosalinds."

"Johnny, how do you know?" Ben cried, unbelieving.

"I saw her, not ten yards from me," Johnny said, "out in the river with her gray horse, nekkid as a fledgling bird, standing for a minute on the horse's back. I couldn't believe my eyes. She saw me goggling, I reckon. Then she jumped in the water, but the gravelly shoal wasn't deep enough to hide her little titties till she squatted. So I gathered the three other horses and come away."

"Are you sure Jack Bonnycastle's a female?" Ben persisted.

"Good God, boy, ain't you been in this world long enough to tell the difference? There she stood, ten paces away from me, balancing herself, nekkid on the horse's back with her shivering arms flung out, her little titties kind of blue from the cold water, nothing, nothing hanging between her female legs but a little tuft of yellow hair."

Ben's face was suffused with dismay. "She could have told us," he said. "I slept with her most nights between Marshfield and here."

"Yeah, and how many times a day along the road did we walk over to a tree, unbutton our dongs, and wet the trunk without thinking of a female in our company? Downright ornery of her. Did anybody ever see Jack Bonnycastle stand to piss?"

Dr. Pingree appeared to be more amused than pained by the surprise discovery. "I told you from the beginning," he said teasingly, "that the name Jack Bonnycastle was false, didn't I?"

"He—she always did smell good," Johnny said. "I allowed it was from some of your sweet soap, Doc. But I reckon it was sweet female smell all along."

"What we going to say to her," Ben asked, "if she comes back now? You think he—she will come back, Dr. Pingree? Are we going to let on we know?"

"She knows I know," Johnny said. "She—"

"Wait a minute," the peddler interrupted. "I've thought of a way we can tell her without saying a word." He turned and strode across to the Chariot of Wonders and entered the rear door.

While he was gone, Johnny peered hard at Ben and said with forced jollity, "When I waked you the other morning, I found you two curled up like a pair of breeding catamounts. No more sleeping with that bed partner, little hoss. You're still a young-un, but you can make a baby even at your age." Johnny grinned. "Maybe you already have."

Ben felt his face burning. He could think of nothing to say and was mightily relieved when Dr. Pingree interrupted by stepping out of the wagon. In the peddler's hand was one of his penny dreadful books.

"She hid it in her blankets," he said.

He lifted the book so they could see the title: *Jack Bonnycastle and the Fiend of Bellingsworth*. Beneath the lettering was a drawing of a handsome young man facing a hooded monster wearing a black cape and making a threatening gesture with a blazing flambeau.

"If you boys had kept your eyes open and were more interested in reading my 'dreadful' books," he said drily, "you would have known she was not Jack Bonnycastle as soon as I did. When she wouldn't bathe with us in the spring, I suspected she was a girl."

"Here she comes," Ben said. "She *is* coming back."

The girl, dressed in her brown linsey-woolsey trousers, brown shirt, and black-and-tan checked waistcoat, was riding bareback on the gray horse. Beneath her old militia cap her straw-colored hair clung damply to her cheeks and neck. Her blue eyes looked directly at Johnny as though challenging him, then flicked across the faces of the others.

When she dismounted and started to pick up her saddle that lay beside the wagon, Pingree stepped in front of her, holding up the penny dreadful. She only glanced at it. "Yes," she said quietly, "you know my name's not Jack Bonnycastle." The peddler made a nodding bow, smiled gently, and backed away.

Ben shouted at her, "Why'd you fool us?"

She shook her head. "I reckon I was afeared of Billy Goodheart. The way he treated me." Her voice was almost matter-of-fact. "I didn't want any of you roosters knowing I was a female. To be mistreated the way Billy Goodheart mistreated me."

"Then who are you?" Ben demanded, his feelings still hurt. "What's your true name?"

Before replying she picked up her saddle blanket and placed it carefully on the gray horse. "When I tell you my true name," she said firmly, "you better not laugh. If you laugh I'll pound every one of you in the nose." She tugged at the saddle girth. "Promise me, all of you. Not to laugh."

They promised, almost in unison.

She stepped away from the horse. "Well, my name is Queen Elizabeth Jones."

Dr. Pingree smiled at her again. "Why, that's a fine name," he said. "But I'm going to call you Princess."

"Are you of royal blood?" Johnny asked her. He was having difficulty keeping from laughing, not because of the name but because of her threat if he did laugh.

"My blood is as good as the blood of any queen or king or prince or princess," she replied, "or anybody named Johnny Hawkes or Ben Butterfield or Dr. Pingree. Or Hadjee."

"Amen," said the peddler. He was about to speak further but was interrupted by a call from the Frenchman across the grove: "*Allo! Allo! Déjeuner! Poisson!* Fish! Break-fast!"

XIX

BEN BUTTERFIELD

~

Thinking about that French artist in the wilds of the Missouri Ozarks reminded me of a postcard that I have kept with others, and I've just found it. After Old Man Fagerhalt died, his daughter Hilda cleared out his desk and ordered me to take it for my own. This damned ancient piece of furniture has such vast numbers of drawers and coffers and cubbyholes in which to store things that I can seldom find whatever I have put away, but I did finally recover my treasured postcards tied up with a piece of string.

The card I was looking for is in the pack, the name, address, and message written in pencil in that mannered schoolgirlish script that she was so parsimonious in using to convey love and kisses, or even a plain matter-of-fact greeting to me. The card is addressed correctly to Louisiana Street, and the message is in two words: "Remember him?" She signed it Queen Elizabeth Jones as she always did when writing to me, in the boldest of letters four or five times the size of the message itself.

On the other side of the card is a reproduction of a painting of a live steamboat, with black smoke pouring from its stacks, at the St. Louis riverfront, and beyond this resplendent foreground vessel is another and then another and another steamboat, each becoming smaller in the receding perspective, until the group forms all together a crescent with the bending of the Mississippi River. With her pencil, Queen Elizabeth Jones had drawn a line and arrow pointing to the name of the artist, Jean Bonaparte, and the lithographer. Below Bonaparte's name and that of the Paris lithographer are a few printed words in French that describe the place and subject of the painting.

The card bears the postmark of Buffalo, New York, but I do not know where or when Queen Elizabeth Jones found it— possibly in Paris, the year that Bell Brothers & French's Circus and Menagerie went to Europe. That was two or three seasons after my first accident, so I missed all that excitement.

Some excitement for the present, however, has been promised me this afternoon, and I am waiting here with modest expectations. The Sisters Grimsley, Maude and Annie, have expended another portion of the considerable fortune left them by their dear carpetbagger father. They have purchased a Columbia Electric automobile. During the past week I have seen the sisters in this vehicle moving silently along such streets as are smoothly paved. They sit quite close together on the driver's seat while one or the other manipulates a horizontal rod that steers this machine at a speed twice that of a horse and buggy.

Surprisingly, they have not yet run over any man, woman, child, or beast, and this morning when they came to invite Hilda and me to ride with them in the afternoon, they boasted that their vehicle runs forty miles on each charge of battery. "Only a few cents' worth of electricity," Maude said. "Guy Blythe is jealous of the superiority of our electric over his snorting, bucking, smelly gasoline automobile. His is always out of order."

Guy Blythe manages the local Studebaker wagon agency, which is beginning to serve as an outlet for automobiles, and it was he who sold the Columbia Electric to the Sisters Grimsley. I have heard that Guy now goes about the city visiting the business and social centers to predict that gasoline automobiles will not succeed but that within five years most of the families of this town will be riding in electric vehicles.

As for Hilda and me, Hilda especially because she refuses all entreaties of the Sisters Grimsley to ride in the electric, we'll settle for one of those neat little spider Stanhope buggies with the dickey seat and rubber-head elliptical springs. We'd need a horse, of course, and that is the obstacle, as we have no stable, and the city fathers oppose any more permits for stables on lower Louisiana Street. So there we are. But who knows? A few months hence Guy

Blythe might be selling us a Columbia Electric so that we may go spinning about the city like millionaires.

And right at this moment I hear the squeak of the Columbia Electric's vulgar-sounding honking horn—reminds me of a mule breaking wind—as the Sisters Grimsley roll up in front of the entrance to the hardware store. I can see them partially from my window. Both are wearing purple bloomers, green goggles, and navy blue yachting caps. Maude is out of the machine, tripping jauntily up the sidewalk, and so I rise to go out to meet them under the suspicious scrutiny of Hilda Fagerhalt.

Two hours later. I am back at the desk, unbruised, unmarked, my bones still sound (except for those already broken and mended), but I am slightly concupiscent. The last is the result of an unplanned, totally unexpected, but very pleasant encounter with Letitia Higgins.

It came about this way. The Sisters Grimsley placed me in a sort of tub chair that is attached immediately behind the driver's seat of their electric, and off we went south on Louisiana Street with Maude's strong mannish hand on the throttle, both sisters singing at the top of their voices:

> *Drill ye terriers, drill,*
> *Drill ye terriers drill.*
> *Oh, it's ride all day*
> *With sugar in our tay*
> *In our Columbia E-lec-tric.*

They repeated this amended doggerel four or five times, attracting numerous startled gapes, neck cranings, and hasty arm wavings. Had the sisters not raised their voices in this way, few people would have noticed our passage because there was no sound of hoofbeats or snarling engines, only the whisper of the tires on the paving, like a gentle breeze through a pine tree.

They turned the machine down Capitol to Broadway and turned south, spinning merrily along, then slowing perceptibly as we approached Mount Holly Cemetery. While passing its black metal gates, Maude hummed a death march, Annie broke into a giggle, and I passed a salute to Old Man Fagerhalt whose bones lie somewhere back in the nethermost reaches of the burial ground. Hilda Fagerhalt would have frowned upon us, and her friend Lora Valentine would have thrown up her little peach-colored hands in horror.

When the pavement ended, Annie turned back to Ninth Street, where she had trouble with the trolley car tracks, which kept throwing the narrow tires of the electric from side to side. After she almost collided with a dray wagon, I tried to steady my nerves by staring directly down from my seat at the odometer fastened to the axle below. The odometer's numbers turned with the spinning of the wheel, and I felt secure as long as I could see digits moving.

At the old arsenal on the east side of town, we sailed under tall persimmon trees and oaks and elms, circled the park, and turned down Scott Street toward the river. At the sight of any pedestrian of their acquaintance (and they know almost everybody in town), either Maude or Annie would sound the dreadful horn. In our wake was formed a flotsam of barking dogs, scurrying cats, jumping mules, stamping horses, and cursing or laughing human beings.

At the corner of Markham Street, none other than the buxom Letitia Higgins stepped off the sidewalk, almost into the path of the silently moving Columbia Electric. Annie turned the steering bar just in time and brought us to such a sudden stop I was partially propelled from the tub chair so that both my hands were resting against Maude Grimsley's sturdy shoulders.

When I turned my head I looked directly into the sparkling black eyes of Letitia Higgins. For a moment she reminded me of Patsy Halfacre the first time I saw her. Her face expressed a mixture of surprise, annoyance, and fear until Annie called out cheerfully, "Our fault, Letty! So sorry. Where're you going? Could we give you a ride?"

Letitia Higgins smiled then, charmingly, and I was amazed to see that she had half a dozen freckles scattered over the porcelain skin of her face. She also had very pink full lips and very clean white teeth.

While I was absorbing this glowing assemblage of femininity, slowly realizing that I had held all of it in my arms while waltzing not many evenings past, Letitia Higgins said that she was walking to a house on Broadway and would be pleased to ride in the electric automobile if there was room for her.

"Mr. Butterfield will make room for you," Maude said. "Come aboard."

I stood up and put my arm out to assist Letitia into the automobile, and she managed to drop into the seat, filling it more completely then I had. She then stood up and I tried to press myself to one side of the seat, but try as she would she could not get more than one half of her bottom into it.

Maude, who had been watching our maneuvers with amused interest, finally declared, "There's nothing for it, Mr. Butterfield. You'll have to hold Letty in your lap."

At this, Letitia murmured good-naturedly that she would get out and resume walking. I could have been a gentleman, of course, and offered to give up the seat and walk home myself, but I was not going to abandon this unanticipated opportunity to hold the warm body of Letitia Higgins close to my lascivious person. I reached out, caught her around the waist, and sat her pneumatic posterior into my lap.

By this time a considerable crowd of curious onlookers, including several horses and dogs, had gathered around, but I was too much of a coward to look at any faces, knowing the odds were that some would be familiar friends or acquaintances.

Satisfied that the seating problem was solved, Annie started the Columbia Electric forward, very slowly so as to gently brush aside the closest spectators, one of whom to my dismay was Brigadier Preston Boggs. Soon we were on our way again. To keep Letty from falling forward I had to encircle her with one arm, and I was surprised by the smallness of her uncorseted waist. Her buxomness I thus discovered was above her waist, and I could not help but wonder, and am still wondering as I sit here, how an artist might paint her bosom uncovered.

Back on Louisiana Street we found Hilda waiting for us at the entrance to the hardware store, an expression of relief appearing instantly across her usually stolid Nordic features. As soon as the electric stopped, Letty Higgins stepped out upon the sidewalk, smiling at the approaching Hilda. I do not know, and probably never shall know, whether Hilda's evident concern had been for my physical safety in the automobile. Or was it for imagined seductions by the well-to-do Sisters Grimsley? The attention Hilda gave to Letty far exceeded her consideration for the sisters, al-

though she did thank them for providing me with the outing and for giving Letty a ride to her destination. I truly believe that she regards Letty as a sort of lightning rod protecting me from the man-eating Grimsleys. If so, Hilda's reasoning is about as close to the mark as a compass needle spinning at the North Pole.

I sit here now wondering if the fragment of life that I experienced some days past during the evening of waltzes at the Grimsley House is blossoming into more than a passing fancy. Would Letitia Higgins have eased herself just as willingly upon any other male's legs as she did upon mine? Or am I an old goat, an aging Lothario, a Casanova, yearning for a return of my lost youth? Is Letitia Higgins only an understudy for my lost love, Queen Elizabeth Jones?

I am looking at the circus poster above this desk, at the equestrienne in white riding tights, her golden hair like a halo, lips parted in that joyful smile that is like no other. I remember the early morning light on the bank of the Gasconade River in Missouri where Johnny Hawkes destroyed Jack Bonnycastle forever, transforming him into Queen Elizabeth Jones, but I can't remember why I was so angry at the time. The others were not angry at all. But I remember how I kept recalling the way she would fall asleep beside me in the hold of the Chariot of Wonders, with little bubbling sounds on her lips.

That bubbliness preceding sleep came to be endearing later. It signified the effervescence of her being. Now I look at her gaudy likeness on the poster and wonder why she still stays with the circus, risking life and limb, as they say. Does she hope she can drive the memory of Johnny Hawkes out of her head? On some days does she remember me?

This evening I have asked myself a swarm of questions, but I can answer none of them.

XX

Mischief and Misfortunes in a Town Called Rolla

~

When they stopped for nooning in a pleasant little valley on the road to Rolla, Jean Bonaparte set up his easel and quickly repaired the painting that had been despoiled by the mountain ruffian, Gabe Byford. Dr. Pingree offered payment for the picture, but the Frenchman refused adamantly, saying it was a *cadeau* in return for *amitié* and explaining that he had made a pencil sketch of the scene and that when he returned to Paris he would paint a more artistic rendering in the leisurely surroundings of his studio.

"You may have anything in my wagon as a gift, sir," the peddler said. "I value this painting more highly than any of my possessions."

Bonaparte shrugged. "I observed that you have *huile de lin,* oil of flax. I have need of a bottle."

Dr. Pingree looked puzzled for a moment. "Oil of flax? Oh, linseed oil. Yes." He motioned for the painter to follow him into the Chariot of Wonders.

For most of that morning, Queen Elizabeth Jones had kept to herself, avoiding Johnny more than the others, riding her gray horse ahead of the wagon or behind Hadjee and the camels. After Dr. Pingree and Jean Bonaparte went into the wagon, she said quietly to Ben, "Do you think my hair is too long for a boy's?"

"It's too short for a girl's," Ben replied.

"Dr. Pingree refuses to cut it for me," she continued.

Johnny, who was sipping the last of his coffee, laughed scoffingly. "You can't turn yourself back into a boy, Princess. You ought to be wearing that dress Doc Pingree offered you from his stock."

She thrust her tongue out at him and turned to adjust the saddle on her horse.

During that morning they passed the stagecoach stop but saw no sign of Tom Thistle or Gabe Byford or the other rogues who had threatened them. Consequently they slackened their pace after the nooning stop, Dr. Pingree assuring them that they could reach Rolla long before dark.

As the little procession followed the twisting trail over a narrow corduroy road, with a bog on each side, the sounds of shouts and mingled hoofbeats somewhere ahead gradually filled the air. At first, Ben feared it might be the mountaineers searching for them, but then he saw movement ahead on a slope that was almost bare of trees.

In a few moments a coiling column of mules appeared. After the lead drovers reached the beginning of the corduroy road and halted the animals—obviously to await the passage of the Chariot of Wonders and its accompanying short train—the mules began spreading across the face of the hill.

"Godamighty, look at them mules," Johnny cried. "I didn't know there was that many mules in the whole world."

Jean Bonaparte was too busy keeping his cart on the rough road to make any comment, and Hadjee was similarly engaged with the camels, which were showing signs of alarm, having picked up the scent of the enormous herd of mules.

When the wagon finally rolled off the corduroyed logs onto hard ground, Ben noted that a mounted man was waiting there. He wore a high-crowned black hat with a band of faded red silk around it. His eyes seemed to glare in all directions, impatient and disapproving. As Johnny approached him, the man glared at him. "What's all this?" he demanded. "Some kind of two-bit circus?"

"No, sir," Johnny replied. "Army consignment. Where'd you get all them mules?"

"Missouri, of course, if you're that green you must ask. Southeast Missouri."

Johnny eased his horse in closer. "You wouldn't be Mr. Patrick Halfacre, would you, sir?"

The man glared even harder at him. "Have we met? Do I know you?"

"No, sir. My partners and me, we stopped at your stockyard in Springfield. Miss Patsy told us you had gone for mules."

Patrick Halfacre rose several inches in his saddle. "What business of yours what I'm doing? Who the hell are you?"

"I'm John Hawkes. The U.S. Army hired me to bring them two camels you been staring at into Rolla."

"Did they now?"

"Yes, sir, and I'll be heading back to Springfield soon after I make proper delivery. I'd like to work for you. Miss Patsy said—"

Patrick Halfacre spat on the ground. "You and my darter must've done aplenty of talking."

By this time the wagon, the cart, and the camels had passed. All were turned off to the right to make room for the mules that the drovers were trying to re-form into a column by waving their hats and yelling at the tops of their voices. Queen Elizabeth Jones cantered her horse up beyond the others, keeping her head down as though trying to avoid notice from anyone.

"Mr. Halfacre, Miss Patsy said you could use another man," Johnny explained with forced casualness. "I could see that your stockyard is busy enough to need a tried-and-true man who knows horseflesh. And I'm a hard worker, Mr. Halfacre."

Patrick Halfacre continued glowering at him. "If I find you messed with my darter, boy, I'll track you down and blow your head off. Now pull out of my way so as I can get my mules moving." He touched a spur to his mount and sprang away.

"See you in Springfield, Mr. Halfacre," Johnny called after him, but there was no reply.

When Johnny rode alongside of the wagon seat, Ben grinned at him and said, "Miss Patsy's pa ain't so friendly, is he?"

Johnny shrugged. "I've taken the sting out of meaner critters than Patrick Halfacre. Even so, a man that ornery might be hard to work for."

Dr. Pingree chuckled low in his throat but kept his opinion to himself.

~

As the Chariot of Wonders rolled through and out of a stand of oaks the town of Rolla came into view quite suddenly. The road ran along a flat-topped ridge with hills all about and on almost every hill were houses scattered as though flung there by a passing giant.

Church bells began ringing, two of them, one acute in pitch like a chiming clock, the other deep and reverberating so that the mixture of tones was almost musical.

"What's that?" Ben asked.

"Church bells," Dr. Pingree replied. "For evening prayer meetings, I'd guess. Today is a Sunday. You never heard church bells?"

"They had a fire bell at Fort Davis. Didn't sound like that."

"No." The peddler slapped his lines to urge the Belgians into a faster pace. "Maybe I'd better take you to church while we're in Rolla."

"How did a town get such a name as Rolla?" Ben asked.

"I once raised that very question myself," replied the peddler. "I was told that this town was named by a Carolina man, who came here from the city of Raleigh. R-A-L-E-I-G-H. This Carolina man pronounced it in the Southern way, and it got writ down R-O-L-L-A. So I was told."

The business structures of the town were lined up along the ridge. New buildings, still unpainted, bore military placards on their high false fronts or above the entrance doors. The railroad station was stained a dull brown. Long lines of canvas-covered military wagons were drawn up on both sides of the shiny rails that ended at an embankment of heavy timbers adjoining the depot. Blue-uniformed soldiers lounged in and around the wagons and the station, awaiting arrival of the next railroad train. A hundred yards away, other soldiers were digging trenches and throwing up earthworks.

Noticing a signboard with a crudely drawn pointing finger and the word CAMPGROUND, Dr. Pingree turned his wagon leftward into a sandy trail that led to a large grove. Tents and lean-tos cluttered the area, but the peddler found a cleared space and brought his vehicle to a halt within it.

While they were making camp, the distant sound of an approaching railway train broke the silence of the late Sunday afternoon. Far off to the east, spirals of gray smoke rose above the trees. The chuffing of the locomotive grew louder.

Johnny dropped his saddle beside the wagon and looked at Ben. "Let's go see her steam in," he said.

They set off toward the station, half running, with Queen Elizabeth Jones close behind. Neither she nor Ben had ever seen a locomotive before. As the huge puffing machine came rolling toward the end of track, they both drew closer together as though for mutual defense. Coal smoke, heavy with the stench of sulfur, boiled over them. Steam hissed in white jets from the black monster's sides to form evanescent clouds. A tinny bell clanged a slow alarm. And then a shrill whistle blew suddenly, startling the girl so that she reached with both arms almost beseechingly for Ben's shoulders, her head pressed against his chest. He pushed her away and shouted at her above the din, "You're behaving like a scared female!"

She scowled furiously, then fell in behind him as he followed Johnny along the sides of the stopped cars. From the forward coaches, soldiers and civilians swarmed upon the graveled platform, jostling, shoving, shouting. Ben was reminded of the confusion on the outskirts of Pea Ridge battlefield during the fighting. Frightened by the noise and crowding, and apprehensive of being separated and lost, the girl reached for Ben's hand but had no sooner caught his fingers then she flung his arm away disdainfully. He turned to look at her; her teeth were biting her lower lips almost to bleeding.

Johnny wheeled and faced them. "We've seen the elephant," he cried. "I'm going up the line where the army headquarters are. You two can go back to campground, or do what you please."

"We'll go with you," Ben said.

"Suit yourselves."

They walked back past the panting locomotive that to Ben seemed as much alive as some wheezing demon of hell.

Halfway down the row of unpainted pine buildings, Johnny found one with a sign identifying it as Quartermaster's Headquarters. The door was ajar, a stream of late afternoon sunlight playing upon a slender young man with close-clipped red hair and a fuzz of reddish beard. His uniform blouse was unbuttoned and his cap was pushed far back on his head. His booted legs were atop the rough pine desk.

When his half-closed eyes saw Johnny enter, he came quickly alert, with annoyance showing plainly on his freckled face. "Yes?" he said as if expecting some unpleasant interruption.

"I'm looking for Captain Solomon Lightfoot," Johnny said politely. "He's a quartermaster officer from Indiana."

The freckle-faced lieutenant waited a few moments as if carefully considering a reply. "And what would be the nature of your business?" he asked.

Johnny patiently fingered the fraying order sheet from his shirt pocket, unfolded it, and handed it across the desk.

Moving his lips as he read the words, the officer glanced up suddenly. "So you're the Hawkes fellow bringing Lightfoot's camels. Where are the beasts?"

"Out at our camp. Now where do I find Captain Lightfoot?"

The red-haired lieutenant showed his teeth in a dismissive smile. "You might find him in St. Louis."

An expression of disgust crossed Johnny's face. "The captain didn't wait for me," he said.

"He was ordered to St. Louis," the lieutenant replied with an exultant ring in his voice.

As he learned to do when dealing with military officers, Johnny kept his composure. He also remained in an almost, but not quite, military posture of attention. "You can see, sir," he said, "the orders state that I am to deliver the camels to the railhead at Rolla for loading into cars, after which I am to be paid in full. I would like to do the loading and collect my pay before sundown."

"I'm afraid that is out of my hands," the lieutenant responded in a manner almost that of elation. For the first time he looked at Ben and Queen Elizabeth Jones. "Are those brats your camel-herding squad?" he asked mockingly.

"They help out," Johnny said flatly. "The camels are in the care of an Egyptian. He is in need of pay money for his needs and I need pay money to get us all back to Springfield."

"All right. That Captain Lightfoot left some instructions for you. They're in the office of the provost marshal. That's Major Thornberry, and he's the lord and master of this town. Two buildings down."

The building was easily found, but to reach Major Thornberry, Johnny had to explain the reasons for his visit to a private soldier acting as door guard, and then to a sergeant in a cubicle outside the major's office. Leaving Ben and Queen Elizabeth Jones on a bench in the cubicle, Johnny entered the sanctum to find a fat, balding, red-faced man wearing a black patch over one eye. The provost marshal was not friendly. He quickly let Johnny know that he held a very low opinion of Captain Lightfoot. "A mountebank," he said. "Backed by Indiana politicians." Reaching in a desk drawer he pulled out a leather sheath similar to the one that Lightfoot had given Johnny in Springfield. "You'll find instructions and a few greenbacks in there, if you will sign for them." The provost marshal's one bloodshot eye studied Johnny with obvious distaste. "Can you tell me the meaning of this damned camel business, Mr. Hawkes?"

"No, sir," Johnny replied. "All I know is I was hired by the army to deliver the animals to the railroad here. And load them on stock cars."

Major Thornberry grunted. "Well that's impossible now. The South Pacific Railroad was ordered to transfer all its stock cars for use east of the Mississippi." He grunted again and then continued. "Does the army truly mean to bring in camels for transport, like Captain Lightfoot claims?"

"I don't know, sir."

Johnny started to open the sheath, but the provost marshal raised one of his pudgy hands and made a thrusting gesture toward Johnny, as if with the intent to sweep him from the office. "Take that bullshit out of here to read it. That's quartermaster's business. If you need explanation, go see that incompetent freckle-faced lieutenant up the street, though I doubt if he could help you." The major snorted and with a fretful grimace adjusted his eye patch. "Good day, Mr. Hawkes."

On the bench in the tiny waiting room, Johnny squeezed in between Queen Elizabeth Jones and Ben. Then he twice read the message from Captain Lightfoot, his anger growing with each reading until he finally burst out in a barrage of profanity.

"Swearing and cussing won't get you nowhere, Mr. Hawkes," Queen Elizabeth Jones said quite primly. "That's what my Uncle Sims always says."

"It *would* get me more satisfaction if Captain Lightfoot was in hearing distance. If I've offended your ears, Princess, I beg your indulgence."

"I've heard all them bad words," she replied. "Out of the mouths of Billy Goodheart and others."

Ben interrupted, "What's Captain Lightfoot done now?"

Johnny sniffed. "Gone off to St. Louis. And we can't load the camels on stock cars because there ain't any stock cars. Worse still, he didn't leave us any of our due pay." Johnny slipped a thin collection of greenbacks from the leather sheath that Major Thornberry had given him. "Traveling funds, he calls this. To get the money he owes us we have to drive the camels on to St. Louis."

"Thunderation," Ben said. "How far is St. Louis?"

"I don't know. Let's go back to camp ground and ask Dr. Pingree."

They found Dr. Pingree asleep under a leafing wild cherry bush, and he was not good-humored about being awakened. St. Louis, he said, was a hundred miles east by north, but he seldom traveled that route. Towns were sparse and not prosperous enough for peddling until Pacific City and on east. For this trip he was going north to Jefferson City, where he could stock up on goods from riverboats and then follow the Missouri valley and meander on east through Pacific City to St. Louis.

"How far would that north track be?" Johnny asked.

"Almost twice the miles by the direct route. Takes a lot longer, but it puts jingles in my pockets."

"How long would you be on the road?"

Pingree took out his pipe and tapped tobacco into the bowl from his doeskin pouch. "Let me figure. Three weeks, maybe four."

Johnny sighed. "I reckon we'd better go the short way to St. Louis. A hundred miles we ought to do in a week."

Ben asked him, "Are we going to St. Louis?"

"Looks that way," Johnny said. "Old Lightfoot's got our pay money there." He looked at Queen Elizabeth Jones, who was lying on the grass scissoring her trousered legs in the air. "What're we going to do with you, Princess? We won't be traveling back west to Marshfield for a long spell."

"You could put her on a stagecoach," Dr. Pingree said.

Queen Elizabeth Jones let her legs fall heavily on the ground.

"I told you I no longer have a place at Marshfield. I'll stay with you."

"With me?" The peddler's deep voice had turned to a rasp. "I didn't take you to raise, Princess."

"Then I'll stay with Mr. Hawkes and Ben and Hadjee."

Johnny shook his head slowly. "Maybe Mr. Bonaparte will take you. Where is the Frenchy and his carreta, Doc?"

"Went into town to see if he can sell the cart and donkey. Said he wants to ride a railway car into St. Louis."

A few minutes later, as tree shadows elongated with the lowering sun, the Frenchman appeared on the sandy road, riding atop the cart and urging the donkey to move faster than its usual walk. He halted the cart a few yards from the wagon.

"*Pourquois la tristesse?*" he asked as he stepped down and strode toward the group of loungers. "Why the glum faces?"

Johnny told him of the journey to St. Louis that had become necessary, and Bonaparte then countered by telling of his disappointment in not finding a buyer for his cart and donkey. The Frenchman also said that he had seen a *colleur d'affiches,* a poster announcing an evening concert by a military band.

"Weeks have passed since I've heard *musique veritable,*" he said. "My soul yearns for *musique.*"

After a hastily prepared meal, all except Hadjee went into the town for the concert, Bonaparte riding his donkey and the others doubling on the gray horse and the mustang. They were late in arriving, but to Jean Bonaparte's delight the band was playing a medley of national anthems, among them "La Marseillaise." The uniformed musicians were assembled around the steps of a new redbrick courthouse, and a considerable crowd was scattered over the grounds—seated, reclining, or standing. Johnny found a few empty wooden boxes in an alleyway and they used them for seats.

As daylight began to fade, the band sped through renditions of various Stephen Foster melodies, a stirring version of "The Battle Cry of Freedom," and had just begun "Hail Columbia" when Queen Elizabeth Jones, who was seated between Ben and Johnny, grabbed the latter by the arm and cried out above the blare of brass instruments, "Look! Billy Goodheart! He sees me!"

Around the edges of the crowd, a rider on a black horse circled the open ground, apparently heading for them. He had certainly recognized at least one of them, for his pale blue eyes were fixed upon Queen Elizabeth Jones, and his thick lips were formed into a frozen, leering smile. Around his long greasy hair he was wearing a dark red Indian headband. Tiny bells that were fitted into the beaded band made a sleety whispering sound as he rode closer. He brought his mount to a stomping halt directly in front of Johnny and the girl. The horse's eyes were filled with terror.

"I see the Jones slut got you by the balls, Hawkes," Billy said in his plaintive falsetto.

Johnny jumped to a standing position. "Dismount, Billy, and I'll close your mouth with my fist."

"She ain't worth it," Billy said, shaking his head so that the tiny bells tinkled. "She ain't a sweet female."

Queen Elizabeth Jones shouted at him, "Why don't you leave me alone, Billy?" The music had stopped, and spectators nearby were watching and listening with curiosity.

Billy laughed crazily. "You tell me where you and Sims Jones hid them Mexican silver dollars, and you'll see no more of me. If'n you don't tell me, I'll follow you to the end of creation." He turned his attention to Dr. Pingree, who had risen and moved closer to Johnny and the girl. "You know where the silver dollars are, don't you, peddler?"

Johnny grabbed the black horse's noseband and held tight. "Nobody knows nothing about any Mexican silver dollars," he said with controlled anger. "I ought to shoot you out of your saddle for bothering us."

"You wouldn't do that with all these soldiers around. Besides, you're a coward, Hawkes."

"Get down and I'll show you who's a coward."

Billy grinned his leering grin. "You and the peddler tricked me once, Hawkes. But I'm too slick for you-all and that Lebanon marshal and his duncehead deputy taking me back to Marshfield. I shot him in the knee with his own gun and took his horse." He laughed crazily again.

The concert had ended, and parts of the crowd were beginning to gather closer to them. Dr. Pingree moved against Johnny and said almost in a whisper, "Let him go."

Johnny looked around, frustration on his face.

"Let him go," Pingree repeated.

When Johnny released his hold on the harness, Billy wheeled the black horse, forcing the curious spectators to make way for him. Turning in the saddle, he called back, "Wherever you go, I'll be watching out." He spurred the terror-ridden horse into a lunge, and the sound of the tiny bells in his headband faded into the pounding hoofbeats.

"Why'd you want me to turn him loose?" Johnny demanded of Pingree. "We ought to've taken him to a lawman."

"They'll catch him soon enough," Pingree replied hurriedly. "We've got to get back to campground."

"What's wrong?"

"Billy's been in my wagon," the peddler said as he urged Johnny toward the mustang. "That headband he's wearing. It's an Osage band. I got it from a trader at Independence. Mighty scarce."

When they reached the campground they found Hadjee lying halfway under the wagon. A lump on the side of his head had swollen to egg size, but he was conscious. His arms and legs were tied with ropes, and the lower half of his face was encircled by a tightly fastened bandanna. As soon as he was freed, he began babbling Egyptian maledictions.

Both the ropes and the bandanna had been taken from stores in the Chariot of Wonders. The back door hung loose, and when Dr. Pingree lighted a lantern and looked inside, he uttered Anglo-Saxon maledictions. The interior of the wagon was a rat's nest, a higgledy-piggledy, total chaos. The most disorganized area was Pingree's bed cubby in the upper section, but Billy Goodheart had not found the lower hold. With lanterns hung at both ends of the interior runway, they all set to work restoring goods to their proper places. When it was possible to move easily through the wagon again, Johnny announced that he was going back into Rolla to find a lawman.

"My guess is," Johnny said, "the Rolla lawmen have already heard about Billy's escape from the Lebanon marshal, but they may not know he's in their town."

Not until well after midnight did Johnny return. Ben, who was sleeping outside, came wide awake when he heard Johnny softly humming a tune as he crawled into his blankets.

"Hey," Ben called in a loud whisper, "did you find the law-men?"

"Nope. Marshal's office and jail closed up. But boy, did I hit a bonanza in a poker game."

"How much?"

"Tell you in the morning."

Next morning, for some reason, everybody except Queen Elizabeth Jones was up before the sun, helping with breakfast preparations. Jean Bonaparte began muttering about his donkey and carreta. "I must dispose of them today. I will—how you say it?—a l'enchère—oxshon?"

"Auction?" Dr. Pingree asked.

The Frenchman bobbed his head, smiling. "I must travel speedily to St. Louis where I have letters of credit. I will sell donkey and carreta for a ticket on the railway train."

"Will you sell them to me?" Johnny asked.

Bonaparte and Dr. Pingree both looked surprised. "For you," the Frenchman said, "I make un bon marché."

The peddler groaned. Frowning at Johnny, he said, "Surely you are not going to put your travel money into a cart and donkey. Your funds are scarcely enough for victuals and grain. Four humans and four animals. You'll all starve."

"Ah, but Doc, last night I tripled old Solomon Lightfoot's greenbacks in a poker game. If these Union soldiers here in Rolla can't fight any better than they play poker, the Rebels got nothing to worry about."

Pingree groaned again. "God! You risked it all, didn't you?"

"Life is filled with risks." Johnny replied and drew the leather sheath from inside his shirt. "How much you want, Mr. Bonaparte, for this bun marsha?"

The next train for St. Louis left at ten o'clock that morning. Dr. Pingree and Johnny went to the station to see Jean Bonaparte off, leaving Ben, Hadjee, and Queen Elizabeth Jones to guard the wagon and the camels. After the passenger train pulled out with a loud shriek of the locomotive whistle, Pingree and Johnny walked up the street to a small brick building that housed the jail and the town marshal's office. A pallid middle-aged man, so lean he looked underfed, was busily cleaning a large Colt's navy pistol. He glanced up and forced a smile. "Gentlemen, your pleasure."

They exchanged names; the marshal was Ed Baines. Johnny told Baines about seeing Billy Goodheart and asked if he had heard about his escape from the Lebanon lawmen. The marshal said that he was new on the job, then hemmed and hawed, scratched the sparse strands of hair on his head, and allowed that he may have received a telegram from Marshfield about this Goodheart outlaw. He fumbled through a pile of papers on his desk. "Too much going on in this town, deserting soldiers and suchlike. Anything military the provost marshal helps some. But I'll keep my eyes open for that outlaw." He thanked Johnny for the information and inquired if there was anything else he could do to oblige.

"I'm in the peddling business," Dr. Pingree said. "I usually ask permission of the law before setting up in the streets. Your predecessor always assigned a place for my wagon."

Marshal Baines hemmed and hawed again, worked his lips frantically as if trying to form words, then finally said, "That would be the provost marshal's department. This town is army now, you must have noticed. You'd best go see him. Name's Thornberry, Major Thornberry. Up in the military quarter."

Johnny had no desire to accompany the peddler to see the one-eyed major. Near the jail was a saloon, already open for late-morning customers, and Johnny told Pingree he would wait there for him before returning to the campground.

A few minutes later the peddler returned, entering the barroom, his face a study in puzzlement. "Johnny," he said as he sat down to take a beer, "when you were in Texas, how did you manage to work for the army and not go loony?"

"I did things my way when I could. When I couldn't do things my way I tried to follow the army's line, but it was not easy and seldom satisfied anybody. Of course, when things went bad I always had to take the blame."

Pingree pulled out his pipe and began tamping rough shreds of tobacco into the bowl. "Trouble is I'm not sure what the army's line is in Rolla. The provost says my peddling wagon has to be on a backstreet, between the hours of such and such, or else I'm subject to 'penal retribution' and various other military punishments. But what is a backstreet? They don't seem to know for sure. Selling door-to-door is forbidden except beyond unspecified boundaries and within mysterious hours. You couldn't ever guess what else that one-eyed popinjay of a provost marshal said to me. He virtually accused me of being a Confederate spy. And went on to impugn my manhood by declaring that honest Yankees would never lower themselves to the level of Secesh trash by taking to peddling as an occupation. What's that remind you of, Johnny?"

Johnny laughed. "That Tom Thistle fellow back there on the Gasconade River. He accused you of being a Yankee spy, because righteous Southerners would never lower themselves by peddling."

"Ah, so." With a long swallow Pingree finished his beer. "The world is turned upside down. Before the war, Rolla was one of my best towns for selling. No more. Johnny, my boy, I'm pulling out after noontime. Are you and your party coming along?"

"You going north?"

"Yes. Today to a place called Clifty Dale."

"I reckon it's east to St. Louis for us. I'll miss you, old hoss."

"The same, Johnny Hawkes."

Shortly after noon, Johnny, Ben, Queen Elizabeth Jones, and Hadjee bade good-bye to the peddler who had befriended all of them many times. Even the insouciant Johnny looked a bit sad for a brief moment, but as soon as the Chariot of Wonders turned onto the road, he clapped his hands sharply and ordered everyone to start breaking camp.

Pingree had gifted them with boxes and tins of food, all of which they packed into the carreta. As Ben had no horse, the duty of driving the donkey and caring for the vehicle fell upon him. He was struggling with the cart's sailcloth cover when he heard horses' hooves thudding shoftly on the sandy road. Turning, he was surprised to see approaching side by side on horseback a uniformed sergeant and a very lean civilian wearing a wide-brimmed black hat.

Johnny had also observed the pair, and he walked out a few yards to welcome them. "Afternoon, Marshal Baines," he said.

"Mr. Hawkes. This here's Sergeant Crumrod. Sent by the provost marshal. Major Thornberry, that is."

Sergeant Crumrod touched the brim of his forage cap with his fingers, but he allowed no human expression to cross his face.

The marshal continued awkwardly. "The major and I work together. Since this here has to do with military property, the major sent Sergeant Crumrod to accompany me."

"I don't understand, Marshal," Johnny said. "What military property?"

The marshal pointed at Johnny's mustang. "That spotted hoss there. With the U.S. brand."

"That's my horse. Name's Little Jo. He'll come if I call him."

Baines lifted his big hat and scratched at the disarranged strands of hair on his head. "I received information that the spotted hoss was stole from a gov'ment corral in Springfield. Major Thornberry crobberated that information."

"Well, I can't stop you and the army from taking Little Jo, but you're making trouble for nothing. I can send a telegraph and straighten the matter out in a short time. Where'd you get this information about my horse?"

"Not at liberty to say," the marshal replied.

"All right. Take my mustang." Johnny's manner was turning hostile. "I'll borrow my friend's horse and ride into town and send a telegraph."

Sergeant Crumrod spoke sharply. "No, sir. My orders are to seize the horse and place you under military arrest, Mr. Hawkes."

"On what charge?"

"Theft of government property in the form of a horse."

Johnny swore a few of his choicest oaths. "Well, as I said," he continued, "you're making a lot of trouble for nothing. I'm on army duty, with orders to proceed to St. Louis."

The sergeant said, "You can take that up with Major Thornberry, mister." He paused a moment, then continued in flat mechanical tones, "Will you saddle that branded horse and come peacefully with us?" As he finished the question, his right hand dropped to touch the pistol in his belt holster.

Johnny did not bother to reply. He picked up his saddle and bridle and walked across to the mustang. Ben and Queen Elizabeth Jones were close on his heels.

In Queen Elizabeth Jones's blue eyes was a hint of tears. "That soldier won't shoot you, will he, Mr. Hawkes?" she asked.

Ben broke in, "When are you coming back?"

"I'll be back before sundown."

While Johnny continued adjusting saddle and bridle, he told Ben that he was now in charge of the camp. "I may not be back in time for us to start for St. Louis today. When the sun drops down, you and Princess get out some of that pickled souse and hard bread that Doc Pingree left us. Keep some water hot for me."

He mounted the mustang and pulled over to join the sergeant and the marshal. The sergeant fell in behind the other two, his face still inexpressive of any emotion.

To Ben, the late spring afternoon seemed even longer than the one he had spent as a prisoner in the woods near Pea Ridge waiting for Captain Lightfoot to come and free him and Johnny or else lock them in a dungeon. This time he feared that Johnny might already be a prisoner in a dungeon.

Queen Elizabeth Jones went for a stroll in the border of the adjoining woods. After a while she called to Ben and he went to join her. She was carrying a bouquet of violets. She wanted him to see a mother raccoon and led him quietly down a ravine where they silently watched the animal teaching her three cubs to climb and descend a tree.

Suddenly the girl turned away. "Will they let Johnny go?" she asked. At the sound of her voice the four raccoons quickly vanished into the brush.

"He said he'd be back before sundown," Ben replied. He noticed that her fingers had squeezed the bouquet of violets into a purple ball.

At sundown they built a fire and prepared food, but only Hadjee ate very much. The Egyptian seemed to be confused about what lay in the future, but he showed no concern over Johnny's absence.

Until late into the night they kept a fire going, and then finally the demand for sleep forced them to abandon hopes that Johnny would come back before daylight. Queen Elizabeth Jones wanted to sleep close to the fire but not too close to Ben and his blanket. Ben slept fitfully. One time he was awakened by short, repressed sobs. She had moved close enough to reach one of his hands. When he felt her slender finger on his wrist, he wanted to draw away from her, back into the privacy of sleep, but he pretended to be in deep slumber. He felt sorry for her.

The sun shining on his closed eyelids brought him quickly awake. Queen Elizabeth Jones had revived the fire and was slicing thick cuts of meat into a pan. Close by her side, Hadjee knelt on straw that he had spread there, and he was watching every move she made with intense concentration.

Breakfast went very slowly; it was as if they believed that by delaying their morning routines they might somehow speed Johnny's return. As the pink dawn turned to yellow sunrise, Ben reached the conclusion that Johnny was in serious trouble. He was certain that he would have sent a message of some sort had he not been prevented from doing so.

"I'm going into town to look for Johnny," he finally declared.

"I'll go with you," Queen Elizabeth Jones said at once.

"No. You stay here. You know what happened to Hadjee the last time we left him alone here."

She glared at him. "You'd leave me here to fight off Billy Goodheart if he comes back? I don't have a gun to defend myself."

"Billy won't come back here. If it'll make you feel safer, saddle Champ and keep him nearby. If you get scared, jump on him and ride fast for the jailhouse."

"Where's the jailhouse?"

"Next to the courthouse, dolthead. Where the band played last night."

She stuck out her tongue. "You think I'm a scary girl, don't you, Ben. Well, I'm ascared of only one thing and that's Billy. If you knowed what he'd done to me, you'd be scared of him too."

"Could be." Ben glanced at the donkey, standing beside the cart, its eyes closed apparently in sleep. "I'd ride that jackass, except I can walk faster'n he can run."

She spoke quietly, "You can take Champ."

"No. You might need him." He turned abruptly and started walking at a fast pace on the sandy road. He wanted to look back at Queen Elizabeth Jones and offer her some reassuring sign, but he could not bring himself to do so.

When Ben stepped from the street into the jail's office, he saw Johnny pacing back and forth, restless as a caged animal, in the single barred cell. The cell was only about a dozen yards from Marshal Baines's desk, so that the marshal, seated in his chair, could look along an angle at his prisoner.

Johnny called Ben's name as soon as he saw the boy, but his voice seemed strained, as if all the jauntiness had been wrung out of him.

Baines gave Ben permission to talk with Johnny, that is, after the marshal searched the boy to make certain he was carrying no weapons that might be passed through the bars. As soon as Ben reached the cell door, Johnny put his hand through the bars to touch his arm. "I'm pleased as a possum to see you," Johnny said and then lowered his voice. "That damned marshal wouldn't even send a messenger to tell you and Hadjee where I am. Is Princess all right?"

Ben nodded.

"How'd you know I was locked up?"

"We didn't hear a peep from you last night, so I knew you had to be here or in an army stockade."

Johnny smiled for the first time. "I was counting on you, boy." He paused a moment. "It was Billy Goodheart turned me in. Told the marshal about my branded mustang. Look, I'm having a hell of a time getting much help from the army. That freckle-faced quartermaster's lieutenant who jumps around like a red-headed woodpecker—well, until near dark yesterday he resisted sending a telegraph to St. Louis for Captain Lightfoot, who can get me out of here. I had to pay for the telegraph even though it's army business. This morning he tells me Lightfoot is on duty down the Mississippi River and can't be reached by telegraph. So I've got to wait, locked up here."

"We'll stay out there at campground till they turn you loose. Dr. Pingree left us things to eat."

Johnny whispered, "Come up closer." When Ben did so, Johnny continued very softly, "Listen, they may hold me here for several days. I want you and Hadjee to start the camels to St. Louis. That red-headed woodpecker quartermaster's lieutenant is talking about seizing the camels. If he does that, we're sunk. We won't get a continental dime from Lightfoot." Johnny stopped and peered around Ben's head at Marshal Baines. The marshal was testing the loading lever of a Sharp's percussion carbine and seemed totally absorbed in his work. Johnny continued whispering. "In a minute, Ben, turn around and look at the marshal's desk. On the far side is a drawer. Has a lock on it. You can't see it from where you're standing, but it's there. In that drawer is my leather sheath with the greenbacks Lightfoot left for us. Patsy Halfacre's Walker Colt is also in there. You'll need them to start for St. Louis."

Ben's face revealed his bewilderment. "You're not stringing me, are you?"

"No. You must get them."

"How?"

"I'm going to tell you how. You'll need help from Princess. When she gets to palavering she can talk the feathers off a chicken. She's our card up the sleeve. You go back to camp and tell her to come for a visit. Right away. Now, go thank Mr. Baines for letting you talk with me and get on back to camp."

Ben wasted no time returning to the campground; in fact as soon as he was off the main street he alternated jogging and running. When Queen Elizabeth Jones saw him coming in at a run, she feared that something dreadful had happened until Ben recovered his breath and told her to mount her horse and ride to jail. "Johnny needs you," he added.

She was gone for about an hour. Ben walked out on the sandy road to meet her, eager to know what Johnny had told her. He had trouble reading her face. A few freckles stood out against her crimsoned cheeks. He wondered if she were angry, puzzled, or frightened.

"What did Johnny tell you?"

She dismounted and held the bridle as she walked beside him. "He asked me to do something I don't want to do."

"What?"

"Be a squalling girl."

"Well, he wants me to get the greenbacks and the Colt," Ben said. "Out of the marshal's desk."

A trace of a smile crossed her lips. "Johnny told me we have to start to St. Louis with the camels, and we'll need the money and the pistol. He thinks I can help you get them. I reckon it won't be stealing. They belong to Johnny." She sighed. "But I don't want to be a squalling girl."

They stopped at the cart. Hadjee rose up from where he had been lying with his head against Tooley's rump. "We go?" he asked. "East?"

She shook her head. "I don't know, Hadjee."

The Egyptian spread his hands. His puzzled face indicated that he had not understood her.

"Well, what are we going to do?" Ben asked.

She put her head against his shoulder. "Ben, Ben, I reckon I'll have to be a squalling girl," she said ruefully. She then related the remainder of Johnny's instructions.

Dr. Pingree had told Johnny that the road to St. Louis could be reached by taking a shortcut that led out of the campground and away from the town. And so Johnny's instructions to Queen Elizabeth Jones were to break camp, start out on the side trail, make a halt in the woods, and there leave Hadjee with the cart and animals. Then Ben and Queen Elizabeth Jones were to ride back on Champ to the jail.

A few minutes later they moved out of the campground. Hadjee and the camels were in front, followed by Ben and the slow-moving donkey and cart, and lastly Queen Elizabeth Jones on the gray horse. The trail ran through a thick virgin forest for a mile or so to where it joined a wider highway. This main road followed a railway track and a telegraph line.

At the first open glade, Ben called to Hadjee, motioning for him to take the camels off the road. After he was satisfied that the animals and the cart were invisible from the road, Ben mounted Champ behind Queen Elizabeth Jones and told her to lope the horse back toward the jailhouse.

When they rode into the courthouse square, the time was near noon. The streets of Rolla were filling with soldiers and workmen. At a hitching rack beside the courthouse, they dismounted.

"Johnny told me to wait for about five minutes after you go in the jail," she said. "How long is five minutes?"

"If you count out loud real slow to sixty," he said, "that's a minute. At least it is in Texas. Five times sixty is three hundred. Can you count to three hundred?"

She gave him a murderous look. "When I was at Marshfield school I was good at sums. I'll bet I can count higher than you can."

Ben shrugged and turned toward the jail. As he was nearing the entrance, the door opened and Marshal Baines stood there in his fine street costume that denoted authority. "Why're you back again, boy? Once a day is enough times for visiting. I'm going home to eat."

Johnny's voice sounded from inside. "Give us just a minute, Marshal. I've got to tell my sprigs how to take care of themselves while I'm locked up in here."

The marshal frowned. "Hurry it up." He sidestepped over to his desk and sat down with a loud sigh. "This damned line of work is more trouble'n I figured. It's past noon dinnertime and I ain't et yet."

Ben went over to the cell door where Johnny was anxiously waiting. "Is Princess outside?" he whispered.

"She'll be here in five minutes. If she can count that far. Are you sure she can do this, Johnny?"

"When she gets chattering she can talk the leaves off a tree. And make a lawman cry. What'd she tell you?"

"Said she was going to be a squalling girl."

Johnny laughed, then added seriously, "When you get started to St. Louis, keep going. Don't wait for me. If I don't catch up with you before you get to St. Louis, go to Camp Jackson on Grand Avenue. I found out from the red-headed woodpecker that's where Captain Lightfoot is when he's not out chasing Rebel guerrillas along the Mississippi River. Remember that now: Camp Jackson on Grand Avenue. When you get to St. Louis I'll find you there."

A slow creaking of the entrance door was followed by a loud feminine wail, and then Queen Elizabeth Jones flung herself toward the marshal's desk. When Ben turned to watch her, he was startled to see that she was not wearing the familiar militia cap but had fluffed out her yellow hair so that she looked female.

"Please let my papa go free," she cried. "I'm a motherless child and need him bad." This was followed by a louder wail than the first.

"Good God almighty," the marshal shouted in astonishment. "I thought this morning you was another boy, like that one." He pointed to Ben. "But you're a gal, sure enough." He stood up and reached as if he meant to comfort her with a pat on the shoulder, but she drew away out of his reach, moving toward the cell door. She began sniffling loudly, and Ben was sure he saw real tears on her cheeks. He stepped away as though the scene was too much for him to bear.

"Oh, my dear papa," she cried and followed her words with another keening squall, seizing the cell bars with both hands.

Marshal Baines approached her, waving his arms helplessly. "I wish I could do something—" He turned to face Johnny. "Mr. Hawkes, I didn't know you was old enough to have a boy—a girl, I mean, old as this one. And that other boy."

"We marry young in Texas," Johnny said.

Ben meanwhile had crossed to the desk. He glanced quickly at the marshal's back. The desk drawer opened easily. He took out the pistol and money sheath and thrust them into the big pocket of his tunic, closed the drawer, and walked slowly to the jail's entrance door. The marshal was still trying to quiet the sobbing Queen Elizabeth Jones.

Activities on the street outside were slowing, with only a few horsemen and a single covered wagon moving in front of the courthouse. Ben walked to the hitching rack, loosened the tie rope, and rose leisurely into the saddle.

After a minute or so, Queen Elizabeth Jones came out of the jail, dabbing at her eyes with a blue bandanna that the marshal had given her. When she reached the horse, she opened the saddlebag, took out her militia cap, and pushed her golden hair up into it as she pulled the bill down tight over her forehead.

Seizing Ben's offered arm, she sprang up behind him, and they rode away from the courthouse square without exchanging a word.

XXI

BEN BUTTERFIELD

❧

Brigadier General Boggs came in the hardware store this morning, fairly early for him I think. I can hear his mellifluous voice, with the sort of forged British accent he uses when trying to impress Hilda Fagerhalt, who is easily impressed by any sort of male physical embellishment that she considers genteel.

Almost every living soul on earth is an actor of sorts—pretending, gilding, flaunting—regardless of whether he ever set foot on a real stage. Preston Boggs is so accomplished at the art that he would probably be accepted by professional stage players as one of their own. I've heard that Boggs was once a member of a local amateur thespian group, but he left under some kind of dark cloud that no one has ever specifically identified for me.

Letitia Higgins is an actor, too, not as accomplished as General Boggs but quite convincing in her role as a benevolent laundress who washes, starches, and irons the soiled clothing only of carefully selected families, doing this solely out of the goodness of her heart she pretends. In her role as loving and faithful wife of Yancey Higgins she is even less believable, especially in the eyes of friends and acquaintances who know her caitiff husband. She does not have to playact at all however, in her effortless presentation of sensuality.

Before General Boggs's arrival this morning, I saw from my window the lovely Miss Betty Hesterly, skipping along, her steps shortened by a long, tight summer skirt of light blue linen. Miss Hesterly had just come from her night's duty as the telephone central operator in a room above the telephone company offices, and she looked fresh as morning dew. In her lacy shirtwaist and wide-brimmed straw hat over her dainty curls, she presented herself as a character of virginal innocence, a true ingenue of the stage.

Nevertheless, the wise men and women of the town know that Miss Hesterly is engaged to Theo Drumgoole, the handsome and muscular young engineer for the telephone company who keeps his equipment on the same floor as the exchange room where Miss Hesterly beds at night with a listening device clamped to her curly head. Night owls of the masculine sex have seen Theo leaving the telephone building very late in the evenings, and there are no secrets in this town. Scarcely anyone believes that Miss Hesterly is as virginal as the image she so artfully projects.

All this leads me to memories of Queen Elizabeth Jones, who might have been one of the world's greatest actresses if she'd had the benefit of proper guidance. After all, in the days of our early acquaintance, she cleverly deceived Johnny and Hadjee and me into believing that she was a boy and probably would have fooled Dr. Pingree had she not taken the name of a character in one of the peddler's penny dreadful books. And he was not certain of her sex until the last day or so of her performance, if it can be called a performance. For a day or two she even deceived the artist Bonaparte, and Frenchmen are said to be like bloodhounds in tracking females. Her first public performance was, of course, as Jack Bonnycastle singing that song "Wait for the Wagon" in the Waynesville, Missouri, courthouse square. Under burnt cork blackface her sweet voice brought wild applause. As for her scene in the Rolla jailhouse, I'm sure that no trained actress could have performed any better than she did that day, humbugging Marshal Baines so completely that he almost joined her in tear shedding, and his tears would have been far more genuine than hers.

Queen Elizabeth Jones, however, never had any guidance in the art of acting. She had nothing but a lot of encouragement from a pair of wild riders from Texas, both of whom loved her so deeply their hearts soared and sang and ached, and one finally was broken.

From my window I see a Columbia Electric automobile gliding to a silent stop, with the Sisters Grimsley aboard, wearing white mannish caps, bright yellow scarves, and purple bloomers. They are alighting at this moment and heading for the entrance to the hardware store. From their smiling faces and gay birdlike chatter,

I assume they are on an errand of pleasure-giving rather than to purchase some commonplace household object.

I must arise from this desk and hobble down the hallway to see what the sisters have in mind for Hilda and me, and perhaps for that lost artist of the drama, Brigadier General Preston Boggs.

Two hours later. The Sisters Grimsley and Brigadier General Boggs have just departed in the Columbia Electric, he in the seat that I occupied a few days ago. For a time this morning he teased me mercilessly about Letitia Higgins being seated in my lap while we spun through the paved streets of the town. While he was bantering me, I stole an occasional glance at Hilda to determine whether she might evidence some sign of jealousy, but I think she was too busy building mental defenses against the Grimsleys to give any heed to the absent Letty. In her view the Grimsleys are dangerous because they are bold and rich and unmanned, while Letty is trustworthy because she is shy and poor and married. Why Hilda places any value at all upon me, why she maintains an alert defense against possible raiding rivals, is all beyond my limited purview.

This morning she seemed to be especially wary of Maude Grimsley, possibly because of the immodest way Maude flaunted her bloomer costume, crossing and uncrossing her legs in the low wicker chair in which Hilda had placed her. Because of the thickness of her thighs, Maude's bloomers did not billow as her sister Anne's did but in certain places clung tightly to her flesh, and the elastics that held the bottoms of her bloomers in place had been pushed above her knees so that the overall effect was of a buck deer that had acquired the ability to sit human fashion with haunches displayed to the world.

I suppose it was because Maude spent more time talking with me than with the brigadier that Hilda threw up a defensive screen, even going so far as to toss a few catty remarks in Maude's direction. Yet if Hilda could have read my mind—which thank God she cannot most of the time—she would have learned that if by some unlikely chance I was offered a choice of one of the rich Grimsleys for a mate, I most certainly would choose Annie above the lusty full-bodied Maude. As it is, neither sister can play in the same yard with Letty Higgins.

What the sisters brought us today was an invitation to the

Grimsley House about a fortnight hence. It seems that they have again summoned the St. Louis dancing master to teach them and their friends a new dance called the cakewalk.

At first Hilda was not too keen on attending another evening affair during which the wealthy sisters would dominate every invited male, including me, but when she realized that Brigadier Boggs was accepting, she made no further resistant motions. The brigadier did offer a mild dissent, suggesting that the Virginia reel might be a better choice than the cakewalk, which he said had originated among plantation darkies before the War Between the States. When Annie asked him how the dance got its name, he replied in his best Edward VII voice imitation that customarily the winning couple in a dance set was given a cake for a prize. At this, Maude slapped her haunches and clapped her hands and then declared that she and Annie would provide a cake for the competition if Brigadier Boggs could find them a historically authentic recipe for a cake that was popular during plantation days.

Selah.

XXII

A Dead Man and a Kindly Lady

~

Somewhere between Rolla and Cuba City the narrow highway they were following turned away from the railroad and its accompanying line of telegraph poles. They spent the night under great oaks that groaned and rasped before an unceasing wind until dawn, when Ben was awakened by the creaking of several ox carts carrying blocks of limestone along the road.

Before noon they were in Cuba City. The town's largest building was a general store constructed of gray limestone, and there they stopped to spend one of the greenbacks for a bag of flour, a slab of bacon, and some barley and beans for Tooley and Omar. Hadjee and the camels attracted considerable attention from the town's citizens, and for the first time Ben began worrying for fear the Rolla marshal might have sent descriptions of them to towns in all directions. He guessed that if Johnny had been in charge he would have been more careful, probably would have bypassed the town. He missed Johnny. And he could see that Queen Elizabeth Jones missed him too and was doubtful of Ben's ability to keep them out of trouble.

As soon as they could pack their purchases into the donkey cart, Ben started the little expedition out of the town. The morning was filled with birdsong and the scent of wildflowers, and the sun-drenched air was so somnolent that neither humans nor beasts were inclined to move with any purpose. When they approached the edge of a natural meadow, a large flock of quail rose heavily from the grass, their wings beating like distant arms fire, the sound reminding Ben of riflemen he had seen firing at a great distance when he was in the woods near Pea Ridge.

At the meadow's farther rim the road made a sharp turn to the right and ran along the base of a slope. A hundred yards up the rise was a large log house around which were gathered several wagons, buggies, and saddled horses. Queen Elizabeth Jones on Champ was a few yards ahead of Ben, who was atop the donkey cart. Hadjee and the camels were close behind the slow-moving carreta. Moonraking and half drowsing, Ben was idly pondering the reasons for so large a collection of vehicles and riding horses around the farmhouse when he was brought wide awake by the firing of a pistol from a thicket to his left.

The first shot was quickly followed by another, and then a third, the last bullet whistling so close that Ben wondered if he was meant to be the target. On the road in front of him, Queen Elizabeth Jones turned Champ about almost instantly, kicking the horse into a lunge toward the donkey cart. As she came alongside she screamed at Ben to jump behind her saddle.

At that moment a black horse, with Billy Goodheart mounted, sprang from the thicket. One of Billy's hands was clutching his bridle, the other waving a pistol. "The death hug's acoming!" he yelled in his mountaineer's accent, his tones high and almost hysterical. He fired blindly at Ben and Queen Elizabeth Jones on Champ until the girl turned the horse across the road and galloped him toward a low rail fence. When the gray horse cleared the fence, Ben was almost unseated. To regain his balance, he squeezed the girl's waist tightly and almost pulled her from the saddle.

"Watch yourself!" she growled.

"Where're you going?" he demanded.

"Up on that hill. Lots of people up there."

He took a quick look behind them. The donkey and cart were motionless in the road. With a stick, Hadjee was hurrying the camels along the rail fence, searching for an entry. Billy Goodheart was trying to force his black horse to leap the fence, but the terrified animal would not make the attempt. Blood streaks from Billy's spurs were visible on its flanks. Billy kept clicking the trigger of his empty revolver and cursing hoarsely.

"He's drunker'n a skunk," Queen Elizabeth Jones said, as she let her horse slow its pace. "Otherwise he would've hit one of us."

"Are we going to leave Hadjee and the camels to Billy's mercies?" Ben asked.

"You can go back and help," she replied flatly and then turned so that her flushed face was only inches from his. "Billy don't want Hadjee. He wants me."

Moments later they were in an unfenced and grassless yard, in the midst of vehicles and horses. They both dismounted. An uncommon quietness surrounded them.

The wide porch was cluttered with old chairs, benches, a pile of loose firewood, and four dogs, all apparently peaceable. If there were vicious dogs among them, they may have been subdued by the presence of so many strangers. One of the dogs, a mustard-colored, mixed-blood hound, raised up and approached them, sniffing at each of their dubiously offered hands. The hound's eyes were moist, as though about to fill with tears. With an air of disappointment it turned away and lay back down on the unpainted flooring.

The front door was wide open. A stack of rifles, with a few pistols arranged on a small table beside them, stood just outside the door. From within the semidarkness a man materialized. He stepped in front of the weapons as though to guard them.

"Who are you?" he asked.

A moment later a middle-aged woman in a black bombazine dress and a straw hat dyed dark blue appeared beside the man. She smiled at them.

"Oh, you must be the boys from Springfield," she said in a soft sweet voice. "We been waiting the services for you."

Ben glanced at Queen Elizabeth Jones, puzzling for a few seconds, and then replied; "Yes, ma'am. We come from Springfield."

The woman made a motion as though inviting them inside, but the man stepped in front of them. "Hold up," he ordered. "Are you boys carrying arms?" Ben suddenly remembered the Walker Colt that was stowed in the inner pocket of his tunic. "Yes, sir. Why'd you want it?" The man grinned, showing a flash of yellow teeth. "To keep the peace, boy. Old Pursglove had Union friends and Secesh friends. They're all packed together inside this house."

After Ben surrendered the pistol, the woman said with a reassuring smile, "Well, come on in the parlor now." She went on talking. "Brother Pursglove, your great uncle, he writ you too late,

I fear. He died yestiddy, but he swore to me, on his deathbed, as how the last of his kin would be here for his funeral."

"Yes, ma'am," Ben said.

"I'm Lydia Bright. I kep' house for Brother Pursglove the last year of his life." She turned toward the others in the room, dozens of men, women, and a few children. "These here boys just come in are Brother Pursglove's nephews," she announced. "His last of kin. Now, tell us your names, boys."

"I'm Ben," Ben replied, "and this is, ah—"

"I'm Jack," Queen Elizabeth Jones said hurriedly.

Lydia Bright smiled prettily and continued in her soft sweet voice. "Now, Ben and Jack, you both come over here and take a last farewell peek at your kindly old great-uncle."

In a rectangular pine box resting upon the arms of facing hand-hewn hickory chairs, Brother Pursglove lay in state. His long gray hair was arranged neatly over each shoulder. To Ben the old man's face looked as yellow waxen as Miz Sergeant Peddicord's face had at her funeral at Fort Davis in Texas.

Arrival of the two supposed Pursglove kin evidently spurred the funeral arrangers to accelerate their schedule. A very fat man, dressed like a gambler Ben remembered seeing in San Antonio, moved behind the bier and read a few words haltingly from a Bible he held in his hands. Then two men in faded brown jeans came forward with hammers and nails. Placing two pine boards over the open coffin, they nailed them down so noisily that a baby, and then a young child, began crying in bursts of sobs. In a moment one of the dogs on the porch joined in with a howl that was plaintive and prolonged.

Shushing sounds in the room were followed by a loud whisper from Lydia Bright. "That's Bednego wailing, Brother Pursglove's coon hound. He knows. Dogs always knows." She moved closer to Ben and Queen Elizabeth Jones, encircling them with her plump and loving arms. "Brother Pursglove said he had not seen you boys or your dead papa since you was tykes, so you wouldn't know what a sweet old man he was. He'd want you to spend the night here before starting home to Springfield. Neighbor folks will bring us lots of victuals."

Four young men were lifting the coffin, turning it toward the front door. Someone shouted from the porch, "Hellfire and god-damn! They's a circus out here on the property, Miss Lydia."

Everyone in the room hurried toward the door at the same moment, sweeping Lydia Bright and her two charges against the coffin bearers and almost upsetting the pine box from their shoulders. Ben pushed his way onto the porch and declared in a loud voice, "That's Mr. Hadjee with two camels in his care, and our donkey cart." The crowd turned silent, attention upon Ben, respecting him because of his supposed bereavement, but then returned to Hadjee and the camels who were waiting beneath a spreading oak a hundred yards down the slope. Off to one side were the carreta and donkey. There was no sign of Billy Goodheart anywhere.

"Me and my brother," Ben continued, "we helped the poor man drive his camels along the way from Springfield. He's Egyptian and don't speak many of our words."

"Where's he going with them beasts?" a large-breasted woman demanded.

"To St. Louis," Ben replied.

"Devil's town," another woman said.

"T'aint," a young man retorted. "It's safe in Union hands."

"Devil's town," the woman repeated.

"Stop that talk," Lydia Bright ordered. "It was agreed there'd be no crimination between Blue and Gray till after Brother Purs-glove is laid to rest."

A murmuring of assents followed, and then many of the younger mourners went venturing down the slope to inspect the camels at close hand. Ben joined them and as best he could tried to make Hadjee understand that he was to stay where he was until matters calmed down.

After the diverted mourners returned to the house, those who owned weapons collected them and began preparing to leave for the burial. Lydia Bright insisted that the "nephews" ride in a surrey with her and Reverend Potts—the corpulent man in the gambler's black costume—out to the Bourbon community's burying ground. They rode on the backseat all the way in silence. A grave had already been dug, and after Reverend Potts read a few more words from his Bible, Lydia Bright nudged Ben and Queen Elizabeth Jones and motioned for them to return with her to the surrey.

"You boys will stay the night before starting home to Springfield, I'm sure," she said in her sweet voice, "and partake of supper with me and Reverend Potts."

"Yes, ma'am," Ben said, slyly winking at Queen Elizabeth Jones. "Me and Jack are powerful weary and hungry from our long journey."

During the waning of the afternoon, Lydia Bright kept up a constant chatter, occasionally displaying various objects that had belonged to Brother Pursglove—a bronze medal bearing the likeness of President Martin Van Buren, a faded red pennant with the number 3 stitched upon it, a daguerreotype of a round-faced young girl, and several Mexican coins of various denominations.

"He left very little," Lydia Bright complained amiably. "When Reverend Potts comes for supper, he will read us your great-uncle's will. The reverend took it down on paper one day last week."

Partly to escape Lydia Bright's incessant prattle and partly to keep Hadjee at ease, Ben excused himself at midafternoon and walked down the slope to join the Egyptian. Queen Elizabeth Jones accompanied him.

"You are living a lie, Ben Butterfield," she said as soon as they were out of earshot of the house, "pretending to be a nephew of that old dead man."

"It's only a taradiddle, a little lie," Ben answered. "After all, you told everybody in that house your name was Jack, still pretending to be a boy. Johnny Hawkes says a taradiddle won't hurt nobody. Besides, we was in a mighty bad scrape this morning, with Billy Goodheart's bullets buzzing by us like bees. Where you reckon Billy is now?"

"Out in the woods somewheres, sleeping off his big drunk. I wish we could get on the road right now and travel as far as we can before dark. Lose him if we can."

"We'll be safer here tonight," Ben said. As they neared the big oak, he noticed that the sailcloth cover on the cart had been opened and partly thrown back.

With hand signs and a few simple words he asked Hadjee if he had opened the cart cover. As soon as the Egyptian understood, he shook his head. "No, no. Bad boy. One who shoot, shoot, shoot. He do."

"Billy Goodheart went into the cart? Godamighty! I stowed the greenbacks in there. Under the oats sack."

Queen Elizabeth Jones sucked in her breath, and then they both ran for the cart. The contents had been tumbled about as though stirred by a giant spoon. Nowhere could they find any trace of the money sheath or its contents.

Ben sat down with his back against the trunk of the oak and held his head in his hands. "What a fool I am. Johnny Hawkes never would've left that money off his person. Now I've really done it."

She came and sat down beside him and gently patted his shoulder. "We'll make out. Don't go blaming yourself, Ben. You thought the money was safer there. You had no way of knowing—"

"Hellfire! Johnny always been telling me to expect the unexpected and be prepared for it. He'd laugh at me now. What the hell we going to do?"

"Grow up and take care of ourselves." She squeezed his arm.

Two buggies had entered the gate and were winding their way up the hill toward the house.

"That must be the neighbors bringing the victuals Miz Bright told us about," she said. "I'm plenty hungry. Let's go, Ben."

"I've lost my appetite," he said.

"Oh, hush your mouth. One thing's in our favor. With all them greenbacks in his pocket, Billy Goodheart won't be bothering us for a while."

They both stuffed themselves on the slabs of roast beef, slices of ham, cornbread, and cakes and pies that were brought in for the condolence feast. With Lydia Bright's permission, Ben took a full plate down the hill to Hadjee, who had firmly refused to leave his camels and come up to the house.

The neighbors who brought the food stayed for a while, swapping stories about the departed Brother Pursglove, and then at dusk they bade commiserating farewells to the satiated but weeping Lydia Bright. Only the Reverend Potts remained, he continuing to eat with the undiminished enthusiasm of a hog, sopping gravy from his plate with large hunks of bread, taking immense bites from wedges of pie, and washing everything down with gulps of clabber from a tall mug.

At the first signs of darkness, Lydia Bright lit two oil lamps and placed them on a table in the parlor and then suggested that they all gather in there for the business of the evening—reading of Brother Pursglove's will.

Patting his enormous belly and emitting a series of satisfying belches, Reverend Potts left the dining room with apparent reluctance and led the way into the parlor. He sat facing his three listeners for a silent minute, his porcine eyes fixed alternately upon Ben and Queen Elizabeth Jones. Then without preliminary explanation he took a folded sheet of ruled foolscap from an inner pocket and began reading in his halting manner. After several obfuscating phrases, a series of *whereases, to wits,* and *to whom it may concerns,* along with several unrelated Latin words, the will and testament proceeded to list the worldly possessions of Brother Pursglove. The house, its contents, and the surrounding acreage was the "sum total" of the deceased man's fortune. Reverend Potts started reading from a list of clothing, furniture, utensils, harness, and trinkets, but Lydia Bright stopped him with a sharp command to cease.

"Ain't no use in going over all that again, Reverend Potts," she said. "Whyn't you just read what was left after his main worldly goods was bequested?"

Reverend Potts rubbed his tongue along his heavy lips, making little smacking sounds as though anticipating the delectability of leftovers in the kitchen. "I have no objection, Miss Lydia. First I should state for the benefit of Brother Pursglove's next of kin that all his worldly goods, with exceptions to be noted, are left to Miss Lydia Bright in compensation for the sacrifice of her later years while serving as his beloved housekeeper. And then it goes on to say, and I read: 'To my brother Orion's living descendants I leave one Mexican silver dollar each, and also to the same I leave my faithful coon hound Abednego, the reason being that Miss Lydia and the aforementioned dog never did get along with each other, and I would not wish to leave the two of them together without my presence to reconcile differences between them.' "

At that point Reverend Potts raised his head and blinked at Ben and Queen Elizabeth Jones. "This last will and testament," he said quietly, "was signed by Brother Pursglove and witnessed by me. Any objections by anybody to the provisos contained herein?"

Neither Ben nor Queen Elizabeth Jones knew what to say, so neither said anything.

"Silence means consent," Reverend Potts declared. "In that case the will and testament stands as it was written."

From a small filigreed box that Lydia Bright had brought with her from the dining room, she removed two Mexican silver dollars, and with successive exaggerated flourishes of her arms handed them separately to the two beneficiaries. "Now as for Bednigo," she said in her sweetest voice, "he belongs to both of you, and I expect you to take him with you when you leave tomorrow."

Again, neither Ben nor Queen Elizabeth Jones knew what to say to this, so they said nothing.

Bedtime was soon at hand. Taking one of the lamps, Lydia Bright led them through the dining room and kitchen to a small pantry that was empty of all furnishings except for a feather bed on the floor. "You boys will have to pallet down here," she said. "Reverend Potts is occupyin Brother Pursglove's room. The outside convenience is right out the back door. Wash pans are in the kitchen, with a pitcher of water if you want to clean up." When she bade them good-night she took the lamp with her, leaving them in darkness.

While Queen Elizabeth Jones went into the kitchen to wash, Ben removed his tunic and boots and stretched out on the feather bed. It was soft but thin, and he could feel his body sinking through the feathers to the floor. He was sleep weary but could not keep from thinking about the loss of Captain Lightfoot's greenbacks. All the funds that he and Queen Elizabeth Jones now possessed were the two Mexican silver dollars—money that did not truly belong to them—and a few odd coins of small value in their pockets. He was wondering how much farther it was to St. Louis and how they were going to feed the camels and themselves when Queen Elizabeth Jones slipped soundlessly into the pantry and sat on the end of the feather bed. He felt her hand touch his knee. "Are you sleeping with your pantaloons on, Ben?"

"Yes."

"I'll do the same, then. You keep on your side now."

He grunted, listening to the rustling of her jacket and waistcoat as she folded them carefully. "We both need better clothes," Ben thought. "Her old jeans are wearing to threads at seat and knees.

She sighed as she lay back to sink into the feathers. "What a day," she said.

The silence of the house was broken by a series of distant giggles and then little shouts of pleasure from Lydia Bright.

"Wonder what tickles her?" Ben said.

After a minute the giggling, partially suppressed this time, resumed and then ceased.

"Well, I wonder what she'd think if she knowed I was a female," Queen Elizabeth Jones said, with just a hint of a snicker, "and sleeping with you."

Ben made no reply. He began thinking about what Johnny Hawkes had said one morning on the bank of the Gasconade River after they discovered that Jack Bonnycastle was a girl named Queen Elizabeth Jones. Johnny had ordered him not to sleep with her anymore because they might make a baby, although he was only fifteen. Ben had seen stallions and bulls presumably doing that with mares and heifers, but he was not too certain how human beings went about it. He was almost sure that Queen Elizabeth Jones knew.

As he drifted into sleep he could smell perfumed soap mingled with the natural fragrance of her hair, and after a while he heard the faint sounds of bubbling from her lips and knew she was falling asleep.

Before morning the late spring night turned chill, but there was no blanket or other covering for the feather bed. When Ben awakened shivering in gray daylight, the first thing he was aware of was a screen of yellow hair over his eyes. For a long moment he struggled to move.

"What are you trying to do to me?" she cried indignantly.

As they disentangled themselves from each other's arms and legs, Ben remembered another remark Johnny Hawkes had made at the Gasconade: "When I waked you the other morning I found you two curled up like a pair of breeding catamounts."

XXIII

BEN BUTTERFIELD

~

Among the photographs in my shoe box is one of Old Man Fagerhalt with daughter, Hilda. It was made in a local studio: Jacob Parnell, Fine Photographic Portraits. Still in business, but poor old Jacob has the shakes so bad that few people have their portraits made by him these days. Some sort of ailment connected with his profession, so they say.

Anyway, this photograph was made at least a dozen years before my sudden entrance into the family household. Old Man Fagerhalt looks much younger than I ever saw him in the flesh, but his face is frozen into a Nordic solidity, and during the few years that we tolerated each other I never saw him smile. Not one time.

On the other hand, Hilda in the photograph has an expression indicating that she would like to smile if only she dared to do so in the presence of her stern father. She was possessed then of a youthful beauty that still lurks in her features beneath a determined manifestation of will to manage the hardware store as efficiently as Old Man Fagerhalt ever did.

I find it pleasurable to sit here and study Hilda's face and form of twenty years past. Two thick braids of flax-colored hair lie loosely over each shoulder, giving her a schoolgirlish openness. She is wearing what appears to be a polka dot print dress. Set back on her square Swedish head is a fashionable sunbonnet, probably pink, as she prefers that color. Her strong, capable hands are clasped over what is not a lady's handbag but instead is a bundle fashioned from a bandanna kerchief. Her large mouth, as I said, appears to be on the verge of breaking into a good-natured smile that was always there during the first days I was laid up in a bed in this very room. What is missing most from the black-and-white photograph is the color of her eyes—blue, sharp, and clear as the pigment of a robin's egg.

I do not know how the circus manager found the Fagerhalts, and Hilda says she does not remember either. After my smashup in that closing bit of action with Queen Elizabeth Jones, where I always jumped my horse from a platform over the stagecoach, Dr. Socrates Drumm pronounced my leg bones so shattered that I could not travel farther with the circus for many weeks. Healing would require considerable bed rest, he said, and several weeks of convalescing with the aid of a nurse. Socrates Drumm may have found a doctor in town who knew the Fagerhalts, although he did not find old Dr. Henry Mortmain, the physician in regular attendance upon the Fagerhalts. On that evening, according to Hilda, Mortmain was sleeping off one of his periodic drunks in a back room of the town's billiards parlor.

Whoever the connecting link was, the circus's offer of liberal remuneration for my care undoubtedly attracted Old Man Fagerhalt's craving for stash as well as provided a chance for him to put his daughter to work earning her keep.

Hilda was, and is, a most capable nurse and attendant. The first two or three days were a blur to me because grubby old Dr. Mortmain kept me floating in the firmament with continual strong doses of laudanum, which is a mixture of alcohol and opium. Doc Mortmain, I discovered, was opposed to my being cared for by so young a woman as Hilda. He believed her to be virginal, which she was, and totally innocent, which she was not. And I, being from a circus, was considered to be a mountebank interested mainly in fornication and the seduction of chaste womanhood.

Hilda, being an only child and female, had a natural curiosity about the mechanism of the male body, and having me at her absolute mercy for several days, she was free to observe and touch and fondle to her heart's content. After we were wed, she confessed that during this period she visited the public library to examine drawings of the human anatomy, but because the pictures were vague in some details she would wait until I fell sound asleep and then would lift the bed covers and use me as a model to complete her knowledge of male appendages. She told me this on our wedding night in the Hotel Arlington in Hot Springs, she giggling as she talked and I expressing mock horror at her past lasciviousness.

The incident that brought us to hasty matrimony, even before my leg was fully healed, occurred late one afternoon. Old Doc Mortmain had been treating my fever with horse pills, and they converted the fever into severe chills that made me shake all over. Hilda tried to stop my chattering teeth with warm towels and then piled blankets over me. When these ministrations failed she simply crawled into the bed beside me and tried to warm me with her body. Considering my splinted leg and bandages, and my trembling chills, there was not much I could do to her, although she treated me most tenderly with her closeness. Exactly what position we were in, I cannot say, but Old Man Fagerhalt chose that moment to enter this room. Perhaps the long quietness made him suspect something, I do not know, but after exhaling loudly he ordered Hilda to her quarters and before he left the room he called me a dozen vile names in Swedish and English.

I did not see Hilda again for two or three days. During that time, Doc Mortmain brought an old lady along with him to attend to me, and then one morning Hilda came in alone, her robin's egg eyes very bright and her flaxen hair combed tight to her head, her braids swinging like the tassels on a circus horse.

With a note of justification in her voice, she greeted me and held a folded newspaper page in front of my face. In the very first paragraph of a column of local social notes was an announcement that bore my name linked with Hilda's. We were formally engaged, a wedding date to be announced later. She explained that Old Man Fagerhalt had ordered her to so inform the newspaper.

My face must have turned even paler than it had become after all those days of drugs and fevers because an expression of concern filled her blue eyes. She babbled something about not binding me to that public announcement, that it was entirely her father's doing. I could do as I pleased, she declared, go back to the circus without her when I recovered, if I liked.

I don't recall exactly what my response was to her at that moment. I was partially in a drug delirium and probably did not say a word, but I'm reasonably certain that I reached out to grasp her hand, and I remember her bending over me to kiss my forehead. These two simple actions sealed our fates. Luckily for me, Hilda *taught me everything worthwhile that I know, especially about words and how to use them. She made me read through her little school dictionary until I knew the meanings of every word in it.*

Last evening we attended the Cakewalk Soiree at the Grimsley House. It began wonderfully well, with a schottische, a polka, and a waltz, and then the dancing master from St. Louis came forth to arrange the couples for a cakewalk. I could tell right off from his descriptions and examples of movements that this was not going to be a dance for old cripple-legged Ben. But I was game to try, mainly because Letitia Higgins was my partner. When she and Yancey arrived, he was already full to the gills, and the efficient Sisters Grimsley quickly steered him into the sunroom where Maude laid him out on a settee and gently stroked his neck until he fell fast asleep.

After three dances with me, Hilda begged for an intermission and literally pushed Letitia into my arms for the first cakewalk. Lordy, does Hilda not know what temptations she lays in my path? Last evening Letty was wearing a new white homemade dress with a decolletage lower than I've ever seen on her. Her rounded pink shoulders were seductive enough, but the tops of her swelling breasts, looking as if they might emerge full grown from fluffy beds of lace, were almost more than I could bear.

The cakewalk, as taught by the St. Louis dancing master, begins with a promenade that is easy enough, with gents on the inside, but then as the music grows livelier both partners begin stepping higher and higher, at the same time maintaining elegance and grace on the turns. Acting as judge, the dancing master eliminated the couples one by one, until at last only one couple remained at the end of a set.

Because of my bad leg I could not step high or turn with the required precision. Although Letty Higgins was doing very well, we were quickly eliminated from the first set. I begged her to find another partner, suggesting Hereward Padgett or Jack Bilbrew who had come as singles by invitation because of an excessive number of single females also invited by the Sisters Grimsley. Letty would not hear of dancing with either one of them, and after a brief sortie into the sunroom to see if Yancey was still sleeping, she took a chair between Hilda and me. Hereward Padgett, she whispered, might be a certified idiot, but she was certain that he remembered every word she had ever spoken in his hearing, and she feared he might embarrass her with an unwanted recollection at some future date. As for Jack Bilbrew, every woman in town knew that he fancied himself to be a lady killer and she did not want any talk arising that linked him with her.

So we sat there and enjoyed the cakewalk music that is called ragtime. This music is new, certainly, although each piece usually starts out like a circus march but then builds harmoniously into varying melodies. A banjoist came down from St. Louis to help in the rehearsals and performances of our little orchestra. To close the evening, Miss Ivy Crowninshield, the pianist, presented a solo of a new piece called "Maple Leaf Rag." Miss Crowninshield studied classical music in the East, and when some of us went up to praise her performance, she said that ragtime is much more complex than she had believed and that she had spent as much time practicing for the Cakewalk Soiree as she had in preparing for recitals of Chopin or Bach.

To assuage any hurt feelings among those of us who chose to sit out the cakewalk performances, Annie Grimsley brought forth a bottle of bourbon, one of the few remaining of a shipment her father imported from Kentucky before his demise from a liver ailment. I had tasted this brand once before, and although I am only a mild imbiber I know that this liquor is as smooth and smoky as any ever distilled.

My first thought was of poor foolish Yancey Higgins, one of the town's true-blue connoisseurs of whiskey. As I've noted, he loaded himself with so much cheap moonshine corn that he arrived bottle blind and lay unconscious on a settee, missing out on the best bourbon in the world.

The word "bourbon" also brought out of the recesses of recollection a place and a long-ago adventure in Missouri. The association of names in a human being's memory is a remarkable thing indeed. Some names cause joy or sadness to flash across my consciousness. Certain words will also bring back a human face, others will re-create a happening. When I hear or see the word "bourbon" I am transported back to that little crossroads community in Missouri that calls itself by that name. Bourbon at that time had only a schoolhouse, church, livery stable and blacksmith shop, some sort of merchandise store, and a dozen or so houses scattered randomly over the hillsides. Three or four miles from the crossroads was the farmhouse where Queen Elizabeth Jones and I found refuge from that half-crazed idiot, Billy Goodheart. No one ever believes us, even today, when we tell of how we arrived at the timely hour of a funeral so that we were accepted as relatives of the corpse. Not even Johnny Hawkes ever believed us. Truth is stranger than lies, however, and every word of that story is true. We never discovered whether the real relatives arrived later to miss the bequests, because Queen Elizabeth Jones and I had departed with the Mexican silver dollars in our pockets and with the coon hound Abednego trailing behind us. In later years, after I became wiser in the ways of greedy human beings, I suspected that the sweet-talking Miss Lydia Bright and the Reverend Potts had euchred a pair of unsuspecting young supposed heirs of Brother Pursglove out of a farmhouse and farm near the town of Bourbon.

To everyone's surprise, the winners of the cakewalk cake that was baked personally by the Sisters Grimsley, from a Civil War recipe provided by Brigadier Preston Boggs, were Hereward Padgett and a gap-toothed girl who is the daughter of one of the town's leading drygoods merchants but whose name I can't recall at the moment. I think the secret of Hereward's and the gap-toothed girl's success is that they are both quite slim and long-legged, physical attributes that lend themselves to the elaborate turning and high stepping necessary for graceful cakewalk dancing. The fact that Theo Drumgoole and Betty Hesterly won second place corroborates my theory. Theo is lean and muscular from climbing telephone poles, and Miss Hesterly, as I have said before, has the unreal ethereal qualities of a virginal, long-winged butterfly, light as gossamer but no doubt delectable in bed.

Yancey Higgins was still snoring with childlike naturalness when the musicians and guests began departing. Maude and Annie Grimsley, Letty Higgins, and Hilda and I all gathered around Yancey at the settee and brought him gradually to wakefulness. Finally I grabbed his legs, set them on the floor, and pulled him to his feet. How such a man can make a baby face is beyond me, but Yancey did, and he yawned repeatedly as he closed his eyes and tried to lie down on the sofa again.

Letty explained that Yancey had been out on a coon hunt with Guy Blythe, the Studebaker wagon agent, and some of his other friends until dawn of that day and had not been able to catch up on his sleep. At this, Maude Grimsley volunteered to take Yancey and Letty home in the Columbia Electric. She had some difficulty bringing life to the vehicle and asked my help in changing batteries. At last we set off into the night, Maude, Letty, Hilda, Yancey, and I, crowded upon one another, the machine moving very slowly because the light on the front of the vehicle refused to burn. To warn off any approaching wagons, buggies, or persons on horseback, Maude kept squeezing the rubber bulb on the horn, its vulgar squawks alarming each neighborhood that we passed through. Eventually we reached the Higgins house, a small cottage on Fourteenth Street, but Yancey was still only half conscious, and it became my duty to assist Letty—tugging him on foot between us into the house. We got him into the bedroom and let him drop upon a bed. He moaned softly until Letty unlaced and removed his shoes. Then he turned over on his belly and began breathing deeply.

She followed me out to the entrance hall, apparently not shamed or provoked but letting it all flow by her quite serenely. In the dim light of the hall, I could see her partially disarranged dark hair falling over her pale oval face, her half-exposed breasts rising and falling with her steady breathing. I took three or four steps toward the front door. Reaching for the doorknob, I swung around to tell her good-night and was surprised to find her standing very close beside me. She encircled my neck with both arms and kissed me, not on the cheek but on the lips, a kiss as sweet and luscious as a ripe strawberry. Then she whirled and hurried away down the hallway.

I went out into the night, inhaling the cool air, glad that the occupants of the Columbia Electric were in deep shadow and could not clearly see my face.

XXIV

LIVING OFF THE LAND

~

Lydia Bright provided them with a fair breakfast and then made up a lunch of bread and meats that she wrapped in a fold of ragged muslin. Just as they were preparing to leave, the Reverend Potts appeared. He placed his hands on their heads and mumbled a prayer and blessing. Lydia Bright squeezed each of them in warm embraces and then handed a length of rope to Ben.

"Put that around Bednigo's neck and take him with you," she said sweetly. "Your uncle will not rest easy in his grave if you do not give the dog a good home."

"Yes, ma'am," Ben said.

When they went out on the porch, the mustard-colored Abednego was waiting for them with a mournful face, his eyes moist. As soon as the rope was attached, he followed Ben willingly down to the big oak where Hadjee had the donkey hitched to the cart, Champ saddled, and the camels ready to move.

Lydia Bright and Reverend Potts stood on the porch waving farewell to them until they started down the slope toward the road. As soon as they were through the gate, Ben tied the dog to the rear of the cart. He looked back and was relieved to see that both the man and woman had vanished into the house.

"I was wondering what they'd think," he said to Queen Elizabeth Jones, "if they saw us heading east instead of west."

"Fiddlesticks," the girl said as she adjusted herself in her saddle. "They don't no more care what we do or where we go. They've got what they want and a hurry-up good riddance to us, for two

Mexican silver dollars and a sorrowful old coon hound." She urged Champ forward, taking the lead on the gravelly road.

The day was pleasant, neither too cold nor too warm, with snowy clouds floating across a pure blue sky. At a midafternoon stop they found a clear ice-water stream curling its narrow way through a sward of wild clover. Soon after they halted, none of the three humans or any of the five animals had any desire to resume the journey. Bees hummed and buzzed over the clover, birds sang from all directions, and a cowbell sounded faintly beyond a strip of green willows. They decided to stay there until morning.

For breakfast they cut into their shrinking slab of bacon, rolling the slices into flour before frying them.

"We ought've bought more provisions at Cuba City," Queen Elizabeth Jones said.

"How was I to know Billy Goodheart would steal our greenbacks?" Ben answered. "Grain for the animals is getting low, too."

"They can eat grass, but we can't," she replied.

Ben did not say so, but he thought that before the day ended one of their Mexican silver dollars would have to be sacrificed.

Early that afternoon, a cloud bank began building in the west. Aware that they faced a scanty dinner as well as a need for some kind of night shelter, Ben kept a lookout for a crossroads store, a livery stable, or a farmhouse with a good barn. The country they were passing through was hilly, with outcroppings of limestone. The farms, the houses, and the barns were all small. Eventually they came upon a neatly kept cottage close by the road, with what appeared to be a combined milking shelter and chicken house a few yards from the dwelling.

Ben called for a stop and jumped down from the cart. He strode up a pathway to the house. No one responded to his knock on the door, and he walked around the cottage, calling out, "Hullo the house, hullo the house!"

While he was circling the dwelling, Queen Elizabeth Jones examined the interior of the chicken house. After a minute or so she came outside. "Eggs," she cried. "Lots of eggs in there."

"But nobody's at home," Ben said.

She pulled a knotted handkerchief from inside her waistcoat. "I have about a dozen pennies tied in here. I remember Uncle Sims buying eggs for a penny apiece. We can take a dozen eggs and leave the pennies on the doorstep." When she turned and reentered the chicken house, Ben followed her through the narrow doorway.

Three or four hens were sitting on nests, but they objected to the invasion of privacy and one by one hopped down and ran outside. Queen Elizabeth Jones began a careful selection of eggs, choosing the darker shells, and using her militia cap for a temporary container.

A feminine voice sounded abruptly from close by, on the outside, a note of irritation in it at first, and then the harangue ended in a fierce scolding. A moment later Abednego let loose a drawn-out yelp of pain, and then Hadjee spoke very excitedly, mostly in Arabic, finally shouting, "No shoot! No shoot!"

Ben turned quickly and started toward the open doorway, which suddenly filled with the form of a large woman brandishing an old Colt's navy pistol. He was so close to her he could see her fingers trembling on the cocked weapon.

"Come out of my henhouse!" she cried, backing out of the door. "You gypsies come here and steal my chickens in broad daylight. I don't know what this odious war will bring next to poor Lizzie Starbird. Come out, come out!"

When Ben stepped outside he saw Hadjee, his dark face distraught, standing nervously beside the camels, his hands in the air. Abednego crouched at his feet, his moist eyes expressing mortification. The stick that had been thrown at him lay nearby.

Ben faced the angular woman directly. She was a foot taller than he, long jawed, long nosed, her dark eyes burning with anger.

Queen Elizabeth Jones came outside, saying calmly, "We warn't after your chickens, ma'am. Just a few eggs." She held up the knotted handkerchief. "We was going to leave pay for them."

"Why, you boys ain't gypsies, are you?" the woman said. "Are you with that furriner there with the camels? You're circus people, ain't you? Worse'n gypsies I'll allow."

"No, ma'am," Ben protested. "We're not circus people. The camels belong to the Union Army, and we've been hired to drive them to St. Louis."

The woman shook her head as though disbelieving what Ben had said. "Who's the master here? That furriner?" When she pointed a long finger at Hadjee, the dog at his feet assumed that he was the object of attention, guilty of some gross iniquity. With tail between his legs, Abednego tried to conceal himself behind the Egyptian.

"You can put your hands down, man," the woman said to Hadjee and made a downward motion with the pistol. "Now you tell me the truth about what you folks are doing here with camels and a donkey cart."

Ben interrupted to explain to her that Hadjee was Egyptian and understood very little English. She wanted to know where they had come from and who had hired them. Ben did not tell her that Johnny Hawkes was in jail; he simply stated that the man they worked for had been delayed in Rolla and would soon overtake them. He then went on to explain that they had been robbed of their traveling funds.

"Robbery is a common occurrence since the outbreak of this odious war," she said. Uncocking the pistol, she slipped it into one of her apron pockets. She looked closely at Queen Elizabeth Jones, her gaze fixing upon the holes in the knees of the girl's brown jeans, and then she studied Ben for a few seconds. "Why, you're both just children," she said and asked their names. After they told her, she said, "I'm Lizzie Starbird."

A steadily rising wind brought a scattering of big raindrops that quickly ceased. Thunder rumbled off to the southwest. "It's going to storm," Lizzie Starbird said, pulling a kerchief over her head. "I reckon you children better take shelter with me in the house. The furriner too, if he wants."

"Hadjee will stay with his camels," Ben told her. "He'd be obliged if he could use your cowshed."

The cowshed is where the travelers spent that night. After a thunderstorm, rain continued past nightfall. Lizzie Starbird gave them permission to stall their animals and sleep there. At one end of the shed's interior was a platform about six foot in length where hay and grain were stored, providing enough room for Ben and Queen Elizabeth Jones and Hadjee to stretch out in their blankets. Abednego also bedded up there, with them, and he was the only member of the company who slept well through the night. In the lower part of the earthen-floored shed, the camels, Champ, the donkey, and Lizzie Starbird's milk cow struggled for sleeping space. The cow distrusted all the strangers and spent most of the night leaning against one wall, keeping herself as far away from them as possible. The camels kneeled, but every time Ben was almost asleep, Omar would growl as though with deep anger, and sometimes Ben was certain he heard Tooley crying. He remembered Hadjee pointing to her udder a few days past and indicating that it was tender because of her condition, that she was going to bear a calf. But Hadjee could not say when.

Sleepy though he was, Ben welcomed first daylight and was the first out of the shed. While he was washing himself on the narrow strip of back porch, Lizzie Starbird appeared from inside the cottage and told him that if he and his friends expected breakfast, they should be seated at her kitchen table in two shakes of a lamb's tail. Ben noticed that she was still carrying the old Colt's navy pistol in her apron pocket.

During the breakfast a black pot bubbled quietly on the woodstove. From time to time, Lizzie Starbird would rise, go over to the pot, ladle out several boiled eggs, and put them in a large bowl. Then she would drop several more fresh eggs into the pot.

By the time breakfast was finished, the bowl was filled with hard-boiled eggs. "I can't give you children anything to put them in," Lizzie Starbird said. "Do you have any utensils?"

Queen Elizabeth Jones volunteered to go and bring their largest pot from the cart. While she was gone, Lizzie Starbird asked Ben, "Is Jack your brother?"

"No, ma'am," Ben replied, "but we are both orphans."

"This odious war has brought sad times to us all," she declared. "It took my husband last year, leaving me all alone in this world. In that battle over by Springfield, where General Lyon also was killed." She sighed. "I can't see all that bloody fighting did any earthly good for the State of Missouri."

When Queen Elizabeth Jones returned with the pot, Lizzie Starbird began placing the eggs carefully inside it. "Boiled eggs will keep for some days. You children won't go hungry for a time." She turned then and looked at Queen Elizabeth Jones. "Boy," she demanded sternly, "why do you always keep your backside away from my sight?"

Queen Elizabeth Jones stepped sideways from her, startled by the question.

"Turn around, boy."

"Why—"

Lizzie Starbird gripped her by the shoulders and turned her around. "You've got no seat in your jeans, just strips of ragged cloth. And you're wearing no underdrawers. In another day or so you'll be bare in the bottom as a newborn. Jack—that's your name ain't it—you come with me." She marched Queen Elizabeth Jones out of the kitchen and into an adjoining room, closing the door behind them.

After a few minutes, Lizzie Starbird returned alone, chuckling softly, her angular face half smiling. "Ben—that's your name ain't it—your friend Jack is a shy boy. I'm giving him my dead husband's army pants. Too long and loose for little Jack, but they'll cover his nakedness. He would not allow me to stay in the room while he changed."

When Queen Elizabeth Jones returned to the kitchen, she was wearing a pair of sky-blue kersey cavalry trousers, rolled up at the leg bottoms and fastened in folds at her waist by a yellow cord.

An hour later they were on the road again. After the night storm, the air had turned quite chill, and whenever racing gray clouds screened the sun, Ben would find himself shivering atop the rocking cart. Each day the donkey seemed to grow lazier, and in order to keep up with the others Ben had to goad the animal into faster movement with a long stick. Occasionally Queen Elizabeth Jones would let Ben ride Champ, but she detested the donkey and the cart and was so reluctant to swap that Ben hesitated to ask her to do so.

By midday the temperature warmed slightly, and Ben began looking for a place to stop for nooning. Judging from the increasing frequency of the houses he guessed that they were approaching a town. From far away a train whistle sounded, and a few minutes later he could see a speeding locomotive pulling a few passenger cars a mile or so to the southeast.

At that moment a stagecoach swung over the crest of a hill in front of them, its driver pulling on the reins to slow its passage and shouting profanely at his four-horse team. Because of the narrowness of the road, the coach was slowed to a crawl when it met and passed the camels and the donkey cart. It was an Overland Stage Company vehicle, but the driver wore a sergeant's uniform of the Union Army. Two officers peered out the side windows.

The stagecoach was only a few yards past when Ben heard the driver geeing and hawing. He looked back and saw the vehicle turning around in the road. In a minute or so the coach was rolling alongside the carreta. A round-faced army officer, grinning amiably, his bare head thrust out the forward window, was signaling for a halt.

Ben shouted to Queen Elizabeth Jones who was halfway up the hill and motioned to Hadjee to turn the camels off the road. By this time the officer, a major, followed by a very young lieutenant, was out of the stagecoach.

"Is this John Hawkes's bunch?" the major asked.

"Yes, sir, it is," Ben replied and stepped down from the cart.

The major looked back and forth along the road, swinging his forage cap in one hand. "I see the 'ships of the desert' up there with a dark foreigner in attendance, but which one of you is Hawkes?"

"He's not with us right now," Ben replied. "He's been delayed in Rolla."

"Delayed? What do you mean delayed?"

Ben explained patiently, deciding that since the man was an army officer and the camels were army business he might was well tell all the facts.

The major laughed. "So Mr. Hawkes got himself in the bastille for stealing his own horse." He pulled his forage cap down tight on his head and looked up at Queen Elizabeth Jones on Champ. "You two boys and the camel driver are the lot, eh?" He grinned. "I wonder what Solomon Lightfoot would think about that." He turned to the lieutenant. "Are you hungry, Zack?" Then he asked Ben, "Are you boys aiming to stop for a noonday feed? Tell you what. There's a grassy spot by a little stream back over this hill. We'll share rations with you."

Major Strawbridge and Lieutenant Hockaday were quartermaster officers from St. Louis, and they had been billeted with Captain Lightfoot near Camp Jackson. Lightfoot had often talked with them about the camels, the Egyptian, and John Hawkes. When Lightfoot discovered that Strawbridge and Hockaday were being sent west on the Springfield turnpike, he asked them to keep an eye out for his camels, and if they met John Hawkes they were to assure him that he would be paid in full for his services as soon as he reached St. Louis.

The two officers and the sergeant were well supplied with jerked beef and hard biscuits, which they willingly shared. When they learned that their guests had nothing but boiled eggs and a small strip of bacon, and that their funds had been stolen, Major Strawbridge gave each of them a silver half-dollar and expressed regrets that he could not spare more.

"You will just have to scrounge your way to St. Louis," he said. "Where do you lads live? You have homes, don't you?"

"We're orphans," Ben replied. "Jack's from west of here. Over in Marshfield. I'm from Texas."

Major Strawbridge grimaced. "Don't ever tell anybody between here and St. Louis that you're from Texas. They'll put you down as a Secesh. You're not Secesh, are you?"

"I'm a Texican," Ben said.

The major chuckled and then began teasing Queen Elizabeth Jones about her ill-fitting sky-blue trousers. "How'd you come by the cavalry pants, Jack?"

Queen Elizabeth Jones told him they were a gift from a war widow down the road, a place where they'd spent the night.

"The widow's Union then," Strawbridge said. He reached inside his jacket and brought out a worn map, unfolding it carefully and holding it so they could see it. He pointed to a road line. "We're right about here. Where it says Mount Helicon. Except now the railroad calls it Sullivan. You've traveled how far this morning? Eight, ten miles?"

"Maybe," Ben said.

"At places where you stopped yesterday and today, did you hear any talk about a gunpowder maker in these parts? About anything unusual?"

Ben and Queen Elizabeth Jones exchanged glances, and then she said, "Only about a shoemaker. Miz Lizzie Starbird said as how we should stop at a shoe factory nearby Mount Helicon town and try to talk 'em out of some cull shoes."

"She said nothing about a gunpowder maker aroundabouts?"

"No, sir."

"Well, there's a hidden one somewhere's around here. I might as well tell you, somebody is making powder and lead bullets for Sterling Price's Confederate Army. We aim to find it and close it down."

"If you find it, what will you do to the gunpowder makers?" Ben asked.

Major Strawbridge laughed heartily. "Shoot 'em if they resist. Take 'em to St. Louis prison if they surrender."

As soon as they'd had their fill of jerked beef and a few of Lizzie Starbird's boiled eggs, the officers and the sergeant boarded the confiscated stagecoach and resumed their journey. As he was leaving, Major Strawbridge declared in his genial manner that if he reached St. Louis and Camp Jackson before they did, he would inform Captain Lightfoot that his ships of the desert were on their way.

While Ben was checking the donkey's harness in preparation for departure, he noticed Hadjee in attendance upon Tooley. The Egyptian was holding a bottle that he'd thrust into the camel's mouth, and the animal was drinking avidly.

Ben moved closer and recognized the bottle as one the army officers had been sipping from during the nooning. The letters RUM spelled out its contents.

"Did Major Strawbridge give you that bottle?" Ben demanded testily.

Hadjee shrugged, and an expression of incomprehension crossed his face.

Queen Elizabeth Jones interrupted. "The soldiers left the bottle in the grass over there. I reckon they forgot it."

"Won't rum make Tooley sick?" Ben asked. He rubbed his stomach and groaningly made signs of illness.

Hadjee grinned and shook his head. "No sick. No, no. Rum good medsin. For enceinte camel."

Sullivan was a very quiet town with so few people on the streets that little excitement was created by the passage of camels and donkey cart. The narrow highway ran close by and parallel with the railroad. As they were entering the woodsy countryside again, Ben noticed a long, high-roofed smokehouse on the opposite side of the railroad track. A large sign was painted on the gable: HAMS AND POTATOES FOR SALE. A lazy breeze brought mixed perfumes of spring blossoms mingled with the aroma of smoked meats.

Ben called for a halt, dropped down from the cart, and with Abednego at his heels crossed the railroad track. As he walked down the slope of the roadbed, he could see hams hanging from rafters inside an open breezeway. Below them and just inside the wide entrance were several other hams lying on a long table. To one side were gunnysacks of varying sizes with mounds of potatoes around them.

The first movement from the smokehouse was the appearance of a young woman wearing a black bonnet and a flowing black dress. Evidently she had seen Ben approaching and had stepped into the breezeway and was looking out at him.

A moment later a large black dog, a mastiff, leaped to its feet beside the girl, and then with a spring began running at full speed toward Abednego. At first there was no sound except for the whisper of its feet skimming the grass, but as the mastiff came nearer—its drooping ears flung back by velocity, its pendent lips drooling with saliva—a low menacing growl rose from its throat.

To Ben's surprise, Abednego stood his ground against the onrushing attacker. Snarls and quick barks were followed by the impact of canine flesh against canine flesh. The two dogs grappled like human wrestlers, rolling over and over down the slope, dark yellow replacing black, black replacing dark yellow.

About this time the girl wearing the bonnet, armed with a long-handled hoe, came running from the smokehouse, shouting something at either Ben or the dogs. Because of the fury of dog noises, Ben could not make out her words. A shrill yelp from the black dog signaled a temporary retreat. It skittered off to the right, avoiding the swing of the young woman's hoe, with Abednego in close pursuit, quickly gaining ground. When the black dog leaped upon the table of hams just within the breezeway, Abednego soared after him. The weight of both dogs and their angles of descent sent the table crashing to the ground, scattering smoked hams all around the front of the open building.

The girl was now directly in front of Ben, her face flushed with anger, eyes glaring at him, the hoe uplifted again. "Get your mean circus dog out of here!" she shouted.

"Your dog attacked mine," Ben replied calmly. "We stopped to buy a ham and some potatoes, that's all."

"Look what a mess you caused!" she screamed back at him. "I'll sell you nothing!"

By this time Queen Elizabeth Jones had ridden Champ across

the railroad track and seemed to be enjoying the wrangling between Ben and the hostile girl. In the midst of the hams that were
strewn in front of the smokehouse, the two dogs stood facing each
other like contenders in a boxing ring, each awaiting a strike from
the other. During the brief period of silence a locomotive whistle
sounded from the northeast.

The truce ended when the black dog suddenly plunged at Abednego. Unable to elude the teeth of the mastiff, Abednego emitted
a bloodcurdling howl that may have startled the black dog just
enough for the coon hound to make a quick escape. For a few
seconds, Abednego sped ahead of his pursuer, but the gap between
them began to narrow. Just as it seemed that the mastiff would
overtake the coon hound, the two camels with Hadjee between
them appeared abruptly upon the railroad track. The Egyptian's
curiosity about the commotion occurring between the track and
the smokehouse had brought him and his charges up the embankment.

It was then that Ben became aware of the rapid approach of
the railroad train from the northeast. The locomotive's whistle was
tooting short blasts. Black smoke boiled from its diamond stack.
The cowcatcher protruded like the black teeth of a monster, giving
the entire engine an image of ferocity.

Waving his arms at Hadjee, Ben shouted to the cameleer to get
his animals off the track. The shriek of the whistle and the roar
and rattle of the locomotive so frightened Omar that he broke loose
from Hadjee's halter and ran down the embankment toward the
road. Queen Elizabeth Jones on Champ immediately began pursuit
while Hadjee contritely led Tooley after them. Ben himself barely
made it down the slope behind Hadjee before the train went hoot-
ing past.

A few yards from the track Ben stopped, wondering what had
happened to Abednego. The last that he had seen of the dog, it
was chasing after the black mastiff, which had been so frightened
by the materialization of camels that it had turned tail to run back
to the smokehouse.

Slowing for the railroad station in the town ahead, the freight
train finally rumbled past, and then Abednego emerged from a
cloud of steam and smoke, trotting proudly across the tracks, the
shank of a ham gripped in his teeth. Without so much as a glance

at Ben, the dog moved unhurriedly toward the donkey cart on the road. Far to the northeast Queen Elizabeth Jones was still visible in close pursuit of Omar.

Ben called to the dog to drop the stolen ham, but Abednego paid no heed, continuing to the cart where Hadjee stood nervously beside a perturbed Tooley. Both were peering up the road at the vanishing Omar and Queen Elizabeth Jones.

Returning to the top of the embankment, Ben saw that the girl in black now held a shotgun cradled in her arms. The black mastiff was nowhere in sight.

"I'll pay for the ham!" Ben shouted to her.

She shifted the heavy shotgun, pointing it in his general direction.

He stood defiant, wondering if he dared take a few steps closer to her. "We'll buy some potatoes, too," he added.

"Git!" she cried and fired the gun.

Pellets showered in a beech tree off to his right. The girl's face showed surprise and pain as she reeled from the recoil.

"I tried," Ben said quietly to himself. He turned about and crossed the railroad embankment in unhurried strides, never once looking back.

That evening they camped in a grove of cedars near the village of Stanton.

While Queen Elizabeth Jones trimmed neat slices from the ham stolen by Abednego, she broke out occasionally in little gleeful bursts of comment. "Thanks to our dog," she said to Ben, "we'll have a good supper. But he is a thief."

"He earns his keep," Ben replied.

XXV

BEN BUTTERFIELD

~

Theo Drumgoole, the engineer for the telephone company, with his two roustabouts, was outside my window early this Monday morning, measuring distances along the sidewalk. On their wagon they brought an auger of considerable diameter and with it took earth samples that Theo studied with the concentrated attention I've seen him apply to Miss Betty Hesterly whenever she is in his company.

After a few minutes of this activity, I was not at all surprised to see Hilda Fagerhalt traipse outside the front of the hardware store to confront Theo in his working clothes. The fact that she did this brought home to me the importance she attached to the installation of a telephone. Ordinarily Hilda would not leave her store to interfere with a man at work, but there she was with her capable arms folded across her magnificent bosom, the morning sun glinting on her braided and slightly fading flaxen hair, her height matching Theo's, looking him square in the eyes as a man would, demanding that he name a date for the installation of her telephone.

Hilda was so excited by all this, she could not wait for noontime to share with me the information she had gleaned from Theo Drumgoole. As soon as she finished attending a customer who had interrupted her researches on the sidewalk, she came prancing down the hallway to announce that as soon as a shipment of tarred poles could be obtained from Carolina, work would begin on extending telephone service to our part of Louisiana Street.

"Did Theo name a date?" I asked, knowing full well that if he had, she would have announced it in her very first sentence.

"A matter of days he said, certainly before the Fourth of July."

As I have previously made clear, I dislike telephones. I consider them more interruptive than unexpected visitors and am convinced that they consume vastly more of humanity's precious allotments of time than they save. I have used the contrivance less than half a dozen times in my life and see no reason why the telegraph cannot serve us better. And without that damned jingling bell to discompose mind and body and to break thoughts into shards.

Alas, Hilda still seems determined to have the telephone situated right here on Old Man Fagerhalt's desk. When I remonstrate and say that it should stand beside the cash drawer in the hardware store, so that she can take customers' orders, she replies that if she is busy waiting upon a customer, it would be impossible to stop and answer the telephone. No, that should be my duty, she says.

Ah, but that will lay waste my cherished style of living, the pursuit of memories in my early life, my study of old photographs of golden moments, my re-creation of the past. Diabolical! In her attempts to placate me, Hilda says that Theo Drumgoole believes the day is coming when we can project our tinny voices to distant locales, to every city and hamlet upon this earth. What a calamity for human privacy! Perhaps, she says, she can exchange words with her only living relatives in Stockholm, Sweden.

She said nothing about my exchanging words with my old cronies of circus days. Most of them, of course, are gone, gone, gone, without addresses, or lost to the grim reaper. I would gladly exchange words with Dr. Socrates Drumm if I knew where he was. And if I could refrain from weeping or from choking in the throat with emotion, I would force myself to talk into that black voice box if it would bring me the liquid music, tinny though it might be, of Queen Elizabeth Jones.

Yesterday, Sunday, I went to church with Hilda and her widow friend, Lora Valentine. I felt the need of sonorousness, and the Reverend Junius Bragg, who looks after the souls of this favored flock, has one of the most resonant of voices. It floats over the congregation's heads like a message of doom from a cave or a deep well.

Hearty though the vocal powers of the Reverend Bragg may be, I find it possible to sleep through some of his sermons, although this is difficult to do when seated in a pew between Hilda and Lora Valentine. At the first evidence of closed eyes on my part, Hilda will jog me with an elbow or knee. If Hilda does not notice my slackness, Lora will. The widow does not nudge me with any part of her anatomy because she has a profound distrust of most males, her exceptions being the ghost of her dead husband and that living gentleman, Brigadier Preston Boggs, whom she believes to be a disciple of the Lord. To awaken me, Lora uses the end of her folded ivory fan with considerable enough force to be painful.

Lora is certain that I am beyond redemption, a product of the licentious world of the circus, and she cannot imagine why a good woman like Hilda Fagerhalt ever consented to marry such a wretch as I. Of course Lora does not know the inside story.

On the rare occasions when I do attend church with Hilda and Lora, I am never certain whether Lora wants me there or not. She is forever urging my attendance in order to save my soul from the fires of Hell, but when I do attend I have the feeling that she sees me as a lost cause and that the pew space I occupy is wasted.

Yesterday's sermon from the vibrant vocal cords of Reverend Junius Bragg caught my interest from the beginning, and not once did the arms of Morpheus bring sleep to my eyes. Reverend Bragg maintains that with the beginning of this new century his sermons should be developed from events of the day. The subject of his sermon yesterday was our individual responsibilities on the eve of the age of electricity as compared to the declining age of steam, the biblical text being from the Book of Daniel. In his peroration, the Reverend Bragg brought in the name of a living Italian marchese, Guglielmo Marconi, who is attempting to send telegraphic messages through the air instead of over wires. At the mention of Marconi's name, Brigadier Boggs, who was seated with his daughter Blossom in a pew a few yards ahead of us, immediately pricked up his large pink ears. I recalled the brigadier's bragging some months past about how Queen Victoria and Prince Edward had lent their support to Marconi's experiments while United States leaders ignored him, and that the Italian had actually sent the Morse code four miles through the air across the Salisbury Plain.

Reverend Bragg declared that it would never be possible to send sound signals across the Atlantic Ocean's countless miles without a wire cable, yet nevertheless he believed the marchese's feats over the land were almost as miraculous as the survival of Daniel's three companions from King Nebuchadnezzar's fiery furnace into which the king's soldiers had cast them because they refused to worship his golden image.

It was Reverend Bragg's naming of Daniel's three companions that caused me to prick up my ears. "Shadrach, Meshack, and Abednego came forth in the midst of the fire." Abednego! For years I have given no thought to that noble canine who surely had been christened by the late Brother Pursglove whom I had never seen in life. Abednego was more intelligent than many human beings; he was as independent as a house cat. Perhaps he was loyal, even subservient, to his original master, but never to me or Queen Elizabeth Jones. He tolerated me; he politely obeyed Queen Elizabeth Jones who never used the initial letter of his name, always calling him Bednego. He was at times a good companion, but he was always his own dog. Selah.

XXVI

SHAKESPEARE AND THE HORSE TAMERS

~

The heat was like midsummer when they came into the outskirts of Travelers Repose. In that time of the year, the days were lengthening, and although Ben knew that they could probably journey another five miles before dark, he willingly acceded to Queen Elizabeth Jones's hint that it was time for a night camp. Hadjee and the camels looked weary in the sweltering atmosphere. Champ was holding his head low, the donkey was more contrary than ever, and Abednego's tongue fluttered with his panting.

On the west side of the road was a fine green pasture with no livestock of any sort in sight. Nor was there a farmhouse or barn in view there, only a rail-fenced stock pen. On the opposite side of the road, however, was a white house of considerable size barely visible through a grove of oaks.

Stepping down from the cart, Ben was just about to tell Queen Elizabeth Jones that he was going up to the big house when he saw a man open the wide entrance gate and start across the road. The man was short of stature and somewhat portly, with gray hair spilling out below a low-crowned planter's hat. His gray beard was cut close and trimmed with a neat exactness. He was the sort of person, Ben thought, that Johnny Hawkes usually described as "venerable."

The man was swinging a fancy walking stick, which he lifted and pointed at the camels. "I say there, young man," he called to Ben, his bright eyes flashing under heavy gray brows. "Whence come these dromedaries?"

"They're property of the United States government," Ben replied, "trusted to our care."

The venerable man stepped closer to the camels and with his head turned to one side studied them intently. Then he spoke to Hadjee. "And whence come you, my good man?"

Hadjee shrugged and spread his hands.

"He's Egyptian," Ben explained. "He don't understand and speak much of our talk."

"Aha. I see. Is he, or are you and the lad on the gray horse over there in charge of this menagerie?"

Ben explained that their leader had been delayed in the town of Rolla, and he added on the spur of the moment, "We thought if we made camp early, maybe he might catch up to us before dark."

The venerable man asked their names and then told them his own, Robert Burns Cambridge. After a few moments of silence on his part he invited them to camp in the grounds east of his house. "I don't care a fig for property of the Lincoln government," he said bluntly. "They send armies into Missouri and stir up our peaceful people against one another. But in neither of you two boys' voices do I detect any trace of the Yankee pronunciation. How you got mixed in with these Union government camels is none of my business. I would grant you the use of that pasture across the road, but Potawatomi Tom has rented it for a herd of wild horses he's driving in here for breaking, maybe tonight. Since Monday the grass is his. But you're welcome to the east pasture. You can sleep in the sheds there if you like. However, some traveling thespians have laid claim to two or three of the buildings. Don't intrude on or bother those cultured people. Good day, my young friends."

The old man turned and walked back to the entrance gate, tugged at it until it was wide open, and motioned with his walking stick for them to come in.

Sloping away from the big two-story house was a series of swards broken by outcroppings of gray limestone. Along one of the flatter ridges was a row of sheds, or cabins, built of barked and stained logs, all with a connecting roof. Beside the cabin at the row's left end stood a canvas-covered wagon with a small sign on its side: VALLEY SHAKESPEARE COMPANY OF ST. LOUIS. THEATER VEREIN.

In front of the end cabin a barefoot young man was sitting in a cypress-wood chair propped against the wall. When he saw the intruders approaching, he lifted his head in annoyance. He had been reading aloud from what Ben later learned was a Shakespeare playbook.

"Mr. Cambridge gave permission for us to use one of these sheds," Ben said to the young man.

"He did, eh?" The young man let his chair legs drop flat on the ground. "Well, well, what a menagerie we have here. Camels, donkeys, dark-skinned lascars, and bright-eyed juveniles wearing discarded military clothing. Just our luck to have a flea-bitten circus come to Travelers Repose to draw the rabble away from our performances."

"We're not a circus," Ben said.

"No, and I suppose you're not intending to display on the streets the talents of yourselves and the beasts."

"No, sir," Ben assured him.

The young man wiggled his bare toes. "Well then," he said and made a sweeping theatrical gesture with one arm, "I bid you take quarters at the farthest end of this row, far enough away I hope so that my companions and I may be spared your insufferable odors and clamors."

As soon as they had chosen cabins and confined the animals and cart to a fenced yard at the farther end of the row, Ben and Queen Elizabeth Jones went exploring down the grassy slope that faced the town of Travelers Repose. The only grazing animal in sight was a large ram with immense horns curving outward from its head. The sheep stared at them for a time, then trotted closer, its malicious eyes regarding them with suspicion.

At the bottom of the pasture was a six-foot hedge, unkempt and ragged in places from lack of care. As they strolled down toward the hedge, the railroad track and station were revealed below.

Through breaks in the hedge they could see the pasture ended there at a drop-off of twenty feet or more. Just below was a small glade where several people were gathered. Some were sitting on stools, others on the grass, all talking and gesturing. A warm wind that blew capriciously carried their voices in fits and starts to the top of the little bluff.

Queen Elizabeth Jones lay belly down on the ground, her arms crossed on a flat lichen-covered stone as she looked and listened through an opening in the hedge.

"Do you suppose they are the thespians Mr. Cambridge told us not to bother?"

"I don't know," he said.

"What is a thespian?"

He shook his head, chagrined that he did not know. "Maybe they're some kind of church people."

"Not if they're like that rude young man back there at the cabins. Church people where I grew up wouldn't treat strangers the way he treated us."

Ben sat down on a mound of grass to face her. "I guess you're right. I don't know much about church people or Bible religion except what Miz Sergeant Peddicord read to me at Fort Davis in Texas."

"If Doc Pingree was here," she said, "he would know."

Ben nodded. "Yeah, that covered wagon back there has a sign, something about Shakespeare. Doc Pingree knows all about Shakespeare."

The fitful wind lifted the words of a conversation between two men below: "If Shoemaker is not on the St. Louis train, Goodloe, d'you think I could have a chance at Orlando?" The reply came quickly. "No, because Arthur outranks you. You can read Orlando as well as Arthur does, but no better. So I'd have to give it to Arthur. We *could* do without Shoemaker, but if he doesn't bring Mary, we have nobody for the entr'actes. We'd have to omit the songs and dances. And the audience won't like that. Even at Hermann the audience was edgy that night we couldn't fill . . ." The wind turned, lost its force, and the words became too faint to be understood on the bluff top.

Queen Elizabeth Jones gently pulled a long stem of new grass from the ground and nibbled its tender end. "I wish Johnny Hawkes would catch up to us," she said. "Do you think he's out of jail yet?"

"I don't know," Ben said.

"If he comes by on the road this evening he wouldn't know we've camped up here," she said.

"He'd find us. Johnny can track anything."

"Even without Johnny here I feel happy," she went on. "Being in a cabin is better'n being in Lydia Bright's closet or Missus Starbird's cowshed."

"They both treated us kindlier than most folks would."

She sniffed. "Missus Starbird treated us like children. I didn't like that. Major Strawbridge, though, he acted like we was his age."

"Well, he is a lot older than us."

"But he respected us for keeping on toward St. Louis."

"What else can we do but keep on to St. Louis?"

Queen Elizabeth Jones sat up and crossed her ankles. "Even if you are kind of contrary, Ben, I do feel happy being here with you. We have a roof of our own this night, so let it rain if it will. I don't mind this hard travel except when we have no roof against the weather."

She began singing, softly at first, and then let her voice rise to its full volume:

> *"The years creep slowly by, Lorena*
> *The snow is on the grass again.*
> *The sun's low down the sky, Lorena,*
> *The frost gleams where the flow'rs have been*
> *But the heart throbs on warmly now*
> *As when the summer days were nigh*
> *Oh! the sun can never dip so low*
> *A-down affection's cloudless sky*
> *The sun can never dip so low*
> *A-down affection's cloudless sky."*

To Ben the sound of her voice was like nothing he had heard before. It was far more melodious than on the day she sang "Wait for the Wagon" on the courthouse square in Waynesville. Of course that was before he learned that she was not Jack Bonnycastle but was instead a girl. Now the sweetness of her music seemed to linger in the vernal air until the world turned completely silent.

A moment later the silence was broken by a clapping of hands from the glade below, a shout of "bravo! bravo!" and a demand for the second stanza.

In the midst of this unexpected applause, which caused Queen Elizabeth Jones to turn pale and cover her mouth with one hand, a locomotive whistle split the air as a train rolled into view on the track and slowed with spurts of steam blowing across the front of the station house.

"Shoemaker's train," shouted one of the men down below. "Let's go meet him!"

Except for two young women who continued to sit in their cane chairs, the group rushed away to the railroad station. Within a few minutes they returned, laughing and talking as they walked, dancing and skipping over the grass. They virtually surrounded a neatly dressed young man whose dark jacket fit tightly to his muscular arms and torso.

"He's handsome," Queen Elizabeth Jones whispered, "but his hair is pink."

"Sort of like that quartermaster lieutenant in Rolla," Ben said. "Woodpecker head."

They were both on their bellies now, halfway through the break in the hedge, fascinated by everything they saw and heard.

The pink-haired young man was Shoemaker, and the others were scolding him for not bringing someone named Mary.

"She has an engagement all month entertaining the soldiers," Shoemaker explained in an accent that reminded Ben of the wounded German soldiers who had traveled in the wagon from Pea Ridge. "Mary wouldn't leave St. Louis for your entr'actes." He set his bag—an elaborately rose-figured carpetbag—down on the grass and looked around appreciatively. "Charming place you've found here, Goodloe. Where are we billeted?"

Goodloe was a slender, rather intense young man, with oiled black hair parted precisely in the middle of this skull. He pointed upward to the bluff. "Plain but gratuitous. Former slave quarters, as a matter of fact. They're ours this week thanks to an old gentleman named Cambridge. He freed his slaves a long time ago and wants to help people like us."

"Atonement?" Shoemaker asked.

"I doubt it," Goodloe replied. "He is loyal to the Rebel cause, methinks. Well, it's getting late. Before we go up, let's pin down the final parts. Are you fully prepared to do Orlando?"

"Yes, of course. Tomorrow night, isn't it?" Shoemaker turned slowly in a complete circle. "Do you know, you could stage it right here among these Forest of Arden trees."

"We thought of that. But there's no place for the audience. A pity. Now let's see. Gretchen as usual is doing Rosalind, and you Katy are Celia. Phoebe and Audry complete the female cast. Arthur Pound is up at the cabins reading for the melancholy Jaques. And Eric is Touchstone of course." His voice rattled on, with the others joining in until to Ben they became a babble.

The sun was almost down, and the last strong beams cut through the hedge, magnifying objects struck by the light. At Ben's feet, bright particles danced on the surface of a large rock. He stood up and backed away to observe it from a different angle.

"Look at the sparkles in this rock," he said to Queen Elizabeth Jones. "When Johnny saw one like this while we were crossing Indian Territory he thought he'd found gold. A man told him it was worthless pirates or something." He leaned forward, hands braced on his knees.

"Watch out, Ben!" Queen Elizabeth Jones shouted. "That sheep! Jump!"

Her last words he heard while in free motion. The big ram's head butted him on the bottom with such force that he was propelled through the broken hedge and over the rim of the bluff. A cedar growing at an angle near the top broke his fall, but only temporarily. He slid for moments against the face of the precipice, dislodging stones and earth. He caught at a shrub, pulling it out by its roots, and then he tumbled to earth, landing on his hands and knees facing a pretty young woman who had drawn her feet quickly into her chair, wrapping her skirt around them. Her face was a caricature of astonishment.

"I say!" cried Goodloe, the intense young man with black oily hair. He stepped forward to offer Ben help. "Are you hurt, boy?"

"I've got to get back up there," Ben said hurriedly as he brushed dirt from his clothing. "My friend is in danger."

"Danger from what?" Shoemaker asked in his slight German accent.

"A sheep, a bad ram."

Goodloe stared at him. "D'you mean a ram shunted you down that bankment?"

When Ben nodded, Goodloe laughed slightly. The pretty woman with her legs still folded under her skirt tittered.

"Not amusing," Shoemaker said. "The boy could've broken a limb, or been killed."

"You're quite right," Goodloe agreed. "We'll lead you up, my boy." In the lowering twilight Goodloe turned to the others. "Gather your things, my dear thespians, especially the play books, and prepare for the ascent."

A zigzag trail that Ben was unaware of led from the glade to the top of the escarpment. On the way up Goodloe asked Ben, "Was it you or your friend who was singing 'Lorena' while ago?"

"My friend," Ben replied.

"Is your friend a girl?"

Ben hesitated a moment. "No. Jack Bonnycastle is his name."

"Fascinating," Goodloe said. "His voice hasn't changed yet. Must be younger than you. I'd like to hear more songs from him."

An hour or so later Goodloe heard Queen Elizabeth Jones sing again. The group of actors invited her, Ben, and Hadjee to share bowls of chowder from a large pot they set to simmering over an outdoor fire. Except for the young man named Arthur Pound, who had been so brusque to Ben and Queen Elizabeth Jones when they first arrived, the actors were friendly as well as entertaining. Franz Shoemaker was especially taken with Hadjee, and when he discovered that the Egyptian understood French, he joked with him until Ben was surprised to see Hadjee break into smiles and subdued laughter.

Later in the evening, Goodloe broached the subject of singing. "Master Jack Bonnycastle," he said, "we heard you sing 'Lorena' this afternoon, and very fine it was. Do you know any other songs?"

"A few," Queen Elizabeth Jones replied matter-of-factly.

"Such as?"

" 'Wait for the Wagon,' 'Swanee River.' "

"Would you sing a verse of 'Swanee River'?"

She shook her head shyly.

"Sing for your supper," he commanded with a friendly laugh.

She sang, hesitantly at first, and then in full voice as sweet as she had sung 'Lorena.'

"We'll take a vote," Goodloe said. "Raise your hands if you want Jack Bonnycastle for our entr'acte singer." All except Arthur Pound raised hands.

Goodloe stood up beside Queen Elizabeth Jones and put his arm around her shoulders. "Jack," he said, "you see facing us a cast of actors, male and female. Good readers, but not one can sing well enough to entertain an audience between acts. We believe you can do that."

Queen Elizabeth Jones put a hand over her mouth and then asked, "Sing to a crowd of folks, you mean?"

"Exactly that. You sing your songs tomorrow evening, and we'll pay you four bits."

She glanced at Ben, who was as surprised as she was. "Can we stay here another day, Ben?"

"If you want to," he replied.

She turned back to Goodloe. "Will you pay me in silver?"

"In U.S. Mint silver," Goodloe promised.

Shoemaker asked her if she could perform a few dance steps, but Goodloe interrupted to say that they could hardly ask a beginner to do more than sing. Somewhat demurely Queen Elizabeth Jones said that she could dance, but only with a partner, and all except Arthur Pound applauded her remark.

When Ben woke the next morning, with Abednego still sleeping on the floor beside him, he smelled horses and the aroma of trampled new grass. The sun was not yet up, but he dressed quickly and went to the door of the cabin. Beyond the oak trees, in the pasture across the road he could see dozens of horses milling—bays, chestnuts, sorrels, blacks, iron grays, nearly solid whites—all with heads up and prancing with that frenzied aura attending animals of the wild that find themselves in unwelcome confinement.

After fastening the reluctant and sad-faced Abednego in the animal pen, Ben observed down near the entrance gate the venerable owner of the house and acreage. Mr. Robert Burns Cambridge was briskly swinging his walking stick as he approached the road. He wore a black duster that reached to his boot heels. Ben hurried to overtake him and did so just as Mr. Cambridge was lifting the chain on the gate.

"Good morning, sir," Ben said.

Mr. Cambridge turned in surprise. "You're an early riser, young Ben. Did your man from Rolla catch up to you last night?"

"No, sir. He must have been considerably delayed."

"Did you and your friends find the sheds suitable for yourselves and the livestock?"

"Yes, sir. Thank you, sir."

"And you did not annoy the diligent thespians?"

Ben hesitated. "That's what I want to speak to you about, sir. They offered my partner, Jack Bonnycastle, pay money for singing at their show, and I want to ask your permission to stay in the sheds another night."

Mr. Cambridge's thick eyebrows twitched as he stared at Ben. "Oh, so that pretty young fellow on the gray horse is a singer, eh. His voice, as I recall, is a bit more than counter-tenorish. Almost girlish. And so he's to sing in *As You Like It* this evening?"

"Mr. Goodloe said something about him singing 'on track,' whatever that means."

" 'On track?' I don't know what that is. I'll have to ask young Goodloe when I see him."

Mr. Cambridge started to push the heavy gate open, and Ben lent his efforts to assist.

"I am just going across the road to take a look at Potawatomi Tom's horseflesh," Mr. Cambridge said. "He drove them in last night."

"They look wild as Texas mustangs," Ben said.

"He collects them from all points. The horse breakers are around somewhere. I find it exciting to watch them tame the wickedest of the beasts. Here's Potawatomi Tom now."

Approaching along the edge of the fence was a heavy-set, dark-faced man wearing a rawhide coat and a dusty slouch hat. He lifted a gauntleted hand to Mr. Cambridge. *"Buenos,"* he called in a raspy voice.

"Appears to be a good bunch of horse, Tom," Mr. Cambridge said.

"Not enough breakers have come in," the man replied. "Best ones went off to join Pap Price's rebel army in Arkansas." He was close enough now for Ben to see that he was part Indian. His long hair was jet black, his face pockmarked, the bone of his nose askew from an ancient break. A small scar thickened his lower lip. One of his legs appeared to be twisted sideways; he walked with a limp.

"The world's turned upside down," Mr. Cambridge said. "Still you can't expect strong young fellows with feelings for the South to stay out of it."

"Uh-uh. But they can never win against the bluecoats," Pota-watomi Tom said and changed the subject. "I may need to stay here more than two days, Mr. Cambridge. Cavalry buyers are coming tomorrow, and they want tamed horses."

Mr. Cambridge chuckled. "Yankee cavalrymen can't ride these wild Missouri broncos, I reckon. All right, Tom, stay till you've finished. My sheep won't need this grass for a little while."

Potawatomi Tom's wrangler, another Indian, very young, mounted on a spotted pony, expertly herded a dozen unbroken horses into a temporary V-shaped corral of poles held together by strips of rawhide. One of the wrangler's arms was strapped close to his chest by a sling. He dismounted easily, however, and with one arm strung a single rope across the corral opening.

"Astonishing," Mr. Cambridge said, "how that one rope, shoulder high to a horse, will hold a herd in that pen."

"It will—so long as they don't spook," Potawatomi Tom said. "But if a shit scare goes through that bunch all at once, they'll down the poles and head for the timber."

The young wrangler strode across the grass toward them, his white teeth showing in a smile. "Them in there is ready for breaking, Mr. Tom," he said.

"This young feller here is Raymove," Potawatomi Tom said to Mr. Cambridge. "Osage he is, but a damn good horseman. Broke his arm when he was throwed off a mean devil horse."

"And my young friend here's name is Ben," Mr. Cambridge said.

The Indians nodded to Ben, but neither offered to shake hands.

"Had to shoot that devil horse," Potawatomi Tom went on. "One of the sort that'll sneak up behind a man and stomp him to death. Even if he could be broke in, he'd be too dangerous."

While they were talking, two men rode up to the corral at a trot and dismounted. One was wearing a wide-brimmed black hat;

the other was bald and hatless. Among the accoutrements hanging from their saddles were lariats, hobbles, and quirts. "We're ready when you are, Potawatomi," the bald man said.

"Go ahead," Potawatomi Tom replied, motioning for Raymove to stand ready at the rope end of the corral.

Methodically, almost mechanically, the bald-headed man adjusted his gear, mounted, and rode into the corral. He spun his lariat out twice in practice throws, then dropped it like lightning over the head of a medium-sized bay mare. In an instant the man was standing on the ground, tightening the lariat around the mare's lower neck. While the horse kicked and reared, the breaker walked closer, tightening the noose until the animal could barely breathe. Over its head the man quickly fastened a hackamore, a bitless bridle, while his partner in the black hat slipped a rawhide hobble around its front legs. The breaker now gradually released pressure on the lariat until the mare could breathe again.

Sensing a return of lost freedom, the animal resumed struggling, but at each attempt the breaker lashed down cruelly with his quirt.

"No, no" Ben cried compulsively. "You'll break her spirit!"

With Mr. Cambridge and Potawatomi Tom, Ben had walked to the corral fence where he was standing with his arms resting on the top pole. When he cried out, the Indian turned to peer hard at him. "How would you tame her, boy?" he asked harshly. "Did you ever break a horse?"

"I've helped break mustangs," he replied. "Johnny taught me how."

"I don't know who this Johnny is," Potawatomi Tom said, "but we're breaking horses for bluecoat cavalry riders. And they want the fear of man beat into 'em."

"Johnny broke mustangs for the cavalry at Fort Davis," Ben replied defensively, "but he didn't kill their spirits. Nor would I do so."

Potawatomi Tom stood silent for two or three minutes. Then he said, "All right, boy. Pick out one of them horses in there."

Ben had been watching a big cream-colored stallion that was nervously circling the pen, its head held high, nostrils flaring.

"That one," he said, pointing at the cream-colored horse.

Potawatomi Tom whistled softly. "The boldest of the lot, boy. He could kill you."

Mr. Cambridge spoke up for the first time. "Are you certain you want to try that horse, Ben?" Then he turned to face the Indian and continued, "He's just a boy, Tom. Maybe he was talking bigger than his britches."

"It's his to choose," Potawatomi Tom replied. "If he breaks the stallion, he gets the regular six bits pay."

"I'll need a horse and lariat," Ben said.

Potawatomi Tom raised an arm and whistled to Raymove, the young Osage. Then he signaled to the man in the wide-brimmed hat to guard the corral entrance. Raymove wheeled his horse and rode over to join them, and a few minutes later Ben was in the wrangler's saddle. He rode up and down the outside of the fence, testing the feel of the lariat. It was finely plaited rawhide, light and easy to throw.

The smells, the sounds, the horses, everything reminded him of his last weeks at Fort Davis when for the first time in his life Johnny and some of the soldiers were beginning to treat him like a grown-up instead of an abandoned brat.

He kept Raymove's horse walking slowly while he grew more and more impatient waiting for the bald-headed man to finish saddling the bay he was breaking. Meanwhile Potawatomi Tom had mounted and moved around to the corral entrance to take the other breaker's place. When the Indian pulled the rope aside, Ben rode in slowly, trying to remember every action that Johnny made when he approached a wild mustang.

Within minutes he had the cream-colored stallion cornered. After one awkward throw with the lasso, he spun a loop that held its circle flawlessly, dropping around the stallion's head, but it slipped back over the animal's ears.

"If he had horns, you'd trapped him," Raymove shouted.

On the next throw, Ben dropped a perfect loop around the perfect neck of the stallion. Dismounting quickly he pulled on the rope with all his strength. The horse reared, then fell back, its breathing growing hoarser as the lariat tightened against its heavy throat muscles. Now it was almost in a sitting posture, its front feet flailing like a boxer's arms, with an accompanying crescendo of snorts, grunts, and bellows.

"Hobble him," Potawatomi Tom shouted from the entrance. "Hobble him!"

Ben heard Raymove's voice from behind him, "Tie his feet!"

Remembering then how Johnny always did it, Ben whipped the loose end of the lariat into a firm loop around the stallion's forefeet.

Without hesitating, he approached until his face was only inches from the horse's face. The animal's enlarged eyes stared directly into his. With his ungloved fingers, Ben touched its forehead gently and began rubbing the muzzle close to the nostrils. Although the horse flinched, he continued caressing up to its ears, playing around them, and then coming down, following the lay of its hairs. Now he began stroking the neck, quite firmly, speaking nonsense words in a slow babble. Johnny Hawkes had said that he always talked in Comanche, but Ben could remember only a few broken phrases, the meanings of which he had forgotten.

Slipping a hackamore very gently over the stallion's head, Ben leaned close enough to breathe into the flaring nostrils, as he had seen Johnny always do in the corral at Fort Davis. Again man and beast stared into each other's eyes, and then the horse lowered its muzzle to sniff Ben's hand.

When Ben released pressure on the horse's muzzle, it appeared to be less frightened. Freeing the forefeet, he tossed the lariat aside. Now he had only the hackamore with which to control the inspirited stallion.

Ben shouted to Raymove, "Bring me a saddle!"

In a moment the Osage boy brought a saddle, swinging it on his unbroken arm.

Ben had forgotten the boy's bound arm. "Here, hold him by the hackamore," he said to Raymove, "and I'll fasten the saddle."

"Stay, stay, stay," Potawatomi Tom called out as he came striding from the corral entrance. "I'll hold the stallion."

Roiled by the pressure of the saddle, the horse began twisting from side to side, kicking furiously. Ben talked softly to the animal, tightening the saddle all the while until it was securely fastened.

He turned to Potawatomi Tom. "If you'll bridle him, I'll ride him."

"You could wait till he's got the feel of the saddle," the Indian said. "An hour or so maybe."

"Johnny always says don't give a wild horse time to ponder about it. Saddle and ride, he says."

Potawatomi Tom shook his head. "This stallion," he whispered hoarsely, "can throw you so far you can't get back in time for your own funeral."

Ben was tempted to give in, but by this time he'd beaten his own fear away, and he did not want any interval of doubt in which to think about getting onto the saddle.

As soon as the stallion was bridled, he mounted in one steady movement. The horse stood stock still as though in shock—astonished, enraged, frightened. Ben held the bridle tight, guiding the cream-colored animal toward the corral exit. The horse shot out into the pasture, stopped abruptly, and began bucking, high, then low, then high. Ben kept talking to the horse, the way Johnny always did, informing it profanely that the weight on its back was its master. Suddenly the stallion began to run, loping at first, then quickening to a gallop. After a hundred yards, Ben bent forward to hold his old dragoon hat in front of the stallion's eyes. The horse slowed to a walk, then halted.

Ben turned the stallion back toward the corral and let it canter the last few yards. Potawatomi Tom and Raymove were both there waiting for him. When he dismounted, Raymove caught the bridle and started leading the tamed horse over to a holding pen.

"Who told you about horses' noses, boy?" Potawatomi Tom asked Ben.

"What do you mean?"

"Your breath in that stallion's nose didn't tame him," the Indian went on. "Old Boog Young over there always wipes his hands under his armpits before rubbing them on a wild horse's nose, but that don't tame 'em. It's just Old Boog showing off his horse-taming tricks for anybody happens to be watching."

"My friend Johnny Hawkes taught me to breathe in a wild mustang's nostrils," Ben said.

"It does nothing," Potawatomi Tom insisted. "But along the way you learned that a horse uses its nose to feel with, the way we use our hands to feel with." The Indian's scarred lip lifted in a half smile. "You want to break some more horses for me, boy?" He asked in his unemotional rasping voice.

"Regular pay?"

"Regular pay," the Indian replied.

During the morning two more horse breakers came in. At noontime the work stopped, and Mr. Cambridge invited Ben to come up to the house to share a meal. "You brought no victuals, son, and likely Potawatomi Tom's got none to spare, so you be my guest."

Never in his life had Ben seen such a luxurious and splendidly appointed dining room as the one Mr. Cambridge brought him into. Although he had dusted his clothes and splashed water on his hands and face in his washroom, he felt ill at east at first. Along one wall of the dining room was an enormous sideboard filled with glass and silver containers, and on the opposite were large gilt-framed paintings of hunting scenes and several portraits of handsome men and beautiful women.

Mr. Cambridge evidently sensed Ben's unease, and he tried to reassure him by asking questions about his origins, not prying, but expressing admiration for his many qualities at so young an age, and inquiring about his experiences at the Texas army post on the far frontier.

"You said you were an orphan," Mr. Cambridge remarked. "Was your father in the army?"

"No, sir," Ben replied. "He was on his way to California to prospect for gold when my mother died on the trail—so I was told later. I was not quite five years old. He was traveling alone then and decided to leave me at Fort Davis with a sergeant and his wife."

"And your father is not still living?"

"I don't know. He sent letters sometimes to Sergeant Peddicord, but then they stopped."

They were interrupted by the entrance of a lanky, slightly bowed black man with a head of close-cropped gray hair, who served them steaming dishes from covered silver bowls. He moved silently through the entire meal, his eyes never meeting Ben's.

Mr. Cambridge toyed with the broiled trout on his plate. "Extraordinary," he said. "And this Johnny you talk about, the horse tamer. Who is he?"

"Oh, Johnny Hawkes is not just a horse breaker. He was a scout for the cavalry at Fort Davis. He knows Indian talk. Kiowa and Comanche, some Cheyenne. He's always looked after me."

"Where is he now?"

Ben hesitated until he'd finished the buttered johnnycake that was the most delicious cornbread he could remember ever tasting. After he took a swallow of sweet milk, he decided to tell Mr. Cambridge where Johnny was. He told first about the mustang, Little Jo, and how the Union Army had seized the horse at Pea Ridge and put a U.S. brand on it, and then how Johnny had recognized Little Jo in the remount corral at Springfield and took him back without so much as a by your leave. And then how later, at Rolla, Johnny was arrested for stealing a horse that was army property and put in jail. "The Union soldiers also took my mustang," Ben continued, "but I never found it again."

"My, my," Mr. Cambridge said, "so your friend Johnny is in the calaboose at Rolla for stealing his own horse. It's just like the damned Yankees to do that." He wiped his lips with a linen handkerchief. "I expect, young Ben, that you and your friend Jack and that Oriental camel driver had best stay here at my place until Mr. Johnny gets freed from jail, or escapes, and catches up to you. When the Yankees take a prisoner they're likely to keep him as long as the French kept the Count of Monte Cristo."

"For years and years!" Ben cried in dismay.

"You know the story?"

"Miz Sergeant Peddicord read it to me."

Mr. Cambridge laughed. "Your experience of life constantly amazes me," he said. "You *will* stay until we can learn something about your friend Johnny's prospects, won't you?"

Ben took another swallow of the delectable sweet milk. "As soon as Captain Lightfoot finds out that Johnny is locked up, he'll get him out. You see, Captain Lightfoot wants the camels in St. Louis as soon as they can be driven there. And I gave my word to Johnny that I'd see that Hadjee delivers them, no matter what. I'll stay here with your permission another day or two to earn some money breaking horses—to buy victuals and feed—but then we must travel on to St. Louis."

Mr. Cambridge carefully folded his napkin and smiled at Ben. "Well spoken," he said. "I take it this Captain Lightfoot is a Yankee officer."

"Yes, sir."

A tall clock at the end of the dining room struck one. Ben hurriedly placed his silverware on the plate and stood up. "I'd better get back to the corral, sir. Are you coming down?"

"No. First, a wee nap to recuperate my heartiness and then I shall stroll over to the schoolhouse to observe the thespians at rehearsals. Will you be attending the play this evening? To see your friend Jack's performance as singer?"

"Oh, I'd almost forgotten. Yes, I have never seen a real show. Just the shows the soldiers performed at Fort Davis." He picked up his dusty flop-brimmed hat, noticing for the first time its shabbiness. "Sir, I don't know how to figure Potawatomi Tom," he said abruptly. "He looks Indian, but he don't act or talk Indian."

Mr. Cambridge had also risen from his dining chair. "He's a remarkable mixture. Some missionaries adopted him when he was an orphaned child. Sent him off to school in the East. He has the educated brain of a white man in the body of an Indian only one jump from savagery. He's a man of his word and honest as the day is long. But there's a cruel streak in his nature. Don't cross him."

During the afternoon Ben broke four horses, one of which was a persistent bucker. Before it finally accepted saddle and rider, Ben's nose was bleeding profusely from the jolting. Potawatomi Tom made him sit in the shade for an hour before tackling another wild horse.

When the sun dropped below the rim of the ridge on which the Cambridge house stood, the horse breakers called it a day, and Ben trudged back across the road and up the slope of the pasture to the cabins. Only Hadjee was there, and he let Ben know somewhat peevishly that Queen Elizabeth Jones and everyone else had gone away and left him with nothing to eat.

In the cart Ben found enough bits and pieces of meats and bread to make a cold supper. While they were eating, he noticed at the end of the row of sheds a hand pump that emptied into an old wooden trough that could be used for bathing.

After pumping the trough full of water, he removed his clothes and shook them free of dust accumulated in the corral. The trough leaked, but he pumped water to its brim and then climbed in and stretched out with his head against the wooden brace. At first the water stung with its subterranean iciness, but after a few moments the coldness permeated his weary muscles and aching bottom, and he felt much better.

He had just closed his eyes when he heard feminine voices,

growing louder as two young persons in strange and brightly colored costumes rounded the end of the sheds, not twenty paces from the water trough. He recognized Queen Elizabeth Jones at once, although she was dressed in very tight red bombazine trousers and a black jacket. Her face was dusted with some kind of powder. The young woman with her was wearing a grass-green dress and a dark green bonnet with a large feather in it, and she was smiling mischievously at the startled Ben.

"You go ahead, Jack," the young woman said to Queen Elizabeth Jones. "I'll wait here."

When Queen Elizabeth Jones approached the water trough, Ben sat up hastily and leaned forward to cover part of his nakedness.

Motioning to the young woman behind her, Queen Elizabeth Jones said, "This is Miss Katy Burton, Ben. She taught me two new songs today."

"Jack sang them both beautifully," Miss Katy Burton declared. "His voice is well suited to the songs of Stephen Foster."

"We came to invite you to the show," Queen Elizabeth Jones said. "Mr. Goodloe gave me a pass for you." She slipped a card from a pocket of the black jacket and offered it to him. "Hadjee can come, too, if he wants to."

"I'm wore out," Ben said wishing the water would quit leaking so fast out of the trough. He took the ticket with wet fingers and laid it on the wooden brace behind him.

"Mr. Cambridge told me you was breaking horses," she said. "Did you get throwed any?"

"Once or twice."

Queen Elizabeth Jones stood silent for a minute, looking aslant from the trough to spare him embarrassment. His face was red as fire.

"They was nice to me, Ben," she said, "but I wanted to go see the horse breaking. I'll bet I can break horses as good as you can."

Miss Katy Burton interrupted. "We'd better start back. Many things to do."

Queen Elizabeth Jones started to turn away, then said, "You come see the show now, Ben."

"Where is it?"

"In the schoolhouse. Other side the railroad depot."

"Maybe," he said.

Hadjee declined the invitation to attend the performance, explaining in his mixture of words and signs that unless the show was spoken in Egyptian or French he would fall asleep as soon as the actors began speaking.

Ben took his spare shirt from the saddlebags in the cart, smoothed out the wrinkles as he pulled it on, and fastened the loops all the way to the collar. He had just finished wetting and combing his hair when the lanky, gray-haired black man, who had served him food at noon, emerged from the gathering twilight.

"Mr. Cambridge he want you, Master Ben, to go with him," the black man said. "To the show."

"Tell him I have a pass," Ben replied. "The thespians gave me a ticket."

The black man was silent for a minute, then said, "You better come with me, Master Ben, back to house. When Mr. Cambridge say you do something, you better do it."

Ben responded with a puzzled laugh. "All right, I'll come."

A two-horse carriage was waiting at the side door when Ben and the black man arrived at the house. Mr. Cambridge stood just inside the open doorway, impatiently tapping his walking stick on the brick flooring. He was dressed in a fine-woven black broadcloth suit and was wearing a tall beaver hat. "Come inside, Ben," he said and pointed to a shirt, a pair of trousers, and a coat all neatly folded on a chair. Nearby on the floor were several pairs of boots. "I think you are about my size," Mr. Cambridge added. "Try these on."

Except for the boots, which were too tight for him, and the trousers, which were too loose in the waist, the clothing was wearable for him, but he was decidedly ill at ease in trappings that were too scrumptious for his tastes. While riding beside Mr. Cambridge in the carriage, he listened politely to his elderly host's description of the play they were to see. The dramatics were to take place in a forest, the old man said, with many misunderstandings and hidden identities, an evil duke and a good duke, and a beautiful girl dressed as a boy. Ben wondered to himself if any of the thespians suspected that Jack Bonnycastle was a girl dressed as a boy; perhaps they had chosen her in some sort of mocking way to sing for this play.

When the carriage stopped at the redbrick schoolhouse of Travelers Repose, a considerable crowd was already gathered outside. The black man, who was serving as coachman, stepped down to assist Mr. Cambridge out of the vehicle, and Ben felt very conspicuous when several people greeted the old man and then stared curiously at him.

From out of the crowd, the slender dark-haired young man named Goodloe came to take Mr. Cambridge's arm, leading him into the schoolhouse, with Ben close behind. They entered a large room filled with benches, stools, and chairs, many of which were already occupied by people of all ages facing a small platform across which a plain black curtain was drawn. Goodloe led them to the middle of the very first row of seats. He pointed Mr. Cambridge to a large leather-covered horsehair chair. Undoubtedly it had been procured by the thespians as a gesture of thanks to Mr. Cambridge for his generosity in providing them with lodgings during their stay in Travelers Repose. With a little bow to Goodloe, who was already vanishing upon the darkened stage, Mr. Cambridge simultaneously waved Ben into a wicker chair beside him.

Within a few minutes the room was totally filled with people murmuring and laughing. Two young women in green costumes, with strange-shaped yellow bonnets on their heads, appeared through a narrow opening in the curtain. One carried a pair of lighted lanterns that she placed at opposite sides of the proscenium; the other carried a small torch with which she lit candles set behind tin reflectors for footlights. While the two young women continued around the room extinguishing lanterns on the walls, a man clad in billowing striped pants with the bottoms tied above the knees stood suddenly upon the proscenium, holding his arms aloft to silence the audience. Although he wore an enveloping feathered cap that concealed his hair, Ben recognized him as the pink-haired actor named Shoemaker.

"Ladies and gentlemen," Shoemaker began, "this evening we present for your approval a young boy whose voice remains sweet with the richness of youth. He will sing for us between the acts of *As You Like It*. And now before the play begins, young Master Jack Bonnycastle will render a favorite by Mr. Stephen Foster."

Slipping shyly through the curtain, Queen Elizabeth Jones bowed to the actor and then to the audience. Ben felt a certain pride in the way she stood so composed in the neat black jacket and tight red trousers. As soon as Shoemaker vanished through the curtain, she began singing, with no accompanying voices or instruments, "Come Where My Love Lies Dreaming."

The music of her voice filled the crowded room. When she finished there was a sudden hush, a total absence of sound. Then the applause broke out, cries and poundings and clapping of hands. Mr. Cambridge shouted several "bravos" before turning to Ben. "Your friend Jack has a remarkable voice, indeed," he said. "A pity he must lose it when his masculinity becomes ascendant and extinguishes it."

The curtains parted abruptly to reveal the painted scenery of an orchard. The actor Shoemaker, as Orlando, accompanied by another of the young male thespians, strolled upon the stage, Orlando giving a long opening speech. Two more males joined the first pair, and after a bit of animated dialogue the curtain closed for a scenery change.

In the second scene Ben was surprised to see Miss Katy Burton, who had caught him bathing in the water trough that afternoon. She was playing Celia to Rosalind. While the two young women conversed, a torpor began permeating Ben's lower limbs, spreading upward through the weary muscles of his body. He fought to keep his eyes open, and came wide awake when Shoemaker, or Orlando, cheered on by Miss Katy Burton, or Celia, engaged in a very realistic wrestling match with an actor playing Charles. After that, Ben fell sound asleep, to be awakened at the end of the first act by loud applause.

For a minute or so members of the audience chattered and stretched themselves, and then there in front of the curtain was Queen Elizabeth Jones again. With her this time was Goodloe in green tights, a banjo in his arms. The song was "Ring, Ring, the Banjo," and Ben could tell that Queen Elizabeth Jones was truly enjoying herself, stamping briskly with one foot to the beat of Goodloe's banjo and the song's natural rhythm.

At the end the audience howled for more, and the pair repeated a stanza before hurrying off as the curtain parted upon scenery of the Forest of Arden.

Although Mr. Cambridge, sunk deep into his horsehair chair, muttered occasional fragments of approval, Ben guessed that the

old man was also growing sleepy. At the end of Queen Elizabeth
Jones's song, Mr. Cambridge repeated the word *castrazione* two or
three times. "Casanova would know," he muttered. "In Italy that
singer would be one, unless like Rosalind she need not be." In later
years, Ben would smile when he remembered the old man's loud
whispering, but at that time, what Mr. Cambridge was saying
meant nothing to him. Through the remainder of the performance
of that Shakespeare play, sleep from weariness blotted out everything except the entr'acte songs and a dream sequence of himself
rising and falling in a saddle. While Rosalind was bidding the audience farewell, Mr. Cambridge shook him awake.

During the following morning, Ben broke three more horses, and
then there were no more to be tamed. Soon after sunrise two uniformed U.S. cavalry officers, accompanied by a dozen or so private
soldiers, had arrived to inspect the herd and choose mounts for the
army. Before noon the first detachment of horses and men began
moving northeastward on the highway toward St. Louis, a city that
Ben had learned from Potawatomi Tom was a long fifty miles distant.

At noontime Mr. Cambridge and his black servant brought
down a pair of iron pots containing beef stew and beans, with
several loaves of freshly baked bread. Mr. Cambridge's attitude
toward the Union officers was rather standoffish, but he did not
appear to begrudge them servings of the savory food. The old man
sought out Ben, inquiring if he had received any news of Johnny
Hawkes and insisting that he and his singing friend, Jack Bonnycastle, remain as his guests at Travelers Repose until some news
came from Rolla. "I shall make discreet inquiries through the Rolla
authorities," Mr. Cambridge added.

Ben promised to talk with Jack Bonnycastle about the offer that
evening.

Early in the afternoon, after Mr. Cambridge returned to his
house, Ben noticed that Potawatomi Tom had separated half a
dozen of the best-looking horses from the herd and placed them in
the rail-fenced holding pen. Among them was the cream-colored
stallion, the first horse he had tamed on the previous day.

When Ben saw the Indian had a free moment, he asked him
what he meant to do with the special horses.

"Sell 'em," Potawatomi Tom replied. "For more money than the cavalry will pay. In the morning me and Raymove will start 'em up to Pacific City where we will make a sale at the railroad stables."

"How much for the cream stallion?" Ben asked.

The Indian turned to look at the horses in the pen. "He's the best of the lot. He'll be bid up plenty." He ran a gloved finger across his scarred lip. "I reckon he's your pick, huh."

Ben nodded and then asked, "Do you aim to pay me today for my breaking?"

Potawatomi Tom frowned as if he'd been offended by the question. "You can have your pay now," he replied coldly.

"How much more would you want besides my pay? For the stallion?"

The Indian's expression was still hostile. "More'n you've got, boy."

"Will you trade for a donkey and cart, added to my pay?"

Potawatomi Tom sniffed as if he smelled a foul odor. Before he could reply, one of the cavalry officers came up with a handful of yellow sheets of paper attached to a wooden shingle. "I've got my figgers ready, Tom," the officer said.

Ben stepped aside, disappointed, wondering if he shouldn't just ask for his pay and go back up to the sheds and see if Queen Elizabeth Jones was there. He had turned his back on Potawatomi Tom when the Indian spoke roughly to him, "Where's your donkey and cart, boy?"

"Other side of Mr. Cambridge's house."

"Go bring 'em down here so I can see 'em."

When Ben brought the donkey and cart down to the pens, he had to wait several minutes for Potawatomi Tom to complete his business with the cavalry officers and pay off the horse breakers. The Indian offered to pay Ben, but Ben refused, saying he wanted to trade for the cream stallion.

"I didn't say I'd swap for that toothless old donkey," Potawatomi Tom replied crustily, "and that creaky worm-eaten Mexican cart."

Ben remained silent while he waited patiently for the Indian to examine the animal and the vehicle. Raymove had joined them and apparently was fascinated by the rig.

After checking the harness and the cart's wheels, and then the teeth and hooves of the donkey, Potawatomi Tom turned to Ben. "I'll trade you that little roan mare in the pen and let you keep a dollar of your pay."

"I don't want the little roan," Ben replied. "I want the stallion or nothing."

Potawatomi Tom gave him a fierce Indian scowl. "Damn you, boy, you're more stubborn than me." He took a deep breath and exhaled loudly. "All right. The stallion's yours."

"Done," Ben said. "If you'll throw in one of the old saddles you've got in your wagon."

That evening Ben did not attend the play, which was *The Taming of the Shrew*. He was too excited about his acquisition of the cream-colored stallion to think about anything else. Soon after sundown he saddled the horse and went for a ride around the pasture. By the time the stars came out, he was too sleepy to think about going to the schoolhouse, and a minute after he lay down in the shed beside Abednego he was sound asleep.

Late in the night he was awakened by a low growl from the dog, followed by a shushing voice, and then he felt a hand gentle against one side of his face. "Ben," Queen Elizabeth Jones whispered, "wake up. I must talk with you."

He sighed and sat up, pulling his blanket around his torso, noticing at once in the slant of moonlight that she was not wearing the stage costume but instead was clad in the oversized kersey cavalry trousers that the widow Lizzie Starbird had given her.

"They're going to Rolla tomorrow," she said.

"Who?" he asked, yawning widely.

"The acting company. They want me to go with them."

"To Rolla?"

"That's what I said."

"Are you going with them?"

She was silent for several moments. "Do you think I should dare?" she asked. "I have had a pleasurable time with them, and except for that rude Arthur Pound they've all been sweet as pie to me. Mr. Goodloe promised that if the company holds together through wartime that this winter I can sing at their performances in St. Louis. If I go with them to Rolla, what are you going to do, Ben?"

"Oh, I'm starting with the camels to St. Louis tomorrow."

When she brought her face closer to his, her eyes appeared liquid in the moonlight. "If I go to Rolla with the actors," she said, "and that old Marshal Baines sees me, he'll for sure throw me in jail. Thunderation, if we only knew if Johnny's still there. Wouldn't it be sickening if I passed him on the road?"

"Well, I'm sure not going back to Rolla. Maybe you better not either."

She sucked air through her teeth with a whistling sound. "Yeah. Soon enough the actors will find out I'm a girl, and that would change everything. The men are beginning to quarrel, too, about the war. I thought Mr. Goodloe and Mr. Shoemaker would come to blows at rehearsal yesterday. Mr. Goodloe said if he joined for the war he'd go back to Tennessee and ride with General Forrest. Mr. Shoemaker called him a traitor. Miss Katy Burton had to make them stop. And then Arthur Pound laughed at both of them and said if they had any sense they'd run off to Canada or England like he was going to do to get away from the war."

"Look," Ben said, "Mr. Cambridge offered to let us stay here till we get some word from Johnny. He also said he was going to make inquiries at Rolla. If he does that he'll just stir up the army and the lawmen. We wouldn't be safe here."

She muttered a word or two that may have been profane and then said, "If you're traveling on tomorrow, I reckon I will, too." She laughed softly. "Anyway, we've got some tin in our pockets. Mr. Goodloe paid me an extra dollar. How much did you earn breaking horses?"

"Some," he said, "but I don't have any of it left."

Her face moved even closer to him, her eyes peering hard into his in the moonlight as if she were trying to determine whether or not he was bantering with her.

"You didn't look in the stock pen when you came back from the show?" he asked.

"No, why should I?"

"I traded for a horse," he replied. "A stallion. A beauty."

She said, "I want to see him." She grabbed Ben's arm and tried to pull him to his feet, and his blanket fell away, and when she looked back at him she cried, "Criminee, you're naked as a new-born jaybird!" and went out the door.

He pulled on his shabby dragoon trousers, and with Abednego at this heels he followed her to the enclosed yard at the end of the sheds. She stood by the rail fence, admiring the stallion. The animal looked almost white in the moonlight.

"He's a beauty all right," she said.

"I had to trade the donkey and the cart away, too," he said.

"No! But they belong to Johnny. He bought them with his poker winnings."

Ben laughed. "If Johnny'd been here, he'd've done the same as I did. That stallion is worth ten donkeys and carts. Potawatomi Tom said he was the best of the lot."

Queen Elizabeth Jones's gray horse came to the fence, offering its nose to her, and then curiosity brought the cream stallion to come close enough for Ben to reach its shoulder. The horse shivered under his touch and drew away with a loud snort.

"He's afraid of you, Ben."

"No. He remembers the smell of his master, but he still has his spirit. Three days ago he was a wild horse."

The moon was lowering in the sky and the stars seemed bigger and brighter against the blackness above.

"How long do you reckon till first light?" Ben asked.

"Some time yet, I guess. After we came back from the schoolhouse, I heard Mr. Goodloe say it was midnight. That was a while ago. I couldn't sleep, wondering if I ought to go with them tomorrow. Now that's settled, but I'm still not sleepy."

"I'm not either," he said. "No use trying now." Again he looked with pride at the stallion. It stood with its head pointed at the resting camels placidly chewing their cuds beside the wall of the shed. "Let's wake Hadjee," he said, "and get on the road to St. Louis. The moon may stay up till the sun rises."

She reached for him with both arms, squeezing his neck and kissing him hard on the cheek. " 'Forward, I pray,' " she recited, " 'since we have come so far. Be it moon or sun or what you please.' "

Ben had not attended *The Taming of the Shrew*, nor did he know that Queen Elizabeth Jones had spent the previous afternoon helping Miss Katy Burton rehearse her speeches for the role of Katherina. Therefore he had no idea what she was babbling about, but he was happy to know she would not be joining the Valley Shakespeare Company and instead would be riding with him to St. Louis.

XXVII

BEN BUTTERFIELD

~

This morning, as I sit here at old Man Fagerhalt's desk, I am wondering if I allowed the events of yesterday afternoon to move faster and farther than was prudent. Or should I rationalize the occurrence as an act of God in the form of a sudden cyclone with cloudburst, or take comfort that self-determination was at work, that it was comparable to what happened between Adam and Eve in the Garden, neither person being more or less blameworthy than the other.

Some responsibility must rest upon the Omicron Eclectic Society, which set the scene. This society meets four times a year, each event occurring at the beginning of one of the four seasons. In autumn the members gather in the Blythe farm's woods above the river at Crystal Hill; in winter they go indoors at the Grimsley House; in spring they meet on the screened verandas of the Crowninshield home on the Arch Street pike; in summer they go boating and swimming at Manlove's Anchorage.

The present season being summer, yesterday's ritual of the Omicron Eclectic Society moved inexorably as clockwork to the Anchorage. Early in the morning two of Percy Manlove's dray wagons, canvas-covered and filled with clean straw, and two buggies for the more elderly members, were drawn up before his blacksmith shop and livery stable on Lincoln Avenue. There the society members gathered leisurely by various means of transport. I had thought the Sisters Grimsley might travel out to the Anchorage in their Columbia Electric, but no, both came to the assembly point by streetcar, wearing purple bloomers, eager to ride in one of the *hay wagons. Annie Grimsley told Hilda and me that they feared the turnoff road from the highway to the boat landing was too rocky for the machine's tires.*

Percy Manlove is an honorary member of the Omicron Eclectic Society, and he attends only the summer session, being uninterested, he has said frankly, in the speechifications that accompany such gatherings. Percy owns the largest smithy and livery stable in town, as well as several dray wagons and other vehicles, and he also built the Anchorage on a knoll at the mouth of the stream that runs quite gently, most of the time, through his woodland to the river. The Anchorage is a roofed pavilion decorated with ornamental scrollwork done in his blacksmith shop. Inside the Anchorage on the brick flooring are tables and benches meant for picnicking. Upstream on the left bank, along which a narrow road runs from the highway to the pavilion, are small wooden stands spaced a furlong or so apart where boaters can tie up and climb a few steps to a bench and railing. These places are meant for resting, fishing, contemplating nature or passing boats, and cuddling or philandering. About two miles upstream near the highway is a small boathouse with a dozen rowboats that Percy rents. Most boaters paddle to the pavilion and then row back upstream, stopping occasionally along the way. Some prefer to leave the boats at the Anchorage from where they are hauled back to the boathouse in a wagon.

No further explanation is needed to make it clear that Percy Manlove is indispensable for the success of the summer session of the Omicron Eclectic Society. He refuses to accept any payment for use of his equipment and facilities. I have heard it said that Percy considers his contributions to be excellent advertising for his businesses, but it is my opinion that he is in awe of the leading members of the society and feels that somehow he will be rewarded, not in legal tender but in social standing, by opening up to them the lares and penates of his element. Yet this does not explain why he fails to attend the other seasonal meetings, unless it is his air of being unable to measure up to his peers, a demeanor almost of subservience whenever he believes himself to be out of his mileau.

The origins of the Omicron Eclectic Society are amorphous in my mind. I have heard Miss Ivy Crowninshield say more than once that someday in her capacity as permanent secretary she is going to write up the history of the society's founding and publish it with its peculiar bylaws that are in her possession. From what I've heard through snatches of recollections, the society was founded in the years immediately following the Civil War. The founders' objective was to meet occasionally for the purpose of discussing cultural topics and thus get their minds off the distressing subjects of the postwar malaise. Among the founders were August Crowninshield, now a wealthy, aging lawyer; Felix Markham, who is Lucy Markham's father-in-law, Hereward Padgett's deceased father; the late carpetbagger Grimsley who fathered the sisters; Guy Blythe, Sr.; Dr. Henry Mortmain; and two or three others whose names I do not recall at the moment.

One of Brigadier Preston Boggs's deepest regrets is that he was not present at the time of the founding and therefore had to become a member by election. Old Man Fagerhalt was also a member by election, his membership passing to Hilda at his death. The society's rules allow each member to bring one guest to the meetings, and as I am not a member I attend as Hilda's guest.

On the occasion of yesterday Hilda was not especially enthusiastic at first about going to the Anchorage. Soon after sunrise both the temperature and humidity began rising by the numbers. After grumbling her usual phrases about the summer heat, Hilda announced that she was going to close the hardware store for the day and attend the society meeting at the Anchorage because she expected that the open pavilion would afford her cooling breezes from the river yet shield her from the burning sun. As for joining the boat excursion, she warned me that she would have none of that. Pesky flies and other insects, sunburn, broiling heat, and blistered hands if we rowed. No, no, she would leave boating to me and such fools as Hereward Padgett and the Sisters Grimsley.

As it turned out, when the canvas-covered hay wagons turned off the highway to the boathouse, Hereward Padgett and the gap-toothed girl, whose name I can never remember, were the first of the couples to drop off the wagon behind ours. I was with Hilda in the forward wagon, in which among others were Ivy Crowninshield, the Sisters Grimsley, and Lucy Markham.

When Hereward and the gap-toothed girl turned toward the boathouse, I was surprised to see Letitia Higgins join them. I could

not recall ever seeing Letty at any previous Omicron Eclectic Society meetings and wondered if she was a guest of Hereward or of
the gap-toothed girl, both of whom are members. Letty and the
gap-toothed girl were wearing white navy blouses, blue navy caps,
and bloomers with wide vertical black and white stripes.

The Sisters Grimsley in their purple bloomers were the first to
leave our wagon, and I quickly decided the diplomatic thing for
me to do before following them was to beg Hilda to reconsider
and join me in a boat ride to the Anchorage rather than continue
there in the wagon. I could see that her cold green eyes were riveted
upon the full haunches of Maude Grimsley and I guessed that she
might be speculating whether they appealed in some seductive way
to me.

Hilda refused to accompany me, however, and I dropped down
from my perch in the hay, feeling slightly guilty for offering myself
as a lure to a platoon of bloomer-clad females in search of male
oarsmen. Upon setting foot on the ground I almost changed my
mind. The air had turned decidedly sultry and oppressive, and the
westward sky above the tree line along the stream was beginning
to boil with young thunderheads. I heard someone say, "It looks
like a rainstorm," and I actually turned around to start back to
the wagon, but the vehicle was already moving. I saw Lucy Markham waving to me, and then Hilda waved in that jerky way of
hers. I should have run hard to catch up with it, but I did not.
Around such indecision man's fate is often woven.

At the boathouse I found Hereward Padgett hurrying about,
beseeching every male in sight to join him as a fellow oarsman in
a four-passenger boat. When he saw me, he plunged toward me
like a jaybird diving for a grain of corn. Chortling in his usual
foolish manner, Hereward slapped me upon the back and declared
that I was just the fellow he was looking for. After all, he added,
I had been Letitia Higgins's dancing partner many times, and I'd
make a good oarsman for her. Hereward remembers everything.
He remembered that he'd seen me riding with Letitia in the Columbia Electric, she in my lap. Hereward even remembered to say
that he knew Hilda wouldn't mind the tiniest bit if I rowed as
Letty's partner in a boat race to the Anchorage.

I must admit that I did not mind the tiniest bit being in such
closeness to so enticing a bit of flesh as Letitia Higgins in her

breast-revealing white navy blouse and the striped bloomers that were remindful of the short britches I had seen used as costumes by members of the Valley Shakespeare Company so many years ago at Travelers Repose, Missouri. The angle she wore her blue navy cap gave her a most alluring appearance, and there was a glint in her dark eyes I had never seen there before. Or was it just my imagination? Her husband, Yancey, she quickly informed us (or me) was far down in the Saline bottoms with a timber-marking crew and would not be back until after dark.

The boat race to the Anchorage, so dearly desired by Hereward Padgett and the Sisters Grimsley, fell completely apart, mainly because Hereward has not the mental ability to organize anything. Yet he refused to allow the sisters or anyone else to take charge, and our boat was the last into the stream. Just ahead of us were the Grimsley Sisters in a boat expertly manned by two of Percy Manlove's young male employees. In a matter of minutes they were out of sight around the first big bend in the winding stream.

By this time the sky above us was darkening rapidly; the low clouds churned furiously and sudden fierce gusts of hot moist wind swept limbs of the bank willows almost down to the surface of the stream. We passed the first wooden stand, and from somewhere around a turn, I heard Maude Grimsley's hoarse voice. "How jolly," she called out. "I feel the first drops of rain!"

The gap-toothed girl, looking nervous, suggested to Hereward that he row faster. I joined him earnestly, but he kept assuring us that it was only a summer flurry and would quickly pass over. Once again we caught a glimpse of the sisters, but they were swept around another bend. And then came the first rumble of thunder, followed by a blast of chill wind.

I do not know how long Hereward and I dug our oars hurriedly into the water while storm winds and a deluge almost swamped us. In seconds we were soaked to the skin. Ahead through the opaque stream of rain I could see the outline of a wooden stand on the east bank and I yelled to Hereward for us to take what shelter it offered.

We had just turned out of the current when I heard the first sound of a falling tree, a root shriek that was almost human. It was a fairly large cottonwood, its foundation eroded by time and the stream. Attacked by too much force of wind, it fell slowly, almost reluctantly, directly down upon the stream. One branch, heavy with wet leaves, struck the boat amidships. All of us threw our weights in the same direction in reflex actions to escape harm. The boat was upset, either by us or the tree branch, and out we went into the water. Fortunately the current there was not swift, the depth not over six or seven feet. I remember seeing Hereward Padgett keeping his head above water by bouncing up and down with his toes on the sandy bottom. The two young women were both clinging to a tree limb. Letty had lost her sailor hat, and her wet hair clung to her neck and shoulders. Sheets of rain swept past, and then the downpour slackened to a gentle sprinkle. The boat, on its side and jammed into the fallen tree, bobbed rhythmically in the current.

I swam a few feet across to Letty and was surprised to find her less distraught than I had expected. She was all right, she said, except one of her ankles ached from a blow of some kind. I took her hand and swam with her to a gravelly shoal at the base of the wooden stand on the bank. Our canvas shoes squished when we stepped clear of the water. She laughed at the sound, then bent forward suddenly with a quiet "Oh."

Hereward and the gap-toothed girl soon joined us, and when they noticed Letty limping up the wooden steps to the stand, they volunteered to walk along the parallel road to the Anchorage and bring back one of the buggies for her. She protested, but after we made her remove her shoe and stocking so that we could examine her ankle, which was inflamed around the joint, she reluctantly agreed to wait with me in the stand until they returned. Hereward assured us that he would be back with the buggy in less than an hour.

After he and the girl plunged through the brush to reach the road, Letty sat down on the bench. She looked like a half-drowned kitten, her clothing so soaked that it clung like a wet glove to her body. An artist could have drawn her in silhouette as a nude. Her bounteous breasts were exposed almost to the nipples. She had removed her other shoe and stocking and was trying to wring water out of her striped bloomers by squeezing them above the knees. A water nymph, I thought to myself. A true Nereid. (I learned that word from reading Old Man Fagerhalt's book about polytheistic gods and spirits.)

And then rain began again, the drops large and heavy and cold. As there was no roof over the stand, I looked around for something to break the downpour. Back in the brush was a young pine. I broke off the lower limb and propped it above Letty's head. It was only a makeshift shelter. Her teeth began chattering, and then her whole body shook. She moved close beside me so that her wet flesh touched mine.

"I would cover you with my shirt," I said, "but it's as clammy as your blouse."

She moved even closer to me, seeking warmth, pressing herself around me.

Twenty-four hours afterward, I tell myself that it was Adam and Eve in the Garden. God did not stand between Adam and Eve. Nor did he stand between us.

XXVIII

BESIEGED IN PIPESTEM'S CAVE

~

As they left Travelers Repose they were aware of the moonlight changing subtly to dawn light. Along one side of the road were little bluffs of sandstone layered in amber and pink, the tints accentuated by the brightening light. Surrounding Ben on the cream-colored horse were two saddlebags stuffed full and a few cooking utensils tied on with rope. Queen Elizabeth Jones refused to burden her horse with any of the hodgepodge they had removed from the Mexican cart. She intimated that she was punishing Ben for trading away without permission property that belonged to Johnny Hawkes. Nor would she agree to use any of the money she had earned from the Valley Shakespeare Company to buy grain for Ben's horse. Barley for the camels and bacon and beans and bread for themselves she felt an obligation for, but if Ben was so foolish as to spend his last penny for a fine stallion, then he must find the means to feed it. Abednego was Ben's responsibility also, but she allowed that the dog was clever enough to fend for itself by stalking prairie chickens or catching some of the cottontail rabbits that occasionally crossed the road in front of them.

During the afternoon the cream-colored horse grew more and more restless, and when they made brief stops for water—where Ben would unbit the stallion for grazing—it refused to eat more than a nibble or two of grass no matter how green and lush it might be. The horse would snort, stamp its forward hoofs, shake its head, and glare reprovingly at Ben. He could not recall Potawatomi Tom feeding grain to any of the horses during the days they were in Mr. Cambridge's pasture, and he was certain that this deprivation was the reason for the stallion's behavior.

Late in the day they came upon the Iron Hill Trading Post, and Ben decided to make a supreme sacrifice. Contrary to Queen Elizabeth Jones's belief, he had not spent his last penny. He still possessed the half-dollar given him by Major Strawbridge, also a few smaller coins. And inside a hidden pocket of his dragoon tunic he carried the Mexican silver dollar that had come to him from the hands of Reverend Potts with the approval of Lydia Bright, both believing him to be one of the two living heirs of Brother Pursglove. Ben had never considered the silver coin to be his; he had secreted it away with some vague notion that somewhere and sometime in the future his path would converge with that of the true heir and that somehow he would recognize him. The coin was unfinished business, but the needs of his steed, the cream-colored horse tamed by his own nerve and brawn, demanded an immediate trade for grain.

And so it was that the Iron Hill Trading Post, a general store located near the railroad bridge across the Meramec River, was where Ben rid himself of the unfinished business of the Mexican silver dollar by exchanging it for oats, corn, and barley, and a few cents in change. When he handed the coin to the sour-faced merchant who waited on him, the man's eyes brightened perceptibly. After biting the dollar to make certain it was genuine, the merchant asked Ben if he had any more like it. "A young fellow new to the community," he explained, "offered me a premium for Mexicans."

Ben shook his head and felt suddenly uneasy. Perhaps he was perturbed by the forbidding countenance of the merchant, he told himself, the pale reptilian skin, the avaricious eyes.

They camped that evening on the bank of the Meramec, and Queen Elizabeth Jones surprised him by placing a small jug on a fallen log that they were using as a table. The jug contained wine that she had purchased at the trading post while Ben was buying grain for the animals.

"The man said his wife made the wine," she explained. "I gave him my pennies for it."

"You got it from the sallow-skinned looby? He may have sold you vinegar."

She shrugged. "He said it was Moselle, whatever that is. Taste it."

Ben took a plug from the top of the jug and sniffed at the released fragrance. "It smells like flowers," he said.

"It tastes like flowers," she retorted with a laugh.

"I've never eaten a flower," he said and took a long swallow from the jug. "A mite sourish," he declared. "Maybe it is vinegar."

Queen Elizabeth Jones, seated on the ground with her back against the log, called to Hadjee, and pointed to the jug. The Egyptian approached cautiously, almost suspiciously, his dark eyes shifting back and forth from the jug to the girl. When she lifted the jug, he pulled a pewter cup from a pocket of his striped blouse and held it out to her.

"Looks like water," Ben said, peering into the cup.

Hadjee swallowed it all, smacked his lips, and smiled at Queen Elizabeth Jones. *"Bon goût,"* he said, *"bon goût."* He held the cup out to her again. Meanwhile the camels, in hopes of receiving more barley, had followed him to the log. Queen Elizabeth Jones stood up to refill Hadjee's cup. She then turned and put both arms around Omar's neck and stared into the camel's eyes.

"Why does Omar have longer eyelashes than Tooley?" she asked. "Being as Tooley's a female she ought to have longer lashes. Like I have longer lashes than Ben." She lifted the jug, took another swig of wine, and then moved so close to Ben there were only inches between their faces. She touched one of his eyelashes and tugged at it until he pushed her hand away.

"What's the matter with you?" Ben asked her. "Babbling like a brat child."

"Look at my eyelashes," she ordered. "Longer than yours, but not as long as Omar's."

Ben glanced at Hadjee, who was shaking his head in puzzlement as he led the camels away.

"It's your turn to cook the beans," Queen Elizabeth Jones said, picking up the wine jar for another long swallow.

"All right," Ben replied. "But you start the fire. I'm going to give my cream horse one more bite of oats. I don't want him to eat too much grain at one time after living on grass for so long."

"Your *cream* horse," she said mockingly. "For God's sake, Ben, why don't you give that horse a name?"

"I have named him," he replied.

She stood with hands on hips, her head turned to one side, mouth slightly open in a slight smile, waiting for him to tell the name, but he did not speak.

"Well," she said, "is it a secret?"

"His name is Jack Bonnycastle."

Her face changed instantly. An expression of bewilderment quickly turned to anger. "You're trying to torment me, ain't you? You're still mad because I fooled you."

"No," he said. "I liked Jack Bonnycastle better than I like Queen Elizabeth Jones. So I named my horse for Jack, seeing as Jack's gone for good. You've been a smarty ever since you shared with the Shakespeare people."

She picked up the jug and drank three long swallows of the wine. "And I'm a dolthead," she groaned, "not to've gone on to Rolla with them. They treated me nicer'n anybody ever treated me in my whole life."

He spoke gently. "You'll get tipsy if you keep swigging that stuff." He paused a moment and added, "Start the fire while I'm feeding Jack Bonnycastle."

When he returned, she was lying with her head propped against the log, her eyes closed in sleep. After he started the fire, he took the almost empty wine jug to Hadjee.

That night he slept uneasily in his blanket roll, occasionally waking to stare at the multitude of stars in the glassy black sky. Each time he woke, he marked the passage of time by changes in the position of the Big Dipper. The sky was a starless charcoal when Queen Elizabeth Jones woke him not long before dawn. She was crying almost soundlessly and whispering, "What is to become of us, Ben? What is to become of us?" She lay very close to him, still whispering, "Hold me, Ben. Hold me. But not like Billy Good-heart did."

Soon after sunrise they were on the road again, climbing for a mile or more and then descending gradually into a valley checkered with woods and small fields. They came abruptly upon a slope that was so precipitous the road was laid out in zigzag fashion. Insisting on taking the lead, Queen Elizabeth Jones on Champ was at times only a few yards directly below Ben, who was riding in the rear.

She called up to him once. "Take a look at that big log house down there. The one backed up against a little knoll. See it?"

"Yes," he shouted back to her.

"There's a shed with a waterwheel under some trees nearby the house. Must be the gristmill the man at the trading post told us about."

"You want to stop there?"

She nodded and started Champ at a faster pace down the slope.

As they approached the log house, Ben noticed that the yard in front of it was filled with several small mounds of earth, varying in color from orange to dark red. When he first sighted the mounds they resembled anthills, but on coming closer he could see that they were excavated earth from round holes about the size of wagon wheels. Then he saw Queen Elizabeth Jones, who was far in front now, reining her horse to a quick stop a few yards in front of the gristmill. Two persons, a young man and a woman, holding rifles at the ready, suddenly appeared beside her horse.

Urging his mount past Hadjee and the camels, Ben hurried down the hill. The stallion shied away from a collapsed bridge of rotting logs and plunged across a narrow, swift-flowing stream that ran down to the mill wheel. When the horse hurtled up behind Queen Elizabeth Jones, the pair with rifles both shouted at Ben to halt.

Queen Elizabeth Jones appeared to be more flustered than frightened. She said hurriedly to Ben, "They asked if the Black Knight sent me."

"Did he?" the young woman demanded of Ben. "Did the Black Knight send you?" Her voice was a childish treble, so inconsistent with her pose of belligerence that he would have laughed had he not glanced past her at the young man who had his weapon in a firing position with Ben as the target. He appeared to be about nineteen or twenty, and his features reminded Ben of a fish because of his pale bulging eyes and the way he kept opening and closing his small mouth.

"We never heard of a Black Knight," Ben said politely. "We stopped here for some cornmeal."

About this time Hadjee and the camels, with Abednego at their heels, appeared out of the deep streambed. When Ben had made his dash down the hill, Abednego was off somewhere hunting, and the dog's face now bore the pained expression of one whose worth has been passed over or scorned.

"Balls afire," the girl squealed. "A circus, Li'l Daniel, a circus!" When Hadjee saw the two strangers brandishing their rifles, he had the presence of mind to halt the camels.

"You be careful, Joy," the young man warned her when she started toward the camels. "The Black Knight might've sent them beasts. You stay right there, Joy!" He kept the muzzle of his rifle moving back and forth from Ben to Queen Elizabeth Jones. The young girl, Joy, had lost all interest in them, however, and was totally absorbed in the camels. With her rifle pointed at the ground, she rocked back and forth on her bare feet like a runner preparing to leap forward on signal.

"I'm going to dismount," Ben said to the young man. "We don't mean to harm anybody. All we want is a bag of cornmeal and we'll be on our way."

The young man sucked in a deep breath and let it out in a half whistle. "Oh, all right. But we got only a wee bit of meal. Mr. Pipestem's so busy at his work he's had no time to grind. And me and Joy so busy digging for the buried gold and fending off the Black Knight, we had no time to grind either."

"You *can* spare us a *little* cornmeal?" Queen Elizabeth Jones asked. She also had dismounted.

"I reckon. I'll ask Joy."

But the girl had already disregarded his warning and was with Hadjee and the camels.

The young man sighed in exasperation, balanced his rifle in both hands, and said in a forlorn tone of voice, "I reckon you boys don't mean us no harm. You've just come back from the Crusades, ain't you, bringing them animals from the Holy Land?"

Ben did not know how to reply to this unexpected query. He glanced at Queen Elizabeth Jones, who rolled her eyes wonderingly but kept a straight face. They walked on to the camels with the young man between them, handling his rifle now as though it were an impediment. Hadjee's facial expression was one of total confusion.

"Looky here," the young man said, working his lips in his fishlike way, "I'll tell you who we are. I'm Daniel Boone." He pointed at the girl who was patting Omar's neck. "She's Joyous Gard."

Joyous Gard smiled prettily while Ben told the names of his party.

"I'm hungry," Joyous Gard said in her childish treble. "Mr. Pipestem promised to cook us some corn dodgers. You-all for sure are welcome to partake." She stepped close to Ben, still carrying her rifle muzzle down, and linked her free arm with his, tugging at him to accompany her. "You're a handsome boy, Mr. Butterfield. But too young for me, I 'spect."

Inside the gristmill, which was open on the side facing the road, a very lean man stood cooking over a sheet of heavy iron beneath which glowed a heap of orange-colored coals. He was Mr. Pipestem, and he was wearing butternut homespun that with the addition of lapels and pockets on the jacket would have resembled the brown uniforms that Ben had seen on some of the Confederate soldiers at Pea Ridge.

After two or three questions about the camels, Mr. Pipestem had little to say. He made no comment on Daniel Boone's explanation that the camels had come from the Holy Land and that the dark-skinned man with them was a captive taken by Crusaders. The skin on Mr. Pipestem's face was almost as dark as Hadjee's. It resembled finely dressed leather, drawn tight like a mask over frail bones of the jaws and nose. He seemed to take pride in serving an abundance of corn fritters to the three guests, and he kept pointing silently to a crock of butter and a large whiskey bottle filled with honey.

From time to time Ben slipped a piece of fritter to Abednego; no matter the sizes the dog swallowed them in a single gulp. After everyone appeared to have eaten sufficiently to satisfy Mr. Pipestem, he joined them at the solid oaken table, wolfing down several of his cakes and then bringing out a jug of cider and asking Joyous Gard to fill the cups. Leaning back in his chair, he finally remarked, "So you folk are traveling to St. Louis."

"Yes, sir, to deliver the camels," Ben replied.

"I shall be going to the city myself," Mr. Pipestem said. "In the morning, if Joy and Little Daniel and I can finish gathering enough fruit from my orchard to make a wagon load. They tell me fresh fruits are bringing high prices this year in St. Louis."

Joyous Gard tittered. "We'd a-picked enough yestiddy if the Black Knight had not come."

After waiting a moment for further explanation, Queen Elizabeth Jones asked impatiently, "Who is this Black Knight you and your brother keep talking about?"

"Li'l Dan'l ain't my brother," Joyous Gard cried out shrilly. "He's my one true love, Li'l Dan'l is." She grinned at Queen Elizabeth Jones, then her face darkened. "The Black Knight is evil. Li'l Dan'l says the Black Knight killed his own king in the Holy Land."

"What does he look like?" Queen Elizabeth Jones persisted.

"Oh, he looks like the devil. Scowling all the time and messing with our diggin's."

Daniel Boone interrupted. "He comes down here most every day, and if Joyous Gard and me are digging, he takes our tools and goes to digging himself."

Ben looked questioningly at Mr. Pipestem, who appeared to be unconcerned with what was being said. Ben asked him pointedly, "What is it you folks are digging for out there?"

"Oh." Mr. Pipestem seemed startled by the question. "Oh, that's Li'l Daniel's doing." He smiled suddenly, causing his parchment skin to break into deep wrinkles around his mouth and nose. "The boy claims to have a map," he explained, "a map showing where the first Daniel Boone buried some found Spanish doubloons, but I've never seen the map. He's most secretive."

While Mr. Pipestem was talking, Daniel Boone got up from his chair and announced that he was going to take a look into the hole that the Black Knight had dug on the previous day. As soon as he was out of earshot, Joyous Gard spoke up tremulously. "Li'l Daniel's name ain't Daniel Boone. But I took oath in blood I would never tell his real name to nobody. My name is not Joyous Gard neither, but I took no oath not to tell I was born Joy Chance."

She had left her chair and moved over to Ben and sat on the flooring at his feet beside Abednego. The dog was resting on its belly, pretending to sleep. "My, you are a handsome feller, Mr. Butterfield," she said, "but I'm promised to Li'l Dan'l."

Queen Elizabeth Jones interrupted, her tone almost rude. "Ben and me, we're not promised to nobody."

With a faint groan, as though the movement was a burden upon his muscles and bones, Mr. Pipestem jackknifed himself erect. He stretched his arms and said, "Well, we must be back to work, in the orchard, soon as we give our visitors a mess of cornmeal. Joy, you find the cornmeal and then round up Little Daniel and come help me gather fruit." He turned and started off at a rapid pace toward the rear door of the mill shed.

"Thank you for the fine dinner, Mr. Pipestem," Queen Elizabeth Jones called after him.

When Ben echoed her words, Mr. Pipestem waved one of his long, thin arms airily and disappeared through the door.

Joyous Gard went over to a wooden crib, took out a small bag of meal, and brought it to Ben. "We'll pay," Ben told her, but she shook her head, put the palm of her hand against her lips, and then placed it on his mouth, giggling. "No need to pay," she replied, trilling the words. "We going to be rich anyway soon as Li'l Dan'l finds the gold."

Daniel Boone, who had rejoined them, began begging them to stay another day, but they politely declined as they prepared to resume their journey to St. Louis. Hadjee had woken the camels and was urging them to their feet.

Ben and Queen Elizabeth Jones were tightening their saddles when a pounding of hooves drew their attention to a horseman zigzagging down the steep hill they had recently descended. After disappearing for a few moments behind a screen of willows, the horse and rider dipped into the streambed beside the broken-down bridge and reappeared directly in front of them.

"The Black Knight!" Daniel Boone shouted.

The rider was Billy Goodheart, and his mount was the same terror-stricken black horse they had last seen at Brother Pursglove's funeral.

Billy slowed to a walk, halted beside the camels, and peered down at Hadjee who was cowering on his knees. "I thought so," Billy growled and then turned to face Ben and Queen Elizabeth Jones who had quickly mounted. He pointed a finger at Ben. "It *was* you," he declared. "The trader at Iron Hill said the Mexican dollar come from a boy wearing old army clothes." He stopped to spit tobacco juice on the ground. "You and that she-panther there had them Mexican silver dollars hid somewheres all the time I been following you." He slipped his big pistol from his waist and pointed it at Ben. "I'll kill the whole lot of you if I have to. I want them Mex dollars now, or I start shooting."

At that instant a rifle fired, the bullet zinging into the trunk of a tree six feet from Billy Goodheart. He swore and spurred the black horse, but instead of springing forward the terrified animal reared and then spun around while Billy jerked cruelly at its bridle.

"Follow me, follow me!" Joyous Gard called in her shrill voice. The rifle she had just fired joggled in her hands. "Come on!"

When Ben turned his horse, he saw her and Daniel Boone both beckoning frantically. Queen Elizabeth Jones, frightened by Billy Goodheart's sudden appearance, was already urging Champ in the gristmill shed. Ben followed on the stallion. In less than a minute they were through the rear door, hurrying along a path beside the millstream, then turning abruptly at a left angle so that Ben was sure they would be trapped against the natural rock wall of the knoll. Instead they plunged through high weeds and brush, following Joyous Gard and Daniel Boone into a limestone cavern. The interior was illuminated by beams of sunlight coming through crevices above them and from a doorlike entrance to their left, about a yard wide and four to five feet in height, that looked out upon the mounds of reddish earth dug from holes in the yard.

"We're safe now!" Joyous Gard squealed, but she stopped abruptly when Mr. Pipestem arose slowly from behind a barrel. He was holding a hammer in one hand. The dark skin of his face appeared to be stretched tighter than before. His eyes, lighted by reflections from a sunbeam, revealed intense anger.

"You both disobeyed me," he charged harshly.

"We couldn't leave 'em out there for the Black Knight to kill," Daniel Boone said. "He was threatenin' his big pistol at them."

Mr. Pipestem put his hammer on the barrel top. "This cave is our refuge," he said sternly. "We don't like strangers here."

"Please, Mr. Pipestem," Queen Elizabeth Jones begged. "I'm mighty scared of your Black Knight. We'll leave as soon as he goes." She dismounted tentatively, as though awaiting permission.

"He's never harmed any of us," Pipestem said. "But he blusters mightily once in a while."

Joyous Gard sniffed. "He don't look at you the way he looks at me," she said to Mr. Pipestem. "I'm ascared of him too."

Ben was surprised by a sudden shadow whipping across the

doorlike front. The shadow disappeared, then reappeared. Billy Goodheart's laughter rang for an instant seemingly within the cavern. He was riding his horse back and forth very close to the opening. Without warning he fired into the cave, the sound reverberating until it was like a pressure within Ben's ears. The odor of exploded powder drifted in the russet light.

"We can't abide that," Mr. Pipestem said firmly.

"I've got a Walker Colt," Ben said, taking the weapon from inside his tunic.

"Put it back," Mr. Pipestem ordered. He took a rifle from beneath a crude worktable and strode toward the entrance. He was halfway there when Billy Goodheart fired into the cave again.

"Leave off!" Mr. Pipestem shouted at him. "I've not killed a man since I was in the war in Mexico," he added. "But if you fire into my cave once more, you're fair game target."

"I got no quarrel with you, Pipestem," Billy called back. He was standing to one side of the entrance, but his voice came strong into the cave. "It's them two trash you're pertecking in there. Maybe you already traded for their stolen Mexican silver dollars."

"We have no treasure in here," Pipestem replied. "It's all buried out there."

Billy's response was a torrent of profanity. "All this digging is just a trick to fool people. You've got the silver in that cave, and you've throwed in with that pair of thieves I been following for days and days."

Ben had crept up close behind Mr. Pipestem, who seemed startled when he turned his head and saw him so close.

"What's this about Mexican silver?" Pipestem demanded. "Are you and your friend Jack carrying booty?"

"No, sir," Ben replied.

The parchment skin of Pipestem's face assumed the characteristics of a mask, tightening around his eyes and mouth. He was about to say something when Billy Goodheart interrupted with a threat. "If one of you don't bring out the treasure, I'll smoke you all out!"

Ignoring the warning, Pipestem relaxed his grip on the rifle and whispered to Ben, "Not likely." He pointed to the streaks of sunlight shooting down through the limestone vault above. "Too many holes." He repeated, "Too many holes."

They could hear the creak of leather as Billy Goodheart mounted and the slow beat of hooves as he rode off a short distance. "He's desperate, crazy maybe," Mr. Pipestem said, looking at Ben and Queen Elizabeth Jones. "I'll not force you boys to leave now, while his dudgeon's up, but you've got to leave sometime, and how're you going to handle him then?"

"He believes we have a bag of Mexican silver dollars. Stolen from the bank at Marshfield," Ben explained. "If you let him come in the cave and search, maybe he'll go away when he can't find the silver."

Anger reappeared on Pipestem's face. "Never! This is a family haven. You and your friend Jack have got no business in here either. I ought to've run you out when you rode in."

When the popping of dry wood burning resounded from outside, Pipestem turned his head slowly, surveying the cave's interior. "He can't smoke us out, but he can shoot bullets in here. Little Daniel, you and Joy start moving that pile of boards down to the big opening, while I roll some barrels into the side entry. Anything to slow him down. Be careful now. If the Black Knight comes back, get out of his line of fire. Quick." He glanced at Ben and Queen Elizabeth Jones. "You two boys better hobble your mounts. Even a little smoke fidgets horses, and any gunfire in here would pain their ears. We don't want horses thrashing around inside."

With a hasty pounding of his hammer, Pipestem finished nailing the top on the barrel that he had been working on when he was so suddenly interrupted. He rolled it and several empty ones into the brush-filled opening through which Ben and Queen Elizabeth Jones had ridden their horses.

As soon as their insubstantial defenses were in place, they all gathered behind the heap of boards at the larger front entrance, peering out through the cracks to see what Billy Goodheart the Black Knight might be doing. He was tossing dead tree limbs and twigs into a pile directly in front of the cave opening, taking care not to expose himself to those inside.

"What can we do now?" Joyous Gard asked. Her fear had been worn down by the boredom of delayed expectancy.

"We'll outlast him," Mr. Pipestem said softly. "When he sees he can't smoke us out, he'll go away."

Time's passage was snail-paced. Little Daniel devised a game with Ben, tossing a knife at a circle drawn into the earth. Joyous Gard, seated beside Queen Elizabeth Jones, worked at a plait in her chestnut hair. "Jack, your hair is like gold," she said to Queen Elizabeth Jones. "It looks like girl's hair. You let it grow a little longer, you could plait it like mine."

"Soon as I can," Queen Elizabeth Jones replied curtly, "I'll find somebody to cut it."

"Hush, hush," Mr. Pipestem said, cupping one ear with a hand. "What's he doing out there?" A grating noise grew gradually louder. "Sounds like one of my barrels rolling over pebbles." He turned and asked, "That barrel I put in the millhouse yesterday? You didn't take it to the orchard?"

"No, sir," Little Daniel replied. "It had a top on it. We thought it was ready to load in the wagon."

"Damn, damn, damnation!" Mr. Pipestem cried. He kept a hand behind one ear. The crunching sound increased in volume. Through cracks in the board defense, they saw a firebrand drop on the heap of brush and wood outside the cavern opening, and then a barrel rolled into view.

"Get back! Everybody get back!" Pipestem shouted. He grabbed Joyous Gard around the waist and half carrying her, led the way in a rush to the side entrance. As Ben ran close behind them, he looked back to see what was happening, but there was only a small blaze atop the barrel.

The explosion was a flash, a bang, and a boom, all occurring with such suddenness that the mental shock of the happening was almost as great as the physical impact. Small fragments of lime-stone rattled down from above; acrid powder smoke flowed inside the cave, further frightening the shaken horses. The front opening was obscured so that the light inside grew dimmer.

Mr. Pipestem began rolling the barrels away from the side entrance. After a minute or so, he called to Ben and Queen Elizabeth Jones to bring their animals outside. To Ben the sunlight seemed inordinately bright. Following the others, he and Queen Elizabeth Jones led their horses through the gristmill shed.

When they came out in front of the building, they were surprised to see a small herd of horses assembled near the dilapidated bridge. To one side of the herd was a stagecoach. A sergeant in blue was in front of the team, trying to hold them in check while a young lieutenant on the driver's seat sawed at the lines. Another officer, a major wearing a forage cap, was watching a horseman on the road pursuing Billy Goodheart, who was on foot. A lariat spun out over Billy, and seconds later he was on the ground.

Ben glanced at Queen Elizabeth Jones who had broken into sudden laughter. "Thunderation," she cried. "What a throw! Who's that rider?"

"Raymove," Ben told her. "He's Osage. Breaks horses for Potawatomi Tom."

"And there's Major Strawbridge," she said. "And Lieutenant Hockaday on the stagecoach!"

A few minutes later they were all gathered in front of the gristmill—Potawatomi Tom, Raymove, Strawbridge, Hockaday, and Billy Goodheart who was trussed up in ropes, with a gag in his mouth to stop his furious cursing. Billy's hair had been singed all the way to his scalp; his eyebrows were gone and his clothing blackened. Strawbridge and Hockaday were beaming with delight because they believed they had captured the powdermaker they had been sent from St. Louis to apprehend and put out of business.

"We've been tracking this blackguard critter for a week," Major Strawbridge said. "He may not be the real powdermaker, but Lieutenant Hockaday and I are convinced that he runs the stuff to the Rebels. When we get him to St. Louis, the headquarters commander will decide if we are to follow his trail back to a supply point. Maybe to a cave like this one he had you folks besieged in."

Mr. Pipestem guided the two officers through his cavern, explaining that he had used it for many years as a root cellar and storehouse for his apples. Major Strawbridge made a careful search of everything in the cave, including the barrels, all of which were empty except the one that Pipestem had nailed shut. The major asked him to break it open, and when Pipestem did so, it appeared to be filled with green apples.

"These are my best pie apples," Pipestem explained. "I have several more barrels of them down in my orchard shed, also a few early summer mellows. The mellows don't keep well, but they're soft and sweet and bring good prices in St. Louis. I'll be driving a wagon load to the city early in the morning."

As the sun was setting by this time, the travelers decided to make night camps upstream from the gristmill. Before darkness fell,

Mr. Pipestem sent Daniel Boone and Joyous Gard down to the orchard for three pecks of his mellow apples. He gave a peck each to the horse tamers, the army officers, and the camel escort. All pronounced the apples to be the most delicious they had ever tasted.

At daylight next morning a caravan began forming on the road to Pacific City. Potawatomi Tom's horses and supply wagon were out on the road first, followed by the army officers' commandeered stagecoach. Inside the coach was the rope-bound Billy Goodheart, his gag removed after he promised to keep quiet. Billy's black horse, looking as terrified as ever, was fastened to the rear of the coach. Mr. Pipestem's mule-drawn wagon, filled with barrels, rolled steadily behind the stagecoach and lead horse. Following this wagon by several yards was Queen Elizabeth Jones on Champ, just ahead of Hadjee and the camels. Ben, on the stallion, brought up the rear, lagging a bit to let the dust of the forward traffic partially settle. Daniel Boone and Joyous Gard followed on foot for a short distance, then with shouts and waves turned back toward the grist-mill.

About midmorning the winding procession came to a wide but shallow ford. The crossing was easy except for the farther bank, which was so steep it slowed the vehicles. Hadjee guided the camels a few yards upstream and let them drink. Ben waited on the south side, impatient in the hot sunshine, watching Pipestem's wagon jolting behind his straining mules. Suddenly one of the barrels broke loose from its ties, banged against the wagon gate, dropped to the ground, and rolled into a ditch.

Pipestem immediately halted the mules, set the brake, and leaped off the wagon seat. Intending to give him a hand at recovering the barrel, Ben hurried across the ford. He saw Queen Elizabeth Jones dismount and start toward Pipestem. She had almost reached him and the barrel when he waved her away with a furious gesture, his dark face distorted with anger. She stopped and waited beside Champ until he had lifted the barrel and fastened it back into the wagon.

In a minute or so Pipestem was cracking his whip over the backs of the mules. They quickly pulled the wagon up to level ground where they put it into such rapid motion that it was soon out of view.

When Ben rode up out of the ford, Queen Elizabeth Jones was still standing beside Champ. "Look here," she said to Ben and pointed to the ground, at a scattered black dusting where the barrel had fallen.

Ben dropped down from his saddle and knelt to examine the black substance; a thin line of it trailed back to where the wagon had stopped. With a moistened finger he touched a tiny bit to his tongue. "It's gunpowder," he said.

"I'll bet Mr. Pipestem's got the stuff packed in the bottoms of all his apple barrels," she declared. Her blue eyes widened as she stared at Ben.

"I expect so." He wished he had not seen the gunpowder.

"You reckon we'd ought to tell Major Strawbridge?"

While Hadjee was driving the camels out of the stream, Ben replied quietly, "Let's think on it."

XXIX

BEN BUTTERFIELD

~

Quite a delegation came into the hardware store this morning, disturbing my musings about the past. A party of five it was— Brigadier Boggs and his daughter Blossom, Miss Ivy Crownin-shield, Maude Grimsley, and Guy Blythe. Blossom was sent to summon me from my chair at Old Man Fagerhalt's desk.

At that moment I was mind-wandering somewhat sorrowfully over the absence of Letitia Higgins from our town. Yesterday evening when Hilda remarked at dinner that Letty had gone to Shreve-port for what might be a protracted stay, the shock must have shown on my face. A rush of conjectures roared through my head. Was her sudden departure somehow connected with what had happened between us following the capsizing of the boat out at the Anchorage? What did Hilda know about that, other than the over-turning and the storm?

"Well, don't look so surprised," Hilda said. "She's been talking about Yancey's prospects with that Louisiana lumber company for the past month."

"Did she go with Yancey?" I asked.

"Of course she went with Yancey. I'll declare, Ben—"

I told her I was sorry, that I'd been woolgathering all day. She nodded vigorously. "You and your papers and pictures," she said, pointing her fork at me. "Once in a while you'd ought to live in the present."

So this morning I was mooning about Letty Higgins when Blos-som Boggs crept up behind my chair and put her hands over my eyes. She smelled of soap, the same scent of tar soap that Hilda uses, and for a moment I was pleasantly surprised in the belief that the intruder was Hilda, returning to her old teasing ways. But when I turned quickly and squeezed her rump, the way I used to do to Hilda, Blossom let out a squeal that surely reverberated down the hall and into the store.

"Begging your pardon," I said, rising with a little bow. "I thought you were Hilda."

Blossom is not a handsome woman, thirtyish I guess, glowing with good health but with a perpetual expression of disapproval in her eyes. Yet she does have a full-lipped mouth that at that moment, for the first time in my life, I thought of as being amorous.

"Do you often do that to Hilda?" she asked in a husky whisper. As she had not moved from her position since I arose, we were standing almost toe to toe. I could see little droplets of sweat on her upper lip and feel her breath against my chin. Before I could move aside, she reached out a long, gangly arm and squeezed my groin. "Now you know what it feels like," she said coldly and added, "Hilda wants you in the store." She wheeled and started down the hall.

Following her lanky figure, I abandoned all thoughts of Letitia Higgins and tried to recollect what I know of Blossom Boggs. Her father seldom speaks of her, although she manages his small hotel, supervising the servants, planning the meals, keeping the books. Everyone knows that. I had a dim remembrance of gossip, a year or so ago, of some involvement with a drummer, a salesman from St. Louis maybe, who stopped regularly at the hotel. The gossip had got out through one of the servants who witnessed something, but I could not remember who told of it in my hearing. I made a mental note to inquire of Hereward Padgett, the certified idiot who remembers everything he sees or hears.

The group in the store was clustered in the semicircle of cane chairs that Hilda keeps at one side of her counter for visitors. When I approached, they made cheerful noises all around. Maude Grimsley wanted to know why Blossom had screamed. Blossom told her frankly that I had pinched her, but that she had retaliated by pinching me. They all laughed, except Brigadier Boggs and Hilda. Both of whom looked embarrassed. I saw no point in explaining that I had thought I was squeezing Hilda.

Leaning beside the end chair where Miss Ivy Crowninshield sat was a bicycle, its metal resplendently lime colored to match the costume of its blue-blooded owner. I knew it was Ivy's cycle because I had seen her riding it on Gaines Street while wearing a divided skirt.

The subject of bicycles was the reason I had been summoned to the presence of the group. Guy Blythe was spokesman. I soon learned from him that Ivy and Maude were organizing a cycling club. The idea was Ivy's; she had been introduced to such a club while visiting relatives in Connecticut. Being clever, Ivy had sought out Maude, who was always an enthusiastic organizer and joiner. Ivy had also asked Guy Blythe to become a distributor for Pierce cycles, her favorites. The lime-colored one that leaned beside her chair was a Pierce. Guy Blythe, the Studebaker wagon and Columbia Electric distributor, already owned exclusive rights to sell Flynn Hurricane cycles. The Flynn company, however, forbade the sale of any other brands by their dealers, and Blythe did not want to give up the Hurricane because he believed them to be the best cycles in the world. He did allow, however, that the Pierce might have an edge when it came to female riders. The balance and seating were first-rate, he said, for women cyclists.

"We've talked with Hilda," Guy Blythe said to me, "about the Fagerhalt hardware store becoming the local agency for the Pierce models, which at present are not sold in this region. If Miss Ivy's club prospers as she claims it will, you'll have steady sales."

"Bicycles are becoming very fashionable," Ivy said. "President McKinley keeps one in the White House."

I glanced at Hilda, who was looking questionably at me.

"If Ben will be responsible," she said, "for everything concerned about the cycles, I have no objection."

"I can ride a bicycle and maybe sell one to a willing buyer," I said. "But I have no mechanical genius for rehabilitating broken ones."

Guy Blythe laughed. "Oh, our smithy friend, Percy Manlove, has agreed to keep the cycle club's machines in good order, eh, Miss Ivy?"

Ivy nodded and smiled prettily at me. She was wearing her divided riding skirt. It was quite tight over her narrow buttocks. I noted this when she circled the chairs to come to the counter with *papers from the Pierce Safe Cycle Company for Hilda and me to sign.*

The gathering soon dispersed, but while everyone was crowding toward the store entrance, I felt a sudden painful squeeze upon the loose flesh beneath my hip pocket. I almost gasped but instead turned silently to observe a saucy grin on the sensuous lips of Blossom Boggs.

At this moment I am making a second mental note to go in search of Hereward Padgett to find out what he has heard about Blossom.

XXX

THE CAKEBREAD MENAGERIE

❧

Pacific City dazzled at high noon under summer sunlight so bright the effect was almost painful to Ben. The town itself was a creation of graveled highways, two railroads, and the Meramec River, still winding its way toward the Mississippi. Mile by mile the road on which Ben and Queen Elizabeth Jones traveled grew more crowded with wagons and carts and herds of livestock. The disorderly throng slowed movement to a crawl.

One by one the travelers they had been following began to disappear. The earliest to go were Major Strawbridge and Lieutenant Hockaday, with their prisoner Billy Goodheart. After the first crossing of the Meramec, the officers accelerated their confiscated stagecoach and rolled away in a cloud of yellow dust.

In the outskirts of Pacific City, Mr. Pipestem turned his wagon load of barrels off on a side road and without so much as a farewell gesture drove his team away at a fast pace. Ben and Queen Elizabeth Jones pulled their horses together and wondered aloud if they should follow Mr. Pipestem's example to escape the crowded road. "He said he was going to St. Louis," Ben declared. "But maybe he didn't mean directly."

"We should've told Major Strawbridge about the gunpowder in Mr. Pipestem's apple barrel," Queen Elizabeth Jones said.

"That's none of my business," Ben replied. "I'm a Texican. If you're a Unionist you ought to told him."

"I'm not a Unionist," she countered. "I'm a Missourian."

"Well, anyway," Ben said, "it's best we stay on the main road so Johnny can find us."

"Johnny ain't never going to find us," she replied bitterly, almost despondently. She pulled Champ away from Ben's stallion and started forward again to close the gap that had opened between them and Potawatomi Tom's horse herd.

Ahead of them, however, under a wide-spreading pine, Hadjee, the camels, and Abednego had turned off the dusty road to recline in the midday shade. Queen Elizabeth Jones turned to glance back at Ben. He nodded and said, "Let's stop for nooning."

By the time they'd sipped swallows of water from a stoppered jug and chewed a few bits of dried bacon, Potawatomi Tom and his herd were barely in view, but Ben could see the horses being driven into a corral near a railroad.

Later, after they resumed their journey, they came upon a long row of pens that faced a line of waiting railroad livestock cars. The pens were constructed of unpainted pine timber, the boards so fresh their rosin smell overlay the rich odor of manure. Workmen inside the pens were driving cattle, horses, and sheep up ramps right into the livestock cars.

Ben wanted to stop and watch the loading, but soldiers stationed alongside the road ordered them to keep moving. After crossing the railroad tracks, they faced a large herd of cattle coming steadily toward them, spreading across and blocking the road not more than a hundred yards ahead. Suddenly a full platoon of soldiers, armed with rifles, swarmed out from behind a line of freight cars on a sidetrack.

"Off the road!" a sergeant shouted at Hadjee. "Get them damned camels off the road!" The soldiers ran forward and began waving everyone off to the right.

They descended into a wide hollow in which a dozen or more wagons stood, some with teams still hitched, others with singletrees and tongues on the ground, and mules and horses resting nearby. Beyond the wagons was a willow-bordered stream, the trees filled with drooping dark-green leaves. Hadjee and the camels, with Abednego at their heels, dashed toward the water.

Off to one side were four unhitched wagons, one containing a caged tiger pacing back and forth. The second wagon was covered with canvas bearing large mustard-colored letters: CAKEBREAD CIRCUS MENAGERIE. The third wagon was surrounded by hitched donkeys, two of which had uneven black stripes painted on their sides.

The last wagon was oddly shaped and barely visible beyond the others.

Above the sounds of a chuffing locomotive, bawling cattle, and shouts of soldiers, an astonishing burst of sprightly musical tones, unlike any that Ben had ever heard before, resounded unevenly from the cluster of circus wagons. The music, if one could call it that, was a blending of steam whistles somewhat like the locomotive whistles he had heard along the South Pacific Railroad, except there was a wider range of intonations.

Queen Elizabeth Jones on Champ was leading the way to a sward of lush grass adjoining the creek. The menagerie vehicles were only a few yards to the right. Ben could now see the odd-shaped wagon clearly. A woman seated before an extraordinary instrument was pressing keys to make the different whistle sounds. Her arms and breasts were fleshy, and she was wearing a man's broad-brimmed straw hat.

Following Queen Elizabeth Jones's example, Ben unbitted the stallion and led it to the creekside where it drank in long swallows. While he was waiting for the horse to have its fill, he heard the whistle music turn into a long one-note wail, and then it ceased abruptly. Almost at that instant a roly-poly man appeared from beneath the flat wagon. He stood up, stretched his arms, and then stared intently at the camels still drinking from the stream. He came striding toward Ben, his body moving like a rolling ball. He wore faded blue cotton trousers that flared at the hips. They were emblazoned with stars and moons cut from bits of bright yellow cloth and sewed on the garment. His fuzzy hair was a bleached gray, and his thick eyebrows were a deep artificial black. He had a flat nose that resembled a pink mushroom.

"I say there, young fellow," he said to Ben. "What's the meaning of these camels?"

Trying not to laugh at the ridiculous appearing stranger, Ben looked directly at him. "I don't know as they *mean* anything," he replied.

"Don't be brassy with me, boy," the man retorted. "Who is the owner?"

"Uncle Sam, I guess," Ben said.

The man's face flushed with anger. "You're an impertinent wisearse," he declared, "like most of the war brats."

"No, sir," Ben insisted. "I was trying to tell you the camels belong to an officer in the Union Army."

"Where is this officer?"

"Supposed to be in St. Louis."

The man grimaced and slammed a fist into the palm of his other hand. In the meantime Queen Elizabeth Jones had approached them, and just behind the roly-poly man the woman who had been playing the whistle music was smiling at them. She was quite large; her plump face and arms were covered with freckles.

Explanations followed quickly, and names were exchanged. The man was Gabriel Cakebread; his wife was Marigold. No, there would be no performance that evening, or any other evening in Pacific City. The town of Pacific City, Gabriel declared, was too frantic. Menagerie shows did not do well in towns where everybody was on the hop, too busy to eat or sleep or go to shows. So the Cakebreads would be moving on toward St. Louis, maybe stop next day at Kirkwood or Webster, that is, if those villages had not turned too frantic from the war business. And, that is, if he could find two wagon drivers to replace the lazy, worthless pair who had left him to go to work in the livestock pens.

"Well, they did get offered twice the wages what we can pay," Marigold Cakebread explained.

When the Cakebreads discovered that their young acquaintances had a bag of cornmeal but no cooked food, they offered to share. Marigold prepared cornmeal mush and turned it into a delicious feast with fresh butter and cream that she had obtained from a nearby farmer.

Next morning at first daylight, Ben was awakened by the resuming clatter from the highway and railroad. He was surprised to see Queen Elizabeth Jones with Marigold at the breakfast fire near one of the menagerie wagons. While he was washing at the bank of the stream, Gabriel joined him. "My good lady Marigold tells me," he said, "that she has invited your friend Jack to join us on our journey to St. Louis. Would you wish to join us, young Ben?"

Ben dried his hands and face on his shirttail and asked, "Did you find drivers for your wagons?"

"No, in God's truth that's one reason for the invitation. If you and Master Bonnycastle will drive two wagons, we'll supply your keep and give you and the dusky cameleer night shelter in the tent wagon."

As they had almost no food or money, Ben saw the offer as a gift from Providence, and he immediately accepted.

Kirkwood was a pleasant village of new houses built of redbrick and whitewashed lumber. Mr. Cakebread was familiar with the place and quickly arranged for a site where he could erect his tent near the town's school. As the weather was fair with no indication of rain, he decided not to bother with the canvas top. He soon had Ben digging holes for tent poles, while his wife drafted Queen Elizabeth Jones to the task of setting up rows of crude pine-board seats. The circle of canvas that Ben and Mr. Cakebread quickly formed around the seats was covered with paintings of elephants, tigers, camels, bears, zebras, caparisoned horses, men in tights, and women wearing flaring ballet skirts.

Late in the day the Cakebreads organized a parade. Gabriel insisted that Hadjee lead the camels right behind the wagon carrying the caged tiger. He drove that wagon while Ben was assigned the vehicle with the whistling instrument played by Marigold. Bringing up the rear was Queen Elizabeth Jones on Champ. Marigold had dressed her in a doublet of sparkling silver, and her gray horse was decorated with trappings of red and gold. Although Marigold wanted to dress Ben's stallion in similar fashion, the plan was abandoned after Gabriel warned against it. Ben's horse was a stallion, Gabriel said, and if he sighted a warm-blooded mare along the way, he might pursue her and bust up the parade.

Ben was surprised to see so many spectators gathered along the sidewalks to watch the passing wagons. Many of them were very young; he had never seen so many children gathered together. That evening he was even more surprised by the large crowd that paid for seats inside the circle of canvas.

In his ragged clown suit the roly-poly Gabriel began the performance with one of the draft horses that he had taught to kneel and bow. Marigold, dressed in a flowing green robe that sparkled with silver, brought in the two paint-striped donkeys, and she rode one of them bareback around the ring. After she dropped gracefully to the ground and danced away, Gabriel bridled the donkeys together and then startled Ben by standing erect with a foot on each donkey's back and circling the ring.

The greatest applause of the evening, however, came when Hadjee entered the ring on Omar, with Tooley stepping nimbly along behind as though she had been a performer all her life.

Later, after the meager show was ended and the somewhat disappointed crowd dispersed into the placid Kirkwood darkness, Ben was sharing a cold chicken drumstick with Queen Elizabeth Jones in the tent wagon. On the heavy humid air of early summer, voices carried farther than the speakers realized.

Gabriel Cakebread was conversing with Marigold. "Best night on the entire tour," he said. His words were followed by the clink of coins.

"Yes," Marigold replied, "but it was the camels that brought most of the crowd."

"True, indeed true," he agreed. "With the camels we could go downriver to Jefferson Barracks, maybe all the way to St. Genevieve and pick up a richness of lucre. Or upriver to Alton or Grafton. They say there's money, war money, along the river these days."

For a minute or so Ben could hear only the continued clink of coins until Gabriel spoke again. "I'm wore out, clear wore out. Let's go to bed." The swish-swish of feet moving across high grass followed, and then there was only silence.

"I didn't think it was much of a menagerie show," Queen Elizabeth Jones said. "A French menagerie show come to Marshfield last year had several wild animals." She laughed. "And real zebras. Not donkeys with painted stripes."

Ben had never seen a menagerie show before, but he did not say so. "Mr. Cakebread told me his zebras died," he offered.

"Yeah, and Marigold said their elephant died. Maybe they never really had zebras or an elephant. Only a lazy old tiger and a trained horse."

Next morning at breakfast, Gabriel was in an expansive and inquisitive mood. "This fellow you say got into trouble with the soldiers at Rolla, you expect him to catch up with you at St. Louie?"

"Yes, sir. We thought he would be caught up before now.

Johnny Hawkes, his name is. He told us if he didn't catch up before we got to St. Louis we was to take the camels to Camp Jackson on Grand Avenue and turn them over to Captain Lightfoot. If he's there."

"And if the captain's not there?" Gabriel asked.

"I hadn't thought much on that," Ben replied. "I guess I'd just wait for one or the other."

Mr. Cakebread rubbed his short-bearded chin. "I know a carpenter works out at Camp Jackson," he said. "I'll ask him if he knows a boss soldier you can talk with."

Later, after they'd hitched the horses and were preparing to move out, the Cakebreads called the three of them, Hadjee included, to give them final instructions.

"Before noontime," Gabriel said, "we'll be coming to the limits of St. Louis city. We'll be stopped there by the military people. They'll want to see your passes—the whole city's under martial law since Gen'l Fremont was there. You don't have passes, but if I say you're part of my menagerie circus, they'll give me transient passes for you. They may take a hard look at that pair of fine horses you boys claim to own. The army quartermasters are hungry for horses, so you better let me claim them as show horses. And if'n they ask, you two boys are my nephews." He made a simpering grin. "Name of Cakebread, same as mine."

In less than an hour the heavy wheels of the wagons were rumbling along a street macadamized with limestone and bordered by elms and oaks in full leaf. An array of small gray tents, a wooden building that resembled a large outdoor privy, and an improvised gate that had been lifted into the air all indicated the presence of military authority. After a wagon loaded with firewood passed through the roadblock, two soldiers climbed upon Ben's wagon and began searching through the tenting and folded chairs.

"Anybody else on this wagon?" one of the soldiers shouted at Ben.

"No, sir," Ben replied.

"You better be telling truth," the soldier shouted back. "If we find anybody hiding in this stuff we'll jail you for sure."

A few minutes later, Mr. Cakebread appeared in company with a Union officer. From beneath the broad brim of his deep-creased felt hat the officer's sharp eyes studied Ben's face. "He's just another young-un," the officer said. "Can't you find no grown-up men to drive your wagons?"

"My pair of rantallions left me at Pacific City. Had to draft in my nephews to get my wagons here. They'll likely be going back home in a few days."

The officer sniffed. "Need the names anyway. I'll give you their transient passes. And one for that darky furriner. First thing in the morning you take the lot of 'em down to the provost marshal's on Locust Street. Old Gen'l Curtis don't like visitors roamin' around St. Louis without passes."

"Will do," Mr. Cakebread said.

The two soldiers had finished searching the wagons. "Nobody in here, sir," one said to the officer.

Two buggies and a wagon loaded high with hay were waiting behind the last of the Cakebread menagerie wagons.

"Move 'em out!" the officer shouted to the soldiers. "We don't want another pileup here."

As they rolled eastward into the city, the redbrick buildings grew more numerous and considerably larger and closer together. The rims of the wagon wheels gritted against the sandstone surface of the macadamized streets. Front yards disappeared, replaced by redbrick sidewalks. People were sitting on white stone steps facing the street, and some stood up, pointing at the camels and the caged tiger. For several blocks a few young boys ran alongside. Market wagons coming from the river landings lumbered past them, and carriages drawn by high-stepping horses were on all sides.

At one busy cross street a policeman halted the Cakebread caravan until a horsecar rocking on its rail track was drawn quickly past. This was Ben's first sight of a horsecar. He began noting the street signs: Olive, Pine, Myrtle, and then they turned into 3rd. The buildings became more and more dilapidated until at last they halted beside a two-story tumbledown structure, with a livery stable and wagon yard adjoining. The evening air was filled with the sulfur smell of coal smoke.

After the horses were unhitched, fed, and enclosed in the stables for the night, the Cakebreads led the way into the house's dining room that was large enough to contain a dozen long tables. About half of the tables were surrounded by people of all ages, chattering noisily as they gobbled their food. Most of them were poorly dressed, their hair tangled, their bodies unwashed.

"Refugees," Marigold Cakebread said. "They're Rebels fleeing Unionists and Unionists fleeing Rebels. Sometimes they get into fights here."

"Yeah," Gabriel said. "The Unionists call themselves Wide Awakes. The Confeds claim to be Minute Men. If you boys see a fight starting between 'em, clear out of here fast as you can."

The five of them sat at one of the empty tables until a lanky woman with gray hair, wetted down over her forehead and ears, appeared from behind a high wooden counter that screened a pair of cooking stoves. "Marigold, Gabriel," she greeted them in a loud nasal voice. "So you've come back."

"Yes, Ma Sandiwater," Gabriel replied. "We made it to Jeff City and Columbia. But the backcountry is all stirred up these days. Most people got no time for us."

From a wide leather belt, a cow's horn hung at Ma Sandiwater's side. The horn was filled with snuff, and from the opening the woman took a large twig that had been frayed at one end. She thrust the brushy end into her mouth to moisten it and then dipped it into the snuff. After taking a dip, Ma Sandiwater said, "I hope you folks brought back some metal coins from outside. A pocket full of tin, as they say. St. Louis is full of shinplasters. That's paper money, if you don't know. It's driving out all the silver." She took a crumpled piece of paper out of her apron pocket. "Says twenty-five cents right on the front, but it won't buy what two bits silver will. Now, you folks bring yore plates and fill 'em up. This eve we have cawn cakes and milk. Come and git it!" She stopped abruptly and peered down at Hadjee. "You know, Mr. Cakebread, darkies don't eat in here."

"The cameleer is not a darky," Gabriel retorted.

"No, ma'am," Ben added. "He's Egyptian. Of royal blood. Hired by Mr. Jeff Davis—"

Ma Sandiwater caught Ben's head within the crook of her arms and squeezed hard. "Hush, boy! You'll have the Wide Awakes down on us if you say that name again." She stepped closer to Hadjee, who ducked his head fearfully. "If you folks say he's not a darky," Ma Sandiwater continued, "then he can eat. Bring yore plates."

After they had eaten the corn cakes and the milk—which Queen Elizabeth Jones declared to be the worst sort of blue john and refused to drink it—Ma Sandiwater showed them their rooms on the upper floor. They were little more than stalls with old blankets on the floor for bedding.

A summery darkness had fallen, a mouse-colored sort of light, but neither Ben nor Queen Elizabeth Jones was sleepy, and at the suggestion and direction of the Cakebreads they decided to walk the short distance to the riverfront.

When they started, Hadjee caught Ben's sleeve and asked, "You go east?"

"Yes," Ben replied and remembered how Johnny Hawkes had told Hadjee that every step he took toward the east brought him a step closer to Egypt. "Come with us," Ben said.

The waterfront lay below a cobblestone slope with a strip of smoke-stained grass along the high point. They faced a crescent of flickering lantern lights and black smoke from the steamboats extending as far as they could see in either direction. At first sight, Ben was sure that every steamboat in the world had gathered there in the Mississippi River, yet he had never set foot on a single one of them.

Hadjee extended his hands as though blessing the boats. "Egypt," he said, raising his arms toward the sky.

"No, Hadjee," Queen Elizabeth Jones said. "This is the Mississippi River."

The Egyptian shook his head and made signs that meant he was going back to the stables. He would not sleep in the big house; he would sleep with his camels.

Queen Elizabeth Jones sat on a short mooring post and sighed, staring out at the murky river that murmured and splashed in the semidarkness. A steamboat whistle made a lonesome sound. "What are we going to do now, Ben?" she asked.

"We'll go to Camp Jackson in the morning, see if we can find Captain Lightfoot and leave word for Johnny so he can find where we are."

"I know all that." Her voice turned testy. "I mean *after* that. We've brought the camels to St. Louis and we'll soon be done with the nasty beasts. What are we going to do then?"

Surprised at her tone of despondency, he looked directly at her and took a few steps closer. "I reckon Johnny and I will be heading back to Texas. Maybe Hadjee too. We'll ask him, but he may want to keep going east toward Egypt."

"What about *me*?"

"You can go back with us to Marshfield."

She made a razzing noise with her lips. "Nothing at Marshfield for me. My uncle is in jail. Where would I go?" She sighed. "I shouldn't've let you talk me out of going with the Shakespeare actors."

"I didn't talk you out of going to Rolla with them. You talked yourself out of it."

She sat silent for two or three minutes and then said, "I'm not going back to Marshfield. I'm going to stay with the Cakebreads."

He suddenly felt as despondent as she was. "Until they find out you're a girl," he scoffed.

"Won't make no difference." She stepped off the mooring post and started back through a gloom of smoky river fog toward the boardinghouse.

XXXI

BEN BUTTERFIELD

~

Yesterday the first shipment of Pierce cycles arrived, their delivery speeded by the intercession of Miss Ivy Crowninshield who claims to have met the president of the company in Connecticut. There are four machines, three for females, one for a male, and the last I have already taken out for a spin along Broadway and Gaines. Maude and Annie Grimsley passed me twice in their Columbia Electric, Annie sounding the squawking rubber horn and Maude shouting jeering remarks, both giving me toothiest of grins. They are both large-toothed girls.

When I stopped at Dewberry's Drugstore on Capitol to allay the awful thirst I'd worked up, whom should I meet at the soda fountain but Hereward Padgett. Hereward admired my cycling knickers and immediately let me know that he had heard all about the cycle club and was eager to join. I told him that I was not yet a member myself and that he should apply to Miss Ivy Crowninshield or Maude Grimsley.

"Miss Ivy disdains me," Hereward said, "and Maude has turned so gaga over old Preston Boggs she no longer has the time of day for me."

"You don't mean that," I said as we picked up our soda glasses and walked over to a wire-legged table to set ourselves on wire-legged chairs. "The brigadier is twice Maude's age," I added.

Hereward assured me that what he had told was God's truth, that the brigadier constantly fawned on Maude, and she could be found in his company morning, noon, and night.

Hereward is a certified idiot, but that does not mean he is a

poor observer of his species or weak at reaching shrewd conclu-
sions. I decided the time was ripe to inquire about the rumors
concerning the brigadier's daughter Blossom, who had pinched a
bruise into my groin.

Hereward's eyes brightened at my query, indicating that the
subject was one he relished. His information had come from a sister
of one of the maids who worked in the Boggs Hotel. The sister did
housework for the Padgetts, and I know that Hereward is on very
good terms with her, probably has been seduced by her, he not
being the type who would initiate a contact of that sort. The hotel
maid had confided to her sister that she had seen Blossom Boggs
skip out of a traveling saleman's hotel room very early one morning. "Nekkid as a jaybird," she described her. "She was carrying
a towel but not wearing it to conceal anything. Nekkid as a jaybird."

"I have never seen a naked jaybird," I said to Hereward.

"Nor I," he agreed. "But that's what the maid said she saw.
She also said that Blossom Boggs does not have a nightgown to
her name. She sleeps every night nekkid as a jaybird."

"Most interesting," I told him and would have said more had
Theo Drumgoole not entered the drugstore. Seeing me he tramped
over to our table in his heavy pole-climbing boots. He was aglow
with the information that a telephone would soon be available for
the Fagerhalt hardware store. He thought I would be pleased as
punch, but all I could manage was a weak smile. Theo does not
know how much I hate telephones, and he would not believe it if
I or anyone else told him that.

After Theo departed, Hereward wondered aloud how often he
got in bed with Betty Hesterly, the night telephone operator.

"They're engaged," I said, "but how do you know she lets
him?"

"Didn't you see him go in the back of the drugstore with Har-
vey Bilbrew? Bought a pack of rubbers, he did."

As I noted previously, Hereward Padgett may be an idiot but
he sure knows how to observe and recall.

One week later. This afternoon the cycle club held its first outing.
The dozen or so of us included Brigadier Preston Boggs and Maude
Grimsley. Hereward Padgett was certainly on the mark about that

pair being beguiled with each other. Maude continually toyed with the brigadier's neckpiece and he with her hat, each touching the other lovingly as they did so. Hereward himself had become a member of the club since we last conversed, and he was accompanied by his gap-toothed girl.

Either Maude or Miss Ivy Crowninshield, or both together, have set about to devise a sort of uniform for the lady members of the club. It consists of a divided skirt, a pair of blue tennis shoes, a wide-striped shirt, and a very wide-brimmed hat known as the wideawake. Most of the males, including me, wore wideawakes and knickers.

We pedaled out to the nearest arm of Fourche Creek, each taking a picnic lunch, until we found a greensward along the bank. Percy Manlove, who had come along on his three-wheeler to take care of any mechanical troubles, powdered the grass with sulfur to drive away lurking insects. We all sprawled out like young children, resting our muscles from the exertion of pedalling.

Maude and the brigadier were reclining on my right, while on my left Miss Ivy was stretched out languidly, looking up at the scattered clouds in a very blue sky. I asked the brigadier why his daughter Blossom was not with us. He seemed astonished that I should inquire about her and replied that the hotel required either his presence or Blossom's presence most of the time, and that on matters merely of diversion both of them most certainly should not be away at the same time.

At this, Miss Ivy spoke up and said that she thought Brigadier Boggs forced Blossom to spend too much time at work and did not allow her enough freedom to associate with young people of her own age.

"You are speaking out of bounds, Miss Crowninshield," the brigadier said sternly, "about matters you know nothing of whatsoever."

I think Miss Ivy was quite taken aback by the response to her criticism. At least she remained silent, which is out of character for her. And a moment later, the brigadier and Maude arose as if disapproving of our company and walked down the slope to their bicycles. They were not out of earshot.

"Pompous old croaker," Miss Ivy said.

Hereward and the gap-toothed girl who had been reclining on

the other side of us had moved away to a sandy spot to play mumblety-peg with Hereward's jackknife. Being alone with Miss Ivy, I decided to see how she would react to Hereward's story of Blossom and the traveling drummer. As I began narrating, she turned on her side to face me, her greenish eyes widening, her voice interrupting occasionally with "I can't believe it" or "I wouldn't have imagined such" or "So bold." Instead of expressing indignation at my ungentlemanly gossip, as I had half expected, Miss Ivy appeared to be aquiver with delight, blinking her eyes, and clucking her pink tongue.

"I wouldn't have dreamed Blossom could be capable of such behavior," she said softly. "How on earth do you men learn all these things about us?"

Before leaving the scene, perhaps I should record something of the Crowninshields. Ivy's father and mother are transplanted New Englanders, he having been transferred southwestward by the great national insurance company that employs him. Ivy was conceived in this city, she told me matter-of-factly during our tête-à-tête on the bank of the Fourche, but she was born in Connecticut because her mother traveled there so as to save her prospective child the disgraceful handicap of a recorded birthplace in this wild and uncultured land, a burden that could follow a child to the end of its days. Miss Ivy's older brother had been brought into the world in the same manner, and he had been shipped back to New England as soon as he became old enough to take a position with the great insurance company that employs his father.

Mr. Crowninshield has a well-furnished office in the tallest building on Main Street from which he supervises dozens of young men who sell insurance across the state. He always wears a jacket and waistcoat, stiff-collared shirts, neckties, and tightly buttoned black shoes even in the warmest weather. Miss Ivy's nose is a duplicate of his, often described as patrician, being narrow and shaped so as to signify superiority and arrogance. Mrs. Crowninshield is a butterball sort of female, her middle parts expanding as the years pass. She bears no resemblance to her daughter who, as far as I can tell through her clothing, is shaped like one of those Greek goddesses at play around the edges of an urn—an icy marble Greek goddess.

As we were collecting our cycles for the return journey from the Fourche, she approached me and spoke so softly that no one else could have heard. "Would you and Miss Hilda come to dinner with my family one evening soon?"

I was so astonished that I could only nod affirmatively, knowing full well that Hilda was bedazzled by the Crowninshields, and because of that sense of awe she was inclined to disparage them when the Crowninshield name was mentioned in private conversation. After all, they were outlanders, Yankees.

"You will of course let me know if Miss Hilda is agreeable," she added with the usual Crowninshield cockiness and went on to explain. "I need some background from you, Mr. Butterfield. I believe the litterateurs call it local color. Your circus experience, which you seldom speak of, has always intrigued me. I am struggling to compose a piece of modern music, with themes based upon circus airs. The pom-pom-pom rhythm, you know. Close to ragtime, but circusy." She probably would have run on for God knows how long had Maude Grimsley not yelled at us to mount our wheels.

As I rode along beside Ivy, I wondered what she might be up to. I knew that she was accepted by the bon ton as the finest musician in our town, if not in the entire state, but I had never heard anyone speak of her composing music.

When the cycle club riders reached Percy Manlove's livery stable to assemble for announcement of further meetings and expeditions, and final farewells, Miss Ivy lingered at the exit until I brought my Pierce bicycle alongside hers. "I do hope that Miss Hilda and I can arrange a dinner soon," she said with a quick smile. "I'm so eager to talk with you about circus life."

I did not tell her that the last subject on earth that Hilda wanted me to talk about was my life in the circus, but I mumbled some sort of affirmative reply.

"If a dinner at our house can't be arranged," she said firmly, "you and I must get together for a few hours."

"Yes," I said.

Before she turned her cycle eastward at Markham, she stopped to say good-bye, giving me what she may have believed to be a coquettish glance but that actually was almost painfully spurious.

"You're such a cute old duffer, Mr. Butterfield. If you weren't almost old enough to be my father, and already taken, I'd ask you to marry me." With a laugh and a twirl of one hand she sped away.

What is Miss Ivy up to?

Ah, well, c'est la vie, as old Socrates Drumm used to say.

XXXII

VANISHING SHIPS OF THE DESERT

~

For breakfast the next morning they were served corn cakes again, with a slightly warm pink liquid that Ma Sandiwater said was sassafras tea. Before they finished eating, a large man carrying a visored cap in one hand approached their table. Perhaps because he was balding, he wore what was left of his very white hair in long strands supported by his lumpy ears. His white eyebrows were thick and shaggy; wrinkles surrounded his eyes and creased his forehead.

"I'm looking for the Cakebreads," he said in a deep voice.

"We are the Cakebreads," Gabriel replied politely. "You must be the official I inquired about."

The man had come from the provost marshal's headquarters to assist refugees. He had been told that some of the Cakebreads were refugees requiring passes.

"Not refugees," Gabriel said. "My nephews, and an Egyptian who assisted me in droving. From Pacific City into St. Louie."

"They will need passes whether they stay or leave. I have a gig outside and will drive such of you as are without passes to the provost marshal's headquarters."

A few minutes later Ben and Hadjee were propped side by side facing the rear in a crude little seat on the back of a two-wheeled carriage, while the St. Louis official and Queen Elizabeth Jones rode in the forward seat. The horse was of an indeterminate grayish color with missing tufts of hair here and there, as though it had been picked over by moths. Apparently the animal moved its legs only with great effort of will.

"What's your name, boy?" the officer asked Queen Elizabeth Jones.

"Jack Bonnycastle, sir," she replied.

"I thought your name was Cakebread," the man said.

"A nephew," she explained.

"And that boy back there is your brother?"

"No, sir, his name's Ben Cakebread."

Ben, who was listening to every word, did not know whether to laugh or start worrying. Queen Elizabeth Jones had a way of mixing facts and taradiddles in ways that got everybody into trouble.

"You may address me as Captain Trinkle," the big man said. The visored cap with its large silver eagle on its front plate gave him an air of indubious authority.

They passed the last of the buildings between them and the Mississippi, leaving the spacious river frontage open to the sky. By full daylight the steamboats appeared to be even more numerous than after dark, an endless crescent of stern-wheelers and side-wheelers. Whirls of gray steam and black smoke pluming above the white-painted sides and decks gave an air of throbbing life to the panorama. Most of the boats were docked, but some were moving majestically on the dark flowing river, the sounds of paddle wheels slapping against the surface mixed with the deep-throated whistles and jangling bells.

Ben was too awestruck to speak, and Queen Elizabeth Jones kept turning her head in a vain effort not to miss a single bit of the bustle.

"Quite a sight, ain't it?" said Captain Trinkle.

Nearby the provost marshal's headquarters the captain halted the gig at a hitching rack and then led his three charges into a crowded high-ceilinged room. A man dressed as a dandy—black beaver hat, lime-green waistcoat, red cravat, and big-checked trousers—motioned them toward a long counter behind which sat three men with bored faces. These clerks were the only persons not standing in the room, which included half a dozen women ranging from young to old, some dressed in enormous hoop skirts with bustles and fancily flowered hats; others were wearing shabby gowns and bonnets. Three or four of the men wore tall black hats similar to the one the receptionist wore. Ben had never seen such hats in Texas, but he had noticed men wearing them in carriages on the St. Louis streets.

Captain Trinkle pushed his way forward and leaned heavily against the top of the high counter. He held up three fingers. A moment later he pulled Ben close in beside him. In reply to the first question from the clerk, Ben gave his name as Ben Cakebread from Pacific City.

"How old are you, boy?" the clerk asked him. "How tall are you? Let me see your eyes? Blue maybe? Reddish hair, I see. Now repeat after me: 'I, Ben Cakebread, accept this pass on my word of honor that I am and will be ever loyal to the United States, and if hereafter found in arms against the Union, or in any way aiding her enemies, the penalty will be death.' "

Ben wanted to tell the clerk that he was a Texican, but when he tried to speak a lump of fear arose in his throat and made him choke.

When her turn came, Queen Elizabeth Jones said that she was Jack Bonnycastle, also from Pacific City. Both of them then had to assist Captain Trinkle in making it clear who the Egyptian was and the reason for his presence in St. Louis.

While they were waiting for a gray-haired man in uniform at the far end of the counter to sign their passes, a pretty woman approached them and handed each a religious tract printed on thin paper. "The Lord reigneth," she said to Hadjee. "Let the earth rejoice." Hadjee at first refused to take the tract, but she repeated her words, caught his hand, and from the stiffly starched canopy of her gray bonnet smiled so sweetly at him that he finally took the paper. But he still looked frightened. Rolling the tract into a small cylinder he placed it carefully inside his striped shirt.

After Captain Trinkle handed them their passes, with a cautioning word to guard them well, he led them out upon the sidewalk. A boy with a bag of newspapers slung over one shoulder was shouting, "Mortar Boats Bombard Rebels at Vicksburg. McClellan Attacking in Virginia!"

The captain stopped the newsboy and gave him two cents for a paper. He read the column heads quickly and said to no one in particular, "I do believe the war will be over before Christmas."

On the way back to the boardinghouse, Captain Trinkle turned down a street that led directly to the river, halting his ancient horse upon a pier adjoining a docked steamboat. After hitching the horse he announced that he would be visiting a friend who was recovering from a wound suffered at Shiloh. Ben noticed the small sign then on the front of the steamboat:

Betsy Rose
HOSPITAL SHIP

"Might I go with you?" Ben asked. "I never been on a steamboat."

Trinkle shook his head, then looked at Ben. "Young-uns are not allowed inside a hospital cabin, but I reckon you all can go on the deck. If you'll stay there." They followed him over the double-width gangplank that was lashed securely to the heavy piling.

As soon as he set foot upon the deck, Ben felt the buoyancy of the vessel, a sensation he had never known before. In a way, he thought, the experience was frightening—the realization of being suspended upon a substance so thin as water. Yet at the same time he felt liberated, freed from the pull of solid earth.

When Captain Trinkle reappeared, the wrinkles in his face seemed accentuated; there was a sadness in his eyes.

Queen Elizabeth Jones asked, "How is your friend, sir?"

Trinkle raised his head. "He still cannot speak, yet he knows who I am, I'm sure of that." The captain continued toward the landing. "My friend was struck by a minié ball. The ball entered one cheek, went out the other. Took most of his teeth." He began unhitching the horse. "War is a terrible thing. But McClellan will capture Richmond before Christmas, and the madness will then come to an end."

A few minutes later, the captain turned the gig into the entrance yard of the old weather-gray livery stable. Hadjee was the first to drop down; he moved off in his rapid gait into the stable. Ben and Queen Elizabeth Jones had scarcely set foot on the ground when the Egyptian came tearing out of the entranceway. "No camel!" he shouted. "No camel! Camel go!"

"Which one is gone?" Queen Elizabeth Jones asked.

"Tooley," Hadjee cried. "Omar go!"

"Maybe somebody moved them into another stall," Ben said.

Captain Trinkle stepped down from the carriage seat. "Perhaps we should go and have a look," he said.

The tiny windows of the livery stable provided only a dull brownish light. They hurried from stall to stall. Midway down the first line there were two dray horses but no other animals. As they passed each gate, Hadjee grew more distraught. His breath came and went in little wheezing gasps.

"Where's Champ?" Queen Elizabeth Jones cried out suddenly. "My horse is gone!" She had been hurrying along just behind Hadjee. "And your stallion, Ben. He's not in his stall."

Very quickly they passed each stall in the livery stable. Not only were their horses and the camels missing, but also the several dray animals belonging to the Cakebreads. A look into the rear yards soon told them that the wagons and cages of the Cakebread Menagerie had vanished.

Queen Elizabeth Jones began choking back tears. "I want Champ," she demanded angrily.

Captain Trinkle said sympathetically, "There, there, boy. We'll go ask Ma Sandiwater about this."

As it was noontime, the dining hall was crowded and Ma Sandiwater and her helpers were busily serving the tables. The captain guided his three wards to seats and kept raising his hand until he attracted the attention of one of the young girls carrying trays. She gave each of them a bowl of soup and a slice of bread. After muttering a brief blessing, Captain Trinkle began eating heartily, dabbing chunks of bread into his soup. Ben and Hadjee nibbled at their bread and tentatively sipped the soup. Queen Elizabeth Jones ate nothing; she sat silent, her eyes swollen. She was very angry.

At last the captain caught Ma Sandiwater's notice. She came to the table frowning. The end of her snuff twig was hanging from one side of her mouth.

"Are you paying for these meals, Captain Trinkle?" she asked. "The Cakebreads have paid up and cleared out."

"You'll be paid, Mrs. Sandiwater," the captain said. "I'm here to help these refugees find out what's happened to their animals."

She frowned again. "Don't they know? Mr. Cakebread said he'd tell 'em."

"They know nothing," the captain said.

"Where's Champ, my horse?" Queen Elizabeth Jones demanded plaintively.

"Oh, the horses. Now that's why the Cakebreads went off in such a hurry. The army men come and took the two riding horses. Mr. Cakebread talked them into leaving his draft horses, but he was afeared they might come back for 'em. He paid up, but he left the young-uns' blankets in the rooms."

"And I reckon Cakebread took the camels, too," the captain said drily.

"He must've done so."

"Did he take my dog?" Ben asked.

"Didn't see no dog after he cleared out."

"Well, where'd he go?" the captain asked.

She grimaced, took out her snuff brush, and dipped it in the cow's horn at her belt. "He didn't say. I reckon he didn't want me to know. That way I couldn't tell it to them army officers if they come back."

Captain Trinkle took some paper money from his pocket purse and handed it to Ma Sandiwater. "We'll just have to start up a search. He can't hide camels and wild beasts and show wagons for long. Meantime, I'm taking these young folks and the furriner over to the Refugees Home on Elm Street. If Cakebread comes back lookin for 'em, tell him where they are."

After saddlebags and blankets were loaded into Captain Trinkle's gig, he drove them to a gloomy old structure of smoke-stained bricks and stone occupying half a block. Two bored soldiers armed with bayoneted rifles stood near the entrance. The captain handed his reins to Queen Elizabeth Jones. "Hold on steady now, boy," he said, "till I come back."

A few minutes later he returned with a big-bellied, gruff-speaking man who looked briefly at Ben and Queen Elizabeth Jones and then peered hard at Hadjee.

"I told you he was Egyptian," Captain Trinkle said.

The big-bellied man sniffed. "I pass him," he said with a heavy accent. "*Aber*, he's dark man. May get heaved out on his end. I bear no blame if so happen."

While they were gathering their bags and blankets, Ben realized for the first time that his worldly goods had been reduced to so small a compass that he could now carry everything that he owned in one hand. And he had no knowledge of where his horse and dog might be.

The big-bellied man had vanished through the heavy door of the dismal building.

"Come on," Captain Trinkle said with forced cheerfulness. "He ain't such a bad sort. Amsterdam Dutch without the Amster."

The sleeping place for refugees was a very large room that had once been used as a marketplace for cotton and grain dealers, and in the cracks of the rough flooring were tiny tufts of cotton and an occasional grain of wheat. The beds were strips of canvas fastened at each end to wooden crosspieces. With a wave of his hand the Dutchman assigned them three of these crude cots that were placed along a bare brick wall.

"You boys, Ben and Jack," Captain Trinkle said, "and the Egyptian, what's his name?"

"Hadjee," Ben said.

"Hadjee. All right, Hadjee, you and the boys go and eat when they ring a bell. I got business to attend before sundown." The captain turned to go, but stopped and added, "I'll look here for you in the morning. We'll go out to Camp Jackson and see if our friend Mr. Hawkes might be there. Or the officer you say owns the camels. Maybe one or the other can help us find the missing beasts."

XXXIII

BEN BUTTERFIELD

〜

Last night Hilda and I went to dinner at the Crowninshields'.
To my surprise Hilda, who was very nervous at first about
dining haute cuisine with the bon ton, quickly took to the mother
and father. Whether they took to Hilda is impossible for me to say.
They are Yankee folk and keep their hold cards concealed. Hilda
did not make any particular comment about Miss Ivy Crowninshield, but I don't think she warmed to her. I'm sure she did not
like the way Miss Ivy towed me away from the after-dinner tête-
à-tête in the parlor and took me off to her music conservatoire.
But after all, we were invited to the Crowninshields' so that Ivy
could glean a few gems from me about life in a circus. To aid in
the composition of her musical masterpiece.

In the conservatory she and I sat facing each other in rattan
chairs stuffed with pillows, with scarcely more than two or three
inches separating our knees. She was wearing a willowy green dress
made of some sort of cloth that clung to limbs, bosom, and buttocks. In her lap she held a school tablet with an Indian-head
cover. Her pencil lead kept breaking as she made notes, so that she
frequently had to stop scribbling in order to sharpen the point with
a penknife.

She asked if I came from a circus family. I told her no, that I
was born in Texas at San Antonio and that I had spent my childhood years at a fort on the west Texas plains.

"Was your father a military man?" she asked, and of course
then I had to tell her the story of my early life. How my father

had come to Texas from Indiana and married the daughter of a
San Antonio trader. How he had joined the wagon train company
bound for California to dig for gold, taking along my mother and
me, a very small child. A day after the wagon train passed Fort
Davis, my mother fell suddenly ill, probably with cholera. Leaving
the train, my father brought his wagon back to the fort, hoping
the army surgeon could save my mother. But she survived only a
few days.

I told her that from what I later learned from Miz Sergeant
Peddicord and a scout named Johnny Hawkes, my father raged
and cursed and debated aloud with himself about what his course
of action should be. Should he try to overtake the wagon train on
horseback with a child slung behind his saddle, or return to San
Antonio? In the end he gave Miz Peddicord some gold pieces and
told her if she would take care of me, he would pay her much more
when he returned from the California goldfields.

"Did he return?"

"No," I said, "he deserted me. No one at the fort ever heard
from him again. After I grew a few years older and became friends
with the Fort Davis scout, Johnny Hawkes, he sometimes assured
me that my father would come to claim me after he'd made his
pile in the goldfields. Some day he'll ride in here, Johnny would
say, but finally I refused to believe him. He would write a letter, I
said, like other people do. And then Johnny admitted that likely
he was gone from this earth. During the summer that my father
rode alone on horseback to overtake the wagon train, Johnny told
me, some wild Indian bucks were out evening up the score and
might have picked off a lone rider just for his horse. I finally gave
up waiting for my father to come back. Without Miz Sergeant Peddicord to look out for me, no telling what would have happened
to a little sprat like me. But look here, Miss Ivy, I haven't told you
a word about circus life."

She smiled at me. "You're so fascinating. I could listen all night
to your talk about your younger days in wild Texas. But how did
you get into the circus?"

As she asked the question, Miss Ivy's name echoed along the
outer hallway. Mrs. Crowninshield, her mother, was calling for
her.

"*I must go help with the coffee and biscuits,*" *she said, brushing her skirt across my knees as she arose.* "*We must talk about the circus tomorrow.*"

When we reentered the parlor, Hilda gave me a baleful look.

This morning I sit here in front of Old Man Fagerhalt's desk, waiting in some trepidation for the arrival of Miss Ivy Crowninshield, who informed Hilda and me as we were leaving last evening that she would be here promptly at ten o'clock to question me about life in the circus. I have been nervously reading through the morning paper, finding only one interesting item, a brief paragraph or two on page 3. President McKinley visited the circus in Washington yesterday. It is the same circus that should be here in a couple of months, the one in which Queen Elizabeth Jones still risks her life each day. I say "risks" because I know she is in her fifties and the senses begin to dull at that age so that eyes and muscles don't respond exactly as is required for her grand finale with horses and stagecoach.

Well, anyway, until ten o'clock I can sit here and dream about Queen Elizabeth Jones and that dreadful night we spent in the war refugees home on Elm Street in St. Louis. That was one of the worst nights of my whole young life. I had lost the camels that I was in charge of, and worse than that my stallion was gone and my crazy dog, Abednego. And so was Queen Elizabeth Jones's gray horse Champ. That night, for the first time, I truly felt like a refugee.

Maybe I'll tell Miss Ivy, when she comes, all about that night and how I almost got into a circus soon afterward, but for the fickle finger of fate.

XXXIV

ACROSS THE GREAT WATERS INTO
THE UNKNOWN LAND OF THE ILLINI

~

Pale gray light seeped through the high windows along one wall of the crowded refugees sleeping room. Noise from doors opening and closing awakened Ben before the clangor of cowbells from opposite sides of the room set the sleepers into sudden motion. Boys, young men, old men, in underwear or work clothing, were arising from the canvas cots.

Ben had slept badly because of constantly recurring awareness of the loss of his stallion and dog. Now he lingered on the cot, clinging to the canvas.

"You better get up," Queen Elizabeth Jones said as she buttoned her shirt and trousers, "or they'll throw you out."

Ben sat up, then sprang erect when he saw two burly men who were still ringing the cowbells as they moved through the big room, occasionally stopping to overturn cots and eject the sleepy occupants.

"Where's Hadjee?" Ben asked as he tightened his boot cords.

"He got up during the night," Queen Elizabeth Jones replied. "He hasn't come back."

"Couldn't sleep, I reckon. Worrying about his camels." Ben glanced at the double-doored exit. "If he's not in the dining hall, we better go look for him."

Hadjee was not in the dining hall. As soon as Ben swallowed a johnnycake and a cup of very weak coffee, he asked Queen Elizabeth Jones if she was ready to go look for Hadjee.

"I'm not going to look for Hadjee," she said. "I'm staying here till Captain Trinkle comes to take us to Fort Jackson."

Ben hesitated a moment. "If I can't find Hadjee right away, I'll come back here."

She nodded and gave him a little wave as he turned toward the outer hallway. At the entrance, one of the guards asked for his pass and his purpose in leaving the building. Ben replied by asking if an Egyptian had come out of the building during the night.

The guard shrugged, then called to the other man. With a grin the second guard said that some kind of foreigner had come out before daybreak talking in an unknown tongue. "Couldn't make out a word," the guard said, "but he didn't want to go back inside. He seemed harmless enough so I let him go after I looked at his pass."

"I must find him," Ben said. He showed the guard his pass and waited impatiently while the man wrote on a lined manila sheet. "I'll be back when I find him."

Ben guessed that Hadjee had gone off looking for the camels. But in which direction? Most likely he would have been drawn toward the river because of the activity there, with many people moving about. For half an hour or so he explored the narrow streets leading to the river, and then to his satisfied delight he saw the familiar faded long-tailed striped blouse that in Ben's mind had become a part of Hadjee since the day he first saw the Egyptian.

Hadjee appeared to be immensely relieved to see Ben and responded to his call with one of his infrequent wild grins. But when Ben began explaining to him that it was time for breakfast, to be followed by a journey to find Captain Lightfoot, the Egyptian shook his head firmly. Reaching in a pocket of his blouse, he showed Ben two hard round objects of about an inch in diameter.

"Camel turds," Ben said.

Hadjee nodded eagerly and pointed toward the river. Then he started trotting in that direction with Ben close behind him. When they came out on the cobblestones of the riverfront, Ben saw the steamboat. A crudely painted scene of circus animals, midway of the upper deck, had faded under a film of dried mud.

As Hadjee broke into a run, two uniformed policemen who were patrolling the river front turned in front of him. Each caught one of Hadjee's arms, lifting him off the cobblestones between them.

"See here now," one of the policemen said. "What would you be running from, eh?"

As he came up to them, Ben cried out, "He don't understand our words, sir."

"So you two are together," the policeman said as he peered fiercely at Ben. The man had a large sausage-shaped nose, reddish and pockmarked.

"Let's see your passes," the second policeman said.

Ben quickly found his pass inside his waistcoat and handed it to the policeman.

The man read the name off loudly. "Ben Cakebread. Pacific City, Missouri. What business do you have on this waterfront, Ben Cakebread?" Before Ben could reply, the first policeman interrupted, "Ah! Look-a-here. Look-a-here!" He was unfolding a broadside that he'd taken from Hadjee's blouse. "Look-a-here. I swear, we've caught us a pair of Jeff Thompson's guerrillas!"

Ben looked hard at Hadjee. "Where'd you get that?" he asked, pointing to the unfolded broadside.

Hadjee muttered a few words, making gestures with his hands.

"Somebody gave it to him," Ben said. "He can't read it anyhow. He's Egyptian."

"Search the boy," the first policeman ordered. The Walker Colt was almost immediately in possession of the policeman. "A wicked weapon," the first policeman said. Except for a few pieces of almost worthless shinplaster money, Ben had nothing else in his pockets.

"That's Patsy Halfacre's pistol," Ben protested.

"Maybe so," the first policeman said as he pocketed the Colt. He handed Ben the foolscap sheet he had taken from Hadjee. "You better read this to your furriner friend."

"It says, 'Strike while the iron is hot,' " Ben recited.

"Read it all," the first policeman ordered impatiently.

" 'Our enemies are whipped in Virginia,' " Ben read. " 'They have been whipped in Missouri. General Hardee advances in the center, General Pillow on the right, and General McCulloch on the left, with 20,000 brave Southern hearts to our aid. So leave your plows in the furrow, and your oxen in the yoke, and rush like a tornado upon our invaders and foes, to sweep them from the face of the earth, and force them from the soil of our State! Brave sons of the Ninth District, come and join us! We have plenty of ammunition and the cattle on ten thousand hills are ours. We have forty thousand Belgian muskets coming; but bring your guns and muskets with you, if you have them; if not, come without them. We will strike our foes like a Southern thunderbolt, and soon our campfires will illuminate the Meramec and Missouri. Come, turn out!

" 'Jeff Thompson, Brig-Gen commanding.' "

"That proves it," the first policeman said. "These fellows are Secesh. Let's lock 'em up before they try to burn us out."

Half an hour later, Ben and Hadjee were entering a three-story building that was heavily guarded at its entrance and along high balconies that fronted rows of barred windows. The two policemen delivered the pair to a blue-uniformed army officer who questioned them briefly and then sent them under the guard of a sergeant to a cell. The room was so small that there was space on the floor for only two narrow, brown-stained straw mattresses. As the door was solid oak with only a two-inch slit, and the single barred window was only a foot square, the light in the cell was quite dim.

They both moved toward the window. Below was an open area, grassless and treeless, completely surrounded by the walls of adjoining buildings and high fences of stone and redbrick. About a dozen men were strolling about without purpose. Guards patrolled along the tops of the walls.

Afterward Ben would have sworn that he and the Egyptian were kept confined in that dismal cell for a week or more, but Captain Lightfoot assured him that they had been there only two days.

Without announcement of his coming, Solomon Lightfoot, accompanied by a military guard, appeared in the doorway of the cell late one afternoon. "Do you remember me?" were his first words to Ben. Bowing a polite affirmative, Ben waited for the captain to explain his presence. Lightfoot did not offer his hand; he just stood there a foot taller than the boy or the Egyptian, looking down at them somewhat haughtily, his eyebrows raised a bit.

"Your friend, Mr. John Hawkes, has told me that it was you who succeeded in bringing the camels through from Rolla."

"Hadjee and Queen Elizabeth Jones did as much as me," Ben said.

"Mr. Hawkes told me the responsibility was yours," Lightfoot interrupted impatiently.

"Sir, would you mind telling me where Johnny—where Mr. Hawkes is?"

Only the flicker of a smile showed on the captain's face. "I'm coming to that, boy."

In his terse manner, Captain Lightfoot explained that he had managed Johnny's release from the Rolla jail, an action delayed because he, the captain, was engaged in fighting Jeff Thompson's Confederate guerrillas along the Arkansas border. Johnny had repaid him for this favor, Lightfoot complained, by refusing to travel farther with the camels and by joining a circus owned by a scoundrel named Cakebread.

"A name that for some reason you have adopted, Master Butterfield," he added somewhat testily.

"I was told by Captain Trinkle to use that name to obtain a pass."

Lightfoot shrugged. "I have no knowledge of this Trinkle. But your change to a false name made it difficult for me to find you."

"Where is Queen Elizabeth Jones?" Ben demanded abruptly.

Lightfoot frowned, obviously still irritated. "That hoyden, you mean? In boy's clothing? She went with the circus people, with Mr. Hawkes up the river by boat." He rubbed his fingers across his chin. "Now, to the point, boy. I've retrieved my camels from that thieving circus owner. I meant to take them myself on to Bright Star. But sudden circumstances—Colonel Phil Sheridan organizing a cavalry regiment—require me to travel posthaste to Washington City." He forced another faint smile as he stared directly down at Ben. "This war will end when Sheridan brings in his cavalry. After that I'll need the camels, you see, boy, to start farming experiments with them." His eyes were fixed on the tiny window of the cell. "I'll hire you and that Egyptian furriner to drive the camels for me. To Bright Star, Indiana."

After pondering his situation for a minute, Ben asked where the circus was, the circus that Johnny and Queen Elizabeth Jones had joined. Captain Lightfoot replied that the last he had seen of them they were all on a boat, a menagerie boat headed up the Mississippi to Alton, or maybe all the way to Hannibal in Missouri. They seemed uncertain as to their destination. In reply to Ben's question about his horse, the captain said that quartermaster officers had seized the stallion and another horse, one claimed by the hoyden girl, and there was no likelihood of the animals being recovered, wartime being wartime, and the shortage of mounts for cavalry. But he, Lightfoot, would attempt to obtain some compensation from the government. As for a dog, yes, he had noticed a dog, a mustard-colored hound lying at Mr. John Hawkes's feet.

Ben suddenly felt as if he had been abandoned, left to survive totally alone in a hostile, unchartered world. Johnny had forsaken him, as his father had forsaken him at Fort Davis. He did not trust Lightfoot, but the captain was the only anchor left in a world that had turned upside down. The captain could free him and Hadjee from the crushing walls of the prison. Yes, he would take the beastly camels on to Bright Star, Indiana.

Next morning very early—the light was dark gray—the three were at a ferry landing on the St. Louis riverfront. Ben and Hadjee were proudly attired in new brown jeans and boots supplied by Captain Lightfoot. Hadjee was holding ropes attached to Tooley and Omar. His dark face had lost the grimness of the past few days.

Approaching from the river was a ferry, blowing black smoke from its two stacks. Three short blasts of its hoarse whistle alarmed the camels, but a soft command from Hadjee calmed them immediately.

Captain Lightfoot moved closer to Ben to shout above the noise of the docking ferry. "That Egyptian sure knows how to handle the beasts. Do you have the map secure that I gave you?"

Ben nodded and patted the side of his blouse above the deep inside pocket where he had placed the map and the purse filled with paper money that Lightfoot had given him.

"The road across the river," Lightfoot continued, "goes straight to a town called Highland. A good place to stop for the night. Maybe tomorrow you can reach Vandalia. You'll be on the National Road there." He glanced with pride at the camels. "Some tradesmen over in Illinois may not want to accept the greenbacks I gave you, but try till you find one who will. Feed my camels well. The Egyptian believes the female is carrying a calf."

A surge of horses, buggies, wagons, men, and a few women swept them aboard the ferry's lower deck. Lightfoot offered his hand to Ben for the first time, and he then clapped him on the back. "Good luck, boy. Remember, when you reach my farm outside Bright Star, Luke and Cozie Broadhead will take care of you. I wrote their names on the map. Good-bye." He turned abruptly then and strode off the boat, his head above the crowd, disappearing into the shadows of the shelter.

Ben had never seen so much water as flowed against the ferry's side, forcing the boat to slant its course to reach the dock on the Illinois shore. All the way across Hadjee appeared to be jubilant, gazing at the rising sun, murmuring a mixture of Egyptian, French, and English words. Ben suspected that he believed Egypt lay somewhere close by. As soon as they landed, the Egyptian rigged a crude saddle on Omar with a new blanket that Lightfoot had given him. He offered the saddle's first use to Ben, who quickly declined.

Ben walked beside Tooley all the way to the outskirts of Highland, sometimes across long wooden bridges, sometimes along a graveled track with marshes on either side. Late in the afternoon Tooley began snorting and groaning, and Ben noticed that her udder was badly swollen and her eyeballs seemed to be protruding from their sockets. Hadjee was alarmed but shook his head when Ben asked if they should halt.

They found a grassy slope for the night camp. A gathering of local people, curious to see the camels, gradually departed with the fading daylight, and then they rolled in their blankets. As he fell asleep Ben realized that he had grown accustomed to Johnny's absence from his life, but he missed Queen Elizabeth Jones terribly.

Next day the sun burned down upon them with an intensity unrelieved until an afternoon thunderstorm off to the southwest brought cool breezes. They did not reach Vandalia that day but found a pleasant oak grove a few miles beyond a town that Captain Lightfoot's map showed as Greenville. When they halted, Tooley obviously was in pain. For an hour Hadjee gently rubbed her udder and belly.

That night Ben had almost fallen asleep when a sharp, almost human cry and a low groaning, followed by Hadjee's excited voice, brought him to his feet. A half-moon and a sky filled with glittering stars shed enough light for Ben to see a prostrate Tooley turning first on one side and then the other. When the camel finally lay still, Hadjee kneeled to help in the birth, pulling the calf away by its head and feet and then lifting it to blow his breath into its nostrils.

Ben had seen a colt born in the cavalry stables at Fort Davis, but he had accepted that occurrence as routinely military, nothing remarkable. The birth of the camel, however, was a miraculous event of the night, the culmination of his and Hadjee's fears and dreams of the journey. And he, Ben, was a part of the miracle, his assigned accountability deepened with the addition of another living being, a beast though it was.

A male calf, Hadjee announced proudly as he gently milked one of Tooley's teats, letting the milk coat a finger that he then offered to the calf to suckle.

At first daylight, Hadjee began talking in a mixture of Arabic, French, and the little English that Ben had been trying to teach him. He knew the word for "beans" and made it clear that he wanted a considerable quantity of beans, as well as some barley. Ben had seen him make a paste of cooked beans for Omar when the male had fallen ill from eating too much bedewed green grass. But Hadjee did not know the word for butter, and Ben did not know the French *beurre*, and not until the Egyptian used signs and gestures was it clear that butter was needed for the newborn calf.

At a crossroads two or three miles to the east, Ben found butter and beans but no barley. The merchant (who was reluctant to take greenbacks in payment but eventually agreed to do so) offered oats, but Hadjee had not asked for oats because there were still oats in a bag on Omar's back.

After Hadjee placed some of the butter on his fingers and fed it to the calf, he greased Tooley's teats with it and persuaded the calf to suckle a few drops of milk.

Ben then asked Hadjee how long they must wait before resuming their journey. Hadjee frowned, looked at the calf that he had wrapped in his blanket and placed beside Tooley, and then said, "One day, two day, maybe three day."

"The calf can walk then?"

"No. Not many steps. I fasten on Tooley's back."

And so they waited there in the oak grove, the tedium interrupted occasionally by visitors who sighted the camels from the road. On the second morning a farmer stopped his wagon and was so excited by the presence of the dromedaries that he asked if they might be for sale. He had read in his newspaper, he said, that camels might be better than horses for certain farm work. Ben explained that the animals were being taken to Indiana for that purpose, and that they were the property of a military officer. When he learned that the farmer was going into Vandalia and would be returning late in the day, he asked if he might accompany him to purchase a few supplies.

They reached Vandalia about noon, stopping at a livery and farm supply store. A block away was a railroad where a locomotive was backing a freight car onto a siding. In the other direction was a parade ground where men in work clothes were drilling in military formations. The throngs of horsemen and vehicles reminded him of the time he and Johnny were in San Antonio. He wondered where Johnny was. Why had he gone off and deserted him? The way his father had deserted him.

After purchasing a bag of barley, some flour, and cured meat, and loading them in the wagon, Ben thought of walking over to the railroad to watch the trains, but the farmer asked if he would like to go into a nearby saloon for a drink and a dish of victuals.

Ben had no desire to visit the saloon, but the farmer insisted on buying him a drink. Although he had sampled once or twice from Johnny's bottles, Ben disliked the taste of whiskey.

"You may be only a boy," the farmer observed, "but you are doing a man's work and deserve a man's drink." To avoid argument, Ben followed the man into the saloon. He stared down a pious-faced drunkard who rose as if to challenge his presence, and in a minute he was sipping from a china bowl. The farmer finished his drink and was wiping his mouth on his sleeve when Ben remembered that Johnny always responded in kind. He ordered another drink for the farmer. He was feeling strangely dizzy when he turned his back to the polished oaken bar and began blinking at a poster affixed to a large post a few feet in front of him.

It was a rather cheaply printed poster about two feet long and six inches wide. It had no color and only one small black-and-white drawing—a balloon with suspended gondola.

BIG SHOW
Colonel Gaylord's Circus
with the celebrated
CAKEBREAD MENAGERIE
of Wild Animals
from Asia and Africa

∽

EQUESTRIAN ENTERTAINMENT
Separate and Distinct from the
MENAGERIE EXHIBITION

∽

The Famous Cherokee Horse
MERCURY

∽

BALLOON ASCENSIONS HOURLY
under Personal Direction of
COLONEL GAYLORD

∽

Appearing in Vandalia ONE DAY ONLY
Wednesday
At the Fairgrounds

Ben was having difficulty focusing his vision, but he was so struck by the words "Cakebread Menagerie" that he stumbled closer to put a finger on the poster. "Equestrian Entertainment," he read aloud. Then he added, "Could that be Johnny and Queen Elizabeth Jones?"

The farmer clutched his shoulder from behind. "Are you feeling well, boy?"

"What—what day of the w-w-week is today?" Ben stammered.

The farmer replied, "Why, boy, don't you know today is a Monday?"

XXXV

BEN BUTTERFIELD

~

Late yesterday afternoon, Theo Drumgoole, a hireling of Alexander Graham Bell, invaded my office with rolls of wire, an auger, and a box containing one of those dreadful voice carriers known as a telephone. Theo is a most efficient young man and in the short interval of an hour or so accomplished a task that I had feared would require at least a day.

After boring holes in the outer wall, and others on a side of Old Man Fagerhalt's mammoth desk, he strung insulated wires from Louisiana Street, affixed them to a telephone that is now fastened securely to the top of the desk, and handed me a small pamphlet of instructions.

During the first working hours of the morning, Theo, with the assistance of his inamorata, Betty Hesterly, conducted experiments to make certain that the telephone upon the desk is properly connected with all the others of its kind in this town. Hilda, my dear wife, spent an hour in here ringing up central (Betty Hesterly) and asking to be transferred to the telephones of various friends and acquaintances. She would not leave and relieve me in the hardware store until Theo assured her that he would inform her of the arrival of that happy day when no person on earth would be immune from the possibility of being rung up by Hilda Fagerhalt, including her never seen and far distant relatives in Sweden.

So there the telephone sits now, an arm's length from my work pad, and it is ringing with all the bad spirit of an afreet, with what Edgar Allan Poe would describe as a tintinnabulation.

To this inanimate black object, I spoke as Theo had instructed me: "Hello."

"Hello, Ben," a feminine, metallic voice replied, but it was not Betty Hesterly making another test call. The voice was an erotic contralto, Miss Ivy Crowninshield.

"How did you learn this number?" I asked.

"I called Betty Hesterly. After I passed your hardware store on my bicycle and saw Theo Drumgoole monkeying with telephone wires."

I waited a moment before speaking. I still do not like to talk to inanimate objects. But I spoke. "You said you were coming by the store this morning with some circus questions. Why didn't you stop?"

"You were busy with Jack Bilbrew."

"Oh."

The telephone was so quiet I could not even hear her breathing. "A change of plans, Ben," she said then. "The cycle club is having a luncheon meeting to arrange a special event. We need to encourage enrollment of new members. We want you there, Ben."

"This is short notice, Miss Ivy."

"Quit calling me Miss Ivy."

"All right," I said. "What time?"

"Exactly noon."

As it was billed as a cycle club affair, I rode the Pierce bicycle over to the Crowninshield place. Wheeling up to the front gate, I looked for bicycles to park beside. There were no cycles in sight. I thought that perhaps they might be behind the house, but I decided not to search. The day had turned extremely hot, and the pedaling ride had drawn sweat so that I dripped from top to bottom. I walked right up to the front door and turned the bell handle.

In less than a minute Ivy was there, a cool-looking sprite, her hair darker than usual because she had combed it wet and tight against her skull. She was wearing a cap with the bill pushed up, giving her the air of a French gamine. A sensuous smile ran along her lips. The robe she wore was of some sort of white toweling.

She prattled a mouthful of hasty words. She confessed to a mistake because she'd been so busy with her musical composition.

The cycle club luncheon was on Wednesday all right, but next week's Wednesday.

I did not know what to say to this, so I said nothing and followed her into the sunlit living room. With an expression of mock pity, she looked at me in the bright light, shaking her head sympathetically and declaring that I must be miserably hot and damp and in need of a bath. She commanded me to follow her into the rear of the house. When she showed me into a tiled bathroom, I protested. Papa Crowninshield had recently planned and engineered the bagno, she said. Puddles of water around the enormous tub indicated recent use. Attached to the ceiling above the tub was a small tank with chain attached for releasing showers of water.

When I began silently shaking my head, she confided that the elder Crowninshields were in Hot Springs for the day, having traveled there on the Rock Island Special that would not return until darkness fell. After supplying this reassuring information, she demanded that I remove my damp shirt so that she could dry it in the sun.

Obeying her orders, I then closed the bathroom door after her and began running water into the tub that was large enough for two or three bathers.

I had no sooner climbed into the water than a knock sounded at the door, and a moment later she was inside the bathroom with an armful of towels. In my life, women and water have played dual roles. At that moment an unexpected flash of memory took me back about forty years to the Cambridge farm beside Travelers Repose in Missouri, where Queen Elizabeth Jones and the Shakespearean actress caught me nekkid as a jaybird in a livestock watering trough. And then there was that recent dreamlike happening of a thunderstorm and overturned rowboat with Letitia Higgins, something that both of us almost surely agreed was irresistible, as inevitable as Adam and Eve. I had not seen Letitia again; it was as if she had found a single use for me and then deserted me as no longer essential.

And now here was Miss Ivy Crowninshield offering to scrub my back with a brush and laughing, laughing at me because my skin was red as a beet from embarrassment, she said. Perhaps it was the overheated bathwater. You're a cosmopolite, Ben, and we're both artistes, we live by our own standards. Without further remarks, she dropped the toweled robe on the floor and stepped into the enormous tub.

As I said, water and women . . .

After we were back into dry clothing, we went to her music room. She brought in a plate of delicious sandwiches and mugs of some kind of cherry fizz, which we consumed with the zest of children.

In a matter of minutes she became as mundane as a doctor or a lawyer dealing with a patient or client. From the top of her piano she took a sheet of unfinished music, peered at it, made a few marks on it with a pen, and then sat and played for a few moments a very lively, rollicking tune. "That's no marching of gladiators," she said. "Don't you think there's too much marching in circus music?".

"That depends upon what is happening in the rings," I replied. "Some animals seem to like marches."

She shook her head firmly. "They would like ragtime better. I know the audiences would."

Remembering the ragtime she played at the Grimsley Sisters' Cakewalk Soiree, I had to agree with her. "A bum-bum bum-bum, bum-bum-bum-bum-bum," she hummed. "To set everyone to dancing. Dancing, not marching." Then she began talking about trombones. She loved trombones, she said, and circus bands did not have enough trombones. She supposed she would have to score her own composition so there would be enough trombones and banjos. I thought she was behaving like a crazy person, and then I remembered that artistes are usually crazy.

"The circus you were with," she said, "that's the one that's coming here, isn't it?"

"In a few weeks."

"How I wish I could have experienced the people and places and pleasures you've known, Ben."

"You would be disappointed."

"Will that girl you knew, the equestrienne, be with the circus?"

"Yes. She is the star attraction."

"And you'll meet her again?"

I nodded.

"I want to go with you, Ben. To listen to their band music. Not to see her."

Ten days have passed since that conversation. At the next Wednesday's meeting of the cycle club, Miss Ivy seemed to avoid me. It was as if she was pretending that I was not there. And then yesterday afternoon, when I met her and Annie Grimsley in front of one of the dry goods stores on Main Street, Annie responded to my greeting with a cheerful smile and would have stopped to converse had Miss Ivy not gripped her arm and literally dragged her into the store without so much as a word to me.

I recently read a piece in Scientific American about a certain female spider that consumes its mate after copulation. I have no intention of being consumed by Miss Ivy Crowninshield, artiste.

XXXVI

FROM UNDERGROUND A DARK MAN COMES

〜

The sun was down and the light was dusky when the farm wagon stopped on the road below the camel camp. Ben lifted off the burlap bag of barley and his other purchases, thanked the farmer for the ride, and started trudging up the grassy slope.

Hadjee met him halfway, moving his arms in an agitated manner. Tooley's calf was ill, not able to keep its mother's milk in its stomach. There was no possibility of resuming travel for three or four days. Ben assured him that a delay was necessary anyhow and went on to explain that Queen Elizabeth Jones and Johnny might be with a circus coming to a nearby town.

"They come? Johnny and Jack?" Hadjee asked eagerly. "Go with us?"

"Maybe," Ben replied.

Next morning Ben made early preparations for another journey to Vandalia. He thought that perhaps the circus might arrive in the afternoon of the day before its scheduled performances, and if so he wanted to be there on Tuesday.

The first offer of a ride came from a man in a buggy drawn by an aged ash-gray mare. On the buggy's rear and the front dashboard, assemblies of angels were painted in yellow. With a strange grimace that belied his mood, the long-bearded man said he was grateful to have someone to converse with, to keep him company on the journey. But he would not be traveling all the way to Vandalia that day. He said his name was Richard Puckle and that he was engaged in a pilgrimage to the farthest end of the Cumberland Road, the National Road. "Baltimore," Puckle said. "Then I shall

proceed to Washington City and visit Mr. Lincoln. Some years ago
I had occasion to meet him at the courthouse in Peoria. I want to
tell him my plan for ending this cruel and bloody war."

Richard Puckle's long brown beard was speckled with silver,
and he appeared to be a man of about fifty years. He wore a high-
crowned black hat and black broadcloth. As Ben soon discovered,
he seemed never to lack for subjects to discuss, often posing a question but seldom awaiting a reply before he shifted to a completely
different topic. When he halted the buggy beside a small stream to
allow the gray mare to drink, he looked straight into Ben's eyes
and asked, "Do you think me mad, young sir, for devoting myself
to this lengthy pilgrimage, this crusade?" Ben would have replied
by asking Puckle what his plan was for ending the war, but before
he could speak, the man was deploring the competency of Generals
McClellan and Pope. "They are fighting the Battle of Bull Run all
over again," he complained. "What is the point of it? What is your
opinion of McClellan, young sir?"

Before Ben could respond that he held no opinion of a general
he had scarcely heard of, the moan of a distant locomotive whistle
drifted across the farmland. "That's another matter I must take up
with Mr. Lincoln," Puckle declared in an irascible tone. "The noise
of the railways. We should begin by making it unlawful for freight
trains to run on Sundays."

Around noontime they came to a trail branching toward the
north, and Puckle hawed the mare off the main road and halted
the buggy. "If you wish to stay on the Cumberland Road, young
sir," he said, "we must part company here." He paused, stroking
his beard and twisting his lips in that strange grimace of disapproval. "On the other hand, you may accompany me into the little
settlement where I intend to spend the night. There is an unim-
proved road that will take you into the north side of Vandalia. Not
much traveled, but if you find no means of transport, the distance
is scarcely four or five miles."

"Then I'll stay with you, sir, if you are agreeable."

Puckle clucked his tongue and slapped the lines lightly across
the back of the mare, and the buggy began moving again. "Did I
tell you, young sir," he said, "that my pilgrimage is supported by
churches? I have a list of pastors in villages along or nearby the
National Road—clear across the nation to Cumberland in Mary-

land. Only in parts of Ohio am I in a fix. I could locate no churches willing to share in my plan for ending the bloody war. For a few nights while crossing the state of Ohio I must out of necessity find my own sustenance and take my night's rest in this vehicle."

Less than an hour more had passed when they reached a small settlement of residences, log and frame houses with a small, stee-pled church in their midst. Puckle pointed to a lane running east from the church and told Ben that it would take him to Vandalia. "I know the country hereabouts well," he said, "but most likely I shall lose myself in the distant East."

Ben waved farewell to Puckle and the yellow angels painted on his buggy, and he was soon on his way along the oak-shaded lane that took him past well-fenced pastures and then to a narrow bridge over a clear running stream. A hundred yards to the left two boys were frolicking in a swimming hole. As Ben watched from the bridge, they climbed on the bank, dried themselves with their shirts, and set off hurriedly in the opposite direction.

The thought of a refreshing swim was too appealing to disre-gard. He stood with his arms resting on the bridge railing for two or three minutes, looking down at the translucent light green water.

Beginning at the bridge's end was a trampled pathway leading to the pool. When he reached the place where the boys had kept their clothes, he undressed, placing on a log his highly prized shirt and pants, with the underdrawers, socks, and boots, all of which Captain Lightfoot had bought for him in St. Louis.

With a gasp for breath, he let himself drop quickly into the cold water and was immediately exhilarated by it. After swimming in a circle, he came back to the bank. Using handfuls of clay and sand for soap, he scrubbed his feet, knees, and hands. He had learned this from Johnny Hawkes on the long march from San Antonio to Pea Ridge. While he was washing he thought of Johnny, hoping he would see him with the circus before the day ended. A glance at the sun told him the afternoon was moving on. As soon as he rinsed himself, he strode ashore to the log.

Only his underdrawers, socks, and boots were still in place. He rushed forward, peering over the log to see if his shirt and pants had fallen there. He could see nothing but the grass and a crowding thicket of brambles and small hickory saplings. He looked toward the bridge, saw no one, and was almost certain that no one could have gone along the pathway without his noticing. He quickly pulled on the underdrawers, socks, and boots, still mystified by the unexplained disappearance of his other clothes.

From somewhere back in the thicket came a snapping sound, like the breaking of a dead limb. He stood straight, listening. No other sound came, but he knew the direction it had come from, and he began moving through the thick brushwood. He stopped two or three times, listening, but heard nothing more. The thicket was now almost impenetrable, and he could see no more than six feet ahead. Then with an abruptness that was startling, his feet seemed to leave the ground. He began falling forward, the brush tearing at his underwear, the brambles lacerating the skin on his arms and face.

He landed on his back in an open strip of high grass along the crooking stream. Standing over him was a young black man dressed in Ben's shirt and trousers.

"You come look for yo' clothes," the young black man said.

Ben tried to sit up, but the black man pushed him back and said flatly, "We both in a fix."

"Don't you have any clothes?" Ben asked angrily.

"Salt mine clothes. Can't run in them."

"What do you mean, salt mine clothes?"

The black man sighed. "You never heard tell about Mistuh Skiles's salt mine? Underground Railroad trap? No, I reckon not." He stepped backward and sat down in the grass cross-legged. "Set up," he said to Ben, who raised himself, resting his scratched hands on his knees.

"I don't live in these parts," Ben said. "I'm a Texican. Passing through." A drop of blood fell from his cheek onto one of his naked legs.

"You don't know nothin' 'bout the Underground Railroad?" the young black man asked, shaking his head in puzzlement. Then he began to tell how soldiers from the North had come into Tennessee to fight the Tennessee 'federates and run them way off. On Master Breakbill's plantation, where he lived, the Yankees butchered all the hogs and beef and hauled away the corn. Then some of the soldiers told Master Breakbill's slave people they were free and could go north to live in freedom if they liked. He—he told Ben his name was Caleb—had heard about the Underground Railroad all the way to Canada. They had stations a night's walk apart where they would feed you and hide you by day and maybe go with you to the next station. After so many days a runaway would be in Canada, where he would be a free man.

Caleb had decided to go north on the Underground Railroad, and one of the soldiers had taken a pencil and drawn a kind of map on a piece of army paper. So he had set out and made his way into and through Kentucky, stopping at mostly Union Army camps. At Cairo in Illinois he became confused and may have been deliberately misdirected. Someone at the Cairo headquarters told him that if he followed the Ohio River to Shawneetown and then turned north he would find a magnificent station known as Walnut Hill, owned by a man named Skiles. There he would be taught carpentry and woodworking and be paid for his labor. Then if he wished to continue to Canada, he could travel there by a real railroad.

After several days and nights of traveling, Caleb found Walnut Hill with its grand house set on a rise and surrounded by high black walnut trees. Beside the entrance gate was one of the secret Underground Railroad symbols that he had been told to look for—three stones, one large, two small, signifying a refuge. Caleb had not yet the courage to make his presence known at a front door. He went to the rear of the house and was admitted into the kitchen by an aged black woman who summoned the man that Caleb would know as Mister Skiles.

Skiles welcomed him with an affability that Caleb suspected of being false, a foreboding that was proved true that evening when he was sent to join a dozen other black men in a dining hall adjoining the Skiles mansion. All of these men were clothed in a sort of uniform of shirts and trousers made of a coarse variety of salt-and-pepper cottonade.

From the others, Caleb learned that he was a captive, a slave again. He had been lured into a trap instead of a freedom station. Next morning he was forced to exchange his converted army clothing for the cheap pepper-and-salt cottonade. As the days went by, he also discovered that one, two, or three of the other men had disappeared. No one knew where they went, but most believed they were being taken down the Ohio and Mississippi rivers to be sold to buyers below the battle lines. Some of the elderly black people who worked for Skiles knew that he had intercepted runaway slaves before the war began, and they suspected he was still engaged in this wretched commerce. Most of the labor that Caleb was required to do was in a salt mine dug into a mound about a furlong behind the Skiles mansion. Guards forced him to dig in a cramped trench that sometimes became a tunnel where the air was foul and salty earth kept falling constantly upon him.

At night he sometimes talked with others about escape, but none believed it was possible. Armed guards were in the woods around the Skiles holdings, and they had orders to shoot to kill anyone outside the designated boundaries. In the past the few who had managed to escape were easily recognized in their pepper-and-salt cottonade clothing and were captured by sheriffs and constables in the area who received rewards from Skiles and who believed, or pretended to believe, his assertion that the black men were criminals assigned to him by the law.

Caleb's chance at escape came unexpectedly one evening when he was ordered to accompany a wagon filled with bags of salt to a switching station on a railroad. Because of a broken wagon wheel that had to be mended, they were late reaching the railroad. In addition to Caleb there was the wagon driver, an armed guard, and another young black man. While the salt was being loaded into a freight car, Caleb simply melted into the darkness. After the driver and guard gave up looking for him and drove off in the wagon, he returned to the freight car and hid himself among the bags. Next day the freight car was in a junction being shuttled to another railroad track. After nightfall he left the car and was making his way northward along country roads, hiding in woods by day, walking by night, when he found Ben's clothes on the log beside the swimming hole.

Caleb told all this somewhat haltingly and in a dialect so unfamiliar to Ben that he was uncertain of the meanings of some words. The sun and the humid air were growing oppressive. The scratches on his face and arms had partially dried, but blood still oozed from a skinned knee.

"You want yo' clothes, don't you?" Caleb said.

Ben nodded. He had never owned clothing brand-new and of such quality before Captain Lightfoot outfitted him in St. Louis. "Yes, I want my clothes," he said.

"You kin go half-nekkid and people give you some clothes," Caleb said. "If I go half-nekkid they put me in jail. If I wear Mistuh Skiles's workin' clothes, they put me in jail. If you wear 'em, nobody put you in jail."

Sweat was beginning to sting the scratches on Ben's body. "The black man is right," he thought, "we are both in a fix. But he is in a worse fix."

"Where are your clothes?" Ben asked.

For the first time Caleb smiled, briefly, his teeth shining white against his black face. "If I give you my clothes, and"—he reached in the pocket of the trousers he had taken and pulled out Ben's purse, a small buckskin drawstring bag—"and this boodle you was carryin'."

"Where are your clothes?" Ben repeated.

Caleb turned and walked over to a patch of thick thorny shrubs. He kneeled and reached gingerly into the briers, retrieving a rolled bundle of cheap cottonade. He shook out the pants and shirt. They were badly worn at knees and elbows and filthy from the grime of the railroad and dust of roads.

Ben quickly got into them, fastening the broken buttons and tying the laces. Caleb cocked his head to one side, looking at Ben. " 'Pears worse'n I thought," he said and handed Ben the purse. "Boodle no use to me," he said. "Soon as I go into store and show green stuff, they caution 'bout me. I have to live off what I can take in dark of night."

"What are you going to do now?" Ben asked.

"Stay in here till dark. I can hear noises of trains over there. Reckon I'll try goin' north in empty car."

Ben shook his head. "That Skiles ought to be macerated." He looked down at his shabby clothes, avoiding another glance at the fine new jeans on Caleb. "Got to be moving on," he said, "to find some folks in Vandalia. Luck, Caleb."

"Thank you, bless you," Caleb said.

To avoid returning through the thicket, Ben followed the stream in its semicircle back to the bridge and started walking fast in the direction of Vandalia. The declining light of the summer day told him he would be unlikely to reach the town before sundown.

XXXVII

BEN BUTTERFIELD

~

That damned telephone was ringing before I could get down the hall from breakfast this morning. I didn't hurry because I don't aim for it to be my master. The tinny voice at the other end of the wire was petulant. "Preston Boggs here. Do you know if the Gazette put an extra on the streets this morning?"

I told him that I had heard no newsboys and supposed there was no reason for an extra. Yesterday's extra and this morning's regular newspaper had told us that President William McKinley's doctors were confident that the attempted assassination would not be fatal. Brigadier Boggs, however, was worried. It was too early to tell, he said, remembering the many soldiers he had seen wounded in the war in Virginia. They might recover from the shock of a bullet the first day or two, but then even small wounds would often begin to fester and could be fatal.

I told him that our modern antiseptics such as carbolic acid should prevail and that he should stop worrying. The brigadier then conjectured on the madness of the act and the identity of the man who walked right up to President McKinley in the Temple of Music at the Pan-American Exposition in Buffalo, his pistol concealed by a cloth over his hand, and fired point-blank. The brigadier wondered if the man could be a Spaniard, a Cuban, or a Filipino in a rage over their defeat in the recent war.

No, I replied, Czolgosz does not sound a bit Spanish. One of those anarchists based in New Jersey, most likely.

Most likely, the brigadier agreed, especially since their international leaders have announced they are going to assassinate the

*heads of all civilized governments including the United States.
They've already shot the king of Italy, he said, and don't know
why our president was so careless to expose himself. They're going
to try to bring down our country, he declared with vehemenence.*

*I reminded him that life was uncertain at all times. As he did
not wish to hear my philosophy, he changed the subject immediately, said he would be seeing me at the next meeting of Omicron
Eclectic Society, and ended the dialogue. Ah, I thought, had that
telephone not existed, Brigadier Boggs would have walked down
here, taking his regular constitutional along Louisiana Street. Will
he remain seated through the day, talking to that black-mouthed
instrument, allowing his legs to wither and his imagination to de-
cline?*

*As Hilda had taken the second half of the Gazette to the store
counter, I decided to walk out there and see if that part of the
paper had any further promotional print about the coming circus.
So far very little mention has been made of Queen Elizabeth Jones,
which disappoints me. The tub-thumping boys of the circus have
been writing puff about a gymnast and aerialist named Holly Bird,
whom they boast the entire world is in love with.*

*When I reached to pick the newspaper off the counter, Hilda
wanted to know if I'd taken an order on the telephone. She had
heard my voice. I told her that Preston Boggs had called about the
shooting of President McKinley. Hilda had lost her warm feeling
for the brigadier since he had fallen in love with Maude Grimsley.
She clucked her tongue and said that Preston, instead of gossiping
on the telephone, ought to be spending his time helping his daughter Blossom run the hotel.*

*As I walked back down the hall with the newspaper I was
wondering what Hilda would say if I told her where Blossom had
pinched me that day she was here in the hardware store.*

*Today's Gazette has another display about the coming circus.
Again there is only a bare mention of Queen Elizabeth Jones, but
there are paragraphs after paragraphs about the clowns. Pete Wal-
lace and Oscar Conklin I remember, but there are a dozen new
clowns from France, Italy, Russia, and Lord knows where else. A
reader of this puff piece will come away believing it is a circus
entirely of clowns. One paragraph notes tersely that the equestrienne Queen Elizabeth Jones will perform her death-defying stage-*

coach jump. Good God, Johnny Hawkes would never have put up with such a slight. In his day the promotion scribblers knew they'd better put Queen Elizabeth Jones in the forefront of every piece of ballyhoo, embroidering and glorifying her skills and beauty to the nth degree. Back then she was the circus.

Ah, well, we'll soon see if she still can't leave the spectators gasping for breath.

In my heart I must admit that I still bleed a little because she has not sent me a postcard for a long time. Johnny always sent me the new posters, and she sent the cards with her little scribbles on them. I've never seen any mention in the papers of her taking on a replacement for Johnny, and if she had so done the circus certainly would have made something glamorous of it. The more I think about her the more eager and restless I become at the thought of seeing her again.

Perhaps it will be like that day more than forty years ago when I found her with that jackleg circus and balloon at Vandalia in Illinois.

XXXVIII

RIDING IN THE SKY

❦

Colonel Gaylord's Circus with the Celebrated Cakebread Menagerie arrived in Vandalia sometime during the night, but Ben was unaware of its presence until he awoke late in the morning. He had slept through the night in the hayloft of the livery stable where he had bought supplies on his previous visit to town.

The warm morning sun coming through an unglazed casement and the braying of donkeys from the street below brought him slowly awake. Remembering where he was and the purpose of his being there, he sprang to his feet and looked out the window. A small wagon with wooden sides painted red, and pulled by the noisy donkeys, was rolling through the street. It was most certainly a circus wagon.

In minutes he was out on the sidewalk following the wagon and another one ahead of it that bore a cage in which a black bear was wheeling restlessly. Along the edges of the street, crowds were gathering, mostly old people and children.

On the parade ground where he had seen men drilling two days before, he found the circus in process of assembly. A gray canvas tent was up on its poles, with workmen taking ropes around the sides. Beyond it he saw a dozen horses held in a rope corral. Johnny Hawkes should be with the horses, he thought, and hurried on to the corral. He knew his lost stallion would not be there, but he looked for it anyhow, studying each horse and wondering which of them might be favorites of Johnny or Queen Elizabeth Jones. None of the animals struck him as likely to be favored by either.

Their coats were dull; they were scarred in too many places. They appeared to be indifferent to the world.

A roustabout carrying a large wooden bucket was circling the ropes, testing their tautness with one hand.

"Sir," Ben called to him, "I'm looking for Johnny Hawkes. You seen him?"

"Johnny what?"

"Hawkes."

"Don't know no Hawkes." He was peering at Ben and seemed slyly amused by his clothes, and for the first time since awakening, Ben remembered the shabby pepper-and-salt cottonade he was wearing.

Disheartened by the roustabout's reply, Ben started back toward the tent, intending to search for the Cakebreads. Perhaps Johnny and Queen Elizabeth Jones had not joined them when they combined with Colonel Gaylord's circus. After all, he had only Captain Lightfoot's word that Johnny and Queen Elizabeth Jones had gone up the river on a circus boat.

"Hey, boy," the roustabout called after him.

Ben turned.

"You want a ticket to the circus tonight?"

Ben nodded, and the man continued, "You take this bucket to that well over there and bring enough water to fill the horse trough and then help me haul some hay over here from the wagon, and I'll see you get a pass."

While he was carrying the pails of water, he was surprised to see up the slope beyond the horse corral an enormous onion-shaped object forming on pasture ground beside a strip of elm trees. From pictures in books he knew it was the balloon advertised on the poster he had seen in the Vandalia saloon.

As soon as he finished carrying the water and hay and received from the roustabout a hearty promise of a free ticket later, he walked over toward the slowly expanding tan balloon. On the ground beside it was a rattan basket, large enough to contain three or four people. Nearby the basket, two men were working a hand pump that fed gas into the balloon. An invisible cloud carrying the stench of sulfur hung over the area. He stopped and watched the men finish pumping. One of them picked up a few small burlap bags, looping their ties to the basket so that they hung outside the rim. And then joining the other man, he hurried down the hill toward the tent.

It was then that Ben saw her, seated on a stump on the far side of the balloon. She was leaning forward, forearms across her knees, her head bent as though in weariness or despair. She was wearing a gray dress, white stockings, and shiny black shoes. Her hair was longer, curlier.

He was almost running when he came close enough to see the surprise on her face.

"Ben!" she shouted and was up on her feet in an instant.

They almost collided.

He caught her by the wrists and squeezed tight. He tried to speak her name but could not. Through her parted lips he could see clenched teeth.

"Thunderation, Ben," she cried, "you look like you been in a dogfight."

"I'll tell you about it," he answered, relieved to see a wide smile breaking on her face.

Each of them had a hundred questions, dammed up, begging for reassuring answers. He could tell that she was anxious, wanting something that he could scarcely define and that he could only partially bring her.

"So Johnny found you," she said. "Where is he?"

"I haven't seen Johnny. Why did you and him run off and leave me in St. Louis?"

"We couldn't find you. The Cakebreads promised they'd see you caught up with their circus. They left steamboat tickets with Captain Trinkle, but I reckon he couldn't find you either. We waited and waited for you and Hadjee to come and join us. Until Johnny found out you was back on the road to Bright Star with the camels."

"Where's Johnny now?"

"He's somewheres looking for you. Rode out three days ago from a place called Carlinville. He went soon as he got word what you was doing. We thought Captain Lightfoot was taking the camels east hisself."

"Why didn't you go with him?"

The smile left her face. "Johnny needed a horse to go find you.

Colonel Gaylord owes him money but wouldn't let him borrow one of the show horses unless I stayed with the circus till he comes back." She drew away from him, glancing down the hill toward the tent. "Look, Ben, you better clear out. I see old Gaylord heading up this way. He's jealous of anybody hanging about me. Thinks he owns me. I'm supposed to be watching the balloon to keep people away."

"I'm not clearing out," Ben said. "I'll just walk over by the trees and set."

He went to the woods' edge and sat down with his back against an elm tree. He looked out at Queen Elizabeth Jones who was fearfully taking her place on the stump where he had found her.

Colonel Gaylord was a stocky man, thick legs in wide-striped trousers stuffed into knee-high farmer's boots. He wore a black wide-brimmed hat that kept the weather off his smooth-shaven pink face. As he strode straight toward Queen Elizabeth Jones, who stood up quickly, he reminded Ben of the strutting rooster he remembered seeing in Miz Sergeant Peddicord's chicken pen behind the enlisted men's quarters at Fort Davis.

Gaylord was saying something to Queen Elizabeth Jones, patting her curls, feeling her bare arms. Then he turned toward the balloon, leaning over to inspect the pump and hose from the gas generator, the basket, and the anchor ropes. When he stood erect, he saw Ben and frowned. Without pausing he swaggered toward the woods line.

"What're you doing here, boy?" he demanded.

"Doing nothing," Ben replied.

"Be off," Gaylord growled. "I don't allow drifters around my property."

Ben was tempted to stand his ground, but he saw Queen Elizabeth Jones motioning with both hands for him to comply. He stood up and turned to go into the woods.

"And don't come back," Gaylord ordered. "This is posted ground. If I see you around here again I'll have you locked up."

Ben walked slowly into the trees, not looking back until he was certain that he was out of sight of Gaylord. Then he kneeled and crept slowly back until he could see the big man stamping down the hill toward the tent. When Gaylord disappeared into the tent,

Ben walked out beside the balloon and called to Queen Elizabeth Jones.

She raised her head, startled, and he saw the shine of tears in her eyes.

"You can't stay here," he said loudly.

She was up, running toward him. "You better go, Ben. He'll do what he said if he catches you."

"Come on," he insisted, "let's both go now."

"He'll track us down."

A light breeze was tugging at the balloon, trying to lift it from its rope ties, but the grappling irons in the ground held them fast.

"You've changed," Ben said. "If you was like Jack Bonnycastle used to be, you'd lead us out of here yourself. You've turned scared."

"I am scared. That man is the wickedest man on earth."

"Why can't we just walk away through the woods?"

"Because he knows I want to leave. He's got somebody watching. He'd have his roustabouts out on horses before we went half a mile. After us, after me, I mean." As she spoke, she kept turning her head, looking down the slope to the big tent's entrance.

Ben could hear the faint hissing from the balloon's gas generator. He looked hard at the rattan basket.

"Do you know how to make this thing go up?"

Her mouth opened in surprise, not wanting to hear what she knew he was about to say. "I've been up," she said. "I've seen what Colonel Gaylord does."

"Get in that basket," he said.

She turned to take a quick look at the tent and then crawled over into the basket. "Lord, if he catches us he'll kill us."

"Jack Bonnycastle wouldn't give a single featherweight damn for Colonel Gaylord," he said harshly. "What do we do first?"

"Unfasten the grappling hooks and drop them in here with me. Then you get in."

Ben did as she said. The balloon began shifting to one side, the basket lifting only two or three feet from the ground.

Queen Elizabeth Jones reached for the tie of one of the bags hanging from the basket rim, loosed it, and let the bag drop to the ground. The balloon lifted another yard or more. "That's what he calls ballast," she said. "Bags of dirt."

Ben followed her example and dropped two more bags. The balloon shot upward in a hard jerk. He looked down into the tops of trees.

"They see us!" she cried.

Ben whirled and saw men running out of the tent that was now almost directly beneath them. The balloon's ascension stopped abruptly. He reached for one of the ballast bags.

"It's the mooring rope," she cried faintly. Her voice held a note of terror, of hopelessness. "I forgot to tell you. They can pull us back down."

He leaned over the edge of the basket. The tether rope was fastened to one of the metal rods that framed the wickerwork. He could just barely reach the tight knot.

"Hold on to my legs!" he shouted and then felt her arms circling his shins as she threw her whole weight against him. Tugging at the knot, fighting it, he could hear the shouts of men below growing louder as they hauled in the mooring rope.

He had almost abandoned hope when the knot gave way under his frantic fingers, and then like a released bird the balloon soared upward.

The town of Vandalia became a picture in a book with painted greens and yellows and browns, and then it was gone, swept away as though by a brush, replaced by a straight line cutting through green trees. The line was a railroad running straight as an arrow past embankments and bridging streams that were tiny curling strips of pale blue ribbon.

The only sounds were gentle wind whispers and faint insectlike chirrups from the friction of the ropes. He could hear her breathing then, her head pressed close to his shoulder, one hand grasping his arm, the other an edge of the basket.

"Are you still scared?" he asked.

"No."

"Well, I am," he said. "How do we get down again?"

She laughed for the first time since they had left the ground. "Simple, simple. I've watched old Gaylord do it when the mooring rope was pulling too hard." She pointed at a cord hanging above them and then reached up and pulled it sharply. Gas hissed from a valve, and the balloon slanted downward toward a grove of oaks. She calmly dropped a ballast bag from the rim. The balloon lifted.

"There's a big field past the woods," he said. She pulled the cord again, slightly this time, and they coasted down, down. A few yards below them a pair of ponies dashed madly toward a farmhouse. And then the basket struck the ground hard, dragging across the pasture until the balloon collapsed behind them, flattening on the grass.

They crawled out, quietly at first, and then they began laughing, laughing crazily, both of them. A sunburned boy wearing a ragged straw hat approached gingerly, pausing after each forward step, his eyes big, watching them warily.

Queen Elizabeth Jones got to her feet, smoothing her gray dress, brushing leaves and dead grass from her hair, and spoke to the boy, who then asked if that was indeed a balloon they had landed in.

"I saw a pitcher of it," he said, "in Vandalia. It's broke now, ain't it?"

"How far is it to Vandalia?" Ben asked.

"Don't know for certain. Twenty mile maybe."

A woman wearing a sunbonnet and a checked indigo apron had come from the farmhouse. "Mercy, one of 'em is a girl," she said as if talking to herself. "Young women do the wildest things since that Southern war come on. Did you ride that thing from Vandalia?"

They both assured her that they had, and then Ben pressed the woman for directions back to the National Road.

"We trade in Greenville," the woman said. "It's beside the big wide road."

Ben remembered passing through Greenville not long before making the last camp with the camels. After repeating the directions she gave him, he promised her that the circus would send someone to take away the balloon from her pasture.

By early afternoon they were on the road to Greenville, and with the aid of a friendly wagoner, a suspicious minister riding in a carriage, and the owner of a canvas-covered van, they reached Greenville late in the day. With its painted pictures of medicine bottles and Indian chiefs on the canvas, the van reminded them of Dr. Pingree's Chariot of Wonders, and for a time both stopped worrying about a furious Colonel Gaylord catching up with them.

From Greenville they walked most of the way to the slope where Ben had left Hadjee with the camels.

The sun had almost set, its slanted light casting long tree shadows. As Ben led Queen Elizabeth Jones off the road, he was surprised to see a horse near where the camels should be. At almost the same instant, a tall figure lifted a saddle above the horse's back.

"Johnny!" Queen Elizabeth Jones shouted, and weary though she was, she dashed for the top of the slope. Ben was just behind her when she sprang into Johnny's arms.

"Holy Comanche!" Johnny cried, and then he wrapped his long arms around the both of them. Behind Johnny lurked a delighted Hadjee, his yellow teeth showing in a broad smile.

"Lucky you come when you did," Johnny went on. "I was just about to start into Vandalia to rescue Princess from old Colonel Gaylord. Under cover of darkness, as they say." He turned to look hard at Ben. "You've growed some, old hoss, but them clothes. You must've found 'em in a rat nest." Ben quickly explained how he had come by the dirty, ragged cottonade, and then he and Queen Elizabeth Jones took turns telling about their flight in the balloon. Johnny was so amused that he began laughing, finally collapsing on the ground, wiping his eyes when he sat up.

"Old Colonel Gaylord must've spent the day cussin' you two," he said. "Maybe he ain't found his balloon yet. If he finds you two he'll see you both locked in jail."

"Do you think we ought to camp deeper back in the woods?" Ben asked.

"No, sirreee. We got to clear out of here and move on to Bright Star, Indiana. If we start now, we can skirt around Vandalia after midnight when everybody's asleep and hurry on to Indiana."

Queen Elizabeth Jones shook her head. "They'll be loading the circus about midnight."

"All the better, Princess. Old Gaylord will be bossing the roustabouts—if he ain't off somewheres trying to find his balloon." At the thought of the lost balloon, Johnny laughed again and then spoke briskly. "Let's pack up and skedaddle."

XXXIX

BEN BUTTERFIELD

~

Thinking about that balloon flight with Queen Elizabeth Jones—so long ago it was—reminds me of my failed life that is filled with lost loves and lost turnings.

On the wall just above the accursed telephone that is sitting on Old Man Fagerhalt's desk is the last circus poster sent to me by Johnny Hawkes. I sit here in this creaky old chair with my attention fixed upon the artist's fanciful face of Queen Elizabeth Jones, mounted upon her white steed, I pondering as I have done more than a thousand times why fate in its unfaithful manner delights in tearing away whatever my heart and soul chose to hold dear.

That late summer day in rustic Illinois, when we two shared an adventure the like of which seldom comes to the very young, I was sure that she and I would never part again. I was too young to read the subtle meanings of attitudes that perhaps even she could not comprehend. From the moment that she saw Johnny on the slope, preparing to saddle his horse to ride like a knight to her rescue, she wanted always to be in his presence. I must have been aware of this in some way, but I also sought Johnny as a sheltering patriarch, a role he never wanted, although at Fort Davis he reassured me numerous times that the black-bearded man I was told was my father would return one day to claim me as his son. And then finally as the months went by and I persisted in my questioning, Johnny quietly and gradually let me know that perhaps the man would never return.

To me as a child it was abandonment. And then Miz Sergeant Peddicord forsook me by dying. But when the fort was closed because of the war's outbreak, and Johnny without employment set off for San Antonio, he did not desert me. And then a year or so later, at that camel camp near the town of Vandalia, I was too young, too unknowing to foresee that if Queen Elizabeth Jones persuaded Johnny never to forsake her, then she must forsake me.

Enough of this maundering. In a few days I shall see her again, not the young girl of the balloon but a woman almost as old as I, a famous equestrienne who once sent me occasional notices and postal cards from the great cities of the nation and the world. With Johnny gone, she may feel more forsaken than I.

This morning's Gazette printed a ballyhoo piece about the Austrian trick riders who recently joined the circus, but there was only a brief paragraph about that daring equestrienne, Queen Elizabeth Jones. Undoubtedly as the day of performance comes nearer there will be much more about her—and perhaps a paragraph or two about her deceased husband, Johnny Hawkes.

Later in the day. As I completed taking a telephone order for a garden rake, my thoughts were interrupted by the voices of young boys crying shrilly, the first one far away, another on the street outside. At first I let the sounds pass around me, but then as I hooked up the telephone receiver, I was struck by the possible meaning of a newspaper's extra edition. I hurried outside and guessed the headline before the newsboy handed me a paper: OUR PRESIDENT IS DEAD.

So Brigadier Boggs had been right. The president's doctors spoke too soon, with the brashness of modern scientists. Not even our perfect antiseptics of the new century could save William McKinley from the deadly bacteria invading his wound. His physicians have been too confident of their godlike powers.

I remember the words of old Socrates Drumm, the Civil War surgeon who ministered to the animals and human beings of the circus of my youth. In the Civil War, he said, a soldier was better off most of the time if he kept away from surgeons. Dowsing a gunshot wound with whiskey was the best remedy, he said. Perhaps President McKinley's doctors should have used whiskey.

I've been waiting for the telephone bell to ring and hear the lamentations of Brigadier Boggs. But no, he has just arrived in person, his face lugubrious.

"My God, Ben," he declared, "what is our nation coming to?"

"This is an uncertain world," I said. "As is the Great Beyond."

He sat down in the little straight chair that Hilda uses when she pauses in her short visits to this room. "You speak as if you had been conversing with the Reverend Bragg," he said.

"No, the reverend has about given up on me. But I'm sure that in next Sunday's sermon he will find a way to comfort and inspire us."

The brigadier sighed. "How can you be so mildly philosophical, in light of what's happened to the nation?"

"I don't fear for the nation. Remember, you and I have seen it at its worst."

He moaned softly. "I have held such high hopes for the new century. Surely we have learned to live and let live through the nineteenth century. What do you think lies ahead of us, Ben?"

"Prophecy is a cheap way to mislead anybody foolheaded enough to listen to a prophet. I could sermonize to you about mankind's good and evil, Brigadier. But I leave that to the Reverend Bragg."

"Yes," he agreed, "you and I are amateurs on that subject." He paused and looked out the window. On the sidewalk, two or three small groups of men, with newspapers in their hands, had stopped to talk.

"What I fear now," the brigadier continued, "is the elevation of Teddy Roosevelt to the presidency. Roosevelt is a wild young man, a cowboy. His recklessness may bring on catastrophe to the nation."

"They say his cowboy Rough Riders turned the tide in the Spanish War."

"We don't need that kind of tide turning in the White House." He stopped, waiting for me to counter what he had said. He knew that I admired Teddy the cowboy.

When I did not respond, he changed the subject. "By the way, I hear that Theo Drumgoole and Betty Hesterly are soon to announce their wedding. To be held at the Grimsley House."

"Yes, Hilda got word of it yesterday. As she always does. I tell her she could be the town crier."

The brigadier shook his head. "You shouldn't tease her, Ben. You're lucky to have Hilda."

"I know," I replied. "I wouldn't tease her if I didn't know I'm lucky."

For a minute he was silent again. "What would you think, Ben, of an old codger like me getting married again?"

"I learned a long time ago never to speak advice on the subject of marriage."

"Well, I'm fond of Maude Grimsley and she's fond of me." His gray eyes had been looking straight at me, but now, like a timid schoolboy, he dropped his head forward. "The fly in the ointment, the rub, the obstacle, is my daughter. Blossom, you know has been motherless since childhood. Blossom cannot abide Maude. Poor child, she has grown up in my small hotel and knows so little of the world."

I wondered what the brigadier would say if I told him what I knew about Blossom and of how she had so boldly pinched my groin.

While I was pondering this, the bell jangled on the telephone. The voice on the other end was Hereward Padgett's. He wanted to know if I had heard the news about President McKinley, and he was well into a discussion of the deserved fates of politicians when I interrupted to tell him I was very busy and would ring him on the telephone later.

The brigadier was rising from his chair. "I expect you are looking forward to the circus," he said.

"Yes. Next week."

"I've heard you speak of friends you knew there. They are still active?"

"One or two."

"I suppose I'll take Maude to see it. Perhaps you'll introduce us to the performers."

"Perhaps."

"Well, good day, Ben. I feel the better for our little visit."

I stood up, grimacing from a sudden pain in my busted leg, and shook his hand. He looked quite happy.

XL

BRIGHT STAR, INDIANA

After Hadjee had fashioned a rigging from bits of pieces of rope and leather that he carried in his poke sack, he fastened the calf to Tooley's back. With Ben and Queen Elizabeth Jones riding Johnny's circus horse, and Johnny on Omar, they started along the National Road to Vandalia.

Both Johnny and Queen Elizabeth Jones had quickly formed an attachment to the calf, which Johnny christened "Uncle Sam" the moment he first saw it.

"Why such a name as Uncle Sam?" Queen Elizabeth Jones asked.

"Because he was born in the United States of America," Johnny replied, "and he deserves an American name. Instead of something like Tooley or Omar."

As they moved on through the deepening umber light of dusk, each of them recalled the days they had been together on the road to the town of Rolla, in Missouri, where everything had begun to go wrong. Only Hadjee voiced his elation—in various idioms—expressing regret that their former benefactor, Dr. Pingree, was not with them.

They came into Vandalia in the middle of the night. From the late summer sky, multitudes of stars, enlarged in the clarity of the atmosphere, were glittering so that altogether they shed as much light over the town as a full moon.

And as they expected, the circus roustabouts were still loading animals and equipment into freight cars standing on a sidetrack beside the railroad station. Ordering Ben and Queen Elizabeth

Jones to dismount, Johnny took the horse on a scout along streets
south of the busy station.

In a few minutes he returned to guide them around the edge of
the town. Soon they were out in the countryside, following the
National Road that ran straight and free of other travelers into the
luminous night. By dawn all of them were frazzled from lack of
sleep, but Johnny kept them moving until near midday.

"Old Colonel Gaylord will be out for vengeance," he said.
"Mad as a bucket full of rattlesnakes because of what you sprouts
did to his balloon. And we're riding one of his circus horses. He'll
have every sheriff in Illinois looking for reward money."

"How much do you think he posted for me?" Queen Elizabeth
Jones asked.

"A ransom of precious gems of the first water."

They camped outside a village marked Ewington, in prairie
grass taller than the average man. "Better not make a fire here,"
Johnny said. "We'll chew on them pig rinds Ben bought in Vandalia."

They awoke one by one as the day came to an end, and at
sundown Johnny urged them on the road again.

Two days later, as they were halting in a churchyard, Ben saw
beside a well a buggy with yellow angels painted on its dashboard.
Browsing on grass near the buggy was an ash-gray mare, and beyond the mare was Richard Puckle, seated on the well's shelf. Puckle was looking up at a man standing at ease on a peg leg. The
crippled man also had lost an arm.

As soon as he dismounted, Ben walked across to the well and
exchanged greetings with Puckle.

This renewal of acquaintanceship turned out to be a boon for
Ben and his companions. The man with Puckle was a war veteran
named Edgar Kegg, described by Puckle as a "well-to-do patriot,"
who had sacrificed two limbs for the Union at Shiloh. Kegg had
also provided Puckle with a generous supply of meats and breads.
Consequently the two men invited Ben and his friends to join them
for supper.

During the meal, Puckle went through the same routine that
Ben had heard before—his pilgrimage to Washington City to see
Abe Lincoln and present his plan for ending the bloody war. "I
have persuaded Mr. Kegg to accompany me, for Mr. Kegg has

suffered the worst ordeal of war. He will show you what he is going to show the president," Puckle said. Mr. Kegg bowed slightly and limped over to the rear of the buggy. He took out a long, narrow wooden box and brought it back, unhooking the fasteners and throwing open the lid. Inside was the skeleton of a man's leg from the foot to above the knee and also a skeleton of a man's arm from hand to above the elbow.

At first sight of them, Queen Elizabeth Jones smothered a scream and then walked away from the group. Ben and Hadjee stepped closer to examine the bones. When the Egyptian reached out as though to touch them, Kegg said sternly, "Do not touch, please."

"I take it these are yours, Mr. Kegg," Johnny said.

"Lost at Pittsburgh Landing, nigh on to Shiloh Church in Tennessee. On the sixth day of April last. I persuaded the surgeon to bag them for me, and I limed off the rotting flesh coming north on the riverboat."

Next morning they formed a small procession and headed into the rising sun. Richard Puckle's buggy took the lead, and he allowed Queen Elizabeth Jones and Ben to take turns in the back of the vehicle so that Johnny could ride the circus horse.

When they stopped for nooning, Johnny remarked on the deteriorating state of Ben's salt-and-pepper cottonade pants. "It's a wonder to me some lawman don't haul you in for exposing too much. Your bare ass is poking through the backside and your knees are doing the same in front. How much *dinero* you got left in that purse Captain Lightfoot give you?"

Ben handed Johnny the purse.

"Not much here," Johnny said. "Lightfoot figured it close. If you spend for new dungarees, the camels and us won't eat."

"You want to keep the purse?" Ben asked.

"Nah. I still got a little tin from what Marigold Cakebread lent me against what old Gaylord owes me. You better keep the *dinero*. Money don't stick to me, somehow."

He returned the purse to Ben. "Speakin' of the Cakebreads, I tell you what we can do. We can sell Uncle Sam to them. They'd pay well for that baby camel.

Hadjee apparently understood the gist of what Johnny had said.

"No, no, no!" he shouted, and Queen Elizabeth Jones joined him in the outcry. She walked over to the calf and sat down beside it. "Anyway," she said, "Colonel Gaylord would take all the money and likely throw us in jail to boot."

Next day they were in Indiana, crossing the Wabash River and then entering Terre Haute. Although the time was early afternoon, Johnny announced that they would stop to recuperate before moving on to Bright Star. "Terre Haute looks to be a prosperous city, with big solid buildings and horsecars in the streets," he said. "Maybe some of it will rub off on us."

In front of the Vermillion Livery Stable & Outfitting Emporium they said farewells to Richard Puckle and Mr. Kegg, and then from his shrinking purse Ben paid the liveryman for stables and bed stalls for one night.

"You know what, old hoss," Johnny said. "We're in Indiana. Where your papa come from."

"I thought of that when we passed the marker," Ben said, "but I don't know where in Indiana he come from. Maybe I don't care. It was little he cared for me."

"Your papa named his town to me when he was at Fort Davis. He told Miz Sergeant Peddicord more'n once, I 'spect, but she can't help us now. What *is* the name of that place where he come from? Maybe I'll think of it."

With part of his loan from Marigold Cakebread, Johnny took them to the Emporium's adjoining tavern for supper. Soon after they returned to the stables, he announced that he had a bit of business to attend to out in the town. Queen Elizabeth Jones declared that she was going with him, but he refused her and turned angry when she kept insisting. A moment later he was gone.

Ben guessed what Johnny's "bit of business" might be, and was not surprised that he did not return until almost morning. At full daylight, he rousted everyone out of their hay beds and took them off to the tavern for splendid breakfasts.

"I'll tell you what, old hoss," Johnny began over his plate of ham and eggs, "these Terre Haute buckaroos can't gauge the difference in value of an ace and a king, or a queen and a jack. This morning I've got a pocketful of Indiana scratch. Now, down the street is a dry goods store where they sell men's dungarees. We're going there as soon as we eat."

Queen Elizabeth Jones immediately demanded a pair of jeans for herself. "It ain't easy to ride behind a saddle in a dress," she said. "It ain't ladylike."

"It ain't ladylike for a lady to wear jeans," Johnny retorted, but when they went to the dry goods store he bought her a pair.

On the way back to the livery stable, Johnny stopped in front of a saloon. "There's something in here I want Ben to see," he said. "Princess, you and Hadjee go on and get the animals ready to head out."

A few steps inside the saloon entrance, Johnny stopped and pointed to a map on the wall. "The State of Indiana," he said. "Every county and town in Indiana." He put a fingertip on Bright Star and then moved it an inch or so to the right. "Butterfield," he said. "I wonder why I couldn't remember your papa's saying his town was the same name as his. He must've been a man of parts to come from a town named for his family—Butterfield."

Ben could not speak at first. He stood there staring at his name on the map. "Well, so," he said quietly.

"Butterfield town can't be more'n three or four hours horseback from Bright Star," Johnny said.

"Well, so," Ben repeated.

The sun was very bright in the morning sky when they left the stables and found their way through the streets to the National Road. They had scarcely turned into the highway when a big man riding a coal-black horse cut in front of them. He held up an open hand as a signal for them to halt.

"You didn't come round to enlist, Mr. Hawkes," the man said coldly. "Like you promised me last evening."

"No," Johnny replied. "Some urgent business come up this morning."

"You could come back in town with me now," the man said, his tone almost threatening. "You said you'd been a cavalryman."

"A scout for the cavalry," Johnny corrected him. "I never been in a uniform."

"The time has come for you to wear one," the man insisted. "A blue uniform. Like I told you, we're filling a Terre Haute cavalry company for a new Indiana volunteer regiment. We'd like to have you, Hawkes, as a volunteer instead of a conscript."

Johnny used a slight pressure on one knee to start the circus horse to prancing. "I'm on army business right now," he said loudly as he tightened his reins. "We're late delivering these camels to Bright Star."

The man did not seem satisfied. "Maybe you don't know President Lincoln has signed a conscription law. You're over eighteen years. I could have you arrested for refusing to register."

Ben, who was riding behind Johnny's saddle, did not like the way the talk was going. "Sir," he interrupted. "Johnny Hawkes and me, we're Texicans. We're not part of your war."

The man frowned angrily at first and then threw his head back as he laughed loudly. "Don't that tad know Texas is Rebel country? All the more reason you need to enlist in a hurry, Hawkes."

"What say I agree to come back here to Terre Haute soon as I deliver these camels?"

"I'll keep you to your word," the man replied. "You'd suffer disgrace if you force us to take you as a conscript."

"Fair enough," Johnny said. He raised a hand in salute and urged his horse forward. After a few paces, he glanced behind to make certain the man on the black horse had turned back toward the town.

"Scalawag," Johnny said softly. "He was in that poker game last night, and I took him for forty green ones. I reckon he wants it back in some manner somehow."

The National Road was now wider and so straight that the farthest visible point seemed to vanish into infinity. Where weather had damaged the graveled surface, washing pebbles onto the shoulders; blocks of stone were visible on the base. Every bridge large or small was built of limestone, often supported by graceful arches.

As the morning progressed, wagon traffic grew heavier. At every crossroads or fork, stone markers stood with carved lettering to show place names and distances. "It's a grand road," Johnny observed to Ben as they rode along together. "All the way to Baltimore, they say. But a man told me last night that since the war broke out the surface has begun to break apart. Railways are the road's enemy, he said. The road builders graded from Terre Haute to Vandalia and surveyed to the Mississippi River, but the railroads got ahead of the highway builders and beat them to the Mississippi River, and they'll never finish it to the Pacific Ocean."

Just before sundown they reached a village called Pleasant Garden and camped at a crossroads beside a small field of sunflowers. The sunflowers were enormous and filled with bees working late. A stone marker told the name of the place, the distances to Putnamsville and Indianapolis. At the bottom an arrow pointed southward: Bright Star, 12 miles.

Early the next morning they were on the dusty road plodding southward. For days and weeks Bright Star had been their destination, a place that Ben envisioned from a drawing he had seen in one of Miz Sergeant Peddicord's books. In the drawing the heavens were ablaze with light, and from between two parallel streams of clouds, a benevolent human face looked down upon a hamlet of a dozen or so houses forming a rectangle. A neat farmstead adjoined the village. Beams of sunlight struck the earth, the farmstead, and the hamlet. In Ben's own vision on that fair morning in Indiana, the human face was framed within a star brighter than the earth's sun.

When they came to the limits of Bright Star, with its limestone marker engraved as though Bright Star was one word, Ben could not believe the ordinariness of the place. The leaves of trees along the road that had become a Bright Star street were fading into dull brown and mottled yellow. On the right, whitewashed outbuildings reached to the edge of the thoroughfare. On the left, the porch of the first house was shabby with clutter and unpainted leaning posts.

As they moved into the small collection of business houses, children too young for school and a few women wearing gray aprons began gathering at first sight of the camels. The women and children followed the little procession until it halted at a watering trough in front of a brick mercantile building. On a wooden sidewalk fronting the adjoining Star Saloon, several men were staring at Hadjee and the camels. When Johnny dismounted from Omar (Ben and Queen Elizabeth Jones were on the circus horse), a tall man in farmer's clothing stepped closer. He was probing at his teeth with a metal toothpick. When Johnny asked him for directions to Captain Solomon Lightfoot's farm, the man's eyes brightened. He slipped the toothpick into a vest pocket and came to the edge of the sidewalk.

"Turn north at the next corner," he said pointing a long finger. "Only a couple of miles." He nodded his head vigorously, smiling knowingly. "We heard about the camels," he continued. "Solomon Lightfoot always was a wee strange. Good boy, though. Good boy. But a wee strange."

After the camels had drunk from the trough, Johnny mounted Omar and they resumed the journey, leaving the failed expectations of the town of Bright Star behind them.

Luke and Cozie Broadhead, the keepers of Captain Lightfoot's farm, came out of the rambling farmhouse a few moments after Ben opened the gate into the approach lane. The Broadheads had been awaiting early arrival of the camels, having read in the Terre Haute *Headlight* the previous day an item about the presence of the animals in that city.

The Broadheads were well along in life, their faces darkened by years of outdoor toil, their hands hardened and lumpy with enlarged veins. As their visitors soon discovered, the pair was not husband and wife but brother and sister.

Whenever Luke laughed, only two or three scattered teeth were visible in his mouth. He laughed often, nervously at first and then obviously enjoying the peculiar business of the camels.

"We never know," Cozie said, "what odd thing young Mr. Solomon will do next. Like these here camels now."

Luke interrupted abruptly. "I reckon you folks heard young Mr. Solomon gone and got himself captured by the Rebels."

Johnny's mouth opened in astonishment. "No, we haven't heard nothing since he was in St. Louis."

"Yessir," Luke went on, delighted that he held information unknown to his visitors. "Yessir, he got himself captured down in Vinginny."

"You heard from him?" Johnny asked.

"No, sir, not directly. From Colonel Whetstone."

"Who's Colonel Whetstone?"

"The colonel handles this county's military matters, takes care of mustering volunteer soldiers. He got young Mr. Lightfoot his captaincy. I'm supposed to notify Colonel Whetstone the minute as you put in appearance. So I reckon I better hitch up the buggy and go."

~

A few minutes later Luke Broadhead was on his way, twirling and cracking his buggy whip as he set his horse off at a trot. In the lazy Indian summer afternoon the weary travelers awaited his return, idling in hickory chairs on the farmhouse porch and along the front steps. Cozie brought out a pitcher of cool spring water and then spent considerable time asking questions in an attempt to determine Queen Elizabeth Jones's part in the strange company that had invaded her small world.

When Colonel Whetstone arrived, he was riding a mount that Johnny immediately recognized and declared to be a Kentucky Standardbred with Morgan blood. "A great pacing horse," he was saying to Ben as the colonel dismounted.

Ben noticed that Colonel Whetstone's uniform trousers were so tight at the waist that even his wide belt could not conceal the loose buttons on the upper part of his trousers. His middle evidently had thickened since he acquired the uniform. Yet his jacket was so magnificent with its double row of polished brass buttons and yellow galloons on the sleeves that viewers tended to overlook any faults in his very military dress.

With obvious relish, Luke Broadhead introduced the colonel to everyone. The colonel kept a solemn face, so absorbed with his own importance that he undoubtedly promptly forgot the names of those he shook hands with as gravely as if he were officiating at a funeral. Then he came to the point abruptly, turning to Johnny as he spoke. "I have official information from the War Department for you, Mr. Butterfield, concerning Captain Solomon Lightfoot. Unfortunately, Mr. Butterfield, Captain Lightfoot has been captured while in pursuit of his duties near Camp—"

"Beggin' your pardon, sir," Johnny interrupted. "I am John Hawkes, not Ben Butterfield."

Colonel Whetstone stopped reading from the telegraph message, puzzlement in his voice. "But Captain Lightfoot informed me before he went to Washington City that all matters concerning his camels were to be directed to a Mr. Benjamin Butterfield."

"That's him right there," Johnny declared, jerking a thumb toward Ben.

The colonel peered at Ben suspiciously as though suspecting

that he was being played for a fool. "That boy? You mean that boy is Benjamin Butterfield?"

"None other," Johnny said with a broad grin. "Ben and that little girl there wearing the pantaloons, and the Egyptian, brought them camels most of the way from Springfield in Missouri. I joined in from time to time, but mostly I was on more pressin' business."

The colonel shook his head wonderingly and then said, "Well, then, there you have it: Captain Lightfoot is a prisoner in Virginia. I can tell you that our governor, Oliver Morton, is doing his damnedest to find a Rebel prisoner of war of equal rank to offer in exchange for the release of Solomon Lightfoot. Until then we must wait with patience and hope."

"I surmise," Johnny said flatly, "that some days must pass before we hear from or see the captain himself."

"Perhaps weeks," Colonel Whetstone replied gloomily.

Johnny arose from the hickory chair in which he had been sitting and walked a step or two toward the colonel. "May I also surmise, sir, that the captain previously arranged for funds to be paid Ben Butterfield."

"I have no knowledge of any such funds," the colonel replied. "Perhaps the Broadheads are aware—"

Cozie interrupted. "The only letter we got from young Mr. Solomon, from Washington City—he said we was to persuade the boy, young Master Butterfield, and the Egyptian—he could not remember his name—to stay on with us—free bed and board—till young Mr. Solomon could get a furlough back here. He wrote nothing about that little girl wearing the britches. But he was sure the war would end as soon as his commander, General Sheridan, went after the Rebels."

Johnny shook his head. "So there's no stash to pay Ben Butterfield or any of us for all the time we spent herding them camels." He reached out and patted Ben's shoulder. "I reckon, old hoss, you and Hadjee got to decide if you stay here and wait for the captain, or head back in the direction of Missouri and Texas with Princess and me."

"Not so hasty, sir," Colonel Whetstone commanded in his most solemn tones. "Not so hasty." From inside his tightly buttoned jacket he withdrew a folded sheet of manila paper. "There is much

graver news, I fear." He paused deliberately to allow the full effect
of his words to hang in suspense over his audience. "This telegram
came by way of my commander in Indianapolis, and is from the
quartermaster general's office in Washington City. It is signed by
Major General Montgomery C. Meigs. I shall now read the telegram:

Whereas it has come to the attention of this office that Captain
Solomon Lightfoot of the Quartermaster's Department while
on duty with General Samuel R. Curtis in Missouri and Arkansas took possession of two camels captured from the Confederate Army. Because of the substantial value of these camels,
Captain Lightfoot is hereby commanded to turn them back to
the Quartermaster's Department. As a market for camels is unlikely to be found in the State of Indiana, the department
hereby authorizes Captain Lightfoot to prepare for shipment
of the animals to the City of New York where a market is to
be found among the proprietors of menageries, circuses, and
museums. Advise immediately as to exact location of said camels. Instructions as to handling, provisioning, and funding for
shipment will follow on receipt of requested information.

> Montgomery C. Meigs
> Bravet Major General

Until late in the day, Colonel Whetstone remained with the
dumbfounded group on the porch of the Lightfoot farmhouse. He
commiserated with Cozie and Luke Broadhead who could barely
speak of the crushing disappointment the telegram would surely
bring to Captain Lightfoot, whether or not he was released from
imprisonment in Virginia.

Johnny began discussing what he and Ben and Queen Elizabeth
Jones and Hadjee should do now that the camels were being taken
from their care. Among the four of them they could raise only a
few greenbacks and shinplasters. As usual Queen Elizabeth Jones
carried a few coins secreted in a knotted handkerchief, which she
admitted were not sufficient to buy more than a few dozen eggs.

Overhearing their conversation, Colonel Whetstone suggested
that they not hasten away from Bright Star. Perhaps one or two of
them might be employed, he said, to oversee transport of the cam-

els to the City of New York. The War Department, he added, paid excellent wages to citizens.

And then Luke Broadhead spoke up and said that his corn crop and the crops of his neighbors would soon need to be harvested. Because so many young men had gone off to war, there was a shortage of workers on the farms, and good pay could be earned by those willing to labor in the fields.

So that night as bedtime approached, they talked lengthily of what the future might hold for them. After the implications of the telegram from the Quartermaster's Department were made clear to Hadjee, the Egyptian appeared to be more concerned than any of them about the fate of the camels. For many months he had lived so closely to Omar and Tooley, and now the calf called Uncle Sam, that he could not bear the thought of being separated from them. Refusing to accept a comfortable bed in the farmhouse, he trudged off to the barn and slept in the hay with his charges.

XLI

BEN BUTTERFIELD

❧

The circus is coming tomorrow, and in the Gazette this morning is a short piece about Queen Elizabeth Jones, a listing of her honors as an equestrienne in Europe as well as in the United States. This is followed by a paragraph about her late husband, my dear old departed friend and mentor, Johnny Hawkes. I am disappointed that no photograph of Johnny's Princess is included. Perhaps the circus ballyhoo peddlers did not wish to print the old photo they have used for some years, and perhaps a current photograph would not be especially flattering. After all, when I look into the mirror nowadays I do not see the dashing young fellow that I was when I rode in Queen Elizabeth Jones's principal act.

In the past half hour, that monstrous telephone on Old Man Fagerhalt's desk has jangled its inharmonious bell at me four or five times. To ensure that all her customers are aware of the wire connection and the number of this telephone, Hilda sent me to the post office the other day to buy five hundred penny postcards. She has been mailing them out all week, and some of the bell rings are coming from people who only want to say hello.

A while ago, when I took some written messages from the telephone down the hall to give to Hilda, whom should I see coming in the entrance but Hereward Padgett. Hilda immediately tried to intercept him by asking what he wanted (she thinks Hereward needs locking up in a loony bin), but he responded in his direct way that he wanted to see me on a matter of important business.

I noted that moisture had formed below Hereward's lower lip, as it always does when he's excited, saliva flooding out in the savoring of his luscious bits of gossip. His dark eyes were also brighter than usual.

He followed me back into Old Man Fagerhalt's office, beginning his flow of tidings the moment we were inside. "I bet you haven't heard about Blossom Boggs," he said, turning the cane chair around backward and straddling the seat.

"No," I said, "I've heard nothing about Blossom for several days."

"On the bicycle?"

"I didn't know she had a bicycle."

"Her papa's bicycle."

"Was she learning to ride it?"

"No. She was riding it. Completely nekkid. Right about midnight. On Louisiana Street."

"You saw her?"

"No. Eulalie and her ma saw her. Eulalie told me."

I remembered that Eulalie Buck is the gap-toothed girl often seen in Hereward's company. He went on to explain that the two Buck women had been over to Lucy Markham's house to take care of her children while she was away for the evening. They were taking a shortcut through an alley that runs by Brigadier Boggs's hotel. Always one for details, Hereward said that Eulalie had told him that Blossom was unusually hairy.

"Are you going to tell Brigadier General Boggs?" Hereward asked.

"No. Why should I?"

"I've observed you to be close friends."

"More reason not to say anything. But we're not especially close friends. We have mutual interests."

"Somebody ought to tell him," Hereward insisted.

"He wouldn't believe it," I said.

Hereward wiped his moist chin with a spotless white handkerchief. "Well, it's the truth. Eulalie wouldn't make up something like that."

He changed the subject abruptly, as Hereward is wont to do. "I suppose you and Miss Hilda will be going to the circus tomorrow night."

"Hilda does not care for circuses," I said. "But I shall be going."

"You know some people in the circus," he said.

"Yes," I replied. "Old friends." And when I said those words I had a very strange feeling. Like on that morning back in Indiana forty years ago when I started on that old circus horse to go to the town of Butterfield.

The telephone is ringing, and Hereward Padgett is bouncing away down the hall, waving his fingers back at me.

XLII

BUTTERFIELD, INDIANA

~

I was awake half the night with bad dreams," Ben said. "Maybe the dreams was warning me to stay away."

"Nah," Johnny answered him. "Most likely you had visions. Old Paroowah, he taught me some Comanche words when I was in Indian Territory—I was no older'n you are now. Paroowah said dreams are visions. What did you dream about?"

"A man with a dark beard and eyes set back in the sockets. He kept staring at me all night, following me, chasing me."

Johnny studied the boy's face. They were standing outside the open double doors of the Lightfoot barn, Johnny holding the bridle of the circus horse that he had just saddled. "It was a vision," Johnny said. "Your father had a black beard and deep-set eyes. He wants you in his town." He pulled on the bridle, dancing the circus horse so that the stirrups were closer to Ben. "Believe me, if I knew a town named for my folks, I'd sure want to have a look at it."

"You and Princess won't start off for Missouri while I'm gone, will you?" Ben asked.

"Lord, no. We got to pick up some stash before we leave here." Johnny rubbed the beard stubble on his chin. "You been actin' mighty skittery, like you're feared of something. Did all them years I spent teachin' you not to be afraid of any man or beast or thing—did they go for nothin'?"

"I'm not afraid of any man or beast or thing," Ben said. He took the reins from Johnny and climbed quickly into the saddle. "See you when I get back." He set the circus horse to prancing and then urged it to a trot down the lane to the gate. Behind him he heard Queen Elizabeth Jones shouting good-bye and good luck from the front porch. He waved back to her but did not turn to look. A dreadful apprehension choked him so that he could not use his voice, a foreboding that he would never see her again.

The road to the town that bore his name took him through a checkerboard of russet and green and yellow fields. While crossing Missouri and Illinois he had grown used to green in the landscape, but on this morning he longed for the stark absence of color, the dead browns and grays of the earth and mountains, and solid black-blueness of the sky.

From time to time he met farmers on horseback, in wagons, or on foot, carrying loads of produce, scythes, or husking tools. They all spoke to him but eyed him and the high-stepping horse with the curiosity of anchored beings looking upon strangers intruding on their lives. Ben envied them. He had not been in their stationary world since the day Fort Davis was closed and he and Johnny started for San Antonio in an old army wagon.

The lively circus horse brought him into Butterfield about noontime. He stopped at a watering trough and a well just outside a blacksmith shop. After unbitting the horse, he pulled up a bucket of water, poured some into the trough, and then unwrapped a sheet of newspaper from around a bacon sandwich that Johnny had thrust into his blouse pocket that morning.

While he was eating the sandwich, the clang of metal against metal came from the smithy. After swallowing another drink of the sweet well water, he led the horse around to the open front of the smithy. The blacksmith finished shaping an ax blade before stopping to look up at Ben. The man's hair was redder than Ben's; his unsleeved forearms were spotted with small healed blisters. He spat a mouthful of tobacco juice into the burning coals and waited expectantly for Ben to speak.

Not knowing what to say, Ben remained silent.

"What do you want, boy?" the blacksmith asked impatiently.

"I'm looking for a family named Butterfield. Same name as this town."

The blacksmith placed his hammer beside his anvil. "So? Well, as I recall they're all gone." He paused. "No, wait a minute. There's an old lady. A widow woman." He stepped closer to Ben so that he had a clearer view of houses scattered randomly on a rise in the land beyond the graveled street.

"See that house with faded green shutters?" He pointed.

"Yes, sir."

"Widow Twillie lives there. I hear she was a Butterfield afore she wed old Twillie." He looked more closely at Ben. "You must be Butterfield kin."

Ben nodded without speaking, then thanked the blacksmith. He mounted the circus horse and started for the house with green shutters.

A wild vine wound along the top of the rotting fence and gate. The yard inside was overgrown with drying grass and weeds. A narrow half-porch had lost much of its last coat of whitewash.

Ben knocked on the weather-worn green door. For a minute or more there was no response. He knocked again, and this time he heard faint rustlings. The door opened slowly, less than a foot, and an aging woman, birdlike in her appearance and movements, looked out at him. "Yes?"

"If you are Mrs. Twillie," Ben said, "I was told you are a Butterfield."

The woman's gray eyes widened. Obviously she had been startled by Ben's words.

"Yes, who are you, boy? Do I know you?"

"No, but I came to find out something about my father."

"Your father? Who are you, boy?"

"My name is Ben Butterfield."

She opened the door all the way and stood staring at him, a thin woman in a black bombazine dress and a white cap with an unfolded brim pressed down upon her gray hair.

"Where do you come from, boy?"

"Texas," he replied. "I was left at Fort Davis in Texas."

"Yes, yes, brother Ben wrote of a child in Texas. We thought the child had died long ago."

Ben shook his head. "No, I was forsaken."

She closed her eyes for a moment. "Wait here," she said then. "Wait just a minute."

Leaving the door open, she disappeared into the shadows of the old house.

As she had promised she was back in a minute, wearing a woolen shawl that had been dyed a streaky indigo. "Come with me," she said, leading the way out to the gate, moving as though on tiptoes.

He followed her along a sandy pathway until the hilltop turned into a downslope. On the slope was an unfenced cemetery, with grave markers of stone and wood, some old, some recently placed. As Ben soon discovered, the graves were grouped by family names.

He followed the birdlike woman to a grave still mounded and covered with grass and dried wildflowers. The headstone was beginning to show traces of weather stains. She caught his wrist and pulled him close beside her so that he could see the inscription cut into the stone.

BENJAMIN BUTTERFIELD
1820–1854
Brought Home by Angels

She leaned closer to him, peering into his eyes, placing her fingers on his forehead, his nose, his chin. "I perceived you to be one of us when I saw your stance and the shape of your head in the doorway." She smiled. "You look a good bit like your father when he was your age."

"Why didn't he come by Fort Davis for me when he returned home to Indiana?"

Her lips tightened before she spoke. "He come home in a tin box. He died of a fever in a California mining camp. He couldn't come for you." She stopped and looked back at the tombstone. "His miner friends made a tin box out of cans and put charcoal around him and sealed him up. They sent the tin coffin and a bag of his things—clothes and a little pouch of gold dust."

"I did not know about that," Ben said.

"He never named the place he left you, what station or fort. I guess he thought he'd be going back there. The army people in Washington City told us they had no record of a child left in their care in Texas."

Ben said nothing. He looked again at the name carved into the graying stone.

"When you come to my door while ago," she went on, "you said he had forsaken you."

"I've believed that most of my life."

She spread her delicate arms. He could see the blue veins distended on the backs of her hands.

"He never forsook you," she said. "If anybody forsook you, it was I. I failed to persevere in the search for you."

XLIII

BEN BUTTERFIELD

~

I am writing this on the day the circus is coming to town. It is a mellow day as autumn days go, filled with slanting sunlight and golden leaves.

For an hour after we opened the hardware store this morning the abominable telephone did not utter a sound. We learned the reason why when Theo Drumgoole appeared with a bulky bag of tools. After he had repaired the faulty connection and tested it with a call to his inamorata, Betty Hesterly, at telephone central, he informed both Hilda and me that we would soon be receiving an invitation to their wedding. The Sisters Grimsley were offering their big house for a grand ceremony, and Theo wanted to make certain that we would be there. Hilda assured him that we most certainly would be there, and I was on the point of seconding her motion when the loathsome telephone rang, sending me back down the hallway to my once quiet and secure office.

Back at the desk for a precious moment of reflection, I feel some anxiety at the thought that in fewer than ten hours I will see Queen Elizabeth Jones. I should be elated, but then I remember that she never replied to the messages I sent to her after Johnny Hawkes was killed in the circus train wreck in Pennsylvania. Upon first learning of the fatal accident I wrote a letter to her and then sent postcards reminding her that she owed me a letter. Her preferred method of corresponding is by postcard, but I know how careless the circus mail people are about seeing that cards, and even letters, are delivered to the proper addresses.

I decided that because of losing Johnny, she shunned any memories of those associated with him, especially someone as close as I had been to both of them. Or had she also found another love? And needed nothing from me, so far back in her past? Well, I will soon find out. Perhaps.

In the late afternoon. Between telephone rings, I limped down the hall to ask Hilda if she'd changed her mind and wants to go to the circus with me. I knew that she would say no, but I am a believer in crossing bridges rather than burning them.

Right now I'm debating with myself: Should I go out to the fairgrounds and look for the private portable wagon of Queen Elizabeth Jones? I wonder if she remembers that this is the town in which I had the accident that ended my circus life. Probably not. Her life has been too much filled with excitement and adventure. Even though I was the number one rider in her famous stagecoach act. I decided to wait until an hour before circus time and visit her then.

Written after returning from the circus lot in the fairgrounds. Dressed in my best Sunday clothes, I walked across to Main Street and boarded one of the new electric trolley cars to the fairgrounds. Because of the early hour, the trolley was only half full, and when it arrived at the fairgrounds gate, the ticket sellers were not yet in their stalls. I explained to the lonely guard at the tent entrance that I wished to visit an old friend, offering him the price of admittance to one of the costliest reserved seats, but evidently he recognized me for the old circus hand that I am and waved me into the lot.

I walked around the outside rim of the tent. Lights were beginning to burn brightly in small clusters here and there. Trusting to memory and the routinized habits of circus people, I swung off to the left and as I expected was soon passing wheeled cages of restless beasts. An unhappy lion roared without passion, followed by a halfhearted trumpet from an elephant. For me, it all sounded and smelled of nostalgia. I began to feel better about meeting Queen Elizabeth Jones.

And then out of the gathering dusk appeared a familiar wagon, the aging dispensary and home on wheels of Dr. Socrates Drumm.

The gilt decorations on the wagon had fallen away; the steps at the rear entrance were held together by rusting screws; the door hung from loose hinges. I would have thought old Dr. Drumm long since superannuated, but there was his name in square block letters on the half-opened door, and I could see the feet of his big boots placed solidly on the wagon flooring in front of the chair in which he always sat.

I stepped up on the rear platform and knocked on the angled door. His gravelly voice was slow in responding, but there was no mistaking whose vocal cords made the sound.

He was still a heavyset man with a broad head, his half-shaved beard hairs, now gray, set in the deep wrinkles of his face. He looked very old and surely was now the oldest man on the circus payroll.

I don't think he recognized me at first. I had to tell him my name and my former role in the circus. He remembered me then. "Yeah, yeah, Butterworth."

"Butterfield," I corrected him.

"Yeah. Tender skin and soft bones. You were a regular customer of this apothecary. What are you doing these days? You live in this backwater town?"

I'm not sure that he remembered the accident that left me here. After all, he had done nothing more than forbid that I travel farther with the circus. I was carried off to a local doctor while the circus was packing up and leaving for the next town.

"Do you see much of Queen Elizabeth Jones?" I asked.

His wide head turned to one side as he peered at me through his rheumy eyes. "Seldom. You wouldn't know this one, would you?"

"What do you mean—this one?"

"They have to book a new one almost every year. This one is new."

"You don't mean the real Queen Elizabeth Jones is no longer with the circus?"

He made a gesture of placing a cupped hand over his mouth. "Oh, God, I must be speaking out of turn. Circus secrets, I can't remember. You being one of us I assumed you knew."

"Knew what?"

"That the lead equestrienne uses that name."

"Where is she?" I reached out and grabbed at his knee as though prepared to use physical force to extract a reply.

"You do live in a whistle-stop burg, don't you?" he said. "I thought it was common knowledge."

"No! The local newspaper told all about her. Nothing new. All the old glories."

He sniffed. "I never read that bilge."

"Well, where is she—the real Queen Elizabeth Jones?"

He sighed. "You were her best horseman. You have the right to know. Although they still try to keep that a secret."

I think I knew then the awful answer, but I asked once more: "Where is she?"

He told me all about it. In detail. When they pulled Johnny Hawkes out of the wreckage of the railroad circus car, a dead man, she was with him, still alive but badly injured. A few days later she died and was buried beside him secretly at night in a little cemetery in Missouri. Not long after that, another horsewoman took her place, using her name. After all, Queen Elizabeth Jones was the star, the greatest equestrienne in the world, the performer who brought people to the ticket sellers by the thousands.

I knew then, of course, why no replies ever came to my letters and postcards.

After old Socrates Drumm and I exchanged glum farewells— the kind expressed by two people who know they will probably never see each other again—I walked back to the entrance of the big tent. A line had formed at the ticket stall, but I decided that I no longer had any desire to see the performance.

As I walked past the line on my way to board a trolley car home, Guy Blythe called my name in greeting. I turned to respond and was surprised to see Miss Ivy Crowninshield with him. She gave me a lovely, full-lipped smile.

Written this morning. Hilda will be surprised, happily I hope, the next time she comes in here to use the telephone. Before I joined her in bed last night, I removed from the wall above Old Man Fagerhalt's desk the big poster of Queen Elizabeth Jones in white tights jumping a horse through a large hoop. I also removed all other mementos of my circus life and placed them in one of the empty drawers of the big desk.

It has been my intention to carry on this account of my misspent life—from Bright Star, Indiana, to the City of New York where we encountered many strange adventures with Mr. Phineas Barnum, Mr. James Bailey, and other moguls of menageries and circuses. Of how I went with Tom Thumb and Queen Elizabeth Jones to see President Lincoln in the White House in Washington City. Of how Johnny Hawkes became a cavalryman in a uniform. Of our renewal of acquaintanceship with Mr. Frank Fogerty of the New York Graphic, *who could write the most entertaining lies. And of how we all, including Omar and Tooley, became circus performers.*

But this will have to wait until the telephone is removed from Old Man Fagerhalt's desk and placed on the store counter beside Hilda's cash drawer. I am confident that this happy day will arrive as soon as Hilda wearies of traipsing down the hall to use this damned evil demon.

There it goes again—ring, ring, ring. The last call was from an old lady on Cumberland Street, wanting to know if we had any copper chamber pots. Who knows who or what this ring will be?

As Socrates Drumm said when we parted last evening: C'est la vie.

"A TENDER STORY OF YOUTH AND INNOCENCE DURING THE MOST
SAVAGE PERIOD OF AMERICAN HISTORY. IT IS A JOY TO READ."
—*TULSA WORLD*

Ben Butterfield, ex-circus performer, is living out his days in a small backwater
town. He spends much of his time dwelling on the past, pondering his glory days
and his first grand adventure—a fantastic journey across Missouri and Illinois
to the town of Bright Star, Indiana, during the Civil War.

In 1862, Ben set out to drive two camels to the farm of a Yankee officer
who had seized the animals as contraband. On the road he would meet many
oddball characters, find startling romance, and be confronted with breathtaking
hazards, all of which would change him forever.

A magnificent tour of 1860s heartland America, *The Way to Bright Star* is a
grand coming-of-age novel in the tradition of *Huckleberry Finn*. It is destined
to become an American classic.

"THOROUGHLY ENTERTAINING, FUNNY." —*NEW YORK POST*

"MORE THAN YOUR BASIC HEARTWARMING COMING-OF-AGE NOVEL.
IT IS A STORY OF YOUTH AND ADVENTURE AND OF AGE AND REGRET.
IT CAPTURES A TURBULENT PERIOD IN AMERICAN HISTORY WITH
HUMOR [...] *ANTONIO EXPRESS-NEWS*

Cover photographs by
Emmanuelle Purdon/Getty Images (cowboy on a horse)
and Angel Herrero de Frutos/istockphoto (sunset)
Cover design by Base Art Co.

ISBN-13: 978-0-7653-2255-5
ISBN-10: 0-7653-2255-2

0-7653-2255-2 • $15.95 ($17.95 CAN)
A Forge® Paperback • Tom Doherty Associates, LLC
www.tor-forge.com • Printed in the USA